A SHADE TOO FAR

A HUMOROUS PARANORMAL WOMEN'S FICTION

DEBORAH WILDE

te da media
vancouver

1

IN JUST OVER HALF AN HOUR, I'D EITHER HAVE pulled off an impossible heist during an illicit underground magic fight, or I'd be dead. Oh, and to make things interesting, I had to accomplish this feat on a private tropical island filled with shady Ohrist guests swanning around sipping champagne while openly flexing their magic in front of each other.

Then there was my employer, Tatiana Cassin, who moved through the crowd like an eighty-year-old shark in a sea of guppies acting like they had teeth.

My boss chatted briefly with everyone, who paid their respects *Godfather*-style. The few who snubbed her received a serene smile with a hint of menace, which made most of them scurry over to correct their misstep. She didn't give a damn what anyone believed of her, actively encouraging all the rumors about her presence today.

I had much to learn from Obi-Wan Corleone.

An Indian woman in an orange saree, who was literally as insubstantial as the smoke from her cigarillo, waited impatiently for her turn with Tatiana next to a man in a kilt with skin as hard and bizarrely defined as an alien exoskeleton.

Tatiana's bloodred silk couture gown weighed more than she did, but her blue eyes were as sharp as the bone spikes magically fanning out from the neck of a Black woman in a fitted tuxedo, who bent to kiss Tatiana's wrinkled hand.

They both looked majestic, whereas I was shvitzing worse than an old Jewish man in a sauna due to my overly starched formal housekeeper's uniform worn by all the servers employed by Santiago Torres. I swear, the combination of sweat and polyester had terraformed a microbiome in my armpits.

Note to self: next time I secretly crashed an event, wear breathable fabrics.

My golem partner nudged my hip, both of us hidden under my magic cloaking. "How much longer?" he whined in a whisper.

Sighing quietly, I showed Emmett the old windup watch on my wrist—exactly like I had the other dozen times in the last half hour. Five minutes to showtime.

He rocked back and forth from his heels to his toes but was distracted by a woman sashaying by in a flowy caftan made of living bees. With his hands, he measured his hips in comparison to hers.

"I could rock that," he mused, looking sadly at his sweatpants and runners.

I tapped my index finger against my lips, directing him to keep quiet. While no one could scent us or detect my heartbeat under the black invisibility mesh created by my shadow magic, they could hear us speaking.

Everyone was taking their seats for the outdoor fight, except for Emmett, me, and the security team, who made no attempt to be subtle. They patrolled through gardens where short bulbous cacti nestled in beds of red rocks, between rows of gently swaying palm trees, along the beach with the aquamarine Sea of Cortez beyond, and around the perimeter of the ring.

Taking calming breaths of warm, salt-tanged air, I pulled out the domino that I'd won in the Kefitzat Haderech and ran my thumb over the single black line carved into the tile face. Neither Tatiana, nor our client, Vancouver's head vampire Zev BatKian, had been able to learn much about what we faced en route to our target: the Torquemada Gloves. The vault containing them was in the basement of Torres's opulent mansion and had a heartbeat-monitored door.

That was it. A whopping two facts: basement and special door. I was literally operating on nothing.

And if my manipulative employer and the most paranoid vampire in Canada couldn't sniff out any more details than that, no one else could.

Did working for Zev leave an oily feeling deep in my soul? Why, yes. Did I have a choice? Also, yes. Though with my family's safety and my continued breathing at stake, it wasn't a difficult one to make.

I wouldn't betray Zev, yet he'd still taken a few dozen opportunities to press upon me the importance of loyalty. Not being a total moron, I'd understood his feelings on that subject at our first encounter. At this point, he was just beating a dead horse about how scary he was. It had taken all my willpower not to affect a terrible Dracula accent during our last meeting and say, "I vant to suck your blood. Blah. Blah. Blah."

Another reason I wasn't all that worried about the vampire if I failed? He'd be late to the party. Torres's people would have already killed me, being trained to suss out threats using both magic and high-tech means. However, if I didn't present the Torquemada Gloves to Zev, I could kiss the ward to keep out demons and other dangerous supernatural baddies goodbye. I'd blown my first shot at the vampire's assistance and this gig was the rare gift of a second chance.

Thankfully, he couldn't accompany us to the island. Even if he'd dissolved into smoke and snuck through the lowered wards alongside Tatiana, as Emmett and I had under my cloaking, the fights were held in broad daylight, precisely so no unwanted bloodsuckers showed up. Zev might be able to go outside under an umbrella on a sunny day in Vancouver, but the tropical sun here would incinerate him.

I curled my nails into my palms to keep from scratching my itchy armpits. Had the makers of these uniforms never heard of natural fibers?

Two minutes left.

Positive thoughts, Feldman. I wasn't coming into this totally unprepared. In fact, my entire life had trained me for dealing with the unknown. Forty-two years of experience, my honor roll chops, ex-librarian meticulousness, resilience from navigating a divorce, and some pretty sweet magic talent made me a force to be reckoned with. I bounced on my toes, as alert as an Olympic sprinter braced for the starting gun.

With a smile as suave as his bespoke linen suit, Santiago escorted Tatiana to her ringside seat, which was in my direct line of sight. He'd been hosting these championship fights for over forty years, and Tatiana had attended every one with Samuel, her aficionado husband.

Though this was the first time since his death seven years ago that she'd made an appearance.

Santiago's wife, Sherisse, a frosted blonde with a distracted air and leathery skin, joined them. Tatiana leaned over Santiago to speak to the woman, who shook her head with quick nervous movements. When Tatiana sat back in her seat with her chin propped on her fist, Santiago turned a hard look on his wife, but was all smiles again when he resumed chatting with my employer.

There was no way to contact Tatiana to learn if there was an unanticipated and unwelcome wrinkle in our mission, because I couldn't carry a phone for fear of it being tracked. Once the fight was over, Emmett and I were to meet back at the private plane she'd chartered, but until then, we were on our own.

A bell rang out and a loud cheer went up.

Emmett grabbed my sleeve and I nodded, putting away the domino talisman and setting the alarm on my watch. We'd estimated a half hour to accomplish our mission, based on the average length of these fights in previous years.

Still cloaked, we jogged toward the pale yellow manor with its array of arched windows, rounded balconies, and colonnades.

Lionheart, a barefoot Asian woman in a faun-colored sports bra and fitted shorts, exited a set of ground-floor glass doors and strode across the lawn. The tawny hair cascading to her shoulders was straight out of a shampoo commercial, but as she passed us, I glimpsed the flat, dispassionate gaze of an apex predator. The fighter ignored everyone in the crowd attempting to give her high-fives, her balletic grace in no way lessened by the myriad of ragged white scars traversing her body.

The ring was elevated to shoulder height so it could be seen by all the spectators. Stairs on one side provided access, but the fighter ignored them. In one smooth motion, Lionheart grasped the lower ropes and swung her body up and over into the ring. She walked to the corner and sat down on the mat cross-legged, her eyes closed.

If the cheers greeting Lionheart had been enthusiastic, the ones for her opponent, Destructo, were downright deafening. Dude was a wall of a man with two beady eyes and a nose that listed sideways as if bolting for greener pastures. With skin that could transform into a rock-solid surface, he stomped to the ring, roaring and grunting, his blue satin boxing shorts stretched to the breaking point.

Were I to judge a book by its cover—and I were—the chances of him speaking in erudite sentences were small, though I'd bet he referred to himself in the third person.

5

For months, Ohrist fighters had competed in a series of to-the-death battles, all in hopes of winning the lucrative prize at today's championship event. Tatiana hadn't given me specifics but apparently it was enough to set the victor up for life.

Lionheart had to be as bloodthirsty and deadly as Destructo to have triumphed over all the other contenders, but I had no doubt that she'd employ strategy. All Destructo had to do was stand there and let his opponents tire themselves out running into him until they fell to the mat like toddlers at nap time and he squashed them like bugs.

"Betting is closed!" cried a sweaty bald man.

Fun as it would have been to watch the two fighters duke it out to the end, work took precedence.

Emmett and I flattened ourselves against the house, careful to stay in line with an enormous bougainvillea tree. It must have been hooked to the same irrigation system that allowed the lush lawn to grow in this desert climate. What a waste of water for grass that was just getting torn up under people's shoes.

After careful calculations back home, based on aerial shots of the property, we'd determined that the tree fell into a tiny slice of land undetected by either the motion sensor over the door or the one over the bank of windows to our right, both connected to monitors in a security hub.

A female guard on patrol set off the motion sensor light. She checked in with her team leader on a headset while I tracked the rotating camera mounted above the door. The second she stepped inside the house, Emmett and I fell into line behind her. The trick was to follow the guard closely enough that the door shut without hitting one of us, while not breathing down the woman's neck, thereby giving away our concealed presence.

Any anomaly would send the guards to investigate with magic blazing.

The golem was so close behind me that he elbowed my back a couple of times, but miraculously, we peeled off from the guard at the end of a long corridor without detection.

A hand-painted ceiling mural of a bloody battle complemented the half dozen pieces of knight's armor, their closed face shields giving the hallway a menacing air. Grimacing, I hoped for his wife's sake that Santiago hadn't carried this design aesthetic into their bedroom.

Emmett grabbed my wrist to check the time, then prodded me to go faster.

The two of us crept down the stairs into the basement in tense silence, checking over our shoulders every few seconds. Some of Santiago's guards were shifters and we'd braced ourselves to face a tiger or a python or something, but we hit the bottom step without incident.

That was even more unnerving because either our intel was wrong, and the vault was on one of the upper floors, which teemed with guards, or Torres depended on magic booby traps to protect it.

If Emmett and I died finding the gloves, we'd disappear without a trace, since I'd bet good money on Torres's team having excellent body disposal protocols. My kid and I had our standing TV date tomorrow night, and I wasn't missing that. Plus, in the event of my demise, my best friend, Jude, was supposed to pluck my chin hairs. There was currently one under my jawline that I'd named Houdini for its ability to escape any pair of tweezers, and I refused to be killed before I'd pulled that little bastard out by the root.

We quickly checked behind doors, finding a private state-of-the art movie theater, a games room featuring a stunning billiard table with hand-carved panels, and both a walk-in humidor and large wine fridge in a lounge area, but no vault.

"There's one more area to check," Emmett said.

"Give me a sec." I unwrapped a protein bar and downed half of it, because keeping us cloaked was running down my magical battery. "Okay." I crammed the rest of the bar in my mouth, and we headed for the open space to the far right of the stairwell, which served as a small art gallery displaying Torres's collection of modern pieces.

"Is that…" The golem's upper lip curled back. "A graffitied toilet? Why?"

"Some people like to push the boundaries of what's considered art." I frowned at a nine-foot stack of chairs towering precariously in the corner.

"Some people are idiots. We must have missed a secret entrance down here." Emmett placed a heavy hand on my shoulders and turned me around.

I stopped, waving a hand at this museum. "This doesn't fit what I've seen of Santiago's personality. He enjoys aggression, the bloodier the better. Fine wines, good cigars, sure. But a bunch of shitty art?"

I tugged the golem along with me, quickly inspecting each piece for a hidden lever or a button or something, but I came up empty-handed.

"Maybe he ran out of cash for the good stuff." Emmett nodded his chin at a white wall with a large frame mounted there. A small mirror hung at eye level inside it. The rest of the basement had low, tasteful lighting, but this piece had a high-powered bulb trained on it from the opposite wall.

Was the point of this work to show a person's reflection inside a frame, making them the art? Deep. I shook my head. "Even if I was rich, I wouldn't waste money on this."

"Forget about it." Emmett checked my watch. "We've got twenty minutes max until the fight ends."

"I know," I murmured, but I couldn't let go of the sense that I was missing something.

My partner stood on tiptoe to read the small sign above the frame. "'Old sins cast long shadows.'" He made a face at the mirror, which, thanks to my magic, didn't show our reflections. "Guess I'm sin-free."

8

"Yeah, right. Let me lose the magic cloaking and see how true that is." I gasped. "That's it! Santiago has light magic. If he faces the mirror and floods the room with light, he won't cast a shadow. This is the way in."

Emmett gestured at the wall behind us. "There's a camera above the light bulb. You have to drop your magic to have a reflection and if you do, we'll be caught."

"Ye of little faith." Facing the mirror, I dropped the cloaking over my face only. From the back—and therefore as far as the security camera was concerned—we were still invisible.

My reflection blinked back at me in the mirror and a door-knob popped into existence inside the frame. I pumped a fist in victory, but on second thought, hesitated to open it. My myth-loving side insisted that nothing would happen to us. We'd solved the puzzle to gain entry and this was our reward. My fairy tale–loving side, however, reminded me that the witch hadn't padlocked her gingerbread house.

But, at the end of the day, we didn't really have a choice

The bright yellow room with cheap laminate flooring hidden behind the art installation obviously wasn't the vault, and there hadn't been a scanner on the door indicating a heartbeat monitor, so we scurried inside.

As there were no cameras here, I recalled my magic, stretching out the tension in my neck and shoulders. I'd never held my cloaking for that long, and even though I'd trained to keep it up for longer and longer periods in the ten days since Zev had hired us, it was different doing it under the stress of the actual mission.

The place was empty save for two more white doors that were identical to the one we'd entered through: one directly ahead and the other to our left.

"Which one?" Emmett asked.

"That's what I'd like to know."

At the sound of the unfamiliar nasal drawl, I whipped

around, my pulse jackhammering, but the jolt of adrenaline wasn't enough for my magic to do more than swirl around my ankles.

A ruddy-cheeked lad with tousled ginger hair had gotten inside with us. The little prat sported rolled-up khakis and a suit jacket with some preppy insignia on it, waggling his fingers in a wave.

"What do you want?" Emmett puffed out his bare chest.

"Same thing as you do," the stranger said, managing to look down his nose at us, even though both Emmett and I were taller.

The clock was ticking, there were likely traps and certainly guards to avoid before we got off the island with our prize, and most importantly, my family's safety hung in the balance. We hadn't factored competitors into the mix.

He held up a hand. Dark streaks snaked across his palm and spiked out through the tips of his fingers. "Get me into the vault and I won't have to let you die from my venom."

I swallowed. When Sadie was little, she'd been fascinated with snakes, and we'd often visited the reptile sanctuary at a local nature reserve. As a result, I knew way too much about venom's horrific effects, like slow paralysis and holes in our blood vessels causing us to bleed to death.

"Good luck tracking us when we can go stealth," I said, putting on more bravado than I felt.

"Please. You might be able to hide from me, but then again, you do look tuckered out." He clucked his tongue. "Have you considered midday naps? They do Mumsy a world of good."

Tell me to go nap, you insolent puppy? Oh, payback was going to be fun. I just needed a couple minutes so I could summon Delilah and beat his punk ass.

Emmett approached the door directly ahead. He laid a hand on it, then crouched down, and rested his forehead against the wood, humming.

"What are you doing?" the stranger said.

"Getting you to where you want to go." The golem strode to the door on the left. "This way."

I grabbed his hand before he touched the doorknob, the two of us wrestling comically, before I clipped him and wincing, he knocked me aside.

There was a faint reddish smear on the door.

"You made me smudge," he said, rubbing his elbow.

"We're in a secret room on an island owned by a criminal," I hissed. "Don't just charge through some random door."

"Hurry up," the young man said, "or *I'll* pick and force one of you through to test whether I was right."

Emmett confronted me with crossed arms. "Do I or do I not have divination magic?"

The stranger narrowed his eyes at that, considering the golem with a shrewd look.

"You do," I said, "but…" His magic didn't work that way, did it?

"I sensed something dangerous behind the other door," the golem said. "You going to trust me?"

The stranger pointed at me. "What magic do you bring to your decision?"

My fingers twitched because I really wanted to summon Delilah to punch him in the face, but he smirked, his poisoned needles extending further from his skin, and I backed off.

The doors were hung totally flush with the frame, leaving no crack to slip my shadow under and investigate.

"I've got logic, not magic," I said. "If we keep track of the outside wall, we can eliminate doors." I felt in my housekeeping uniform for a pencil, but there wasn't one, so I drew in the air. "According to the blueprints I saw, Torres's house was square. This room seems to end in line with where the outside wall was back in the gallery space. Which means..." I tapped the left door. "This leads outside."

"You're wrong." Emmett put his hand on the door ahead. "I have a bad feeling about this one, and the door behind us leads back to the gallery. We have to take the left one."

The young man looked between us, tapping his foot. "Magic trumps logic. Left door it is." His finger needles glistened with inky toxins. "Don't follow me."

"You can't get through the vault without the golem," I said. "There's a heartbeat monitor on it."

Emmett stepped forward. "And I'm not going through without her."

"Then you can carry her dead body with you after I poison her," our nemesis said. "Or come with me and leave her behind. Alive."

The golem's shoulders slumped. "Sorry, Miri."

"Good choice." The young man opened the left door revealing an identical empty yellow room, and I frowned because it should have led outside.

Before I could tell them to wait and figure this out, Emmett sprinted for it, attempting to grab the man before he could get through. They got wedged in the doorway.

"Emmett! Stop!" I didn't want him running blindly into a room that, by my logic, shouldn't have been there.

The stranger wriggled out into the new room first, smirked—and was engulfed by a ball of flame hot enough to burn the tip of my nose.

His charred and blackened corpse hit the ground with a dusty thunk and the door slammed shut.

I stood there wide-eyed and hyperventilating.

"I lied," Emmett blurted out. "I only said I had a bad feeling because I wanted to protect you. I figured if we disagreed, then he wouldn't hurt you, and once he'd gone into the next room, we'd bolt the other way. But I killed him."

"No," I croaked out. "Torres did that. It's not your fault." I'd been so certain that the left door led outside. If Emmett and I had gone through it instead of the young man, we'd be dead. I shuddered. How were we supposed to survive if logic didn't apply here?

Emmett nervously eyed the door to the right. "What do we do if both rooms are booby-trapped? How do we get to the vault?"

I fought through my shock back to the problem at hand. "We must have missed something back in the gallery. A clue. Let's go back out and search that area again."

Nodding, he threw open the door we'd originally entered, only to now find it blocked by a wall. "I hate this so much," he said.

"Eight minutes," I said anxiously, checking my timer that was counting down until the fight was supposed to end.

The door behind us was a wall and the left-hand one was Tiki Torch Palace. Defeated, I opened our only option, willing myself to move my feet and step into the next yellow room.

Emmett pushed us both inside and the door closed behind him.

I yelped and threw up my hands as if that would save me from immolation, screwed my eyes shut, and waited. When nothing happened, I peered around the room.

We were both fine. Grateful as I was, why had the original door led back to a brick wall, and why didn't the one on the left lead outside? I paced in a tight circle, sorting through possibilities. "Fuck me. The rooms must rotate."

"On top of that, we've got the same problem as before." Emmett rubbed his chin, eyeing the two new doors in this room. "How do we decide which to take next?"

I unstrapped the wristwatch.

"What are you doing?"

"Pick a door," I said. "I'll toss this through and if it sets off a booby trap, then we go through the other one."

13

Emmett opened the one on the left again and I tossed the watch in.

The watch hit the ground, remaining totally intact. Mainly because it didn't have a head for the giant intruder-decapitating blade that came swinging out of the ceiling to remove.

"All righty, then," Emmett said, and went through the non-bladed door.

Shocker, we stood in our third empty yellow room. However, there was only one other door here. It was taller and wider than normal, the thick wood ornately carved with "S.T." Santiago's initials.

Emmett high-fived me. "Made it."

Like the other heartbeat alarm that we'd previously encountered, this door featured a sensor panel—cutting-edge biometric technology. Anyone stepping through it had their heartbeat scanned, and if it didn't match the owner's, an alarm sounded.

"There's no visible lock, just the sensor." I depressed the handle partway. "It's not even a bank vault door. Why make it this easy?"

"Easy? We were almost burned and decapitated."

"Exactly. Why wouldn't there be an even worse trap to stop the people who got past everything else?"

"How many other people without heartbeats are going to make it this far?" Emmett scoffed. "We got lucky, vampires have to be invited into Torres's home, and even Delilah can't go in."

Ohrist magic came from their ability to tap into "ohr," a supernatural life force. It allowed them to manipulate light and life energy. At least ninety-five percent of everyone with magic was an Ohrist, but they were hugely outnumbered by Sapiens, powerless humans who had no clue magic existed.

I was one of the rare Banim Shovavim, the rebellious children of Lilith and Adam whose powers were rooted in death and darkness. My talents included cloaking and an animated shadow, which was incredibly cool, but a faint heartbeat—the echo of mine—beat inside Delilah, and she couldn't enter the vault.

"Be careful." I grabbed Emmett's wrist because he'd already reached for the handle, an excited gleam in his eyes. "Don't touch anything other than the Torquemada Gloves. Got it?"

"You never let me have any fun," he grumbled and trudged inside.

2

———

EMMETT GOT INTO THE VAULT WITHOUT A HITCH, and as soon as he was safe, he became a little kid on the first night of Hannukah, eyes alight at the bounty before him.

The vault was much larger than I'd expected and crammed with a motley collection ranging from bizarre to grotesque.

"Whoa! Check it out." The golem stopped in front of an oval gem on display in a glass case on a pillar and crouched down to read the small plaque. "'Blood diamond made of real blood. Year 1852.'"

I hovered outside the threshold. "Charming. Get the gloves, Emmett. There. On the right."

There was a hissing sound. I sniffed the air but couldn't smell anything.

"Yeah, yeah. Calm your tits." Emmett gave a wide berth to a scaffold with a rusty saw hanging off a hook and a horizontal wagon wheel with spikes sticking up at regular intervals. A length of old pipe was tossed next to it. My partner shuddered. "It's got dried gristle on it."

The hissing grew louder.

I blotted my forehead, feeling hot and dizzy. "Get out of there." My words sounded weirdly elongated.

"Yeeeeeaaaaah, yeaaaaaah." Why was he speaking in slow motion? He reached for the wrinkled, leathery, yellowed-with-age gloves by his fingertips—and missed, swaying like a tree about to fall.

"Gas!" I threw my sleeve over my nose. My eyes watered and my lungs burned. "Hurry!"

With a jerky swipe, he grabbed the gloves, but toppled forward, hitting the ground with a thunk.

"When I was a girl in Sicily," he mumbled.

If they'd dispersed gas, then the jig was up. No wonder there hadn't been a lock. Holding my breath, I ran inside the vault and grabbed Emmett's ankles, hauling him out.

The yellow room narrowed and lengthened, dark spots dancing at the edge of my vision. Why couldn't Jude have made a child golem who weighed less? I collapsed against the outside of the vault door, shutting it, my polyester finery stuck to my skin.

Emmett slurred his third chorus of the *Golden Girls* theme.

Once my head had cleared, I dropped to my knees, and slapped the golem across the face with the gloves, swallowing against the rush of bile. "Getupgetupgetupgetup!"

He staggered to his feet. "Okay, pussycat."

We had lurched halfway across the room when Emmett's head lolled sideways. "Too many doors."

I stomped my foot because while we'd been in the vault, the rooms had rotated again. Instead of simply the vault door and the exit, there was an extra door. "How the fuck do we get out of here?"

"I'll get you to safety," a man with a posh—and familiar—English accent said, "but it'll cost you." Naveen Kumar, the handsome Indo-British man in his late thirties who'd entered, wore the same security outfit as the rest of Torres's crew.

Stuffing the gloves in the pocket of my housekeeping uniform, I squinted at him, hoping he was a hallucination, but he remained maddeningly real. "Nice staff. Compensating, are we?"

Naveen twirled the long weapon made of hard light through his fingers. "Give me the gloves, BS."

I'd run into Naveen on another case of mine and we'd immediately hit it off. He'd given me a safe place to crash, let Emmett hang out with him, and even introduced me to his niece, Evani. However, everything changed when he learned I was Banim Shovavim. After that, we were kicked out and Naveen's treatment of me had turned decidedly cold.

Even if I didn't desperately need the gloves, I wasn't taking orders from someone who hated me for what I was, not who I was. That, I could have lived with.

"It's better if I hang on to them than Torres." My magic danced under my skin.

"No doubt." He dropped into a crouch, the staff held diagonally in front of him. "But I intend to destroy them."

"Did you tell your employer that?" I slammed my mesh cloaking over Emmett and me, but Naveen was faster. He swung his staff into my ribs and knocked me to my knees, shattering my magic.

I hit the ground with a cry.

"It's on a need-to-know basis. And Torres doesn't." Naveen flicked a lock of platinum blond hair out of his eyes with an annoyed gesture, his staff resting on his shoulder. His eyes, only slightly darker than his brown skin, had been so warm and friendly at our first meeting, but they sent chills through me now. "Laurent won't forgive you if you don't hand the gloves over to me to destroy. You know he barely trusts anyone to be his friend. Does that mean so little to you?"

Emmett helped me to my feet, holding me steady by the elbow because it hurt to put weight on my injured leg.

Damn you to Hell, Kumar. Laurent's friendship and respect meant a great deal to me, but if I didn't give Zev these gloves, I was screwed. The vampire was the only one who could protect me from the demon parasites that had already invaded my home once. They'd possessed a Lonestar who was part of my parents' murders twenty-seven years ago, and after I'd recently confronted the magic police officer, he'd been murdered in the same way as my mom and dad.

I was taking zero fucking chances with my family's lives.

"I'm on a job and we have a satisfaction guaranteed policy," I said. The door Naveen had come through remained open. All we had to do was get past him.

"For a vampire. Did you look at the mark inside the gloves?" Naveen's tone had become suspiciously conversational. He shifted his weight onto the balls of his feet, watching us intently.

"No." I held on to Emmett like I still didn't have my balance back, using it as a cover to slowly inch us toward the exit.

"People think the half circle is the logo of the company that made items out of human skin, but it's not." Naveen jabbed his light staff in my direction, waving me away from my partner.

"Human skin?" Emmett dry heaved.

Had Zev and Tatiana known this?

Naveen was faster than me and I needed to rejuice before using my powers again.

I tapped Emmett's back twice, using a code we'd come up with in case we faced one of the security team. "Are these gloves made from Torquemada's skin?"

Tomás de Torquemada was the Grand Inquisitor during the Spanish Inquisition, infamous for his cruelty, fanaticism, and religious intolerance, and devoted to ridding Spain of all heresy. This led to the decimation of the Jewish population in the 1400s through both death and forced conversion, Torquemada sending his inquisitors throughout the old and new worlds to hunt nonbelievers down.

It also resulted in Jewish pirates but that was a whole other story. And none of these facts made having a dead person's flayed-off body part in my pocket any better.

I held up three fingers behind my back for Emmett to see.

The golem scratched his chin and yawned, but I knew he was waiting for my signal.

"No one knows for sure whose skin it is," Naveen said. "But the half circle is a demon mark."

"Could Torquemada have been a demon?"

"Does it matter?" Naveen said.

"You tell me. Sure, the human skin part is gross, but what's got your panties in a twist?" I stepped forward, happy to see Naveen's jaw clench, his focus on me, and lowered a finger down to two.

"The gloves are cursed," Naveen said. "When a person puts them on, they become convinced that they no longer wear their own skin."

I swallowed my nausea at this atrocity. Zev had omitted several crucial details, but even so, I had to give him the gloves, because I was on my last chance with him. I shoved my self-loathing into a hard ball and padlocked it. The vamp would get the demon artifact. End of story.

One finger.

"That sucks," I said mildly.

"Bit of an understatement, poppet," Naveen sneered. "That obsession drives them mad, and they eventually die trying to rip their skin off."

I closed my fist.

Emmett ran at Naveen, picking him up and throwing him sideways across the room, where he hit the wall with a grunt.

The golem and I sprinted for the open door, my knee shooting needle-sharp bursts of pain the entire time.

Naveen's staff flew overhead, slamming the door shut before ricocheting back into his hand. If I hadn't pushed Emmett down, we'd have been impaled.

"Any other questions?" Naveen was already on his feet again, his weapon at the ready.

My heart thudded in my chest and my magic prickled wildly inside me. "Nope."

Naveen circled Emmett and me, once more putting himself between us and the door. "Laurent had almost convinced me I was wrong about you." A wistful look flitted over his face for a fleeting second before his expression hardened.

A few more feelings that I didn't dare examine too closely got locked down as well.

Delilah exploded out of me, but Naveen was ready. He swung his staff into her, and I doubled over with a gasp, pain blazing through my gut.

He dropped into a crouch, still blocking our exit. "My first instincts were correct. Your kind has no compassion and no loyalty."

"You have no idea how deep my loyalties run and what I'm doing to protect people," I wheezed, "so how about you take all your preconceived notions of me and shove them up your ass? Use the staff to make sure you pack them nice and tight."

Mesh in place, I grabbed Emmett and threw us both sideways. The golem executed the move perfectly, thanks to all our practice.

Naveen's strike clipped my shoulder.

My magic rippled and holes gapped in the mesh. I visualized a giant crochet hook patching the cloaking in a blur. The speed at which I mended it pushed me to my limit, sweat running down the back of my neck and dripping off my temples, but we slipped past him and out the door.

We found ourselves outside. Sucking down fresh air, I walked quickly—but not so fast as to arouse suspicion—across the great lawn to the ring, keeping my partner hidden.

With the fight over and staff milling about cleaning up the

high bistro tables used during cocktails, the housekeeping uniform helped me blend in. I hoped the security team would assume Naveen had dealt with the thief. Every step lit up my nerve endings in new and agonizing ways, and it was all I could do to stay upright, but we made it back to the ring without incident.

Santiago Torres presented Lionheart with a trophy and a check while the cheering crowd gave her a standing ovation. The lion shifter bled freely from several wounds, including a nasty gash across her temple, almost every inch of her skin was bruised, and her breathing was labored.

There was no sign of Destructo, only a blood-soaked mat.

All we had to do was avoid Naveen on our way to the plane and we'd be home free. We were safe. Ish.

Tatiana met my gaze and I nodded.

Lionheart accepted her prize with a quiet "Thank you" and left the ring, leaving Santiago to officially close this year's match and wish everyone well.

I attempted to steer clear of the people heading back to their planes or yachts moored on the other side of the small private island, since it wouldn't do to bump into someone and reveal Emmett's presence. I'd narrowly avoided crashing into a couple wearing enormous hats with birdcage contraptions on them when a man bellowed in pain.

Emmett grabbed me, hauling me back against his chest, the impact making him visible, but everyone was too busy gawking toward the source of the cry to notice. "What's going on?" he demanded.

Since I couldn't see over other people's heads, I jumped on a chair toward the back of the audience.

A dybbuk, a crimson ghostly mass, assumed a jagged knife-form and violently stabbed at Torres. It pulsated in fury, slashing his skin and clothing. The man whipped off his sunglasses, his light magic erupting from his eyes, and while I had to throw up a hand to protect myself from the brilliance, his powers did nothing against the malevolent spirit.

This wasn't possible. Dybbuks attacked but only once they'd been freed from their host body. There was no corpse around—not even Destructo's—so where had this one come from? And why didn't I sense it beforehand? I should have been vibrating like a tuning fork, my magic urging me to destroy the abomination, but upon a closer probe of the spirit, I felt nothing.

"You think he's having a seizure?" a woman passing by me said to her friend.

"Karma, baby," her friend replied and the two laughed.

I almost reached out to shake them for their indifference, but I couldn't explain the truth without giving away my magic because Ohrists were unable to see dybbuks.

Several of Torres's guards jumped into the ring, attempting to help their boss, seemingly under the impression this was a medical emergency of some sort, only to be attacked. They busted out their magic, except not seeing where to retaliate, fired wildly.

One guard called up vines to grab Santiago, hitting his colleague instead.

Some of the crowd fled, while others, already amped up by bloodlust from the fight, broke into smaller skirmishes. *Really? You guys took this as an enticement to wail on each other?*

Chaos reigned, and I was the only one who could stop it.

I jumped off the chair and almost collided with Tatiana.

"Miriam." She tugged sharply on my arm. "We have to get out of here, before the wards on the island are raised again and we're trapped." Her stiff-backed anxiety was undercut by her raspy New Yorker accent that turned "wards" into "wahds" like the finest of Wise Guys.

Tatiana showing concern meant that being trapped here would be extremely detrimental to our well-being, either from the guards or Zev. I almost ran for the plane without a second look back, but I forced myself to stay the course. I just needed a few minutes.

"It's a dybbuk attack," I said, marching into the fray. Except, I immediately got held up by a knot of people running away from the melee, and no amount of pushing and shoving got me clear.

We were in the middle of the Danger Zone, the period between sundown Friday and sundown Saturday where dybbuks were released from being tortured in Gehenna to come to earth and find a host with lowered inhibitions to enthrall.

Even though the wards around the island had been lowered and dybbuks could show up, people had been drinking all afternoon. Tatiana had told me this event was a giant game of chicken where any show of weakness resulted in hostile takeovers—or worse. Thus, the desperate need to prove one had the biggest balls. I got that. But I still thought it was stupid.

Wards weren't common, even for this crowd. I was only getting mine in payment for a dangerous mission. So how much magic—and money—did it take to ward up an entire island?

Alert for magic and stray punches, I pushed forward, Tatiana nattering angrily at me, with Emmett bringing up the rear.

I couldn't make sense of what was happening because Santiago's attack was too violent for a possession.

My boss clamped her hand down on my shoulder, spinning me around with surprising strength for her age. "We have to go."

Torres was driven to his knees by the homicidal specter, his right leg bent under him at an unnatural angle. A couple guards got close but the dybbuk whirled on anyone who came within range, ripping into them, but not attempting to inhabit them.

The guards not breaking up fights were grabbing whomever they could, presumably to interrogate them.

I shook Tatiana off. "This is wrong."

Torres cried out and Tatiana briefly glanced his way. "No kidding."

She didn't understand and I couldn't explain it to her because the dybbuk's deviant behavior was unparalleled. If I couldn't predict how it would act, how was I supposed to vanquish it? Would my scythe even work on it? It wasn't inhabiting the Ohrists, but what if I was a tastier target and it chose to inhabit me?

And yet, how could I stand by and do nothing?

Mrs. Torres, understandably hysterical at her husband being attacked by seemingly nothing, was carried off to safety by two female guards.

"Five minutes," I told Tatiana.

"You can't help him without revealing you're Banim Shovavim, which will attract a whole host of trouble with this crowd. Use your common sense and get out while you can." Tatiana blazed off.

Emmett looked at me, then hurried after our boss, not caring that he was visible to everyone. Who'd give a damn in this melee anyway?

Torres lay on the mat screaming, a watery gurgling sound. The dybbuk enveloped him with an angry buzzing.

Out of the corner of my eye, I caught a flash of light across the lawn. A blindspot had flared up, catching three brawling Ohrist guests in its crescent of light.

The blindspot victims froze into stunned awareness of their plight, their fists still held high, before the supernatural energy consumed them, leaving nothing. The ohr, the well of magic that these magic users tapped into, had devoured them to replenish the power supply.

Frankly, it was shocking that with this much magic flying around that the ohr wasn't erupting like geysers. That thought must have occurred to the others because the already chaotic scene went ballistic, people scurrying to safety.

With everyone sucked into their own self-preservation, no one would care I was Banim Shovavim. I glanced over at Tatiana, making impressive progress for someone her age and in that dress. One guard waylaid her, but she jerked her head at Emmett, who threw the man into a cactus.

Yikes. His violent side was really blossoming in her employ.

My shadow magic swirled around my feet. That plane was my only way home. For some reason the Kefitzat Haderech, a shortcut shadow transport used by Banim Shovavim, wasn't accessible here on the island, and if I wasn't at the airfield when Zev met us back in Vancouver in a few hours, he wouldn't ward up my property.

But I was the only one who could save Torres. A quick rescue, then I'd cloak myself and race for the plane before anyone clued in to what had happened. I was already compromising my morals by giving the gloves to Zev; I couldn't let a man die. Not even a man like Torres.

Thrusting my elbows out, I shoved through people to the quiet bubble of space directly in front of the ring.

I glanced around for any guards who might stop me, but they were all otherwise occupied.

Oddly, in all the frenzy, one woman stood off to the side, watching Torres. She had a sensuous figure, her diaphanous gown clinging to her curves. A scarf in a similar silky material was wound over her head and neck, with only a peep of dark red hair showing, like a Hollywood star from the 1950s, the look completed with a pair of oversize black sunglasses that hid most of her face.

Was she the dybbuk's host? How was she still alive since it was free?

I rose onto tiptoe, straining for a glimpse of her shadow, but from what I could see, it was completely normal, with no trace of crimson or sickly gray flecks. I frowned. She couldn't be the host if her shadow was fine, but she also couldn't see the dybbuk. Standing around and rubbernecking at this spectacle could put her in harm's way from a guest, a guard, or the dybbuk itself.

There was no time to lose.

If I hadn't hopped onto the first stair to the ring, intent on stopping this madness, I might never have felt the touch, featherlight as it was. That wasn't some magic skill, it had been honed from Sadie trying to sneak lemon candies out of my pocket one summer.

I gripped the gloves tight while Delilah elbowed Naveen in the throat.

Coughing, he swung the staff and knocked me to the grass, my calves burning from his strike. His shadow fell over me, blotting out the sun, the staff raised high.

Delilah grabbed his weapon and yanked, buying me a few seconds to roll sideways and jump to my feet. A group of Ohrists ran past, putting more space between myself and Naveen.

Save myself and the deadly demon artifact or save Santiago?

I got all of three steps closer to Torres when his screams cut out with a suddenness that made me shiver.

The dybbuk flew off Santiago's lifeless body like a mini tornado and into the woman with the sunglasses. Her shoulders slumped momentarily, but she shook it off and left.

I gasped. That weird dybbuk had just enthralled her. Why her and not Torres?

I pivoted sharply, intent on saving her—if that was even possible with this spirit—but there was a faint squeak of a shoe at the edge of my awareness and a refracted prism of light hit my eyes. Naveen was moving in once more.

"She's enthralled. If you don't let me save her, Laurent

won't forgive you." I snidely parroted Naveen's words back to him.

He raised his light staff. "Laurent has his mission, I have mine. Give me the gloves."

"You hypocrite," I spat. How dare he accuse me of being heartless and then go right ahead and do the same thing?

A quick glance toward the inhabited woman revealed that she was walking normally, no sign of the spirit having temporarily gotten the upper hand as they did during enthrallment.

Even if I couldn't go after her now, I had one week to find her and save her—I hoped. Though nothing was certain where this dybbuk was concerned.

I ran as quickly for the airfield as my wounded knee allowed, cloaking myself along the way. The battle was lost, but I was alive, and this war wasn't over.

3

THE DOOR TO TATIANA'S CHARTERED PLANE WAS already closing when I reached the airstrip. I yelled at the men wheeling the staircase away, furiously waving my arms and limping as fast as I could.

My boss's face appeared in the window, replaced by the female flight attendant, who saw me and nodded.

One of the men on the ground brought the stairs back. The door opened once more and the flight attendant instructed me to be seated for takeoff.

I claimed the farthest chair from Emmett, who was snoring like a congested bagpipe. Private jets were a wonderful thing, with roomy leather seats and a lounge area at the back with a sofa and television, but they were still metal tubes held in the air by the power of faith. Oh sure, and physics, but I was an arts grad with a healthy respect for gravity and the hard fall.

It meant that for all that I adored traveling, planes were a nightmare requiring Ativan. I popped one under my tongue, feeling it dissolve into that familiar mush.

The engines rumbled to life, the plane sped down the runway, and I clutched my armrest, keeping my mind as blank as possible. My stomach lurched into the soles of my feet when the wheels lifted off, so I focused on the tropical paradise, the plane circling the island once to get on the correct flight path. If I ignored the knocked-over chairs, the bloody mat with the sheet covering Torres's corpse, and the guards huddled in tight knots around stranded guests, it was lovely.

The second the "fasten seat belt" sign clicked off, I grabbed a change of clothes and hit the bathroom. After knocking back some Tylenol, I peeled off the uniform, recoiling at my own stench, then sat on the closed toilet lid in my underwear to wipe myself down and assess the damage.

My calves were bruised from Naveen's attack, and my body ached like I'd spent up close and personal time with a washing machine—inside it bouncing around, versus leaning against it for the vibrations. Accidentally. Like before I'd bought batteries for my vibrator Lady Catnip. Listen, beggars couldn't be choosers.

I scrubbed at a smear of dirt on my uninjured knee. The mission was a success, but any exhilaration got swallowed by the hollow chasm in my chest. Zev would get his gloves and I'd get my ward, but Naveen's accusations about my lack of loyalty played on a loop in my head. I was willingly handing an atrocious demon artifact over to a vampire and two men had been killed, Santiago and the young man with his poisoned needles.

I blinked away the memory of the fireball engulfing him and the resignation on his face, unsure of whether the greater tragedy was how callously people died in the magic world or their acceptance of that fact. I didn't want to become inured to either.

Abraham Lincoln famously said that a house divided against itself cannot stand. But what happened when *I* was the house? Should I have prioritized Torres's life, a man I didn't know and who was, let's face it, a criminal, over my own daughter's? Should I have given Naveen the gloves to destroy because that served a greater good, but faced the vampire's wrath, once more putting my family and myself in danger?

If I'd been able to destroy that dybbuk, I'd have gained points with Laurent to mitigate his reaction when he learned about the gloves, but once again it came down to the good of the many over the few. Were my loyalties allowed to be first and foremost to me and mine, or did I have a responsibility to humanity at large, even when it put the ones I loved in harm's way?

It was easy to have a strong moral code when it was never truly tested.

Worse, even my personal loyalties were in conflict with each other. Laurent would have plenty to say about working for Zev. The vamp hated the wolf shifter and vice versa. Emmett and I were under confidentiality agreements, but Laurent would find out. He always did.

But I'd been hired to do a job and had to respect my employer as well, regardless of what that entailed for Laurent and me. I flicked a clump of grass off of my ankle.

I was a house of cards on the brink of collapse, and I wasn't sure how to shore up the trusses for a more stable foundation.

I tossed the damp paper towel in the trash and got dressed, careful to move the domino into my change of clothes. The tile that I'd won in the Kefitzat Haderech had become a good luck charm for me.

Unfortunately, there was yet another problem worrying me, namely that Santiago's death didn't make sense. Even if there was a dead host somewhere on his island, that free-range dybbuk hadn't been trying to possess Torres, it had intended to kill him. Was this a terrifying possibility that even Laurent didn't know about?

Standing up, I splashed water on my face and shook out

my ponytail, raking my fingers through my hair to comb it before facing my reflection, searching for some clue on how to move forward. No beacon of justice or light of goodness shone forth from my brown eyes, though the bags under them smudged purple with exhaustion really made them pop.

And now that poor lady was enthralled and would spend the next week battling the dybbuk for possession of her body, knowing her inevitable fate.

Unless I found her. Me, a middle-aged woman with a zit burrowing up on her chin like a demented groundhog, a left shoulder that kept clicking, and dried pee in her underwear.

When I reclaimed my shadow magic a few weeks ago, it was meant to be the start of a brilliant new chapter in my life. One titled "Yaas, Queen!"

Okay. I'd do what I did best: collect facts, using them to make smart choices, which would bring my loyalties into alignment and strengthen that house of cards. I'd be objective and not allow my feelings for those close to me to color my course of action.

I raised a fist. "Royalty, bitches," I said weakly.

Tatiana patted the leather seat next to her when I returned to the main cabin. Her dress sat on the floor, having retained its shape like she'd molted it off. She wore red leggings to match her oversize red glasses and a black smock minidress with a giant bow under the bosom. Put that outfit on me and I'd look like a psycho child from a horror movie, but she rocked every ensemble I'd ever seen her in.

Royalty, bitches.

"Your friend is dead," I said softly, ready to hand over the tissue I'd taken from the box in the bathroom.

Tatiana pursed her lips. "Men like Santiago Torres don't have friends."

"You knew him for years. You must feel something."

My boss was a world-renowned artist with a passion and insight into the human condition few could rival. But as a fixer for the magic community, those qualities dimmed, and she took on a more hard-edged cast. I didn't like it. No one knew someone for forty years and then felt nothing at their death.

I balled the tissue up and shoved it in my pocket.

"I've outlived a lot of people, bubeleh," she said in a gentle reproach. "One learns to prioritize the grieving." She squeezed my knee. "I'm glad you did the smart thing and saved yourself."

We were silent for a while, save for the golem's snores and snorts.

Fact: self-preservation was Tatiana's golden rule.

Did my boss ever suffer a crisis of conscience over conflicted loyalties or was there only her agenda with everything else falling to a distant second place? Had she always been this hard or had she once been idealistic like me, time and experience scabbing her heart over with calluses?

I didn't want to become that version of myself.

The flight attendant served us a delicious entrée of whitefish with a lemon sauce, accompanied with piping-hot rolls and real cutlery. Suddenly starving, I devoured every morsel, even taking seconds of the bread to mop up the sauce.

Only once we were enjoying tea and cream puffs did Tatiana speak again, looking more like herself. "A dybbuk killed Santiago?"

"Yes." The ice pack I'd requested earlier had grown warm, so I unfastened the Velcro straps holding it against my knee and set it aside.

Tatiana tapped her nail against the armrest. "Is that what Laurent faces every time?"

She'd never seen him in action?

I rubbed my arm, feeling an indefinable melancholy that she'd missed out on the wild beauty and savage mastery that Laurent displayed when dispatching dybbuks. "Yes."

She nodded but her face twisted in pain for an instant.

Tatiana was Laurent's honorary aunt. His grandparents had been her best friends and she'd known him since birth. She'd expressed displeasure about him killing dybbuks on more than one occasion, and I could only guess it was because she worried about him.

Fact: she wasn't totally unfeeling.

"He's really good at what he does," I said to put her mind at ease. "And he's in wolf form when he kills them. Plus, this one behaved oddly in the way it attacked."

"I couldn't see the dybbuk, but Torres was fighting tooth and nail." She clucked her tongue. "I expect that the dybbuk got away since you made the flight."

Her worry was apparently short-lived.

"Uh, yeah." I licked a blob of cream off my lip.

Tatiana placed her cup on the saucer. "Tell me how you got the gloves."

I recounted the tale, ending with Naveen's interest in the demon artifact.

"Oy. Laurent will kvetch about us giving them to a vampire. Well, Naveen won't get them before Zev does, and at that point, it won't be our problem anymore." She finished her tea. "You did the right thing. I'm proud of you."

"Thanks. I think." Praise was better than hearing I'd screwed up, but *I* wasn't proud of me. I picked up another cream puff but immediately set it down, my heart heavy.

"This day was inevitable. Santiago had a lot of enemies," Tatiana said. "No wonder Sherisse was more uptight than usual. He should have hired me to protect him. Silly man." She motioned to the flight attendant for more tea. "He was always convinced that between his magic and his security, he was invincible. But there's always a way."

"And you can't fight what you can't see."

She nodded. "Pride and longevity do not make good bedfellows."

I debated whether to tell her about my suspicions

concerning the woman at the fight. It was one thing for Tatiana to set up a hotline in Vancouver for people to phone in suspected cases of enthrallment, but this woman could be anywhere in the world. My boss would not consider finding her a good use of resources. And yet, it wasn't better to ask forgiveness than permission with Tatiana either.

I adjusted my seat, seeking the best position for my aching body. "The dybbuk that killed Santiago enthralled one of the guests."

"A na'ar geyt tsvey mol dort vu a kliger geyt nit keyn eintsik mol." The Yiddish Yoda serenely stirred sugar into her drink.

I declined more tea, thanking the flight attendant for taking away my meal. "Goes twice? Goes not? Huh?" My cousin Goldie, who'd raised me, had spoken Yiddish when I was younger. Now married to a goy, she rarely did, and I'd forgotten most of it.

"'A fool goes twice where a sensible person doesn't even go once.' Don't be that fool, Miriam." Content that she'd had the last word, Tatiana picked up the art magazine sticking out of her giant purse.

Disappointed yet unsurprised, I moved the pillow from behind my back to my shoulder, thinking of a way to convince her, but within seconds, I gave a giant yawn and fell asleep.

The moon was out, the sky clear when we landed back in Vancouver. The night air smelled like diesel and bitter coffee thanks to the plane, but the tarmac still retained a vestige of heat, keeping the breeze at bay.

As expected, Zev BatKian met us on the landing strip. He wore another elegant suit, this one a dark gray. Not a single hair of his short mahogany strands was out of place and his goatee was impeccably trimmed as always. Did vampires' hair not grow or did this dude have a daily standing appointment with his barber?

I flexed my fingers with their ragged cuticles and nails bitten down to the quick, comparing them to his short, buffed nails. Damn. Outshone by an undead male.

Next to me, Emmett yawned loudly, not bothering to cover his mouth.

The master vamp was accompanied by his human henchman Rodrigo, a hulking man with no sense of humor, unless you counted the chauffeur's cap with the gold braiding that he wore because it was kind of a joke.

"Undertaker, it's a joy as always to see your beaming visage," I said.

His expression, already pretty stony, went positively igneous. I grinned.

Zev tapped his foot. "The Torquemada Gloves?"

"Sorry," I mumbled. Woe betide anyone who fell afoul of his beloved protocols. Carefully, I pulled the shriveled yellow pair out of my bag and placed them in his outstretched palm.

He didn't laugh maniacally or stuff them in his suit pocket with a satisfied smirk. For a moment, he simply stared at them like he couldn't believe they were real. He touched his index finger to them, then recoiled as if burned, that hand balling into a fist.

I'd seen him destroy priceless art without any emotion and ooze more menace in a simple pleasant smile than a chainsaw murderer. In fact, the only time he'd gotten visibly angry that I'd witnessed was in reaction to something Tatiana had said. I had yet to figure out their relationship, but it was layers upon knots upon more layers.

So, when Zev took a single ragged breath, his body bowed slightly over the gloves as if they occupied a much larger physical presence, and rocked back and forth, my eyebrows shot up. This emotion wasn't anger, however, and while his movements reminded me of something, I couldn't put my finger on what that was.

Zev stilled, and I got the sense that he'd just remembered that he wasn't alone. He folded the gloves gently and tucked them in his breast pocket. "Thank you," he said. "I shall be in touch about the ward."

Tatiana watched him with a faint frown, her brows drawn together. At least I wasn't the only one in the dark about what was going on, but she didn't ask, and he didn't elaborate.

Rodrigo escorted the vampire into a Town Car with black-tinted windows, and the two of them drove off.

That's when it hit me. His rocking was akin to a religious Jew when davening—praying. Zev had been a rabbi back in his human life, but he'd been a vampire for a long time. There was no way that someone turned by an estrie—which were demons—still believed in his Jewish God. Was there?

I followed the taillights' progress until they faded away, doubt slithering through me. Had Zev transferred his faith from a god above to one down below? The Torquemada Gloves were a demon artifact. Did the vampire want them to further some agenda for a demon lord?

Or was it the reaction of a Jew seeking to document an awful chapter in our peoples' history, perhaps even gleeful at outliving the monster behind it all, especially if it was Torquemada's skin? Zev might even be old enough to have been alive during the Spanish Inquisition. Having been a rabbi was still very much tied to Zev's sense of self, and as such, these gloves would have enormous personal value to him. If that were the case, I couldn't fault him for that.

But which was it? My character assessment of Zev thus far had been pretty spot-on and it bothered me that I couldn't derive what was behind his behavior with the gloves.

My boss snapped me out of my troubling thoughts with her insistence on driving me home in her death-mobile, a huge gold Buick from the 1970s. Emmett clambered into the back seat with no fear, but I strapped in already white-knuckling the "oh shit" handle in anticipation.

Tatiana never met a green light she didn't want to slow down through, stop signs were merely suggestions, and the horn was an important part of inter-driver communications—even in the middle of the night when there was no one else on the road.

She honked at a tree's shadow, slamming on the brakes and jerking me painfully against the seat belt.

"Let me drive!" I screeched.

The golem cackled in the back seat. "Humans. So breakable."

I twisted around. "Shut it, or I'll have Laurent rip your leg off again."

He harrumphed, crossed his arms, and stared out the window.

Tatiana scrunched up her face, squinting at the yellow line. "No wonder. I'm not wearing my night driving glasses." She took one hand off the wheel and all her focus off the road to root around in her purse.

"Ahhhh!" I grabbed the wheel, trying to keep us on course. Tatiana took this to mean that I'd steer while she searched for her glasses. "You're crazier than Santiago and his Funhouse of Horrors, you know that?"

She calmly switched out her oversize glasses for round granny frames.

"Smaller lenses? Is that really the way to go?" I said.

"Sha." Scolding me to be quiet in Yiddish, she pried my fingers off the wheel. "Ah. That's better."

The rest of the drive was uneventful in terms of my having a heart attack but hearing an eighty-year-old sing along to Taylor Swift's *1989* album, complete with sassy shimmying and finger wagging, induced its own kind of trauma.

Jews wandering in the desert for forty years wouldn't have

been as relieved to find a lush oasis as I was to pull up to my duplex in East Vancouver. A neatly pruned rosebush in full bloom complemented the green siding and white trim of the townhouse. I'd put colorful cushions on the two chairs gracing my half of the front porch and hung baskets overflowing with tiny flowers on both my side and that of my ex-husband, Eli. It was my trade for him mowing my lawn.

Tatiana bumped over the curb, parking the behemoth on the diagonal, and almost taking out the sideview mirror on my sedan.

"Safe and sound. Really, Miriam—" She accidentally elbowed the horn as she twisted to face me, and I jumped. "You worry too much."

I tensed, swiveling to check my neighbors' homes for lights switching on. All I needed was to wake one of them and explain my new friends.

"I'll try to adopt your laid-back attitude," I said, scrambling out as fast as I could, once I was assured that we hadn't disturbed anyone.

"Do that." She threw me a finger wave. "Sweet dreams, bubeleh."

I shut the car door with a sigh of relief. I'd been wound up over this mission and couldn't wait to get a good night's sleep.

And sleep I did. The price of that deep slumber, though, was waking up Sunday morning to find that I'd gotten my period. Add musical accompaniment to my spurting and gushing and I could have rivalled the fountain at the Bellagio in Vegas.

Perimenopause was a cruel joke. If I had to suffer through hot flashes that left me wetter than my gym towel the one time I'd tried a spin class, then my periods could end already. Though speaking of that spin class, it wasn't my fault I collapsed into the fetal position when it was over, in so much pain between my legs that I swore I had my own burning bush. That class had been the seventh level of Hell and was taught by a cyborg. Not even the hot cyborg, Sean, that my bestie, Jude, had sworn would be there.

I sighed. I missed the days when Saturdays meant a weekly brunch with her, but since I'd learned about the Danger Zone, drinking was a no go. We'd moved it to Sundays, but one or the other of us had scheduling issues, like she did today. For now, we'd abandoned our standing date, and it sucked not seeing her on a regular basis.

Between missing my best friend and currently wearing more padding in my underwear than a loose-bowelled baby, I was in a foul mood that could not be dispelled by my latte, the two (okay, four) blueberry Eggo waffles that I'd hidden at the back of my freezer, or cracking into my fun jigsaw of the *New York Times* front page showing the news from the day I was born.

My puzzle mat was unrolled on the kitchen table, and my empty coffee mug and plate with waffle crumbs were pushed to one side as I completed a section in the bottom left. It was a photo of a meteor shower that had happened on that day. I didn't know much about them, and curious, I looked it up.

Meteor showers were streaks of light across the night sky that were caused by bits of rock and debris called meteoroids. Cool. I scanned the next paragraph. The popular name for them was shooting or fallen stars. In shock, I dropped my phone.

The sun's rim dips; the stars rush out / At one stride comes the dark

"The Rime of the Ancient Mariner" was my favorite poem and truly beautiful, but the line that had popped into my head wasn't relevant to this. Dozens of these showers happened every year. This wasn't some prophecy about me and stars. Nor was the dark some allusion to my shadow magic. The meteor shower on the day I was born was a coincidence and no reason to break out the tinfoil hat.

That said, I abandoned that part of the puzzle to tackle the opposite side, scrawling a rough to-do list while I worked on it. The easiest way to narrow down that enthralled woman's identity was to get hold of Santiago's guest list. I underlined "find incentive for Tatiana."

After a brief hesitation, I added another item: find out why Zev wanted the gloves. The vampire didn't need a demon artifact, no matter how cruel, to torture a person. If he planned to flay someone alive, he had minions aplenty up to the task, if he wasn't in the mood himself. Besides, his reaction to the gloves continued to bother me.

A quick search on Ohrist forums didn't yield anything about the Torquemada Gloves beyond Naveen's story of madness and people trying to rip off their own skin. I tapped a puzzle piece against my lip.

Naveen assumed Zev coveted the gloves for obvious reasons, but he was prone to incorrect assumptions, I thought spitefully, fitting the puzzle piece into the headline. Tatiana could probably connect me with a paranormal expert who could shed more light on them, but she also might forbid me from prying into Zev's private business.

My gut instinct said that the answer was more complex than the gloves being demonic. Fellow librarians to the rescue. I typed a quick email on my phone to a colleague at the main library at the University of British Columbia, seeking direction to learn more about a potential religious or historical artifact. They had to be known as the Torquemada Gloves for a reason, but I didn't have time to scour the various academic databases for a lead, especially when a vital clue could easily be a footnote in some obscure scholarly journal.

Someone rapped out a "Shave and a Haircut" knock on my front door as I hit send.

Cursing anyone that perky for existing, I peered through

the peephole, then lightly banged my head against the wall, debating the odds my visitors would go away.

"I know you're home, Mir," Eli called out. "Open up."

"I brought ginger molasses cookies," Ryann Esposito trilled.

I cracked the door, the chain pulled taut. "Homemade?"

"You bet. Super chewy." She held up one of those Danish cookie tins. Excellent. I needed a new sewing kit holder.

I removed the chain and opened the door wide. "Twenty minutes and if your harassment supersedes my enjoyment of the cookies, this ambush is over."

4

DETECTIVE ELI CHU, MY BABY DADDY AND EX-husband, a brawny homicide cop who'd faced down killers without batting an eye, jingled as he stepped into the foyer. That was new.

Curious, I unbuttoned the top button of his short-sleeved dress shirt, avoiding his swatting hands. A cross, a Star of David, and a hamsa for warding off the evil eye were all strung on a gold chain around his neck. I laughed, flicking the necklace. "You know what all this is called? Apotropaic magic. From the Greek meaning to ward off." I simulated spitting three times with a *ptu ptu ptu* sound to ward off the evil eye. "There. You're good."

"Leave him alone." Ryann slung an arm over Eli's shoulder. With her electric grape hair shaved on the sides, her anime-large blue eyes, and peacock print palazzo pants, she looked like a refugee from Burning Man, not the chief Lonestar in Vancouver. I wondered if she owned a hula hoop. "It gives him comfort and a much-needed sense of security during these changing times," she said. "My dad did the same thing when he found out."

Eli gripped his pendants defensively. "Thank you."

I shut the door, leading them into the kitchen. "Comfort isn't going to do shit if he comes across a vampire, and neither is any of that."

My ex pulled a chair out from the table and straddled it backward, clinking mightily. "Which is exactly why we're here."

I put my dishes in the sink to make room on the table for the cookie tin next to the puzzle and opened the lid. Inhaling the spicy tang of ginger dissipated my crankiness by a solid thirty percent. "As I explained during our last four discussions on the topic, it's handled."

Apparently, it was time for the 1:45PM fountain show because my nether regions kicked into active sploohing. Sitting down with my legs firmly crossed, I shoved half a cookie into my mouth. Damn, that was good. Not too heavy on the ginger, with the molasses balancing it out rather than overpowering the taste. The crystalized sugar sprinkles on top provided the final perfect touch.

Ryann examined the cover of the jigsaw box.

"Sadie is my kid too and I own half the property that's going to be protected," Eli said. "Trust me, it'll be a cold day in Hell before some undead serial killer works his magic mumbo jumbo on it."

"It's not like Mr. BatKian lives in a double-wide in the woods," I said.

"He wouldn't be able to fit all his suits in one." Ryann nibbled on a cookie.

"Right? His tailor must be on call 24/7."

She sighed. "That man deserves every penny."

"If you've both finished your little *Twilight* moment?" Eli raised an eyebrow until we'd both nodded.

"Word of advice?" I licked sugar off my finger. "Don't ever make a *Twilight* reference in BatKian's hearing."

"Totally," Ryann said. "He's pretty rigid about his sense of self. If only he'd be flexible and recognize that we don't just carry one persona but many, he wouldn't be mired in such a dark aura."

I stared at her. "Yeah, I meant that he'd tear out your throat."

"Oh, that too." She patted the container. "Told you the cookies were good."

Eli dropped his head in his hands. "Will you please listen to Ryann's proposal?"

His voice was strained, and I felt bad for ragging on him when he was clearly so stressed. The least I could do was hear Ryann out for Eli's sake. It was good that he'd reconnected with her, both a cop like himself and someone else to help guide him in this magic world. However, while Ryann hadn't shown any prejudiced behavior toward me, who knew what she said when I wasn't around? Eli was already predisposed to listen to her over me because of their shared police bond.

I crossed my arms. Then uncrossed them and took another treat. "Knock yourself out."

Should I have shown more compassion? Sure. Very few Sapiens ever broke through the perception filter to open their eyes to the existence of magic, and all things considered, Eli was dealing with it quite well. A couple weeks ago, he'd helped me take down a corrupt Lonestar who was trying to frame Laurent and me for murder. To his cop mind, a killer was a killer, magic or not.

That was great, but then I'd made the mistake of telling him about the demon parasite who'd come through my walls and thus had begun his trip on the Paranoia Express. I sympathized (truly, no one was more freaked out than me, the person the parasite had been gunning for), but when he refused to accept the fact that my way was the only way to get properly warded up, I'd gotten annoyed. Which morphed into outright pissed off when he'd brought Ryann into it.

I had experience and knowledge of this situation that he

didn't. I respected his police skills, and he had to do the same for my understanding of the magic world and my unique and precarious position in it.

"Okay, so last time we spoke, I thought it would be impossible to find anyone to ward against demon parasites because I mean, how mad is that?" The Lonestar's facial expressions and gestures were the same expansive ones that my sixteen-year-old used when she got excited.

I didn't buy her innocent act for a second, because I'd seen her reduce Laurent to a puddle of goo with her magic. She'd done the same to me.

"Super mad." I snapped another puzzle piece into the *New York Times* headline. This discussion was pointless, but at least I could get more of the jigsaw completed while it happened.

"But ta-da! I found someone."

I didn't bother looking up, sorting through to find blue pieces for the sky in one of the article photos. "No, you didn't."

Ryann insisted she wasn't out to get me, and I believed that on some level, but I wasn't an idiot. I would never have made this deal with Zev and gone through that shit show on the island if I harbored even a seed of hope that anyone else could accomplish this.

Eli nudged me. "She did."

I stacked some pieces into a pile. "Okay, I'll bite. Who is this warding marvel?"

"She's a total recluse." Ryann shook her head. "I'm amazed I tracked her down."

"Mazel tov. Have another cookie." I pushed the tin closer to her.

"Mir," Eli said. "You're being a bitch."

"No, you're being an ass. I was very clear that Zev is doing this." I wasn't suicidal and refusing this gesture of help would be an insult the vampire wouldn't overlook. Especially not a second time. Plus, he really was the only one with the abilities to create this kind of ward. I suspected it had to do with his demon bloodline.

Ryann put her hand on my arm. "I appreciate that you're in a terrible position, but we can protect you from him."

Not when he had free rein in my home. "I already have a protector, thanks. My quota is full."

"Your boss? Another trustworthy one." Eli hooked his ankle around my chair, pulling it slightly toward him to make me look up from the puzzle.

It jostled my arm and a piece fell on the floor. "So long as I'm of use to her, she'll do whatever she can to keep me safe," I said tightly.

Ryann retrieved it. "The Lonestars have more power than you give us credit for."

I laughed without an ounce of humor. "Trust me, I don't underestimate your reach. Besides, it's not like you're assigning Lonestars to guard me full-time."

"I wouldn't have to," Ryann said. "One word from Elizabeta and you'd be safe."

"This is the warder?" Off Ryann's nod, I set down the puzzle piece.

Was Elizabeta a demon? Someone higher in the evil supernatural food chain than Zev? Would I take the devil I didn't know over the one I did if that meant I could give Naveen the gloves?

I'd win some likeability points with him, which would make Laurent happy. I'd had two best friends in high school who'd despised each other and it wasn't a pleasant experience for me. Eventually, I'd chosen between them. Not that Laurent and I were besties, but I didn't want to cause him any pain.

Plus, it would be one less demon artifact in the world.

"Why is she so powerful?" I said.

The Lonestar pressed her lips together, looking off as if weighing a decision. She exhaled slowly. "This isn't something many people know, but in the interests of you trusting me..." She steepled her fingers together. "Lonestars operate like packs. Each chapter has an alpha, or a head, and is autonomous from the others, but in case of...issues, there are continental alphas. Elizabeta once ruled all of North America."

I shot out of my chair so fast that it fell over backward. "You want me to trust my safety to a Lonestar?" I gestured at the gold star tattoo on Ryann's wrist that was the emblem of her authority, while speaking to Eli. "Just because she has some kind of cop badge and you babysat her, you're going to ally yourself with her over your ex? The mother of your child? Ryann had no compunction putting me in danger to assess her partner's guilt."

Ryann shrugged. "Guilty as charged. Those were extenuating circumstances, though."

"You did what you had to." Eli patted her shoulder. "No officer wants to believe their partner is dirty."

I moved over to the counter to put some space between us. "You're unbelievable. And this Elizabeta? Got a handy justification for me to trust a stranger when at least one Lonestar was complicit in my parents' murders?"

Ryann had figured out my interest in Fred McMurtry and when confronted about it, I hadn't denied it, so there was no reason to hide the facts from her now.

"One bad cop doesn't mean all of them are." Eli spoke with the exaggerated patience he'd used on Sadie when she'd thrown tantrums as a toddler.

Delilah swelled to life behind me, her shadow elongating to the height of the top cabinet.

Eli darted a nervous glance at her.

"Since the original phrase is 'one bad apple ruins the bunch,'" I snapped, "extrapolate."

"Let's all take a deep breath and calm down." Ryann edged out of her seat, using her hands to demonstrate the flow of her inhales and exhales.

Delilah inflated even more.

Ryann didn't bat an eye. "Take a moment of mindfulness before continuing this conversation."

Behind me, Delilah crossed her arms, the two of us ignoring Ryann.

"You're letting your emotions over the past run away with you," Eli said.

"My *emotions*?" I slammed a hand on the counter. "No, it's a cold, hard fact that at least one Lonestar covered up Mom's and Dad's murders. But if you want to discuss emotions, can I get you an ankh for your terror necklace? Because I think you're missing a few religious artifacts there."

Eli made a "bring it" motion. "If it keeps a vampire far away, then yeah. Keep those artifacts coming, sweetheart."

I yanked open a drawer and chucked an ornate dessert spoon at him. It nailed him in the chest and bounced onto the ground. "Here. Don't forget to carry silver for the were-wolves." I waved my hands around, moving into his personal space. "Ooooh, scary."

"All righty, then," Ryann said, holding up her hands. "Maybe we should try some conflict resolution?"

"How about we don't?" I whirled on her. "I don't need cops coming into my house and telling me what to do."

"Okay," Ryann muttered and sat down. "I'll be taking some deep breaths over here if anyone wants to join in and be calm again."

"Better any corrupt cop than a vampire!" Eli roared, nose-to-nose with me.

The air crackled with hostility. It deepened and grew until it snapped with the slam of the kitchen door.

We spun around to find Sadie gripping her overnight bag. She'd been at her aunt's cabin for the weekend celebrating her cousin Nessa's birthday and had returned at the worst moment possible.

"Vampire?" she said. "Dad, is this a joke? But...why are you and Mom fighting about it?"

Eli turned away with a soft curse, rubbing a hand over his bald head.

The one thing we'd agreed on was that our discussion with Sadie about the existence of magic and things that go bump in the night would be conducted in a calm, stress-free environment, conveying the appropriate amount of seriousness without scaring her.

I grabbed the cookie tin. "Hi, honey. Ginger cookie?"

Ryann stood up. "It's homemade."

Delilah shrank down to normal. *Nothing to see here, folks.*

Sadie's bag hit the ground. She rubbed her eyes with her fists, gaping at Delilah.

Way to break the perception filter, Mom.

Ryann took her leave soon after, telling me to call her if I wanted to contact Elizabeta. I nodded absently, watching my daughter sitting in the living room staring at her feet, her hair falling forward to hide her face like a curtain.

I filled the kettle and set it on the gas burner. Delilah became another shadow on the ground, but instead of the usual faint hum under my skin, my magic was dull.

Eli hovered anxiously in the kitchen doorway, his hands stuffed in the pockets of his jeans. "You're making tea?"

No, I was buying time in case my daughter flinched when she saw me and my entire life shattered. If Sadie was horrified by my powers, I wouldn't use them again.

I pulled a container of English Breakfast out of the cupboard.

You think you can stop now? Quit on Tatiana when Zev has free reign in your home? Go back in that magicless closet?

Sadie had her back to me now and she hadn't made eye

contact since she'd seen Delilah, nor had I gotten any kind of hug even though she'd been away all weekend.

The round tin slipped from my hand, loose black tea spilling across the floor.

"Miriam. We have to speak to her."

I jerked my gaze up from the ground and turned off the stove. "Yeah."

Eli sat on the sofa next to Sadie. He frowned at me when I hesitated, so I took the spot on her other side.

"Sades?" he said gently. "Can we talk about this?"

Neither of us wanted to thrust her into the harsh truth that monsters were real, but we'd agreed that not knowing was far more dangerous. It was time for her to face facts.

She lifted her head, a dazed expression on her face. "I'm not crazy. He had fangs, didn't he?"

"Who?" I said.

"That man. The night our place was broken into. He said he was a neighbor and I invited him—" She gasped, her hand clapping over her mouth.

Eli looked shell-shocked, but a sense of calm settled on me. Sadie had seen magic of her own accord and the first thing she sought was reassurance about her mental state, not horror that her mom was a freak.

"That was Zev BatKian. He's the head vampire here in Vancouver." I brushed her hair off her shoulder. "You didn't do anything wrong. He and I have an understanding and he isn't going to hurt us. In fact, he's going to ward up our house so that nothing bad can get in."

Eli opened his mouth to protest, then looked at Sadie and kept silent, but the look on his face promised further discussion.

Sadie pushed my hand away, but half-heartedly like normal, not like she recoiled at my touch. My shoulders descended another notch. "What are you? What am I?"

51

Curious, not scared. Better and better.

"You're human," her dad said.

I glared at him.

"Your mom is human, too," he amended, "but she has magic powers."

"Like what?" she said.

"I'm a Banim Shovavim, which is basically a descendent of Lilith who can animate their shadow and go invisible. Neat, right? The name itself is also pretty cool," I said, babbling on. "It means rebellious or wayward children, and…" I trailed off, seeing her eyes glaze over.

All right, then. When Sadie started sex education in elementary school, parents had been told to be concise when answering questions, instead of nervously rambling out long-winded answers. Kids were simply interested in the specific question they'd asked, and if they wanted more information, they'd follow up. It seemed like as good a guideline as any.

Sadie twirled a strand of black hair around her finger, sucking her bottom lip into her mouth. "Are there a lot of vampires?" she asked after a moment. "How dangerous is it?"

"There are more humans with magic than there are vampires," I assured her. "And way more people such as yourself without any powers. You'll be able to always see vampires now that your natural perception filter has been breached, and that's important because vampires can only turn people without magic. But if you're vigilant and smart, there's very little danger. Even less for you because of Zev."

She unzipped the front pocket on her overnight bag and pulled out her phone. "I have to tell my friends. Nessa. Caleb."

I closed my hand over hers. "You can't."

"Why not?" She pressed the phone to her chest.

"Because magic has to remain hidden. It's not my rule and I don't agree with it, but anyone who knows could land in trouble."

"Dad knows."

"I ended up working a murder case involving magic and I was given special dispensation to find out about it," Eli said.

Our child's chin jutted up, a familiar stubborn glint in her eyes.

"Sadie," I said, "I'm not kidding. You can't tell them. Promise me."

"So I'm supposed to let everyone I care about be vamp food?"

"That won't happen," I said. "Zev isn't about to target kids who are friends with a cop's daughter."

"That's your reassurance?" Sadie crossed her arms.

"Yeah. He's practical. That's the best guarantee. Now, I need your promise."

The loaded silence stretched on so long I scrambled together ways to keep Ryann from charging her with violating the Lonestars' prime directive.

"Please," I said.

"Is this why you had me watching *Buffy*?" She tossed her hair. "Some kind of primer?"

Eli pressed his lips together and looked away. It didn't matter if it was in the middle of a serious talk or an argument, should Sadie's melodramatic streak rear its head, her dad would want to laugh.

Generally, I carried on in a rational manner until he'd recovered enough to participate, because it was kind of funny, but right now his uselessness and my daughter's theatrics put my temper over the top.

"Busted," I snapped. "It was my deepest wish that you take it as a how-to guide. Careful who you date, make sure I get checked regularly for brain aneurysms, and remember that sister of yours I always joke about?" I shrugged, spreading my arms wide.

The two of us glowered at each other before the child caved.

"Fine," she muttered, dropping her defiant glare. "You have my stupid fucking promise." She kicked her bag across the room and stormed off.

Eli lost it, his shoulders silently shaking.

"And you! Way to help me navigate a tough parenting scenario, Detective Chuckles." I smacked him with a cushion. "Quit laughing already. Seriously. God, I hate you."

"That was worth it." Wiping tears from his eyes, he went into the kitchen.

What a disaster. Sadie didn't seem to care about my magic, and I don't think she was scared for herself, but I hadn't predicted that her friends would be the variable to set her off.

Eli returned with Ryann's cookie tin.

"Is this what we're doing instead of joints these days?" I joked weakly.

"I could bust the kids smoking up at the skate park on Tenth."

I shook my head. "Better not. One of them is Helen's son."

"Helicopter Helen?" He shuddered and bit into a treat.

I'd selected one with the perfect ratio of sugar crystals to cookie when Eli spoke.

"Do you remember what it took for me to see magic?" He touched the faint scar on his arm from where Laurent had clawed him. "Sadie saw it simply being around that vamp. You still want to go through with this? What if he did something to her?"

I put the box on the coffee table, my stomach sour. "He didn't. He gave me his word."

Eli shot me a look like I was being stupid.

"I've shared with you how and why I've come to this conclusion multiple times." I crossed my arms. "You're one of the people who knows me best. I've always considered things carefully, can't you trust that I'm doing that now more than ever?"

"I'm trying, Mir."

I plumped up a pillow with a bit more force than necessary and settled it behind my back. "Really, because you seem pretty keen to listen to Ryann, despite everything I keep telling you."

"You want me to align myself with a vampire when you won't give the same courtesy to this Elizabeta, who's a former officer."

"I'm not asking you to exchange friendship bracelets with him. I'm saying that in the interests of not insulting the dangerous supernatural creature, we should accept his help with a smile and a sincere thank-you. And it's totally different with the Lonestar. You haven't been harmed by vampires."

"Yet," he said.

"Okay, yet, but you've been alive forty-four years without incident. I got fifteen with my parents before someone or something killed them, and Fred McMurtry covered it up."

"Which is one more thing you want me to accept after years of thinking they died in a house fire."

I did a double take. "Are you blaming me for not having told you the truth? I grew up so terrified that their killer might come after me that I cut ties with the one person I had left from my old life, my uncle Jake, so excuse me for not making honesty a priority with you. Is that how you handle victims, Detective Chu?" I said coldly.

"Obviously not."

"Just me, then. Good to know."

"I'm a damn good officer," he said waspishly.

"Yeah, you are. You're also a good leader because you don't second-guess and dismiss your detectives." I threw him a tight smile.

"They're trained."

"Would that help? If I waved a GED from Hogwarts in front of your face, would you trust my capability?"

"I don't know." He crossed his arms.

"Exactly. You don't. But I'm trying to tell you that I do. Or," I amended, "as much as Sapien cops do when dealing with criminals. There's an element of unpredictability in both worlds, but I'm doing the best to mitigate that as much as possible with facts and experience."

"Then let me mitigate it with you. Use my experience to help decide the wisest course of action."

It took all my willpower not to clench my fists and to speak calmly. "I did, remember? When it came time to take Oliver down, I deferred to you. Now you need to do the same."

He made a frustrated sound, his body tensing.

I folded my hands in my lap. "Is the issue me, Miri, or me, a Banim Shovavim?"

"From where I'm sitting, there's no difference between the two."

I squeezed my fingers tightly together, my old engagement ring digging into my skin. "That sounds a lot like an Ohrist prejudice."

"I've said as much to Ryann about her magic, so I'm pretty equal opportunity prejudiced." Eli looked up at the ceiling and took a contemplative breath. "I don't want to fight. Look, I'm grateful that I know about magic now. If I'm being honest, it explains stuff that never added up in certain investigations, little things that I pushed to the side or outright dismissed."

"You think you had other homicides involving magic?"

"Yeah, and if dealing with this vampire is truly the only way to proceed, then I'll suck it up. But I want to be there when he comes over. Okay?"

I nodded. "That's fair."

He shook his head sadly. "I don't know if anything about

this is fair. Guess I'm getting a taste of my own medicine from when I broke up our marriage."

"This isn't some kind of revenge, Eli. Don't frame it that way."

"I didn't..." He gave me a faint smile. "We'll talk later."

For years the secret of my magic and my parents' deaths had weighed down on me. When I accepted my powers back into my life a few weeks ago, those secrets had widened the gulf between me and my family. But now everything was out in the open and that space hadn't shrunk. How did people with powers navigate close relationships with Sapiens? Were they destined to be out of alignment because the difference between the magical and the mundane was simply too great?

I shook my head. That was more negative thinking and unproductive. I'd suggested to Eli before that we see an Ohrist therapist, and given his comments today and Sadie's reaction, I'd better get that name from Jude sooner rather than later.

I spent the rest of the day finding reasons to pass by my daughter's bedroom, but her door remained closed, and I didn't hear anything inside. She didn't even come out for our weekly TV date, which was unprecedented. Generally, when she was mad, she'd stomp around the house, making sure I saw her.

I went to bed early, because it beat living out more of this shitty day, but I couldn't sleep, a host of nightmare what-ifs looping around my brain. After reading the first chapter of the mystery I'd been so excited to dive into without taking in a word, I gave up.

Sadie had given me her promise about not telling anyone else about magic, and I had to trust her to keep it. Eli might think he and Ryann had a bond because she was the daughter of his boss and he'd babysat her when she was young, hiding a special Oreo stash for her, but should Sadie violate the Lonestars' prime directive of keeping magic hidden, Ryann would come after our kid with the full weight of Ohrist law enforcement behind her.

I crossed my fingers. *Please keep your promise.*

Moving my domino from the bedside table to under my pillow, I repeated my wish until I fell into a fitful slumber.

5

MONDAY KICKED OFF EVEN WORSE THAN SUNDAY had. Sadie woke up uncharacteristically early, so I ran downstairs to the kitchen to talk to her while she ate breakfast, but she brushed me off, saying there was a meeting for all the camp counselors before work that she had to get to.

She clomped upstairs to grab her stuff and I planted myself on the stairs to confront her before she left. It was important we reached an understanding and that I defused her anger.

I was so preoccupied with talking to my daughter that I didn't want to answer my phone when it rang, but after the person called back for the third time in a row, I hurried into the kitchen to check the screen. It was Tatiana. I made a face because I didn't have time to deal with her right now, but she'd get pissy if I ignored her call yet again.

"Hello?" I did my best to keep my impatience out of my voice.

"Call off my nephew or I won't be responsible for my actions," she said tersely.

I blinked. Tatiana, riled up? "What happened?"

Sadie was still stomping around upstairs.

"He—"

There was a grunt. "Someone put a death curse on her," Laurent said, having taken the phone away. "And she's not taking it seriously."

His French accent had grown stronger, as it did when he was angry or worried. Even so, hearing it centered me. It was like I'd been wandering in the middle of a vast unknown land, but I could tilt my head back and enjoy the passing clouds for a moment instead of constantly scanning for danger. He was the one person who not only had my back but believed in me.

I'd have smiled if I wasn't in shock.

"What kind of death curse?" I mentally slapped myself. Dead was dead.

"Oh, are you not willing to help unless you have the specifics? The proper paperwork? Alors, woman, you are not leaving this house." This last to Tatiana, who was presumably making a break for it.

I clenched my fists. By all means, be an asshole. Because I wasn't getting enough of that from my kid. "Yeah, give it to me in triplicate with proper bullet points."

"I'm taking it as seriously as every other attempt," Tatiana said in the background.

"Precisely my point," he growled.

"It's an occupational hazard." She'd wrested the phone away again.

"And you didn't think to mention this?" I said. The Moka pot on my glass stove top burbled and I dumped both shots of espresso into my warmed milk, the phone cradled between my ear and shoulder.

"I told you—" Laurent had come back on.

"Not the time for sanctimony, Huff 'n' Puff." I took that first delicious sip, my body singing hallelujah as the caffeine hit. "Are you certain?"

Something thunked onto a table on their side of the call, followed by the clatter of glass.

"You need your wits about you," Laurent said. "No Kahlua in your coffee."

Tatiana made a loud noise of disgust. "Deviating from my routine isn't going to make it go away but it might keep me from strangling you, Lolo."

"Laurent," I repeated, pacing back and forth, my coffee mug in hand. "Are you positive?"

"Oui. Yes. She got the letter."

"Letter?" I did a double take. "Are we talking typed? Letters cut out serial killer–style? Wait. I know, was it hand-written in a formal calligraphy? How etiquette forward of the death curser. Hang on." I paused, my mug halfway to my mouth. "Is that what happened to Santiago?"

Outside, a car horn beeped twice.

"The letter was printed, and we don't know yet if Santiago got one," Laurent said. "Tatiana is waiting for a call from his widow."

"Fuck. Okay, but what does it say? Are there demands or—"

Sadie clattered down the stairs, beelining for the door, her backpack slung over her shoulder.

I ran into the foyer, almost sloshing coffee onto my hand. "Stop right there."

"Stop what?" Laurent said.

"Not you." I jerked a finger from Sadie to the stairs. "Sit yourself down this instant."

"Can't. Asha's waiting." She shrugged, jamming her foot in a canvas sneaker.

"Huh?" Laurent said. "No, come over here now."

"Not. You." I kicked Sadie's other runner out of the way before she could put it on and mouthed, "Sit."

"Yes. Me." Laurent made a frustrated noise. "This is your fault."

I almost dropped the phone. "Are you freaking kidding me?"

"You think I am pranking you?" he said.

Sadie took advantage of my distraction and slipped out the door, hopping into her other shoe.

"Hey!" I bolted after her, still in my pj's, feeling a warm gush as I bled through my pad. I stopped on the bottom stair of the porch and stomped my foot.

"Sadie May Chu, get your butt back here this instant!" Great. I was officially the crazy neighborhood mom, with bedhead, mismatched pajamas, and waving a mug that read "I Love to Wrap Both My Hands Around It and Swallow."

Luka Horvat, my super conservative neighbor, looked up from reading the paper on his porch with an annoyed look.

I turned the writing on the mug around to face me. Not everyone shared Jude's and my sense of humor.

Meantime, my daughter not only ignored me, she achieved a velocity usually only reserved for running from the parking lot to the amusement park when she was younger, practically diving into the car idling across the street.

I narrowed my eyes. That little shit.

Her boss, Asha, a cheerful young woman in her mid-twenties, waved at me through the open window and off they went.

Knock-kneed, I backed into my house, wondering the safest way to get up the stairs without leakage. That's when I realized that Laurent had been silent this entire time.

I slammed my front door and deposited my empty mug on the small table. "You may elaborate on your groundless accusations now."

"Are you no longer too busy to listen to how you put my aunt in danger?"

"Such sweet concern for a woman you don't trust and didn't want me working for. Also, I didn't do anything." I lay on the stairs on my right side, my legs still pressed together, humping my way to the top like a pissed-off inchworm.

"Ah, so you agree. You did nothing and let the dybbuk enthrall some woman after murdering Santiago Torres."

"That's not what I meant, and you know it."

"No? My mistake. Must have been another BS."

I mimed throttling him, which was harder than it looked while contorting my body up the stairs and willing the geyser in my pants to stop erupting. "Use that slur again and die."

There was a terse silence.

"That was uncalled for," he said sincerely. "I apologize."

"Thank you," I said stiffly.

"However—"

"Nope. You were good."

"I never imagined you'd let a dybbuk live," he said snarkily, "but then again, you did give BatKian those gloves, so perhaps I shouldn't be surprised that your loyalties are different than presumed."

My hip now bruised, I made it to the landing, resting while I worked through arguments in my head so that I'd counter his sarcasm with a logic that ground him to dust. When nothing suitable came to mind, I went with the tried and true. "Fuck you."

Then I hung up, flinging my phone into my bedroom as I hobbled into the bathroom to assess the damage. It was "take a shower, maximum stain remover" levels of not pretty.

Between Sadie, my period, and that big dummy, I still hadn't gotten any concrete details about the curse, so I steeled myself to go over to Tatiana's place. By the time I'd gotten dressed and stuffed a pad the size of a saddle in my underwear, I'd ignored three more calls from Tatiana's number and four from Laurent's. Sadie, however, had ignored two calls and a text from me so I wasn't certain if I was winning or losing the pissed-off phone Olympics.

The people in my life sucked, big-time. Wound up to the point of almost shaking—though that may have been my lack of food—I got into my car, craving a fight even more than the double mocha and muffin I bought along the way. Given my restless leg and constantly darting eyes, that second double shot might have been a mistake. On the other hand, my jitters would need to be unleashed on someone. Brace yourself, Laurent, because it was on.

I screeched to a stop at Tatiana's curb and pounded on the door of her old-money monstrosity with my fist. Neither the neighborhood nor the house suited my boss. The artist was color and joie de vivre. This place was everything but that. Quaint gables and a brown and cream decorative façade made me want to put on a snooty British accent and address myself in the third person as Lady Snivelton. No, wait. Countess Kickhim-Intheballs. Heh.

Tatiana threw open the door, her vintage chiffon dressing gown and the hem of her silk men's pajamas swirling around her kitten-heeled slippers, and plucked the mostly empty takeout cup out of my hands. "Don't eat in the car, bubeleh. You'll get terrible indigestion. Food, like sex, should be savored."

I sighed. "Sometimes I just want a quick Triple O."

"The burger or the…" She made a pounding motion with her fist.

"Either. Mostly the latter." *Triple. Big talk, Feldman.* I'd take one solid single O at this point.

"Good for you. Aim high." She pushed her oversize red glasses back up her nose.

I slipped off my shoes, examining her for any signs of anxiety or fear, because her silver pixie cut was all spiky, as if she'd been raking her fingers through it, but her overall vibe was relaxed. The woman was eighty, and as much as I wanted to murder Laurent, I didn't want Tatiana harmed. "Is this for real? Why are you so calm about this death curse thing?"

"It's called the Pulsa diNura."

"It has a name?"

Tatiana locked the front door. "Fah. Old Aramaic word for 'lashes of fire.'"

"That's doesn't make it better." I shook my head. "Maybe a random unspecified death curse is nothing to get worked up about, but one with branding and stationery? We need to get you somewhere safe."

"I have wards. Come." She led me down a hallway that smelled like pancakes, her kitten heels slapping lightly against the floor in an even rhythm.

"You're sure that will protect you?"

Her footsteps faltered for a second and she rubbed a finger over the inside of her wrist. "Of course," she blithely tossed out. "Like I said, it's happened before and I'm still here, aren't I?"

Keeping any reply to myself, I followed her into her kitchen and blinked in surprise, because it was like I'd stepped into a snapshot from the 1950s. There was a bold checkerboard floor, mint-green cabinets and appliances, cherry-red furniture, and a retro glossy refrigerator. Standing at the stainless-steel double oven in a frilly yellow apron was Laurent, terrorizing pancakes with a spatula and a ferocious scowl.

I made a big show of pulling a notebook and pen out of my purse, turned to a clean page, and clicked the pen. "Laurent Amar's list of prejudices." I spoke as I wrote. "Pancakes and Banim Shovavim. Not necessarily in that order."

Laurent's back muscles tensed, then he flipped the food. "Don't forget demon artifacts and Zev BatKian. I know your fondness for complete lists."

I'll give you a list. It started with "rat bastard" and went downhill from there. But man, was it written in record time.

Tatiana tore off a piece of cooked pancake and popped it in her mouth. "Miriam did the right thing. Zev was our paying client."

"That doesn't make anything right, and you know it."

Laurent gripped the plastic spatula so hard I waited to hear it crack. "I expect this from Tatiana, but not you. I thought you were better than that."

"Oy," Tatiana muttered, pouring water into a kettle.

I threw my pen at Laurent's head. Sadly, I missed. "And I thought you were better than judging a person before you had all the facts. Zev gave me another shot at warding up my house against magical bad guys."

"Yeah, everyone except him," Laurent said darkly.

"Which is why I took him up on his offer." I held up a fist. "Protected house and no follow-up visit to Zev's dungeon for the win."

Laurent stilled and I shook my head. "Oh no," I said, wagging a finger. "Don't you dare get all overprotective and contrite. You should have backed my call in the first place simply because I'm your friend and I've never given you any reason to doubt me."

Delilah shot up, bouncing on her toes like a boxer, her fists up, and a low growl burst out of Laurent. I slid into her green vision, noting his nose was temptingly close. I unclenched my fists and forced Delilah back a step.

Shoving my notebook back in my purse before this powder keg—i.e., me—went off, I stormed out the back door and down to one of the rattan chairs grouped around a firepit.

Dumping my bag on the ground, I closed my eyes, my hands bunched in the fabric of my casual black jersey sundress, and tilted my face up to the sun, taking deep breaths.

Why couldn't the men in my life trust me on every single thing with fifty percent less arguments? Skip all the bitching and jump straight to the part where I was right?

The stone fish spouting water from its mouth into the small goldfish pond provided a soothing white noise and I relaxed enough to loosen my death grip on my poor dress. I touched my pocket, only to remember that I'd left the domino under my pillow, so instead, I kicked off my sandals, curling my toes into the scratchy grass.

Eventually there was a rustle and the faint whiff of Chanel No. 5.

"If you're here to defend him, forget it," I said.

Tatiana gave a throaty chuckle. "Please. He had it coming."

I scrubbed a hand over my face, then opened my eyes, watching clouds drift across the summer sky. There were two pressing questions, but I asked the one that I wasn't scared to hear answered. "Did you hear back from Mrs. Torres? Did Santiago have a Pulsa diNura placed on him?"

"Unfortunately, yes. His letter was identical to mine." Balancing a large mug of tea on her armrest, Tatiana handed me a piece of fibrous tan paper with rough edges. Written in bold strokes in thick black marker was the message: "You have been cursed with the Pulsa diNura. Unless you hand over the Torquemada Gloves in three days, you will die."

"Concise, nice presentation." I nodded. "Though I'm deducting points for vagueness on to whom and where this handover should happen."

"Never fear, there will be a follow-up," Tatiana said.

I held the paper up to the sun but there were no hidden watermarks. Beyond that, I wasn't sure what to look for. "Was there a postmark on the envelope?"

"Postmark schmostmark. The letter was slipped through my mail slot." She was rubbing her wrist again.

I gently caught her arm. "What's that?"

Tatiana swatted my shoulder. "I burned myself. Really, Miriam."

I pushed up her sleeve. Three twisted lines rose like flames, carved into her skin. "Hmm," I said, deep in thought, "that's a very stylized burn. I'd almost say it looks like three lashes of fire joined at their base to form a trident. Huh. It reminds me of something."

She yanked her arm away. "It showed up after I read the letter. Happy?"

"My joy knows no bounds. Did this happen the other times you were cursed?"

"No." She pursed her lips, her eyes narrowed as if daring me to comment.

I backed away from that fight and took a kinder approach to get behind her walls. "Does it hurt?"

"It's nothing." She caught herself rubbing it again and dropped her hand into her lap.

"How about I call Juliette?"

Tatiana regarded me with such intensity that I could hear the synapses firing in her brain as she worked through all the permutations of how to answer. She'd waltzed through a crowd of dangerous Ohrists and been treated like their queen. The woman was tough as nails and after decades of being a magic fixer, she'd ruthlessly sanded off any trace of vulnerability.

I was prepared for her to decline my offer.

"Juliette already tried. And Laurent doesn't know, so don't make a big production of it." She plucked a piece of lint off her lilac robe.

I nodded, matching her nonchalant body language with my own instead of giving any indication how much I appreciated her taking me into her confidence.

It was almost as much as my curiosity about why she wouldn't tell Laurent. There was some story behind their test of wills and shows of strength, and for the life of me, I couldn't figure it out. I honestly believed that it was more out of habit at this point because they so obviously cared about each other.

"Okay, well," I said, "there's an easy fix. Zev is still asleep, so you'll ask him for the gloves tonight and that will be that."

"He won't part with them. I don't know why they're so important, but he's been searching for them for years." She covered the burn with her sleeve and shrugged. "But I guess you could inquire."

I ducked my head, biting down on my lip to hide my smile at this major concession, and added asking Zev about the gloves to my to-do list. "What's the deal with the curse?"

She blew on her tea. "Uttering a Pulsa diNura became all the rage in the '90s after some nutjob threatened Prime Minister Rabin with it two weeks before his assassination in Tel Aviv."

"Does everyone who's been cursed die the same way as Santiago?"

"No, people die in different ways, but most don't die at all. It's a scare tactic."

"It's a warning that you've had a hit placed on you."

"And most of the time it never goes beyond that." She fixed me with a stern look over the top of her frames, which had slid down her nose. "Not for Ohrists at least. Sapiens are another matter. Anyone can shoot them and then blame it on a curse."

"I hate to break it to you, but Ohrists aren't bulletproof either."

She sighed. "I keep forgetting how much you don't know. This may come as a shock, but we would never go after another magic user with something as common as a gun."

I fell back in my chair, a hand to my heart. "Ohrists? Arrogant? You don't say."

"Regardless." She pushed her glasses up. "There aren't many magic users powerful enough to take out people like me. The first time I got one of these letters I was terrified. Now, what am I going to do? Beat my breast and wail?" She ran a hand under her skinny boobs. "My handfuls have already shrunk to peanuts. Like I want to make it worse?"

She was back to her usual acerbic manner.

I sighed, but it was what it was. I handed the letter back and she folded it and put it in the pocket of her voluminous robe. "Whoever did this," I said, "got past all of Santiago's security, both magic and hi-tech, as well as made mincemeat of his powers."

Tatiana sighed, putting her glasses on her head so she could rub her eyes. Enveloped in that cloud of fabric, her thin frame looked frailer than usual. "I know."

I followed up with the question that I couldn't put off anymore. "Be honest. Is this my fault somehow? You took the job because that would get me the ward."

"I took the job because Zev paid me handsomely. Stop giving me these altruistic motives." She drank some more tea. "Besides, if anyone is to blame, it's Naveen."

My eyes widened. "That doesn't make sense. If he was going to put a death curse on someone, it would be me."

"I meant that he ratted us out to Lolo and with all the kvetching that one did, I have a headache like you wouldn't believe." She massaged her temple with a fingertip. "From what I gathered from my nephew's initial yelling, because he was speaking quickly and my French isn't what it used to be, Naveen had been working his way into a position of trust with Santiago for a while in order to get on his security team and get his hands on those gloves."

"There's trust and then there's trust," I said. "It's one thing to be hired as a guard, but Naveen knew his way through the booby-trapped rooms to the vault."

Tatiana sipped her drink, clearly intending to tell this story her way and not give me the pertinent facts up front like I'd prefer. "He's a crafty young man with a purpose. It doesn't surprise me that he figured it out."

A fat bumblebee flew between the dainty pink and purple fuchsias on the shrub next to us.

Smiling at its drunken lurching, I picked a fallen flower off the grass and twirled it between my fingers. "How was Naveen planning to get past the heartbeat alarm? He didn't know there'd be a golem handy on the exact day that the crowds from the fight would provide cover for him to steal the gloves."

"I'm afraid that's exactly what happened. Everyone attending the fight was thoroughly vetted and when Naveen saw my name on the guest list, he got suspicious about why I'd go back after all these years." Tatiana girlishly tucked her leg underneath her.

My anger at all the annoying people in my life, and yes, that included Naveen, subsided under the peace and calm out here. Two chickadees sang merrily to each other from nearby trees while a dragonfly flitted between tiny tomato plants crawling up some lattice and a garden bed filled with tiger lilies in full bloom. It took off in a hurry when a sprinkler on an automatic timer turned on, water droplets jetting through the air like tiny rainbow prisms.

"Apparently Naveen has been after these gloves for some time." Tatiana settled the mug on the armrest. "He knows his competitors for them and, upon seeing my name, added me to their ranks."

I brushed the flower against my cheek. "He also knows Emmett. That's on me."

There was a small splash from the pond, one of the goldfish briefly surfacing at the edge of a clump of rushes.

"No harm done," Tatiana said. "Naveen didn't get the gloves. But neither did someone else."

"But—"

Tatiana held up a hand. "Had you screwed up our mission, I would have put a death curse on you myself."

"Why would someone curse you and not me?"

"I'm the fixer. You're the help. It always falls on the person of most power."

"You might be more powerful than me, but my magic is rarer."

"Be grateful you don't exist on most people's radars yet."

Tatiana glanced over my shoulder and put her glasses back on.

My lovely, relaxed shoulders tensed up. "Here we go again."

"Should I prostrate myself in apology now or can I feed you first?" Laurent set a large tray down on the firepit, which was currently converted into a table, his lean biceps flexing. He had the lithe build of a soccer player rather than a quarterback, but he was still a shifter and incredibly strong. In addition to plates, cutlery, and glasses, there was a platter piled high with pancakes, a jug of syrup, a silver bowl of freshly whipped cream, another glass bowl of blueberries, and a carafe of orange juice. I'd have dropped the tray in about five seconds, but he didn't look like he'd exerted himself at all.

He also didn't look or sound sarcastic, but before I could ask if he was serious about apologizing, Tatiana clapped her hands.

"This brings me back," she said. "Lolo used to make this for his grandmère and me on our Sunday morning visits."

"You lived with your grandparents?" I asked.

"I spent weekends with them," Laurent said. "Maman and my father often had business or social engagements then."

From the distinction between how he referred to each of his parents, I gathered there was no love lost between him and his dad. Not that I was going to feel sorry for him. "Are your grandparents still alive?"

"Gila died about three years ago," Tatiana said.

"I'm sorry," I said to both, helping myself to orange juice.

"Her passing was as good as it could be." Tatiana grabbed a plate, forking a couple of pancakes onto it. "Even better, she outlived Yoel like she always said she would, so she didn't have to worry about how he'd survive on his own."

Laurent shook his head. "She had everyone around her dancing attendance, just the way she wanted."

"True." Tatiana added another pancake to her stack. "Gila

unleashed her inner diva on her death bed. She was impressive."

"You say that because you were spared," Laurent groused. "Do you know how hard it was to find fresh pomegranates in Paris in March?"

"It was highly entertaining watching her come up with ridiculous tasks for you." My boss winked at me, and I pressed my lips together so I didn't laugh. "He always was a soft touch where Gila was concerned."

"Fous le camp. Both of you." Laurent accompanied his words with a double flip of the bird, but Tatiana cackled, and I mimicked his gesture right back.

I picked up a fork and knife wrapped in a linen napkin and secured with a napkin ring, eyeing the pancakes. This guy knew how to present a meal, though that was probably Tatiana's and his grandmother's doing.

"Were you serious earlier?" I said to Laurent. "About the apology?"

"Yes." He straightened his shoulders. "I'm—"

I held up a hand because a knot in my chest had given way, like a landslide. In my former profession as a librarian, I'd been mansplained to by colleagues and bosses, and kept quiet on far too many occasions. When I did speak up, I often felt unvalidated. Yes, I'd had to call Laurent out, but he was ready and willing to say sorry.

Aside from the occasional moment of objectification— because the man was ridiculously sexy with those dark long lashes framing his piercing green eyes, and the olive skin of his Moroccan Jewish heritage a few dusky shades lighter than his shaggy chocolate curls—I'd kept him firmly in the friend zone. An important friend, but a bond built on respect and collaboration, not romance.

And sure, given the chance, I'd screw his brains out, if only so he stopped featuring in my masturbatory fantasies, but that would be a one-time thing. This was a new level of attraction, snaring me like barbed fishhooks, and threatening to do as much damage if I ruthlessly yanked it out.

It would be best to keep any attraction in the fantasy zone.

Delilah walked slowly around me as if reminding me that I believed lots of things were best kept in the fantasy zone, but that didn't mean I had.

Or should.

Fuck.

6

LAURENT FURROWED HIS BROWS. "MIRIAM?"

Wrangling my annoying shadow back to the ground, I brushed my bangs out of my eyes, ensuring I forced the right note of nonchalance into my words, because I felt steamrollered by my attraction to him. "Save the apology for after breakfast."

"As you wish."

Oh God. He quoted *The Princess Bride* at me. I crossed my legs tightly and swallowed hard. "Mmm, food," I said with a ridiculous amount of enthusiasm.

Laurent put two massive pancakes on my plate and handed it over, our fingers brushing.

A zing shot through me. "Thanks," I mumbled.

Luckily, Tatiana was too focused on drowning her food in syrup to comment on my weirdness, and Laurent mistook it for apprehension because he assured me that whoever had placed the curse wouldn't get to me.

I was happy to enjoy the pancakes, which were cooked to a fluffy perfection, the tartness of the blueberries cutting through the sugar of the syrup and cream. Men who could cook or bake were so sexy. Eli had won me over the first time he'd made me dinner. It was ramen noodles, same as I'd been living off, but his offering had fat chunks of tofu, tiny spears of broccoli, and spinach leaves all steeped in a spicy broth that was topped off by a fried egg. I'd put my attraction to guys in bands aside once and for all and decided this shy boy with the sweet smile was my new bar for hotness.

Laurent was off to a good start.

I speared a blueberry too hard, sending it flying off my plate. My *friend* had made brunch for his aunt and me because we had work to discuss. This was nothing like the situation with Eli.

Even so, it was a delicious meal. The only thing that could have made it better was a text from my daughter, though she'd be busy with the camp kids right now.

"Are you sure that Ghost Minder didn't have the ability to control dybbuks and that it was destroyed?" I recounted the dybbuk attack on the island for Laurent. "Without a host body, hell, even with one given how violent that attack was, that ring is the only thing that makes sense."

"Positive on both accounts. Ghost Minder is no more." Laurent spooned more berries onto his plate. "We can ask Naveen if they found another body."

"You sound doubtful," I said.

"Because the host corpse should have been close to the dybbuk."

"Then what was going on?"

"I don't know." He loosened his death grip on his fork.

"What about magic?" Tatiana said. "I once met an Ohrist with the ability to expel air from his lungs like a forceful gust of wind. What if this is similar and this woman's powers allow the dybbuk to leave her body at will?"

Laurent rubbed his forehead. "That's even worse." His eyes darted up, flicking from side to side like he was visualizing how to combat this dybbuk.

My fork clattered to my plate. "Shit. She *was* just standing there while it attacked Santiago and I didn't sense the dybbuk at all. That's why I believed she was enthralled, but Tatiana, if you're right, it's even more imperative to find this woman and stop this madness from going further."

"We stop it no matter what, if this is in fact the case," Laurent said. "A dybbuk getting hold of those gloves?" He shook his head.

"Yes." My employer grimly pushed her food around. "They inflict a lot of pain and would be pretty irresistible to a dybbuk."

"And it's far less work to use the gloves than have the dybbuk constantly leave the host's body to kill its target," I said.

"Or it'll do that *and* use the gloves," Laurent said. "Two different ways to inflict misery upon people."

"How likely do you think Tatiana's theory is?" I dumped a liberal amount of whipped cream on my plate, hoping the woman was merely enthralled and could be saved.

"It's plausible." He nodded. "And it's a simple, clean explanation. It makes sense to pursue this line, but I don't think she's enthralled. I think she's possessed."

"Why?" Tatiana said.

"Can't be." I wiped syrup off my lip. "Her shadow was normal."

"I can't explain that," Laurent said, "but if she was merely enthralled, how did the dybbuk stay in control while it left her body to attack Torres? No, she would have cried out for help at that point, not stood by and watched him die. An Ohrist who knows they're enthralled will grasp at any straw to save themselves," he added in a dark voice.

Tatiana set her fork down, shooting her nephew a concerned look, but she didn't say anything.

Braced for the worst-case scenario that this was a straight-up case of possession, I speared a forkful of pancake and smeared it in a puddle of syrup. "Laurent…"

He swallowed, nodding at me to continue.

I half-heartedly poked at my food. "So, I'm going to say something, but I want you to keep an open mind because—"

"You think Nav was working with that woman." He wiped his mouth with a sharp, frustrated motion, but when I tensed, he held up a hand. "That's not directed at you, Mitzi. I want to say it's impossible, but..."

"Nothing is impossible when it involves people." Tatiana's fork squeaked against her plate. "No matter how well you think you know someone, there's always some situation in which they can and will surprise you." She dropped her cutlery on her dish with a suddenness that smacked of resignation. "And usually not for the best."

Laurent shot his aunt a hard look, but she didn't elaborate, handing him her plate to dispose of. He placed it on the tray with his own.

"But what?" I prompted him to finish his earlier thought.

"I will always prioritize killing dybbuks over everything else." The shifter glanced up, as if trying to pluck his next words out of the air.

Much as I wanted to blurt out a whole bunch of questions, I methodically kept eating, waiting patiently for him to fill the silence. A tactic I'd learned from Eli.

"The thing is, I have no conflicting loyalties," he said.

I glanced down at my lap so he didn't see my frown. If it came down to killing a dybbuk or saving Tatiana—or me—he'd go for the dybbuk? He might think that, but there was no way if push came to shove that would be the case. I'd heard his agitation when he'd called about the letter.

Did he require that belief to keep functioning or something? What was this guy's deal?

I set my dirty dishes on the tray, moving some cutlery so the plates didn't topple over.

Laurent leaned forward with his elbows braced on his

thighs. "I appreciate things are more complicated for you. You have a family."

Now I was just sad. I opened my mouth to tell him that he had family as well, but Tatiana shook her head at me with a weary sigh. "I'm glad you see that," I said instead.

His brows got a little crease between them like that hadn't landed exactly as anticipated. "My point is that I'd have sworn Nav's commitment to protecting people would rule out any chance of him working with someone who was dybbuk-possessed. Especially given…" He rubbed his shoulder, like a heavy weight had settled upon it. Before I could press him, he blinked and shook his head. "If Nav deemed the artifact a big enough threat to humanity, then yes, he'd team up with this woman in order to get his hands on it and destroy it."

"Even if Naveen wasn't working with her?" Tatiana crossed her legs, primly smoothing out her housecoat. "He should be able to identify her since he was part of the security team. Pay a visit to Mr. Kumar and get her name and location from him. By whatever means necessary."

"Is he back from the island?" I said.

Laurent gave a resigned nod.

My phone buzzed with my long-awaited text from Sadie. It simply said that she was fine and she'd see me later. That level of terseness from my kid meant she was still mad. However, she'd made contact and that was the most important step.

Since I wasn't a security expert, I put on my mom hat about how best to handle the death curse situation. "Someone needs to stay with Tatiana at all times."

My boss groaned but didn't fight me.

Laurent nodded. "Between the three of us—"

"Three? You mean Naveen?" I shook my head. "Hard pass."

"Emmett." Laurent beamed at Tatiana. "He can stay here

while we investigate."

Tatiana had hired the golem and installed him at Laurent's place. Seems Emmett had worked his usual charm on his new roommate. Jude and I had laid bets on how long the golem would remain in one piece while living with Laurent, and to our surprise, he'd surpassed my generous estimate of four days by almost two weeks.

Jude hadn't even given Emmett twenty-four hours, but she was a bit biased since he'd driven her up the wall during their stay together.

"What's a golem going to do to an assassin that I can't?" Tatiana said.

"It's true," Laurent said. "You're far more powerful, but you also get lost in your work. The golem will do everything in his power to protect you, leaving you free to paint."

"That's what I have wards for," she reiterated. Tatiana was one of the few Ohrists who had the means and ability to ward up her place. Laurent and Naveen had them too, but that was due to connections in their respective lines of work. I'd asked my friend Ava if her bowling alley Stay in Your Lane had them and she'd laughed. Even the Bear's Den, Vikram's speakeasy, was ward-free.

"Be smart about this," I said. "If nothing else, Emmett can alert us to anything weird while you're busy painting."

Tatiana glared at me like I'd stabbed her in the back. "I can't create with people constantly around."

Laurent pointed to an upstairs window where her assistants, Marjorie and Raymond, were walking past, their arms full of boxes from an art supply store. "They come and go regularly. And given how much shit you give them, they probably wish you dead on a regular basis and yet the wards let them through. Wards aren't infallible if you don't maintain them properly."

"Then I'll shore them up." Tatiana's eyes narrowed. "I don't have the space for overnight guests."

"I'll clean out one of your four spacious and underused bedrooms," Laurent replied, unruffled.

I swung my head to Tatiana.

She pulled her robe tightly around her and crossed her arms. "What about the hotline I installed at your place so people could report suspected enthrallments? If Emmett isn't there to answer it, that would be a real shame." She said it with the same smug certainty as a poker player laying down a royal flush.

Ooh, nice play.

"I switched the number from a landline to a cell phone," Laurent countered. "More convenient that way, and it ensures Emmett can be anywhere and never miss a call."

Tatiana's face fell.

Laurent winked at me, and I barely contained my laugh.

"I'm not paying you." Tatiana was grasping.

"Ma chère tante." Laurent kissed her hand. "I wouldn't dream of taking money for this."

"You're too much like your father for your own good," she said crossly, but her hand lingered in his for a moment.

Whistling jauntily, Laurent picked up the tray and carried everything into the house.

"Miriam." Tatiana squeezed my arm.

"No way. I've pushed my family far enough. A golem would send them over the edge. If things become unbearable with Emmett, Laurent and I will take shifts here at your place."

"Very well." She stood up with a swoosh of fabric. "Naveen has been a good friend to Laurent when many others failed him. Don't kill him. Anything short of that is acceptable." Head high, she sailed into the house, passing a returning Laurent with a haughty sniff.

He gently caught her arm, his dark head bent close to her silver one, and said something quietly. Her posture softened, then she tossed her head and continued inside.

81

As Laurent's shadow fell over me, I picked up my purse. "I can stay here and keep watch while you get Emmett and then we'll go together to Naveen's house. Sound like a plan?"

He opened his mouth, but instead of speaking, rolled his shoulders back as if steeling himself, which was odd, because if anyone had reservations about going to see Naveen, it was me. Then Laurent bit his lip, studying me.

I ran a hand over my mouth in case I had a smudge of food there. What the heck?

He flexed his fingers at his sides, inhaling deeply before exhaling into a kneel in the grass and looking up at me through his dark lashes. "I believe I owe you an apology first."

Whoa. I glanced around, ready to tell him to stand up because this was embarrassing and overkill, but no one else was outside. I gnawed the inside of my cheek. All right. I deserved it, so why not hear him out? "Proceed," I said, waving my hand in royal benediction.

He schooled his expression into a grave seriousness. "I—"

I cleared my throat. "I was promised prostration."

He sat back on his calves. "I'm on my knees. Is that not enough?"

"It might be with some, but I hold you to a higher standard of follow through."

He sighed in an exaggerated fashion and bent over, his forehead touching the ground and his arms out in supplication. "You were right and I was wrong." As corny as his actions were, his voice was serious, his words matter-of-fact. "I am deeply sorry for my hurtful accusations. I should have believed in you because you always put the best interests of the people you care about ahead of your own. Next time I'll do better."

He didn't make excuses or try to justify himself. It was a true apology.

I reached for his head but stopped shy of touching him.

We didn't have the kind of relationship where I could sink my fingers into his curls and tell him he was forgiven. "Thank you and I'm sorry for throwing a pen at your head." I paused. "And the mean things I wrote about you."

"Did I warrant a list?" He laughed.

"You better believe it. Mazel tov."

"Quelle horreur." He moved at the same moment that I stretched out my leg to shove my foot in my sandal, resulting in his hand brushing up the back of my bare calf.

I froze and Laurent lifted his head up.

The space between us felt prickly, but in a good way, like it was waking me up, while the faint trace of cedar that always clung to him wove around me, drawing me closer. I leaned forward, unable to resist its lure. I didn't want his apology.

A hot spark flared in his eyes, his hand warm against my skin. He splayed his fingers out, making the tiniest stroking motion.

A strangled moan came out of the back of my throat, and mortified, I clapped my hand over my mouth.

Watching me through half-shut lids, he danced his hand higher.

My breath hitched.

Behind us a window slammed, and he jerked away, staring at his hand for a second before abruptly dropping it.

The sensation of the press of his fingers on my calf was fading, and I wished I could capture it, or better still, have him touch me again. "Laurent?"

He took a deep breath like he was steadying himself and sat back on his calves. "You had a bug."

"Huh?" I patted down my arms and chest but didn't find one.

"On your..." He skimmed his hand lightly against the back of my leg, his eyes tracking the line of his movement.

"Oh." I ducked my head so he didn't see my confusion.

Laurent slowly pushed to his feet. "I'll go retrieve the

golem and then we will go speak with Nav. Attends ici, d'accord?" He raked his hand through his hair. "I mean—"

"I got it." I clenched my thighs against the roughness of his voice. "I'll wait, but I'm going to contact Zev. He can end this."

"He won't. Not even for Tatiana."

I slid on my sandals. "Do you know the deal between them?"

"Many theories, no actual idea. Be back soon."

I watched him leave, torn between reluctance and relief.

Okay, there seemed to be mutual attraction, but that didn't mean either of us would act on it, especially if Laurent had resorted to using bug excuses instead of admitting it. It didn't mean we wouldn't either. Besides, getting involved with Laurent, even for sex, would be heady, but possibly overwhelming since he operated at such an intense level for everything.

I trailed my fingers over the goosebumps on my arms. What would it be like to be laid utterly bare for him to worship me? If he was game, could I keep that kind of carnal encounter emotion-free when we were already so tangled up in different ways? After all the upheaval in my life lately, I'd chosen to put relationships on hold. Laurent didn't seem like he was in a place in his life for that either, but I had a lot of doubts about us pulling off friends with benefits.

Regardless, any decisions around our sexual tension had to wait until we dealt with the Pulsa diNura. I pulled out my phone to research it, but the few results merely reinforced what Tatiana had told me about Prime Minister Rabin and the popularity of the curse, especially toward Israeli politicians.

I dove deeper, going into the Ohrist forums on the dark web that I'd found when stocking up on some weapons a while back. Sentiment on those boards was torn between the belief that the curse was a hoax and that anyone slapped with it was doomed. Overall, there was little discussion on the topic, with no mention of either anyone specializing in carrying out the threat or how to neutralize it.

My librarian colleague hadn't gotten back to me yet, so I contacted Harry, a gargoyle bartender, to set up a meeting with Zev. Gargoyles were treated as neutral parties in the magical community, and provided you used one as an intermediary, you wouldn't get hurt. Neither would the gargoyle, lest the attacker wanted to experience swift and lethal repercussions as gargoyles were an endangered species. Harry was the latest to hold that position.

He agreed to arrange it, adding that at this rate, he should get me a punch card. With every ten meetings get a free coffee. It would be filled in no time. He wasn't wrong. Geez. What did that say about my life?

"Miriam?" Tatiana's assistant Marjorie sat down beside me once I'd wrapped up the call. Fresh faced and dressed in a cute romper, she looked like she'd be equally at home on a college brochure or a trendy makeup ad. In comparison, I felt like I should be in the woods, leaning on my cane and holding out a poisoned apple. "Am I interrupting?"

"Not at all." I put my phone away. "What's up?"

Apparently, the assistants had been briefed on the golem, and in typical Tatiana fashion, it was expected that they accept his presence without reservation. The girl fidgeted with her bracelets, asking halting questions about what to expect.

I put her mind at rest, glad to have a task to focus on—and that when Emmett waved at me from the window, Marjorie went in to meet him with a straight spine.

After a quick stop to shore up Ladytown's flood protection, I headed into the kitchen to greet the golem.

"Hiya, partner!" Emmett shone in a kilt and sparkly flip-flops. He grabbed my arm and steered me into the hallway with a pointed look. "It's a good thing I'm needed here, because I was two seconds away from killing the wolf."

"You don't say." I flinched as Laurent slammed a suitcase of Emmett's things on a kitchen chair.

"He doesn't have a television. I had to beg Jude to give me her old laptop so I could watch shows on it. He cleans. Obsessively." Emmett ticked items off on his fingers. "His taste in music is horrible. I got excited when he sat down at the piano, thinking it was finally karaoke time, but he played some snore fest that didn't have lyrics. Called it a...concerto. You know what I called it? Shit. I told him he could bite my smooth red aaaah—" There was the sound of footfalls behind me and Emmet's eyes widened. "A-Team. I'm almost finished the third season and the similarities between me and Faceman are scary."

Dream on.

"Hey, Laurent," I said without looking over my shoulder. "You ready to go?"

The shifter slammed a hand against Emmett's solar plexus, shoving him up against the wall. "You have the attention span of a fruit fly, but if you don't want the life span of one, you will ensure no harm comes to my aunt. And make sure she doesn't leave the wards. Those are direct orders."

Emmett blinked in a quick rhythmic sequence, like a machine registering some programming. Once a golem was assigned a task, it became their prime directive. Well, that's the way it was supposed to work. Emmett always grumbled when I brought him along. "She's safe with me," he said. "You don't have to go all B. A. Baracus."

Laurent looked at me with an expression of utter bewilderment, then shook his head, before I could explain, and took off at a brisk pace. "No. I don't care. Allons-y."

I'd made it halfway down the corridor before calling back. "Hey, Emmett. Who am I?"

He popped his head out of the kitchen. "Hannibal, obvs."

The leader of the A-Team. I nodded. Good man. "Carry on."

7

LAURENT DROVE US IN HIS TRUCK TO NAVEEN'S house. Before, when he'd only had his motorcycle, I'd coerced him into my sedan more often than not, and he'd nap, so I figured after our weird encounter in the backyard, I'd flip the dynamic, close my eyes, and feign sleep.

There's no way he bought my act. I kept forgetting to slow down my breathing and as a shifter, he could hear my heartbeat, which was anything but relaxed, but he didn't call me on it. We had bigger things to deal with.

The Arts and Crafts bungalow that Naveen shared with his sister and niece in the neighboring city of Burnaby was absolutely charming, from its low-pitched eaves and wide front porch that reminded me of a welcoming cottage in a fairy tale, to the narrow, stained-glass panels on either side of the door.

However, just like in "Hansel and Gretel" with the candy house that was every child's dream, the reality might be a nightmare. I dragged my feet up the walk, Laurent already knocking.

A chubby woman in scrubs, her black hair piled in a messy bun, opened the door and yawned in his face. Blinking, she gave a deep and joyful laugh that brightened up my day, and hugged Laurent. The top of her head only hit midchest on the shifter, and yet she tugged him down so that she could knuckle the top of his head like an older sister.

"If my patient hadn't rescheduled her C-section, I'd have missed you," she said. "Again."

"Daya," Laurent whined. "Quit—" He flinched because she'd caught sight of me and screamed. Right in his ear.

I screamed back and the two of us ran to each other, grabbing each other's hands, and babbling a mile a minute.

Naveen bolted onto the porch with a screwdriver in his hand, his eyes flashing, ready to battle whoever had harmed his sister, but at the sight of the two of us he muttered "For fuck's sake, Daya" and marched back inside.

Laurent opted to follow Naveen rather than stay here with us, which was fine by me.

Dr. Daya Kumar looped her arm through mine, chattering brightly up the front walk. "I couldn't believe it when Evani told me about the guest that Uncle Wolf had brought over." Her upper-crust English accent was the result of her parents' hard work to send both their kids to top schools when they'd immigrated from Delhi to London. "You must show me photos of Sadie right away. What is she now? Twelve? Thirteen?"

I already had the photo album open on my phone. Daya had been my obstetrician, delivering Sadie after my unfortunately drug-free labor. To this day, I resented never having gotten the laughing gas. "Sixteen."

Daya was one of those people who made others smile and my joy at our reunion—and the fact that she didn't seem to care that I was a Banim Shovavim—meant everything to me.

My friend grabbed my cell, swiping through pictures of my daughter. "Impossible. I am not that old. Does she still sleep with her hands like this?" She held them up to either side of her head as if they were antlers.

I laughed. Sadie had come out of the womb with one of her hands pressed to her head that way, resulting in Eli and me calling her Moose when she was little. "Sometimes, but she gets put out if I say anything. I can't believe you decided to have one of your own after insisting that motherhood was not for you, but Evani is adorable. Is she around?"

Their home was infused with Daya's natural warmth from the comfortable furniture made of honey oak to the attention-grabbing pieces from all her travels: Turkish tiles in earth tones that formed a border about three-quarters of the way up the living room wall, a Russian samovar sitting on the ornate dining room set imported from France, and a spectacular blown glass lampshade from Murano.

Naveen had told me about many of these pieces the first time I'd met him, before he'd learned what I was and our newly formed friendship had gone to shit.

"No, my little handful is at my parents' place," Daya said with a fond smile. "But having a child at forty-one was an insane idea. My friends are all rubbish because not one of them stopped me."

"Good thing you were never big on sleep," I teased.

"No kidding." She ushered me into the kitchen, then sighed. "I'd offer you an iced tea, but our refrigerator decided to bite the dust last night and we're struggling."

While magnets from Madrid to Macau crowded the fridge securing finger-painted masterpieces by Evani, it had been pulled away from the wall, the back panel lying on the ground next to a toolbox. Laurent and Naveen were crouched down, peering at the motor or whatever was back there.

"We are not struggling. I can definitely fix it," Naveen said. "The problem is in here. I'm about 85% sure."

Laurent pointed at something. "I think you have to take that out."

"You're worse than he is," Daya said. "No guesswork on my fridge. Call in a professional."

"Agreed. Will you hear me out now?" Laurent said.

"No," Naveen said. "But you can hand me a ratchet."

Daya crossed the kitchen and kicked the toolbox out of Laurent's reach. "Miri, what kind of tea would you like?"

I stifled a laugh. She was awesome. The pediatrician I'd taken Sadie to when she was little worked in a group clinic with Daya, so we'd often run into each other, though once I'd gotten divorced and moved to our current duplex, I'd switched doctors, and we'd lost touch. I promised myself that wouldn't happen again.

"She's not staying." Naveen reached for the toolbox, but Laurent got there first.

He planted himself in front of it and crossed his arms. "Don't be a dick."

Naveen returned to sullenly poking around behind the fridge with the screwdriver.

Daya pulled a bright box out of the cupboard. "How about lemon ginger?"

"Sounds good," I replied.

"Didi," Naveen said from behind the fridge. "It's time for her to go." He grunted, the screwdriver scraping against something.

Daya mugged at me. "Ooh, he's broken out the Hindi." She planted her hands on her hips. "You're being incredibly rude, chota bhai. And you're going to break the refrigerator."

My footsteps faltered. Oh. She had no clue about my magic.

I'd hidden who I was for so long and it was such a relief to have it out in the open. Daya had been a good friend at one point and if we were going to resume that relationship, I wanted to move forward on a foundation of truth. I'd made peace with who and what I was, and though my stomach twisted at potentially losing her friendship for good, at least I'd lose it with my head held high. Nor did I want to continue to catch up if she shared Naveen's prejudices.

I cleared my throat. "I'm a Banim Shovavim."

Daya slammed the box of tea on the counter.

In my head, my house of cards shook.

I twisted my old engagement ring around my finger, my happiness leaking out of me like a deflating balloon. However, I could deal with my emotions later. "Naveen, please hear Laurent out, because one person has already died, and another is in danger." I motioned toward the front door. "I'll wait outside."

Daya narrowed her eyes and raised her hand.

I flinched, anticipating a magic attack, but she smacked the counter.

"Did you honestly believe I would toss a friend out of my home for that?" she said.

The house of cards stilled and held.

Naveen swung his head to me, holding the screwdriver like he was going to shank me, and his brows furrowed like I'd pulled a Jedi mind trick on his sister. Shaking his head, he turned back to her. "Are you not listening? She's a BS, just like—" He pressed his lips together.

Laurent sighed and looked down at the floor.

"The person who killed my Rishi." Daya's tone could cut glass.

I gasped. "Oh, Daya. I'm so sorry." The two of them had been a couple forever. I'd met Rishi once and had a vague memory of an intelligent man with a wry sense of humor.

While it was unfair to paint all Banim Shovavim with the same brush, understanding why Naveen hated my kind lessened the insult somewhat. I rubbed my palms against my thighs. Had I done the same to him by writing him off as another prejudiced Ohrist without bothering to learn if there was a genuine reason behind his feelings?

Daya nodded at me absently, her focus on her brother. "Don't ever use Rishi as an excuse for your hate again. You dishonor everything he stood for when you do that."

Naveen's head bowed lower and lower under her words, as if they very precisely flayed strips off him.

"Sit down, Miri," she said gently. "We will have tea and you and Laurent will tell us what you need."

Tears welled up in my eyes. Had our situations been reversed, I'm not sure I could have managed the level of grace and forgiveness she exemplified. With a watery smile, I hugged her, hard. "Thank you."

She patted my back. "Don't be daft. Now sit." She pointed a finger at Naveen and Laurent. "That means you two numb-skulls as well."

Laurent slid into the chair closest to me.

"Scared, are we?" I said quietly.

"She once gave Nav a detailed rundown on the order and manner in which she would break every bone in his body." Laurent didn't bother lowering his voice. "Daya doesn't need magic to be terrifying."

She put the kettle on the stove and blew him a kiss. "That's why I adore you, Laurent. You always say the sweetest things. And for the record, I'm perfectly happy that both myself and Evani dodged that bullet." Banim Shovavim powers didn't kick in until puberty, but Ohrists were born with theirs. Huh. So, she and Evani were Sapien. "In my experience, magic doesn't make people happier." Daya opened a cupboard. "Baby brother, I'm giving you until the count of three to stop being a git and join us."

He didn't stop sulking, but he did grumpily take a seat.

"Can I help with anything?" I asked.

"There's nothing to help with," she said. "We're just having a cuppa."

I snorted. She'd already unearthed a giant chocolate bar that she'd broken into pieces on a plate in front of me before nudging a fruit bowl overflowing with grapes and plums closer.

"Let's get this over with." Naveen tilted his chair back,

one foot resting on another chair for balance and a lock of platinum blond hair falling into his face. "What do you want?"

"Were you complicit in Torres's death?" Laurent said.

The chair thunked to the ground and Naveen's expression darkened. "Get out."

Daya placed teaspoons and a dainty sugar bowl on the homey table that easily sat eight people, then boffed her brother across the top of his head.

Laurent held his ground. "It's a reasonable question."

"You did want the gloves pretty badly," I said. "If Santiago had stood in the way of you getting them, would you have hurt him? Or worse?"

"First of all," Naveen said, "I didn't get the gloves. And second? If I didn't kill you?" He leaned forward, speaking in a voice that was saccharine sweet. "I certainly wouldn't have killed him."

Laurent hooked a foot around Naveen's chair and jerked it closer. "Ah, but mon ami, you'd only have had Torres's security to contend with if you'd hurt *him*." The smile he gave his friend was feral.

Daya narrowed her eyes at Laurent and me, but the kettle whistled, and she walked over to the stove to deal with it.

Good, because I had enough to worry about without any matchmaking tendencies. Naveen already didn't like me; I had no desire to become his personal Yoko Ono. Though, in my opinion, Yoko didn't even break up The Beatles. John wouldn't have left if he didn't want to, but she got scapegoated for the fallout. Typical.

"Stop it, both of you." I jabbed a finger between them. "We need your help, Naveen, because whoever put the Pulsa diNura on Santiago, put it on Tatiana."

"Bloody hell, mate," Naveen said, shoving Laurent's chair with his foot. Oy vey. The two of them were like seven-year-old boys. It wouldn't surprise me if one of them noogied the other. "You could have led with that."

"You could have helped me because I'm your friend."

I rolled my eyes at Laurent's use of the words I'd thrown at him earlier and reached for a piece of chocolate at the exact same moment as the shifter. Our hands brushed and I motioned for him to go ahead, Canadian politeness hardwired into my DNA.

He took the piece but placed it in my hand. "I know the dangers of standing between you and chocolate." His fingers lingered on mine for a second longer than necessary, but he wasn't gazing into my eyes. He was getting another piece for himself.

Okay, then. I murmured "Thanks" and returned to the topic. "Did you find any other corpse? Was a host killed, releasing the dybbuk that took Santiago out?"

"No," Naveen said. "You're positive it was a dybbuk?"

"One hundred percent," I said.

Laurent filled him in on our working theory that the host was alive and well, her Ohrist magic causing this unwelcome twist to allow the dybbuk to leave her body.

"At the fight you thought she was enthralled," Naveen said.

"That still might be the case," I admitted. "But possessed or enthralled, there was no other host for the dybbuk to inhabit and they don't float free. This explanation is cleaner."

"Actually?" Naveen propped an elbow on the back of the chair. "The explanation that's cleanest is that my boss was killed, and an innocent woman enthralled, because a BS controlled the dybbuk."

I added sugar to my mug in anticipation of the tea so I'd have something to focus on, forcing myself to keep my tone polite for Daya's sake. "I'd prefer if you call us Banim Shovavim."

"Nav, apologize," his sister said.

"It's what you do, right?" Naveen's cold brown eyes bored into mine. "Death and darkness and all that? I mean, you did let the man die."

A hot funnel churned under my skin, and I let go of my teacup because I was rattling it on the saucer. "While I didn't save Santiago, even if Banim Shovavim could control dybbuks —if *I* could—I wouldn't."

"And we're supposed to take your word for it, are we?"

"Yes." Shadows swam over me like animated tattoos. I was stuck in a loop of tight rage, sick and tired of my kind being framed as evil.

"I'll say this yet again." Laurent's tone was steel. "Nothing and no one can control them. If one got free from that woman thanks to her magic, she's fully possessed and it's in control." Laurent brushed a hand over my arm. "Can you shut your magic down? Nav's not worth hurting yourself."

Daya checked the tea, tossed in another bag, and placed the lid on the pot. "Agreed."

Shame for my outburst warred with my anger, and I stood up abruptly, opening the back door to let the breeze cool me off. I gritted my teeth against the desire to let loose on Naveen, forcing myself back into a semblance of calm.

The shadowy tattoos faded away, bringing down the emotional temperature of the room.

"Right, then." Daya carried the teapot to the table, smiling at me to come join them.

I couldn't help the flush on my cheeks, but I nodded gratefully and sat down once more.

She poured the fragrant gold beverage into cups. "Going with the assumption that you're correct about this Ohrist woman, how did she get past all of Santiago's security?"

"Why would she have to get past us? That crowd was hardly pillars of society and they were invited." Naveen's fingers tightened on his mug.

"Then why let them past his wards in the first place?" I

ate another piece of fancy Belgian chocolate that might as well have been cardboard for all I tasted it, but I was unwilling to let Naveen get under my skin any more than he had.

"Santiago knew the importance of showing his dominance by gathering everyone together at these fights." Naveen matched my civil tone.

"Pride." Daya clucked her tongue.

Great. The one time that some caution would have been handy, Santiago had to go swinging his dick around. "Is it possible someone got hold of an invitation and crashed the party?"

"Every invitation was embedded with a code specific to each invitee that was also tied to a fingerprint scan." Naveen added honey to his drink. "All the guests checked in without incident." He raised an eyebrow at me. "The invited guests who didn't magically sneak in."

I shrugged. Sorry, not sorry. "Ohrists can't cloak so she must have had an invitation."

"Scans can be faked." Laurent waved off the offer of tea and bit into a plum with even white teeth, his tongue darting out to catch an errant drop of juice. He nodded at me. "Describe the woman you saw."

"Dark red hair, taller than me, but she was in heels. She had giant sunglasses hiding most of her face and a scarf over her head, so hard to guess her age, but I don't remember wrinkles... Oh. Kind of flowy dress."

"It's a start," Naveen said. "The security team can narrow down the guest list to possible suspects."

"You know the collectors in these circles," Laurent said. "Does anything about her ring a bell?"

Naveen snapped a large piece of chocolate in half. "I'm supposed to know all the players, right? But this woman blindsided me. I'll speak to Wendy, who's head of security, and Mukisa, her second. They're Torres's personal bodyguards. If he discussed the curse or who was behind it with anyone, it was these two."

Did I need to warn Zev now that he had the gloves? The sip of rich lemon ginger tea I'd taken soured.

Daya squeezed her brother's shoulder. "No one expects you to have all the answers."

Laurent and Naveen shared a look that all too clearly said they expected themselves to have them.

I frowned, absently munching on grapes. "Let's go at this a different way. Assume we're correct and this Ohrist woman is dybbuk-possessed. Did she go there specifically to kill Santiago because of his previous refusal to hand over the gloves or had she intended to steal them at the fight as well? And if so, how would she have gotten past the heartbeat alarm? It's not like golems are a dime a dozen."

"I only put it all together because I'd met Emmett," Naveen said. "Thought it would be the easiest way to achieve my goals."

I refrained from gloating that he'd thought wrong.

Laurent nudged my foot, his eyes dancing with amusement.

Naveen was glaring at me.

Whoops. Wherever had my smirk come from?

Daya covered her mouth because she'd eaten some chocolate. "Speaking of which, Evani keeps asking about her play-date with Boo and the baby."

I chuckled, stirring more sugar into my tea. Emmett was going to hate that so much.

"Emmett is staying with Tatiana," Laurent said. "Sadly, that can't happen."

"It can and will as soon as Tatiana is out of danger." I nudged Laurent. "I made a promise to Evani, and I intend to keep it."

"He's not coming back to live with me," Laurent grumbled. "I don't run a home for wayward golems."

Naveen knocked on the table. "Forget that. How did you get through the booby traps? Did Tatiana or the vampire have information on them?"

"I wish." I tore off another bunch of grapes and popped one in my mouth. Summer fruit was the best. "It was luck and..." I shivered.

Naveen nodded. "The remains."

"That young man didn't deserve to die. I mean, yeah, he wanted the gloves, and he'd taken us hostage, but we didn't kill him. It was one of Torres's booby traps."

"I know," Naveen said.

A text came in on my phone, startling me. It was Harry informing me that I could drop by Blood Alley anytime tonight. I set the screen facedown on the table. "We got a lot more careful after that, but still. The outcome could easily have been very different." I twisted my hands in my lap.

Laurent draped his arm on the back of my chair. He wasn't touching me, but it was a comforting gesture, nonetheless. It was done so casually, without him even looking at me, that I'm not sure he was aware of it.

"If neither Tatiana nor BatKian had that info," Laurent said, "how likely would it be that this dybbuk-woman unearthed it?"

"Unlikely, but not impossible," Naveen said. "Those rooms were built in sections, each one by a different group, and Santiago didn't leave loose ends. However, his personal guards had the route in case they ever had to get him out."

Jeez. He'd murdered his workmen? My failure to save him was getting easier to live with.

"You think one of his guards betrayed him?" Laurent said.

"For the right price?" Naveen shrugged. "It'll make sussing any intel out of them trickier."

Daya shook her head. "Why couldn't you become an explosives expert like you declared when you were a kid? I don't let you live here out of the goodness of my heart, Nav, and if I have to find another babysitter for Evani, I will be extremely put out."

He raised his eyebrows. "And leave her alone with you? Please. I wouldn't do that to the child."

"You're a right shit."

He grinned.

Their fierce loyalty and loving manner sent a pang through my chest. Daya didn't seem to have any difficulties with magic, even with the tragedy it had brought into her life. Would Sadie, Eli, and I get to this same place?

When I'd left my librarian position at the law firm a few weeks ago, my work friendships had fallen away. I was slowly building a new circle with people that I didn't have to hide my magic from, and it would have been nice to include these two, but I wasn't sure how realistic that was.

"Even so." Daya mussed up her brother's carefully groomed locks. "Be careful. You told me Santiago was extremely powerful and that dybbuk, wherever it came from, still killed him."

"Yeah, he was," he said thoughtfully, smoothing out his hair. "If an Ohrist's magic can make someone's head explode, it's a problem if they get possessed. But if all they can do is slide a glass across a table, the magic itself doesn't make the dybbuk dangerous. The dybbuk's desire to inflict pain would have to take different forms."

"Like Mei Lin manufacturing drugs," Laurent said, referring to a dybbuk we'd tracked down a while back.

"Right," Naveen said. "But if this woman's magic let the dybbuk leave her body, then that's the full extent of her power. It doesn't explain how she killed Santiago. Or rather, why he couldn't defend himself from the attack since she had nothing else to boost the dybbuk's strength. Can Ohrists not kill dybbuks?"

"Santiago being attacked, rather than inhabited by a dybbuk, is new territory for me." Laurent absently traced a circle on the table. "Ohrists can't sense dybbuks or see them, so if we get enthralled, we aren't aware of it until they make their presence known by trying to take control of our bodies. This was different. Santiago would have felt the attack, but he couldn't see his assailant to strike the dybbuk directly with his magic."

"Santiago's magic flared out like a net. There's no way it would have missed the dybbuk, and you're avoiding my question, mate." There was a pointedness to Naveen's easy smile and friendly tone that put me on edge, and I braced myself for more accusations. Naveen stood up to lean over the table. "Can Ohrists kill dybbuks? Yes or no?"

Laurent didn't answer, his head bowed.

Naveen's eyes widened, his brow furrowed, and he took an unsteady step backward. "Ohrists can't kill the bastards, can we?" He slammed the table. "Can we?"

I glanced between them in confusion, which only grew when Daya looked away guiltily.

"Only BS magic can." Naveen exhaled in a single hard breath like he'd been punched and a cold mask dropped over his features. He clenched his fists, his arms shaking. "You son of a bitch," he snarled and lunged for Laurent.

8

THE MEN COLLIDED, SENDING THEM SPRAWLING onto the floor. Laurent's shoulder clipped the edge of the toolbox and though I winced, his only reaction was to pinch his lips tight and knock the thing out of the way.

It flew into the fridge, rattling bottles inside.

"That's enough," Daya snapped.

Naveen straddled Laurent and slammed a punch into his jaw.

The shifter didn't retaliate. He didn't even defend himself, keeping his body loose and open to injury.

Naveen stood up. "Fight me," he growled.

Laurent pulled himself into a seated position, his knees drawn into his chest, and touched a finger to his bloody lip. His eyes were clouded with hurt and betrayal, which made no sense.

Delilah hovered behind me, her vibrations echoing my anxiety. Naveen hadn't known about Laurent's magic and instead of waiting for a time when tempers were cool, Laurent had dropped it now at the worst possible time? We needed Naveen's help. Tatiana's life was in danger.

And why wasn't Laurent defending himself?

"He doesn't owe you answers," Daya said,

"His silence is answer enough."

Daya winged her brother in the shoulder with a plum from the fruit bowl.

"Back off." The ferocious glower Naveen turned on her was probably nightmare fuel for more than one demon, but his sister merely winged another piece of fruit at him.

Naveen grabbed a fistful of Laurent's shirt and hauled him to his feet. "You're a B—"

I swung my chair into Naveen's back, knocking him off Laurent, but the Brit roughly shoved me away and I hit the counter with my tailbone, the chair clattering sideways to the floor.

Laurent swung his head my way, his eyes darkening and his fingers turning to claws.

"No," I whispered. If he shifted to defend me, this would get so much worse.

But I didn't have to worry, because when he looked at Naveen, he morphed his fingers back, his eyes dull.

His refusal to fight caused an angry flush to dot Naveen's cheeks. With a roar, the Brit snatched the wrench out of the toolbox and raised it over his head.

Daya got to her brother before either me or Delilah could, jumping in front of him and forcing her brother to pull his swing with a sharp twist away.

He lowered the wrench, and a long, hard, wordless look passed between them.

Naveen's shoulders slumped and Daya closed her eyes with an expression of relief, but it was a fake out. Her brother sidestepped her and punched Laurent, snapping the shifter's head sideways under the force of the blow.

I gasped and Delilah puffed up, grabbing the discarded fridge panel. It was one thing for Naveen to be an ass to me, but to turn on Laurent?

Anger bladed through me. I was so done with this.

But then Laurent groaned, rubbing his head, and Naveen froze. His eyes were wide and horrified, looking down at his hands and back at his bruised best friend.

My shadow dropped the panel though we both watched warily for any hostile move.

"You told me you'd been trained by a Banim Shovavim to detect and kill dybbuks," Naveen said, not caring that he'd split the skin on his knuckles with that last punch. "Not that you'd—" His voice cracked, and he sounded as battered as Laurent looked, but although he still held the wrench, the fight had seeped out of him. "What are you?"

"He's the same man he's always been," I said. With the fight over, my adrenaline had worn off, leaving me with the pain from when Naveen shoved me into the counter. I rubbed my lower back against the sting.

Laurent glanced at me, almost wistful, then his chin notched up in challenge and he advanced on Naveen. "How do you think I can kill dybbuks when no other Ohrist can? I took on Banim Shovavim magic in addition to my Ohrist powers."

"That's not possible," Naveen said.

"There are no absolutes when it comes to magic," Laurent retorted, pushing Naveen a few steps back with a finger to the chest. "You're not stupid, *mate*. What exactly did you tell yourself was happening?"

"So that's why you've allied yourself with her." The air charged with an electric bite as Naveen laughed bitterly and the wrench in his hand crackled with little rivulets of power. "No wonder you—"

"Watch yourself," Laurent growled.

Naveen strode to the other side of the kitchen and punched the wall. "Did you know?" he said to his sister.

"Yes." Daya examined Laurent, but he edged away, stopping her with a wan smile. Sighing, she gathered up some of the cups and put them in the sink. "Laurent told me after

Rishi was killed. I didn't care then, and I don't now. Pull your head out of your ass, Nav." She draped an arm over my shoulder. "Come on, love. Let's get a breath of fresh air and if anyone is so inclined afterward, we can bury my brother's body."

Rishi. How horrific had his death been? Chagrined, I wrestled my powers under control as Daya led me down to a swinging bench under a tree.

Was there any hope for true acceptance in the Ohrist community when these old prejudices still existed? On the other hand, Laurent knew Naveen would react badly, so why not deflect his suspicions? And why had he looked like the wronged party?

Daya rocked the bench slowly with one foot. "I take it this wasn't news to you?"

"No, I found out recently." I'd learned of it thanks to the Lonestar who'd tried to frame us for murder. And that cop had known the score because his family were hunters, dedicated to eradicating Banim Shovavim from the world.

I glanced at the kitchen window, but I couldn't see the men, and even though the door was open, I didn't hear arguing. I rested my head back against one of the chains attaching the bench to the tree. My tailbone was bruised but I was unable to muster up any anger toward Naveen. All I felt was a smothering sorrow. For all of us. "Will their friendship survive?"

"I'd like to think my brother isn't so thick that he'd throw away his best friend, but much as I love the little wanker, he's never been the most open-minded when it comes to Banim Shovavim." She paused like she was going to add more, then shook her head. "It got worse after Rishi."

"Sorry for all the emotional carnage." I watched a sparrow flit between branches above us. "I'm so happy to see you again, but our reunion sucked."

"I don't know. I thought it was very enlightening." She elbowed me playfully. "So, how did you and Laurent meet?"

"Nope. Not up to the third degree now."

"I'll let you off today, but it will happen."

Laurent stepped out of the house, his determined stride faltering into more of a resigned trudge once he'd come down the back stairs and out of sight of the kitchen. He caught his bottom lip between his teeth with a look of utter heartbreak, which he exchanged for a bland expression when he saw us.

Maybe my sigh was a bit too loud, or my relaxed pose a bit too feigned, because next to me, Daya suggested that I console the poor boy, accompanied by a lascivious waggle of her eyebrows.

"I hate you," I muttered.

"Is he alive?" Daya called out cheerfully.

"Unfortunately," Laurent said. "Ready to go?"

"Yeah." I stood up. "I'm going to pay Zev a visit. Harry is arranging it."

"Will you be accompanying our lovely Miriam?" The woman quickly losing all friend points leaned forward, her hands clasped together and a secret smile on her lips.

I expected Laurent to say that of course he was and braced myself for arguing that I'd be better off going alone since the vampire couldn't compel me. It was better than the argument that I required space to get my head together before I did something stupid like take Laurent in my arms.

The shifter shook his head. "Mitzi can handle him. I'm more of a hindrance."

"I'm sure *Mitzi* can," Daya said sweetly.

I gave her the finger behind my back. "I'm an expert in not offending Zev. My request shall be conducted with the utmost tact."

Laurent snorted.

Given that the alternative was an emotional sixteen-year-old, I'd take my chances with the vamp. That reminder was as good as a cold shower for all my feelings.

After I bid Daya farewell with promises to get together soon, Laurent drove me back to Tatiana's to retrieve my car.

I rolled down the window of his truck, staring out aimlessly for the first half of the journey. Laurent didn't talk, didn't put on music, and my chest grew tighter and tighter. He could easily have answered Naveen in a way that wouldn't arouse suspicion, or even flat out lied. He'd kept this secret for this long, why tell his friend now?

I stuck my hand out the window, air streaming through my fingers. Laurent should have done this at some other time when the two of them were alone and tempers weren't heated. He had to have known it would go badly and now Naveen had another reason to hate me. It was like a playground fight over who was the real best friend, except everyone had dangerous magic and I hadn't asked to be part of the conversation.

Laurent switched lanes with a burst of speed. "Why are you mad?"

He sounded affronted, which kicked in my own burst of anger, because that felt more productive than guilt and confusion. "Did you hear my heartbeat again?"

"You're glaring at my glove compartment."

I grabbed some lip balm out of my purse and applied it. This was where I should have run through arguments in my head until I'd assessed one that was calmly logical, but the words tumbled out of me. "You shouldn't have dropped that bombshell on Naveen like that."

"You're taking his side?"

"No." I slumped against the seat. "It's not about sides."

"Then what is it about?"

"Other than Daya, who else knows about your magic?" I recapped the tube and put it away.

"Tatiana might suspect." A car cut in front of him and

Laurent slammed his hand on the horn, following it up with a few rude hand gestures out the window. "No one. You. I told you this before."

"I didn't think that included your best friend."

There was a long pause and then Laurent quietly said, "I didn't either."

My heart twisted. "You thought he knew." Or hoped he did. If I felt raw after that fight, Laurent would be the equivalent of exposed nerve endings. I flicked my thumbnail against the seam of the seat belt. What I wanted to say wouldn't be easy for him to hear, but it was important enough that it couldn't wait. I sorted through the kindest way to broach the topic.

"That was expecting a lot of him, don't you think?" I said gently. "It's one thing for Naveen to accept that you trained to take on a second power when most Ohrists couldn't, but for him to have made the connection that it must have been Banim Shovavim magic? Why didn't you tell him in the first place?"

"He knows that Banim Shovavim magic kills dybbuks."

The stubborn set of his chin and defensive tone sent a wave of frustration through me. I pressed my hands flat against my thighs until my irritation had passed enough for me to continue in a calm manner.

"Laurent, I didn't even make that leap and I am one. Your training could have involved anything, not to mention that you're in Ohrist magic wolf form when you kill them."

"I expected you of all people to understand. Guess not." He blew through a yellow light, slamming me back against the seat.

How shaky had Laurent's house of cards become once he'd taken on this other magic and started killing dybbuks? He'd been scared that Naveen's prejudices extended to him. His friend was one of Laurent's few pillars of support. How much more damage would losing that relationship do to Laurent?

Hoping my next words didn't send his emotional state—or this truck, given how erratically he was driving—into a tailspin, I pressed on. "I didn't tell Eli until it was absolutely necessary."

"That's different." Laurent adjusted the sun visor. "You were hiding from your parents' murderer."

"True. For five years. Ten. But twenty? Thirty? Eli was out there possibly going up against dangers he couldn't fathom. And why? I didn't want him to see me differently, to think I was monstrous." Self-awareness wasn't fun, or easy, but hiding our heads in the sand was pointless.

"I don't care about other people's opinions," Laurent snapped. He'd let his best friend tenderize him, but yeah sure, he didn't care. "Don't overcomplicate everything. I assumed Nav knew, but I was wrong. When I realized that today, I told him." He turned on the radio, cranking up the volume on some boy band song that he would never in a million years voluntarily listen to.

My phone rang, and thinking it was Sadie, I answered, but it was Jude.

Laurent continued driving to Tatiana's while I spoke to my friend, digging in my purse for a stick of gum.

Jude said that my daughter was coming to stay with her overnight and wanted to know what kind of fight had precipitated this.

My thumb tore through the wrapper, dumping the red cinnamon-scented stick in my lap. Sadie had never avoided me, even when she was in trouble.

I picked up the gum with a clammy hand. She needed space. That was her choice and I had to respect that, even if every second that passed without us reconnecting felt like a wedge driving deeper and deeper into our relationship.

Had I really found the one thing my kid couldn't handle?

Jude called my name and I gave her the rundown on what had happened so she'd be prepared for any questions about magic or vampires, proud of my steady voice.

Laurent occasionally glanced over, but he remained silent.

My best friend assured me she'd leave out all details about Zev wanting to kill her for a (wrongly) perceived betrayal and that she'd take good care of her niece. As genuinely glad as I was that Sadie had this support system, I couldn't help the melancholy that settled over me.

When we got to my employer's house, Laurent asked if I was coming in, but I shook my head, too distracted to say bye to my boss or Emmett.

Thankfully, Laurent didn't pry for more details or make some empty, sympathetic statement. He simply asked me to phone him once I'd seen Zev.

I tried to take Jude's advice not to worry to heart, but I drove home with a hollow feeling inside me. Sadie had never actively avoided me before. Had I been too quick to believe that she'd accepted my magic simply because I wished it were true?

I flicked on some music, focusing on the lyrics of a forgettable pop song and getting myself home without rear-ending another car. However, inside my townhouse, I drifted aimlessly from room to room.

If my magic was too much for Sadie, would I do what was best for her or for myself? What if what was best for me triggered my daughter's anxiety? It was one thing to tell her to suck it up if I was going to date again and she didn't want to share, but magic was a whole other—and far more deadly—ball game. Even if I stopped using my powers—

Delilah jumped from the floor to the ceiling to the top of the television like a manic squirrel before grabbing me in a headlock. Our psychic connection right now had a sharp, dark edge, like teeth, and my skin suddenly felt paper-thin.

"Stop!" Grimacing, I forced Delilah back onto the ground. "You're not going anywhere."

Somewhat mollified, she lost her solidity, becoming a dark mass that twined around my ankles like a cat.

"Yeah, yeah." The shadow became inanimate, but I rubbed my ankle, loath to lose the lingering sensation of her touch.

Lonestars had the ability to modify Sapien memories. Technically, that was a possibility for Sadie if her anxiety wouldn't let her deal with her new knowledge, but it made my skin crawl. Yes, I'd waited for the perfect moment to tell her about magic, but sending her blindly out into the world wasn't an option. Not anymore.

Going upstairs into my bedroom, I retrieved the blank domino tile, turning the smooth block between my fingers. Emmett had tagged me as a domino in a prophecy at our first meeting, and a game of memory with a shapeshifter called Poe had implied that I was a wild card. There was infinite possibility in being a blank. In being unpredictable. I could be an agent of chaos or an anchor to turn the tide of events in my favor.

But there was such a thing as too much freedom. Blanks could hook to any other tile, which was great in theory, but all the combinations pulling at me from every direction were overwhelming. I shoved the drawer closed again, feeling restless and edgy.

Since I had to shake it off before my visit to Blood Alley and I had some time to kill before night fell, I changed into workout clothes and headed for the Zumba class at my local community center.

I'd been a regular at this class for a few years though my attendance since I'd gotten magic had become a bit spotty. The workout was attended by women of all ages, ethnicities, and body types, and after greeting a bunch of other regulars, I took my usual spot in the back row while our instructor, Kate, fired up the warm-up song.

The choreography was always fun, and I generally did a pretty good job of zoning out to the music, but tonight was different. I couldn't stop watching the other participants. Sure, the young woman ahead of me had a great body and dance training, but she gave an encouraging "whoot" to an older woman with an explosion of gray curls who only got about twenty percent of the choreography but danced like this was the most fun she'd ever had.

No one here was judging anyone. After everything that had gone down recently, why was I still exiling myself to the back row with the other people who were self-conscious about moving their hips and getting into the groove? No one here was going to look askance, and if they did, so what?

I was out there touting my ability to handle myself in the magic world and yet hiding away in a fun dance class because I didn't believe I was good enough? I shook my head.

For the first time ever, I threw myself into the music with the same abandon as when I danced around my bedroom. Even Kate noticed, shimmying over during one song to slap my butt with a scarf while I ground lower and lower in time to the beat.

When a remix of "Proud Mary" came on for the last cardio number, I hit it with everything I had, shaking my hips, wagging my fingers, and strutting my stuff.

The exhilaration stayed with me through the changing room and the drive to Gastown, where I parked a couple of blocks away from the entrance to Blood Alley. Humming under my breath, I did a little two-step along the sidewalk, until the gates to the vamp's territory appeared in front of me.

Blood Alley existed both as a real two-block stretch of restaurants in Vancouver and a much larger hidden space that the vampires operated as a renowned Ohrist attraction. Our own Sin City.

I'd gotten a lot better at seeing these spaces, which took

the same kind of mental energy and visual gymnastics as revealing those annoying 3D stereogram puzzles. I didn't even require my cloaking to see the entrance anymore. It was like a switch flipped in my brain, and the metal sign spelling out "Blood Alley" with gargoyles at each corner appeared.

Beyond it were four narrow crooked lanes lined with black lacquered doors, each with one to three red light bulbs above them, denoting the level of danger (as perceived by vampires, not humans) behind each one. At the top of the hill where all the roads converged was a huge, round limestone nightclub called Rome. The name smacked of Zev's rarely seen wry sense of humor.

His office was in its basement, so I pushed through the crowds seeking the night's entertainment and headed uphill. Two Ohrists tumbled out of one of the many bars, one using psionic power to blast her opponent into a wall. The second woman managed to flick her fingers before she crashed into it, and the psionic's legs broke with loud snaps. Screaming, she hit the ground.

At this point, two vamps showed up, grabbing the women and throwing them over their shoulders, before speeding up to Rome in a blur.

The crowd went quiet. Very, very quiet. People meekly shuffled into various rooms, doors closing behind them and bulbs washing the street in a red glow. A Red Sea, so to speak.

And on that topic...

When I was a kid, the three biggest dangers I expected to face in nature were quicksand, killer bees, and being eaten by sharks while swimming in the ocean during my period. While the latter was disproven to happen, would being around a vampire in this condition set him off? It's not like I could google scientific studies on it.

Some women worried about cramps and bloating, I weighed the odds that walking into Zev's office tonight was the equivalent of inviting him to feast on a champagne and filet mignon buffet. My life was so weird.

By the time I decided I was probably safe on that front, I'd hit the unkempt lawn leading to the front door of the club. All I had to do was cross the grass and wind my way through the hunched forms of the gargoyle statues, their shadows elongated into sinister forms.

In my experience, real gargoyles were a tad eccentric but helpful, so even if any of the statues were alive and faking a Medusa-victim impression, there was nothing to be afraid of. I wiped my palms on my dress, because it didn't matter how often I walked this path, that first step always required a jolt of courage.

Stupid Doctor Who Weeping Angels. That "Blink" episode was all I could think of every time I walked through this place. I blinked my eyes rapidly for a solid ten seconds, getting that urge out of my system. But even with my lids open comically wide, I didn't move, positive that this time, one of the gargoyles would go rogue and take me out.

Two tipsy girls who had "opening credit kill" written all over them passed me to walk through the statues and into the club unharmed. I chided myself that I was being ridiculous, rolled my shoulders back, and stepped onto the lawn. Still not blinking, mind you.

That's when the dybbuk appeared out of nowhere and attacked me.

9

THE DYBBUK WAS SO FAST THAT I BARELY HAD TIME to see it before it knocked me over. I hit the grass and rolled sideways, its next attack missing me by inches.

The crimson whirl of rage honed its amorphous shape into a razor-sharp point, becoming a living knife. It had no face, no features, no discernable sentience other than its violent need to hurt me.

It slashed my forearm, burning a bloody gash across the skin. Swearing, I shook out my poor limb. I'd seen one cut Laurent, but it hadn't happened to me before and it freaking hurt. Talk about the wrong day to wear a sundress.

A magic inky shadow funneled down my left arm into a scythe and I uttered the Hebrew word to make "die" appear on the blade, before swinging it into the dybbuk's center.

Yaas, queen!

But instead of withering and dissolving under the crushing blow of my scythe, the dybbuk just split in two like one of those old cartoons and reformed unharmed to my right.

I stepped backward in shock, almost turning my ankle on

the uneven lawn. That wasn't—they weren't supposed to behave like that.

I should have been vibrating like a live third rail with it this close, yet as it swooped and darted at me, expertly side-stepping all my attempts to destroy it, I felt no sense of its presence. In the darkness, it was little more than a blur that I was too slow to track. How long could I hold out against this thing? It was like it moved at warp speed while I was molasses.

I was tempted to jump through the shadows into the Kefitzat Haderech to safety, but the strain of revelers down in the lower section of Blood Alley grew louder. Rolling out my sore shoulder, I bolstered up my tired left arm with a two-handed hold, squinting into the gloom for my foe.

Where had it gone? I cocked my head, listening, but heard only the faint throb of music and voices of Blood Alley patrons. I crept forward, my shoulder blades prickling, jumping at a twig cracking underfoot.

The dybbuk shot out of nowhere, herding me back against a gargoyle carved with its wings outstretched and a look of vague constipation on its hideous visage. Caught between a wraith and a hard place.

I ducked and dodged, sprinting through a narrow gap between the dybbuk and the statue, but the spirit expanded to crowd me against the cold marble. This made no sense. Dybbuks on their own didn't have intelligence, much less battle strategy. Until they fully possessed their host and had access to the person's intelligence, their sole aim was to cause pain.

Its angry hum surrounded me, giving me an idea. Humans could hear much faster than we could see so, closing my eyes, I let the buzzing sounds guide my hand, abandoning myself to the same easy movements as back in Zumba class. Something inside me clicked, my actions taking on a new level of fluidity. Swing, duck, pivot, swing... I danced with my foe, my nonvisual senses wide open, and my weapon an extension of my arm.

The smell of my sweat mingled with that of dried grass and soil.

I spun like a dervish. My body ached and my scythe-wielding arm weighed a million pounds, but the dybbuk wouldn't die. I ducked behind a large statue to catch my breath. The night breeze ruffled my hair and grass tickled my calves. Where was that woman from the island hiding? As its host, she had to be here, but try as I might, I couldn't spot her.

The dybbuk gave me about three seconds of respite before it drove me back out into the open. I was growing tired, and it seemed able to bombard me from everywhere at once.

"Hey, lady! Are you okay?" a man called out.

I yelled at him to stay back, but the poor guy advanced, asking if I was drunk or sick. Of course, he couldn't see the dybbuk.

The evil spirit hesitated and I brandished my scythe.

"Come and get me," I said, intending to keep it away from the Ohrist.

Unfortunately, the young man took that as a threat directed at him and with a flick of his fingers like a conductor, gathered a cloud of mosquitos to attack me. Swatting at them, I jumped backward, clipping my eyebrow on the beaky nose of a gargoyle. Blood dripped into my eye.

The dybbuk got tangled up with the swarm of tiny blood-suckers. It extracted itself, its humming louder, and shot after the Ohrist and his friends.

I sprinted for the young men, commanding them to get into the club. Luckily, they didn't take much convincing because not seeing the true threat, they figured the crazy lady was out to get them.

Getting close enough to land a hit I swung my scythe, but the dybbuk switched course in midair, ramming into my arm and sending my attack wide. The scythe barely grazed it, allowing it to double down on one youth who'd hung back to rubberneck.

A crimson smile bloomed across the youth's neck. He frowned, swiping a thumb over a drop staining one of the crisp gold buttons on his blazer, then he fell to his knees and pitched forward into a clump of dandelions.

He'd ironed his khakis into sharp pleats. I pictured him excited about his night out, taking great care to get them that crisp.

A rush of adrenaline shot through me, and taking a deep breath, I jumped back into the fight. The dybbuk and I parried across the lawn, my assailant driving me in circles until I tripped over the corpse.

The dybbuk closed in for the kill with a new brusqueness like everything up until now had been a game that it had wearied of. My dress was plastered to my skin and my left arm burned, the weapon shaking in my hold. Santiago's last moments roared up to assault me, and while I couldn't make my cloaking materialize, I refused to die here.

I dredged up the last of my energy for one final attack, hacking at empty air until I noticed the furious hum was gone —and so was the dybbuk.

All that remained was a blessed silence. But had I actually killed it, or had it simply vanished? There hadn't been any sign of it imploding and winking out like normal, but nothing about it adhered to my previous experience.

I collapsed to my knees, my forehead almost resting on the ground, and my magic spent, praying the dybbuk didn't reappear. Finally, I willed myself to move and make sure the other men who'd been here were unharmed. I swallowed a gasp of pain and clutched my ribs with both hands. Every part of me throbbed, but I staggered to my feet.

A large group of Ohrists on their way to the club stood on the lawn in a semicircle, held back by a cadre of vampires. My weary sigh released them from their stupor and the people broke into worried murmurs. Someone took a photo of the corpse and promptly had their phone broken by a vampire. He looked ready to break more than that, but the crowd parted, revealing Zev. The master vamp briefly touched his minion's shoulder.

I bit the inside of my cheek to dispel any lustful thoughts, because Zev wore loose black workout pants and no shirt, displaying a body far more muscular than his suits hinted at. The sheen of sweat on his ripped abs gleamed in the moonlight and his short mahogany hair was tousled from exercising.

An alarm wailed inside my head. Zev didn't look like a god, far worse. He looked like a devastatingly handsome human. Was this another calculated disguise design to have us lower our collective guard and forget his true nature?

If so, gold star, Zev, because the entire crowd stared at him.

Their perfume and club sweat scents weren't enough to chase the spilled blood and death from my nostrils and their whispered conversations grated against my skin like the dybbuk's buzzing had, making my poor body ache that much worse.

"I guarantee that unless a guest breaks the rules, they will leave Blood Alley alive." Zev addressed the gathering calmly.

I almost snorted. Notice you didn't say "unharmed," buddy.

"But one man's transgression should not dull everyone else's enjoyment." The vampire waved his hand with a flourish. "Join us in Rome and we shall provide drinks on the house for everyone."

The crowd cheered, his underlings barely having to do anything to herd the people into the club.

I crouched down by the deceased and closed his lids,

waiting for the coast to clear before speaking. "He was innocent of any wrongdoing."

"I'm well aware of the situation, Ms. Feldman," Zev said.

I jumped, not having seen the vampire move to come stand next to me. His shoes were thin-soled, made of flexible material with ankle protection like boxer's boots. That was part of his stealth, but I bet the vamp could sneak up on me in tap shoes.

"Someone has made a liar of me," he said, "and we can't have that getting out."

Well, wasn't this a pleasant development in our relationship? For once, I wasn't being blamed, nor had Zev unearthed a napkin, rubbed his hands in glee, and exclaimed that he liked his meat raw and extra bloody before tearing into me for causing a disturbance or some other protocol violation in his territory. That was a huge win.

Good thing too because my patience was in shreds. I hadn't almost been torched and beheaded by Santiago's booby traps, harassed by Naveen, and attacked by the rogue dybbuk to lose my shot at getting my house warded up.

I stood up, wincing at the sharp burn that bounced inside my battered self like a pinball, and wrenched my eyes from the divots in the vampire's hipbones, because seriously, a woman could drink champagne out of those. "Allow me to offer my services and find the person behind this egregious breach."

Zev narrowed his eyes as if trying to determine whether I was being sarcastic, but I was deadly serious, and he nodded. "Very well. Considering they came after you."

"Are you sure about that?" I said.

Another vampire arrived, scooped up the corpse, and sped off. I didn't ask what he intended to do with it.

"Meaning?" Zev motioned for me to accompany him.

His legs were longer than mine, and I was tired, sore, and

rocking rubbery limbs. Zev must have noticed how hard it was for me to keep up, but he didn't adjust his pace to mine.

"You're not the only one who wants the Torquemada Gloves," I said. A thrum of unease snaked under my skin because if I hadn't killed that dybbuk, and I didn't think I had, it would be back.

"Of course I'm not." Zev veered left toward the outermost lane. "But I'm the one who has them and possession is nine-tenths of the law."

I shivered, my ears still ringing from the dybbuk. "Could we not use a possession metaphor right now?"

He chuckled.

"How did it even get through? Is Blood Alley really not warded?"

"Wards imply that the person behind them has reason to fear. Do you think that applies to me?" A fly buzzed too close to his face and the vampire grabbed one of its transparent wings and flicked the insect away.

I rolled my eyes—making sure he couldn't see me. Okay, Big Bad. But also, fair enough. "No," I grumbled. "Do you have any idea why that dybbuk didn't behave like the rest I've faced? I fought it for ages and the thing wouldn't die. It was like it had strategy."

"I'd like to know that myself."

Someone screamed and I flinched, but she laughed. It was just a woman jokingly berating a friend about sneaking up on her and almost giving her a heart attack.

"Was Torquemada an actual demon?" I asked hesitantly.

Zev opened a black door. "He was a monster like many fanatics. With that level of evil, does it matter if someone was human or not?"

Perhaps it didn't. I wanted to ask more questions, but I fell silent at the sight before me.

The room was empty save for five bare-chested vampires who stood with their legs planted hip width apart and their arms clasped behind their back, like soldiers "at ease." These dudes were huge, like The Mountain from *Game of Thrones*.

"I will ward your house up tomorrow night," BatKian said. "Have something to report by then. You may go." He dropped into a crouch and made a "bring it" motion at the other bloodsuckers.

As his minions rushed him, I said, "Tatiana has been cursed by a Pulsa diNura. She'll die unless you give up the gloves."

Zev gave no indication that he'd heard me. He slammed his elbow into the first minion's windpipe using momentum to lever himself around and break the kneecap of another one with a hard kick. Sorry, smash it into kindling, tiny shards of bones protruding from the pale, waxy skin.

I smothered a yelp, but I wasn't leaving without the gloves.

A third vampire choked Zev out from behind, but BatKian flipped him to the ground, stomping on his gut so hard that the other vampire spurted blood from his mouth.

Zev's bland expression didn't change during any of this.

Hunching into myself, I tried to stay out of the splatter zone, but I had a front row seat to the fight and I couldn't stop watching.

Every movement of Zev's was methodically and coldly carried out, with none of the manic bloodlust that Laurent would have displayed. Which was kind of ironic, given which one of them was the vampire.

Underlings one, four, and five regrouped, pressing in on Zev. He feinted right, then ducked in close to the vamp on his left with an uppercut to the jaw that shot the blood-sucker into the ceiling headfirst, his legs dangling down uselessly.

I was so busy being in awe, that I'd forgotten to be absolutely terrified that this monster had access to my house. I swallowed around the lump in my throat and backed up until

I hit the wall, trying to make my brain work in actionable steps. *Step one, breathe.*

I'd been useful to Zev, that was a point in my favor, but what happened when his goodwill dissipated? And with his mercurial temperament, it would. Would my death at least be merciful, or would I get special torture treatment as his personal acquaintance?

Still stuck on breathing properly, I briefly considered moving homes so he wasn't invited into my new place, but then I wouldn't have a ward, and he'd just get me another way.

He'd sworn not to harm anyone I cared about, but I wasn't included in that promise. I rubbed away some blood on my cheek from the dybbuk, my hiss as much for my possible fate as the pain that bolted through my cheekbone.

The largest and ugliest of the vamps grabbed Zev like a rag doll and slammed him over his knee with a crunch that bounced off the walls.

Zev went limp and I gasped. Was he down for good? Had all this been a challenge for dominance? Why would Zev have allowed me to see it?

Ugly stared at me coldly, smirking when only the barest flicker of a shadow swirled around my feet. *Please don't let him be the new boss.* Then he dropped Zev to the ground, forgetting the first rule of bad guy warfare—always take the headshot.

Zev's hand shot up and grabbed Ugly's calf. Yanking him forward, Zev bit his Achilles' tendon, ripping it out and spitting it onto the ground.

The vampire toppled over with a scream. I would have felt sorrier for Ugly but a) he was a dick, and b) he'd bounce back soon enough.

Zev rose to his feet, swaying like a cobra, blood coating his mouth.

Had I pressed back any harder against the wall, I'd have mated with it.

His final opponent roared and blurred forward. The attack happened too fast for me to catch, but the lackey hitting the wall face-first hard enough to shatter the concrete was clearly visible.

Zev faced me, barely breathing hard, though rivulets of sweat rolled down his pecs.

I remembered enough of my manners to close my mouth.

His lips still bloodstained, he frowned faintly at the ear he now held, then threw it to the floor with a grimace of distaste where it bounced off the vampire whose kneecap he'd broken.

I tensed my pelvic floor muscles with everything I had, because I would not humiliate myself by peeing in fear.

"No." Zev picked a towel up off a chair and blotted the blood off his lips like was attending high tea.

I looked around, in case I'd missed someone asking a question, but that was apparently for me. "No, what?"

My voice was a tad squeakier than I'd have liked. I cleared my throat, but that made me taste all the blood and fear stinking up the air and I decided that squeaky me was A-okay.

"No," he repeated. He checked the towel, then folded it and lay it back on the chair. "I will not give up the gloves. For any reason. Find another way."

"Is that what this demonstration was about?" I clenched my fists. "Making your point about what will happen if I fail? You're dangerous. Believe me, I understand. This wasn't necessary." I hung my head, overwhelmed by the overt violence when I was trying to save Tatiana. "It just wasn't," I repeated softly.

His eyes, when they raked over me, were cold and distant. "How very self-centered and human to assume this was for you." He dusted off his hands. "It wasn't. Now, I would suggest haste. Your dear Laurent cares for so few people in this world and one of them is in danger. Tatiana," he added, in case I hadn't gotten it.

Zev prodded the vampire whose guts he'd stomped on

with one foot, careful to avoid the puddle of spewage. "What do you think will happen to the wolf if his family member is murdered? He lost himself once already and barely returned from the brink of being forever trapped in his animal side. Are you willing to gamble on his ability to do it a second time?"

The minion got to his feet, but remained bent double, clutching his belly. "Good—" He coughed, and more blood dribbled out. "Fight."

Zev touched his shoulder. "You too."

The vampire hobbled out of the room.

How did Zev know this about Laurent? Had he caused it? Did it have something to do with the scar he'd given the shifter? The vampire was right that I wouldn't chance that happening, but everything else about this situation was wrong, and I resented the hell out of his emotional manipulation when there was an easy solution.

"Like you're really concerned about that."

"I treat everything as a concern," Zev said. "That way I'm rarely surprised." Control freak much? "What's more relevant is that you worry about him. Your daughter, your ex, Jude, the wolf, how many more exploitable weaknesses will you add to your list?"

My magic swirled frenetically into a half-formed scythe. "Is that a threat or simply another concern?"

"Merely an observation." He raised an eyebrow until I'd made the scythe vanish and clasped my shaking hands behind my back.

The vampire that had been stuck in the ceiling tore loose with a grunt and dropped to the ground. He bowed at Zev, uncaring of the shard of wood sticking out of one eye. "Good fight."

Zev clasped his shoulder. "You too."

Ceiling Vamp bowed again, then grabbed his buddy with the obliterated kneecap and the one with the gnawed-on tendon by their arms and dragged them from the room, leaving a bloody trail like slug slime.

Each of the other two croaked out "Good fight," with their boss acknowledging them in turn.

I held the door open for them, my manners and the desire for fresh air kicking in. Ceiling Vamp nodded at me and all three left.

"Let me make this abundantly clear," Zev said, "you will not let Tatiana die from the Pulsa diNura."

There was some connection, some history, between the two of them. He called her Tanechka, and yet he valued a demon artifact over her life? Either he was fooling all of us with how important Tatiana was to him or those gloves mattered a hell of a lot more than I'd given them credit for. But which one was it?

I swallowed a few curses, forcing myself to adopt a pleasant tone. "I want to keep her alive as much as you do." *Or more, since I'm actually trying to do something about it, you ass.* "Help me out here with somewhere to start. Please."

If he said no one more time, I was going to lose my—

The vampire who'd hit the wall face-first slid off with a wet sucking noise.

My stomach lurched at the sight of his face, scrambled eggs forever off my menu.

Zev made a tutting noise.

Less than a minute later, BatKian's vampire friend Yoshi opened the door and handed Zev a small vial of colorless liquid. Where Zev was a jungle cat, Yoshi was a willow tree, strong and lithe with a dancer's grace.

"Thank you," Zev said.

Yoshi's dark eyes darted around the room, and he smirked. "Only five? You're getting soft in your old age."

Zev pressed a hand to his chest with an expression of mock horror and Yoshi laughed.

I gaped at the two of them, which only made Yoshi laugh harder.

"I'll see you later," he told Zev and left.

"What's with the vial?" I said, glancing at the unconscious vamp on the ground. "Are those smelling salts?"

The lackey's fingers twitched, so he wasn't in body bag territory yet, but it was rather optimistic that smelling salts would wake the guy up.

"Do you know why Jude named the golem Emmett?" Shoving the vial in a pocket, Zev grabbed a clean towel off another chair.

I tilted my head, following the clench of his glutes, tempted to bust out a quarter and see how high it'd bounce off those puppies. "She named her attempts alphabetically like hurricanes and the first four tries didn't take?"

"To bring a golem to life, the Hebrew word for truth, "emet," must be etched upon their body." He wiped himself down with the same careful attention he gave everything.

Forcing my mind out of the gutter, I scrunched up my face, teasing out a half-buried memory. "The Golem of Prague. He had it on his forehead and when they needed to stop him, they erased one of the letters in the word, turning truth to death. But Emmett doesn't have that word on him."

"He does," Zev said, "just not on his forehead."

I grimaced, picturing tramp stamps—or worse. Note to self: never ever ask to see it.

The vampire held up the vial. "You want answers to Tatiana's plight? This is the easy way of getting them. Have the golem drink it and for roughly two minutes, his divination magic will tap into the collective unconscious of all known things."

I eyed it warily. "Why would you give this to me? You could have used it on Emmett yourself when he worked for you."

"I only recently chanced upon this potion and I'm giving it to you for obvious reasons."

"Uh-huh. What's the catch?"

"This liquid suppresses his Ohrist magic, bringing his Banim Shovavim powers into focus." Emmett's divination talents came from Banim Shovavim necromancer magic, and it was believed that some of the dead could see the future.

I shrugged. "Jude could unsuppress them and balance Emmett back out."

"You misunderstand," Zev said. "Should this potion quash the golem's Ohrist power for good, he could not be reanimated. He'd be using it at the peril of his Ohrist magic."

"You said this suppresses his Ohrist magic, not kills it entirely."

"In theory, that's how it should work. Practice is another matter entirely. This is, after all magic, not rocket science."

"So, he could end up a giant paperweight? Out of the question."

"Who is worth more to you, Ms. Feldman? Sentient clay who could finally fulfill the purpose he was created for, or Tatiana, the woman who affords you protection?"

I would never pick and choose between my friends. That's not how I operated. I crossed my arms. "It's not an either-or situation. I want a different option."

His eyes darkened for a moment, and I braced myself for one of his violent outbursts, but he rattled off an address. "Go see the Wise Brothers."

"In Los Angeles?" I read back the address I'd hurriedly typed into my phone to make sure it was correct. "Who are these guys?"

"They run a bookstore."

"You could have given me that option first."

"And I didn't because the golem was the easy way." He slung the towel over his shoulder.

"Will this visit cost me my soul or something?"

"Don't be so melodramatic." Said the undead being who'd recently munched on Achilles' tendon. "Your soul is hardly that valuable."

My stomach dropped into my toes. Then what was?

He pressed the vial into my hand. "Tatiana's life depends on your success. Don't make any rash decisions out of a misguided loyalty."

I shoved it in my purse. "What about my ward? When will you set it up?"

"Tomorrow night." Zev crossed the room and knelt by the fallen vamp, his head cocked.

The fiend spoke, but his face was too mushed up for anything other than garbled sound.

"Shame," Zev said, and snapped the dude's neck.

"Wh-why didn't you let him regenerate?"

"Some things are beyond repair." He nodded at the door. "That will be all, Ms. Feldman."

Bile rising in my throat, I bobbed a hasty bow and fled into the night.

10

————

AFTER A LONG SHOWER WHICH LEFT ME PINK, pruney, and positive that I could still smell vamp innards, I lay in bed examining the vial. Emmett didn't have a lot of love for his wonky divination power, but even if he agreed to it, I couldn't let him ingest something that could kill him.

On the other hand, what would the Wise Brothers demand in payment?

I set the vial on my bedside table and flicked off the light. Hopefully I'd have more clarity in the morning.

It was a nice thought, but daylight failed to give me some grand epiphany about my next move. Adding to my frustration was the fact that I'd missed a voice mail from Sadie saying that she was going straight to work from Jude's but promising to come home tonight. At the end of the message, she paused like she'd been about to add "love you" but simply said "bye."

A knock at the front door startled me out of my funk.

Still in my short pj's, I peered out to find Laurent on my stoop with a motorcycle helmet tucked under his arm.

I hurriedly brushed a hand over my bedhead, hoping I didn't have huge bags under my eyes, and opened the door.

"Tatiana wants us to come—" Laurent braced a deceptively casual hand on the doorframe, scanning me intently. "Good talk with Zev?"

It took me a moment, but I touched the cut on my face, glad my pj's hid most of the other injuries. I'd gotten off lightly, all things considered. "Vamp shmamp. You may bow to me."

"Really?" Laurent played along with my light tone. "Why do you deserve the honor this time?"

"I went twelve rounds with a dybbuk and survived." I kissed my biceps.

He gently nudged me inside and closed the door. "Ha. Ha. Very funny."

I shook my head, my expression serious. "I'm not kidding, and I don't think I killed it." I paused, working it through in my head. "I feel like this clinches it that the woman I saw at the fight was the one who killed Torres. It's too much to believe that some other party sent the dybbuk inside this woman when it didn't try to inhabit Torres at all."

"And you agree with my theory that she's possessed not enthralled, because she didn't try to stop the dybbuk when it attacked Torres?"

"That and it fought like it was experienced."

Laurent swore under his breath.

"How is she doing this?" I said. "Her magic allowing the dybbuk to leave her body is one thing, but can she guide it?"

"I don't know."

"Why not?" I snapped a loose thread off my pajama top. "You trained with a Banim Shovavim, right? Why didn't this mentor of yours fill you in better on the whys and wherefores of all things dybbuk? You didn't even know for sure that I could save enthralleds. Why don't you ask him?"

"Her. And she's dead. Trust me, if she'd known about this kind of dybbuk possession, then I could counter what we were dealing with now."

130

"I have a feeling it'll be back," I said.

"Of course it will. Both the woman and dybbuk know you're here." Laurent shook his head, his expression tight. "You have to be extra careful." He gingerly tilted my jaw up with one finger.

I let him examine me, not only getting used to it, but kind of enjoying his concern. "I will, but in one piece of good news, I got a new avenue from Zev to pursue about the curse."

"He didn't know what the dybbuk was?"

"No. And he wasn't thrilled about that."

After one more cursory look, Laurent dropped his hand. "You're sure you're okay?"

"Positive. I'm toughening up like aged leather. So, about his idea—"

"Wait until we get to Tatiana's." Laurent shook out his curls, which were squished from his helmet, and glanced at my bare legs. "Get dressed. Jeans and proper shoes."

"I'm not going on your bike." My period had slowed down from a blood bath to a relatively clean abattoir, but with my luck, the motorcycle's vibrations would open the floodgates again. Plus, my body had rejected the tampon I'd put in. Ladytown was in one of its periodic phases where it was all about the evictions, no new tenancies. No motorcycles, thank you.

"You look like you need cheering up and this will do it." His expression was soft, his eyes clouded with concern.

Zev's comments came to mind, and I longed to lay my hand on Laurent's stubbled jaw and ask how long he'd been stuck as a wolf, and how he'd come back with this deep well of compassion intact, but I lightly curled my fingers into my palms.

"You didn't know I needed cheering up before you got here," I said. "You just don't want to ride in my car."

"That's always true," he said, "but you were distracted

131

over something yesterday. Well?" He held the helmet out.

I rubbed a hand over my lips. Drive through annoying traffic, obsessing over Sadie and how dangerous the Wise Brothers would be, or let this wolf give me a wild ride.

Phrasing.

Laurent blinked at something on the small table in my foyer, and doing a terrible job of not laughing, picked up the mug that said "I Love to Wrap Both My Hands Around It and Swallow."

My cheeks flamed. Shit. I'd totally forgotten about the discarded item. I reached out to grab it. "Give it back."

He tapped the ceramic, holding the mug out of reach. "An older woman with questionable morals. How intriguing." He leaned close with a wicked grin. "Admit you want to go for a ride, Mitzi."

I crossed my arms, grateful that the motion hid my hard nipples.

His eyes were luminous with delight, his lips in a lopsided grin, and his body relaxed with an almost palpable amusement. He was so vitally alive, his usual guardedness absent, and watching this playfulness to him after his fight with Naveen took my breath away.

The rush of attraction hit me like a tsunami, literally forcing me back a step. Mentally slapping myself upside the head, I pointed at the kitchen. "Put the cup in the sink, please, and wait in the kitchen."

Racing upstairs, I did a quick but thorough cleansing, praying that I'd remain downwind of the wolf shifter. Feeling about as sexy as a puddle of toxic waste, I popped a couple of painkillers and threw on jeans and a T-shirt, making an effort to look pulled together. I raked my dark hair back into a low ponytail that would fit under the helmet, and after concealing my bruises with foundation, swiped on some shimmery eyeshadow, mascara, and light gloss.

A notification chimed on my phone. The colleague I'd

reached out to had emailed me back to say they'd passed my email on to another librarian at a theology library at Oxford. Fancy. I sent off a quick thank-you, hoping this second person could illuminate why Zev wanted the Torquemada Gloves. If I had a concrete understanding of the situation, more facts, perhaps I could reason with the vampire to prioritize Tatiana's life over the artifact.

After lacing up my runners, I added necessities to my small, crossbody purse, including my good luck domino and a sanitary pad. After a moment's hesitation, I threw in the vial and flew down the stairs. "I'm ready."

Laurent thankfully refrained from any more teasing as I locked up and we walked over to his motorcycle, a leather and chrome monster that sat between my sedan and an SUV like an alien predator.

I patted the seat. "Hi, pumpkin."

Paper rustled, my neighbor Luka giving me a dry look as he sat down in his porch chair, newspaper in hand.

Laurent rubbed the seat off like I'd infected it with cooties. "Don't call her that."

"What should I call her?"

"She doesn't have a name." He double-checked that my helmet was adjusted properly.

"Liar." I swung my leg over the seat behind him, the bunch and flex of his back muscles filling my vision, and I wiped my hands on my jeans. Our previous ride had been conducted with two layers of leather between us. Neither of us wore jackets now, which meant the only thing separating us was the thin fabric of our shirts.

"Ready?" he called back.

"As I'll ever be." I wrapped my arms around his waist, my cheek pressed against his spine.

He started the engine, his free hand resting casually on my clasped fists, before giving them a squeeze and taking the handlebars.

I snuggled closer against him, butterflies getting the best of me, but Laurent took it slowly at first to ease me back into the sensation, and while I didn't have my eyes closed behind my sunglasses this time, my heart beat as loudly as the bike's rumble.

Little by little, I relaxed, and Laurent opened her up, the pavement streaking by under our feet and the city rushing past in a blur.

A bright blue dragonfly zipped toward my helmet, bobbing close before darting away and I sat up straighter, the volume on the world turned up. It was like my senses had gone from sepia to rainbow-colored. Was this what it was like to be a shifter? My breathing evened out to match Laurent's, and I drank in his scent, that ever-present cedar underneath the muskier aroma of sandalwood soap.

We pulled up in front of Tatiana's house far too soon, parking behind a metallic blue Porsche. Its door opened and I half expected James Bond to exit, but it was Naveen, his platinum blond hair brushed carelessly away from his forehead, and his tailored slacks and silk shirt hugging his frame. So, close enough.

The three of us eyed each other. Laurent and I windblown in contrast to his cool, unruffled vibe.

"Tatiana didn't mention you'd be here," Laurent said.

"Or you," Naveen said.

If they were going to behave like children, I might as well have some fun. I walked around the car, cooing "so pretty."

Naveen grimaced. "My car is not pretty. It's magnificent."

Laurent snorted. "It's a midlife crisis ten years early."

"At least I don't have size issues." Naveen jerked a thumb toward the motorcycle.

See, there were plenty of things for the boys to fight about besides Laurent's magic. I peered in the back window and clapped my hands. "You have a car seat." I pitched my voice all sex kitten and pouty. "That's so badass."

"Evani is required by law to have one," Naveen said. "And it's a pain to keep putting it in and taking it out."

"Poor poppet," I said blandly. "There's medication for that nowadays."

Naveen gasped. "I'm speaking about my niece's safety and you're making inappropriate comments?"

"Really, Mitzi." Laurent shook his head. "Too far."

I cupped a hand to my ear. "Did you two just agree on something?"

They stared sullenly at me in an identical crossed-arms position, which turned to scowls toward each other, and then they dropped their pose at the same moment.

"This is ridiculous." I threw my hands up. "You're both upset and angry and you both have good reason to be, but now you're going to see it from the other's perspective."

They looked away.

"Don't make me break out the mom countdown," I said, "because I assure you, you won't like it."

"I'm still mad," Naveen muttered.

Laurent said something in French.

Naveen shoved his shoulder. "Speak English."

"I should have told you." The shifter looked at me with a raised eyebrow. "Happy?"

"My cup runneth over with delight," I said. "Your turn, Naveen."

"Upon further reflection," the Brit said stiffly, "your magic acquisition was not, perhaps, a huge surprise to me."

I slow-clapped them. "Was that so hard?"

"I've killed demons for less," Naveen said and marched off.

Laurent fell into step with his friend. "True. Remember the one in Zurich?"

Naveen laughed, the two of them entering Tatiana's home without knocking.

Mortal enemies one minute, best friends the next. Just

like children. Whistling, I headed inside. Damn, I was good.

I followed the sound of raucous laughter into the kitchen. Emmett and Tatiana sat in the sun-drenched room at the large round table, attempting to discard the cards in their hands onto small piles in front of them as quickly as possible.

Tatiana rid herself of her stockpile first and slammed her fist on a card, a second before Emmett did the same to one of his piles.

"Old, my ass!" she crowed.

"Rematch!" the golem demanded.

Tatiana gathered up the cards. "My winning streak will have to stand. We have company."

Emmett glanced over his shoulder at us, providing us with a proper look at his outfit.

"Bloody hell," Naveen muttered.

"Looking good, buddy." I flashed Emmett a thumbs-up.

"I know." He stood, showing off his bellbottom velour pantsuit that was obviously a Tatiana borrow, because the purple fabric strained around his bulkier chest. He didn't have a wig on his bald red head, but someone had done a nice smoky eye on him.

My boss on the other hand, wore a loose pink sweat suit with the word "juicy" bedazzled across her butt. Jude was going to kill Emmett for stealing that.

"Emmett thought we should swap clothes today to fool anyone who came after me." Tatiana smiled at him indulgently.

The men's disdain for this idea couldn't have been more obvious if they'd tattooed it across their foreheads.

"Very clever," I said.

Something heavy dropped overhead and then Raymond called out an "All good."

Tatiana rolled her eyes but did not yell back that he was fired. "Let's meet downstairs."

Emmett hung back to grab my arm, keeping me in the

kitchen while the others left.

"What's up? Everything okay? Are you getting along with Raymond and Marjorie?"

"I'm teaching Marjorie to stand up for herself and Raymond to..." There was another thump and Emmett glanced at the ceiling. "That stump isn't teachable. But he's harmless. No, that's not it."

"Then what?"

"Tatiana keeps spacing out. It's freaky." Emmett wasn't the most astute being so for him to notice Tatiana's deviation from her usual behavior meant she was really worried about the curse.

"You want me to talk to her?"

"No," he said. "I'm distracting her. But it's a good thing you got here because there was nothing else of hers that I could fit into and we'd played that same card game six million times."

"You're a good egg, Emmett." I squeezed his shoulder.

He puffed up with pride and ducked his head. "Just doing my job."

I let him go ahead of me. Emmett had been a pain in my ass since day one, either getting drunk as a skunk on missions with me, zoning out at inopportune moments to prophesy, or stealing clothes from my best friend, boss, and very nearly my kid. He had a foul mouth and dangerously little color-matching skill, and he was fast becoming one of the noblest people I knew.

And yet here I was, debating if I could bear to save Tatiana if it meant reducing him to a two hundred pound lump. My hand ghosted over my purse with the vial and my shoulders slumped.

I was the last one into the small basement room. It didn't have windows and Tatiana said it was impossible to bug so we could speak freely.

Laurent looked slightly mollified by her precautions, but

when I sat down next to him, he touched the small of my back. "You okay?"

I nodded, the vial growing heavier by the second. "Let's compare notes."

The humans huddled around a metal folding table while Emmett barred the door. Naveen shared his intel first.

Wendy, the Ohrist in charge of Santiago's security, was aware of the death curse, but Santiago had refused to even consider handing over the Torquemada Gloves. He'd planned to gift them to one of the guests, Estrella Cabral, after the fight, as a goodwill gesture to move a proposed business venture forward. That was why he'd held the championship event despite the curse. Santiago was determined that Estrella not suspect any weakness in his operation.

"Santiago was a fool to do business with that snake." Tatiana had brought the cards. She'd been playing Solitaire while Naveen updated us, but running into a dead end, she gathered up the deck and shuffled. "No wonder Sherisse was so worried. She didn't know about the curse, did she? She was anxious that she was going to be replaced." My boss made a tutting sound, setting up the next round by distributing the deck into eight piles. "Estrella always mixes business with pleasure a little too much."

"It's true. Sherisse had no idea about the curse," Naveen said.

"What about Estrella? Did she know she was getting the gloves?" I placed the discarded jokers in the box. "Has anyone spoken to her?"

"Can't," Naveen said tightly. "Lonestars found her body Sunday morning. They estimated she'd been killed twenty-four hours earlier. Guesses as to whose invitation the dybbuk-woman entered Torres's party with?"

"Dead end," Emmett said. When everyone turned to him with varying looks of annoyance, he shrugged. "Like you weren't all thinking that."

"What's your sense on Torres's bodyguards betraying him?" Laurent said.

"I'd bet my life they're loyal." Naveen checked a note on his phone. "As was the guard who checked the invitation. Even from Miriam's vague description, the intruder could be confused for Estrella. And as you said, fingerprint scans can be faked. We've spoken to Estrella's inner circle. None of them know anything about this other woman. Or are claiming they don't."

"They probably don't," Tatiana said. "Whoever that Ohrist who killed Santiago is, she'll keep her secrets close. Telling Estrella might have been necessary to her plans, but she tied up that loose end." She frowned at her cards and abandoned the half-finished game.

"She wasn't enthralled and then flipped to full possession during the fight either," Laurent said. "The letter Santiago received, stealing the invitation, killing Estrella, this was methodic. A premeditated murder, and within the range of behavior of a dybbuk-possessed host."

Even if that was the case, the dybbuk's actions once free were all kinds of wrong. I should have sensed it and I should have seen the woman's diseased shadow at the fight.

Above all, I should have been able to easily kill the dybbuk when it attacked me. My ease at dispatching them formed a rare solid corner of my house of cards. No longer.

"I'll put out feelers among some people," Tatiana said. "Find out if they've heard anything about a new hitwoman using dybbuks."

"Why do you think she's a hitwoman," Naveen said, "and not someone with a personal vendetta over the gloves?"

"Killing Santiago in front of that crowd was designed to make a statement," Tatiana said. "She was establishing herself in a big way. If she isn't an assassin, then it's some other criminal ploy."

"Oh good, that narrows things down." I gathered up the

cards, stacking them in an orderly pile. "Zev won't hand over the gloves either." My pronouncement was met with three versions of "I told you so" and a golem snort. "But he did give me a way to get answers. Tatiana, what do you know about the Wise Brothers? Are they a viable option?" My leg bounced restlessly.

"I haven't heard that name in years, but I can't tell you much, aside from the fact they have a reputation for being the preeminent dealers in information."

"Visa, Mastercard, ten years of my life…what payments do they accept?" I said.

Tatiana shook her head in frustration. "The most anyone ever told me about their visit was that they lost more than they gained. I suspect visitors aren't capable of discussing the encounter after the fact."

"That's out, then," Laurent said and placed a hand on my jittery leg.

"It's the only way," I protested, stuffing the cards back in the box.

"No, it's not," Emmett said. "Mr. BatKian has a vial that will let me tap into all knowledge."

I blinked. How had he found out? Did Zev go behind my back and tell him? "You're talking nonsense," I said, hoping I could shut Emmett up and debating whether to have Delilah knock him out to keep him safe.

"Am not."

"Great." Laurent gave me a weird look and raised his hand. "I vote for that."

"The vial isn't an option," I said.

Naveen's eyes darted from me to my purse, and I put my hand protectively over the zipper.

"Jude didn't tell you the vampire came to visit her a couple weeks ago, did she?" Emmett said.

I did a double take. It's not like Jude had to report back, but didn't I deserve to know about any follow-up encounters after rescuing her from Zev's bad books? She'd promised she was through with all that.

"Is she working for him again?" I said in a light voice, vowing to throttle my best friend if she was.

"Get real. Mr. BatKian said he had something crucial he needed to know and offered her a lot of money to give me whatever was in the vial, but she refused." The golem frowned and looked down at his fat bare feet. "It was before he hired Tatiana. I think he wanted a surefire way to get the gloves out of the vault."

I tightly interlaced my fingers. "Did he threaten either of you?"

Emmett shook his head.

"Zev gave you his word that he wouldn't harm them," Tatiana said. "He'll stand by that."

"BatKian told you about this?" I asked her.

"Yes."

I stood up, pacing the small room. "Zev's promises are like laws. If he wanted something in direct opposition badly enough, he'd stick to the letter but not the spirit."

Naveen scratched his stubbled chin. "What's the big deal? Give the golem the vial."

"No!" I moderated my tone at everyone's surprised looks. "His Ohrist magic will be suppressed while he's getting answers. Don't you know what that means to a golem?"

Laurent shrugged. "I still vote yes. It's useful."

"Me too." Naveen nodded.

"Me three," Emmett said. "I wouldn't have done it for the vampire, but I like Tatiana."

"I like you too, Emmett," she said with a sweet smile.

"And if it's permanent?" I smacked the table. "Should the Ohrist magic not come back on its own, that's it. Jude can't fix you this time. You still want to take it?"

Emmett hugged himself. "No," he mumbled, looking away from Tatiana.

"It's okay, tattele," she assured him.

Laurent opened his mouth, then wisely shut it at my scowl.

"Now what?" Naveen said.

I was missing something. Zev considered himself honorable, so given his promise about not harming my people, he wouldn't force Emmett to take the liquid and learn how to get into the vault. But he wouldn't risk his opportunity to procure those gloves either. Not after searching for them for so long.

I stopped in front of Tatiana. "What was his Plan B?"

"Sorry?" she said.

"You heard me. You claim you don't know why Zev is so attached to the gloves, and I believe you, but he did want them. Badly. You saw his reaction when I handed them over, so what would have happened if Emmett and I weren't successful? Emmett hadn't drunk the liquid in the vial, so he hadn't divined the way in. How would Zev have gotten hold of the gloves if we'd failed?"

Tatiana blew on her glasses lenses before wiping them with a corner of the sweatshirt. "How would I know?"

To my shock, Laurent's hands shifted to claws and Naveen summoned his light staff, resting it carelessly across his lap.

"Answer her," Laurent said softly.

Emmett shielded Tatiana from them with his thick clay body and she patted his shoulder.

"This is getting gonzo," I said. "No one is hurting anyone. Just tell me what Plan B was."

Tatiana wagged a finger at her nephew. "You know, Lolo, one of these days you constantly thinking the worst of me is going to hurt my feelings." She put her glasses on. "I was Plan B," she said loftily. "If for any reason you failed to get the gloves, I agreed that I would...force Santiago to hand them over."

"Can you compel people?" I said. "Holy shit."

"Last time you forced someone to do something?" Laurent's fingers morphed back to human. "You had a stroke."

"A mild stroke. I'm well aware of what happened," Tatiana said in a steely voice. "And I can't compel anyone."

"How badass are you?" Emmett asked with wide eyes.

"Extremely." She winked at him. "If absolutely necessary, I can control someone's body like they are my marionette, but it's very taxing and I am a woman of some years, so I don't."

My mouth opened and closed several times like a fish gulping for air. Tatiana was a puppet master? I mean, yeah, she could manipulate organic material, I'd seen that, but this was serious next level stuff, *since the only other creature I'd seen do this was a demon.*

Emmett grabbed me with one meaty hand, fanning me with the other. "Are you stroking out?"

Swatting him away, I tore free and smoothed down my shirt. "You agreed to this for me?"

She notched her chin up. "I agreed because I owed Zev and it's none of anyone's business why."

Naveen poked his staff into Laurent's shoulder. "Guess you're going to the Wise Brothers."

"Where are they these days?" Tatiana said.

"Not far," I replied. "I can get there in no time."

The letter sent to Tatiana had given her three days to produce the gloves and twenty-four hours had already passed. Even if I got the first flight out to Los Angeles, that would eat up most of today. I had to use the Kefitzat Haderech, however, as far as I was aware, only Emmett and Laurent knew of its existence, and I intended to keep it that way. Let everyone think that I meant to go through a travel agent. My magic didn't need to be some open book.

"We're both going." Laurent narrowed his eyes when I spoke up to disagree. "Don't even think of fighting me on this, because I guarantee you'll lose."

11

THE MEETING WRAPPED UP SOON AFTER. EMMETT remained with Tatiana, while Naveen left for a call with the security team to go through more of Torres's business affairs in hopes of getting more answers.

I squinted against the bright sunshine, almost missing the helmet that Laurent tossed me.

"Can we take the bike to go see these guys?" he said.

"Not really. They're in Los Angeles, which is why I—"

Laurent blanched.

I stepped closer because he looked seriously ill.

His expression became distant, his eyes rolled up but flicking from side to side like he was doing calculations. His shoulders tensed, then he nodded. "Get us on the first flight out. There is no time to waste."

I waved a finger around his face. "What was all that about?"

He spoke over me, his long strides to the motorcycle forcing me to half jog. "We'll go business class. I will pay for both tickets."

"No, that's not—"

"Yes."

I grabbed his arm. "Stop. We're not going business class."

"I cannot go any other way," he growled.

I was about to make a crack about His Majesty not sitting with the great unwashed, until I noticed he was white-knuckling his helmet straps. "Are you scared of flying?"

"Don't be ridiculous." He looked down his nose at me haughtily, then his gaze dropped to the twisted straps in his hold. "I just—I don't do well being locked in cages."

I squeezed his hand, hating plane rides as well. "We're not flying. We're not driving, we're not taking a train."

He planted his hands on his hips. "You're not going without me."

The truth was that I didn't want to face the Wise Brothers on my own, but things were getting too tangled up between Laurent and me. The Kefitzat Haderech was the one space that was mine. Not co-owned with Eli or shared with Sadie. But if I took Laurent, he'd fill it with his presence, like he'd done with my home and my car.

However, Tatiana was his family, so my desire to set boundaries for myself didn't trump his to do everything he could to ensure she stayed alive.

"I am losing patience, Miriam," he said. "Do you really not want me there?"

Sighing, I put my helmet on. "I do. Let's head back to your place and go from there."

He frowned but nodded.

The ride back to Hotel Terminus wasn't so much a freeing rush as a slow build of dread, but I talked myself down. Laurent hadn't forced himself into any part of my world, I kept inviting him. Badgering him to partner up. I wasn't married to the guy, hell, we didn't even technically work together. If I had to step away from spending time together and sort my head out, then he'd respect that.

I'd wanted to get my divided house in line, which meant bringing all aspects of my life and loyalties into alignment.

Some parts would admittedly take more work but shoring up the foundation between Laurent and myself involved a relatively simple first step.

One that wouldn't force him to suffer through a flight. The Kefitzat Haderech had nothing to do with territories or boundaries. It was simply an expedient means to an end.

Feeling better, I strode confidently into his place and positioned myself in the center of a slanted shadow. "Do you trust me?"

Now that I'd made up my mind to take him, I wanted to see the look on his face when we stepped into the Kefitzat Haderech. It was one thing to hear about magic and quite another to see it firsthand. Might as well dazzle him.

"I did until you asked me with that strange gleam in your eyes." But when I held out my hand, he took it, his callused fingers folding tightly over mine.

I pushed through the shadows, bringing us into the dimly lit cave.

Pyotr was hunched over the tablet I'd bought him to watch movies on, chanting "Go! Go!" at another *Fast and Furious* flick.

"You enjoying that?" I said.

The gargoyle nodded seriously. "Very much." In his Russian accent, he pronounced it "wery." He spied Laurent and snapped his gray gargoyle wings out. "You bring new pet?"

Laurent had ducked so he didn't have an eye gouged out by a wingtip. "Pet?"

"Hmm. Not pet," Pyotr pronounced. He was dressed in his customary brown plaid shirt and brown pants. "This one has heartbeat."

I grimaced. What kind of pets were you used to, dude? "This is my friend."

Pyotr set down his tablet and shoved his bulging eyes and gaunt face into Laurent's armpit. "Smells like dog."

A low growl burst from Laurent's throat, but the gargoyle didn't stop smelling him, his nose now in the hollow of Laurent's neck and a frown replacing the usual sorrow carved into his stone features.

I muscled in between the two of them because the shifter was bristling and the gargoyle was still in freaky sniffer mode. "Laurent, this is Pyotr. He's the gatekeeper here in the Kefitzat Haderech."

Pushing Pyotr away, Laurent raised an eyebrow. "No kidding."

I'd told Laurent about this place when I was still at risk from eternal torture here. Once I'd seen through what the angels had attempted to do to all Banim Shovavim, I'd shared the rest of the story and that I was no longer in danger traveling on it. Right now though, Laurent didn't look as impressed as I'd hoped. Time to call off the gargoyle.

"If I gave the Kefitzat Haderech a name, would it take me to that person?" I said. It was worth asking if we could skip a step in finding the killer.

Pyotr shook his head. "Location, not name." Oh well.

"Can Laurent choose the sock?" I winked at Pyotr. For some reason, single socks ended up here, so to get rid of them, the gargoyle and his boss, the neon sign, told new Banim Shovavim that they needed a sock to use the KH. It was a little silly, but it was part of the fun.

Pyotr sniffed again. "Don't know." His voice was slow and thoughtful, more so than usual.

I tsked, in no mood for any more delays than we were already dealing with. "Please? It'll be fine," I promised, grabbing Laurent's hand. "We'll just take a sock and be out of your hair and you can forget all about us."

Laurent, meanwhile, was not being helpful at all. His arms were rolling with fur, like his magic was surging to the surface.

"Calm down, dude. Just pick a sock and we'll jet," I hissed, and plunged his hand into the sock pile.

Lightning flashed under his skin, like looking at a storm from an airplane, and fangs sprang down from his upper jaw, his curls turning fluffy and white.

I sucked in a breath at the sight of his Banim Shovavim magic warring with his Ohrist magic.

"Stop," Pyotr ordered, raising a stone hand to swat him as the neon sign burst into life.

Its lights sputtered on and off, the sign jerkily cycling between its face and the images of the angels who cursed the Banim Shovavim.

An alarm wailed, the noise bouncing off the rock walls.

"Bad, very bad," Pyotr whispered. He fluttered his wings frantically, knocking over the table, and the tablet flew across the room. The gargoyle dove onto the pile of socks, gathering as many as possible into his hands.

I clapped my hands over my ears against the deafening siren, searching for the narrow green door to get us out of here.

Laurent roared, fully wolf save for his legs, and fell to his knees, his front paws hitting the ground. His bones crunched, his limbs reforming into hind legs while a brilliant white light snaked over his body.

The gargoyle looked terrified, the sign was going berserk, and my friend was transforming into his dybbuk-killing self, howling in helpless fury.

I summoned my magic to make my scythe appear, but we weren't under attack, and it didn't manifest. I grabbed Laurent by the scruff of his furry neck but couldn't transport us out either, so I ran to where the door should be and pounded on the rock face.

A gust of wind and a low moaning sound shivered up my spine. I beat on the rock harder, but when the alarm cut out with a silence loaded enough to go off like a gun, I slowly turned around.

The wolf was blindingly lit up, almost painful to look at, and still he was a preferable sight to the enormous skeleton ghost face made of smoke hovering over the growling shifter.

I shook my hands and stomped my feet, desperate to activate my shadow weapon against the return of the weird phantom that I'd encountered the first time I traveled the Kefitzat Haderech.

"Abomination!" Its voice sounded like dry leaves skittering over rotting wood. It unhinged its jaw to reveal pointed teeth that could crunch through bone.

The wolf leapt at it, snarling.

A skeleton hand appeared in midair, made of the same smoke as its huge face. It lifted the wolf in its palm, weighing him. Judging him.

My lungs had seized up, and my legs didn't want to work properly, but I lurched over to Pyotr, who hunched on the slab containing the socks with his wings covering him like a blanket. I banged on his back with my fist. "Help me."

His wings quivered but he didn't respond.

"Who brought the sullied one into my hallowed space?" Smoky squeezed its palm and a high-pitched yowl tore from Laurent's throat.

The light rippling over the wolf's fur tightened into barbed wire, lashing him. Blood dripped in a steady plop on the ground from all the gashes on the animal's body.

Every protective urge I had went into overdrive and I stormed over to the face. "I brought him, and he's not sullied. Banim Shovavim are not abominations!"

Delilah puffed up, almost filling the entire space behind me.

Yes, Laurent possessed some Banim Shovavim magic, but this reaction was completely uncalled for. I refused to let some shadowy douchebag make this bullshit pronouncement and get everyone wound up.

The face zoomed in close to me and although I swallowed a sour metallic taste, I held my ground.

"Ohrists are the abominations! And this one has taken powers it should not," it proclaimed.

I blinked. "Say what now?"

"Kefitzat Haderech is Banim Shovavim space," Pyotr stage-whispered.

Of course. That's why the sign had given me that riddle to see past the conditions that the angels had cursed Lilith's progeny with. If I solved it, I wouldn't wander the darkness in eternal torment.

Oh fuck. I'd been afraid of the wrong thing.

Smoky dropped the wolf onto the ground—spine-down— with a painful-sounding thud, but the animal still thrashed against the barbed-wire light mangling his fur. He flipped onto his side with a keening sound that tore at my heart.

I edged in front of the wolf to protect him. "He took on our magic at great cost to himself because he kills dybbuks, the same as we do. He's on our side."

"How dare he think himself worthy of that?" Even without lips, it conveyed a sneer, which was remarkable. Its hand turned into a scythe that was as large as I was. Not that I had size issues but come on. "The wolf dies."

"Wait!" My hand crept to the zipper of my purse. "What if I got rid of his Ohrist magic? Would you accept his presence?"

"You speak in hypotheticals." It swung the scythe.

Without thinking, I flung myself over Laurent, knocking us sideways. The blade whistled past my ear slicing off a lock of my hair, which drifted onto the cave floor.

Smoky's cry of rage thundered off the walls, but I didn't dare spare a second to see what he was doing. I forced Laurent's muzzle open and dumped the vial down his throat.

One of his canines nicked my finger and I jerked, my shoulder hitting the scythe's blade.

There was a second of pain and then nothing.

My spine had been severed.

Or...the blade had turned to smoke the second I hit it. I patted my shoulder to ensure it was intact.

I jumped at a loud crack, but it wasn't another assault. Laurent's arms and legs had reformed without any transition. He howled, curling in on himself and pawing at the ground with his hands and feet, because he was in too much pain to realize he'd partially shifted back.

The skeleton face, the neon sign face, and the gargoyle all stared slack-jawed at Laurent as his wolf body elongated and then snapped like a rubber band into human form. White fur rained to the ground.

A single desolate cry tore from the wolf's throat, but before it had even died away, Laurent's muzzle bashed backward into the rest of his furry face. In the moment of impact, his human features exploded outward, tears streaming from his eyes.

He huddled amid his discarded fur taking labored breaths, his clothes torn and blood drying in crusty trails on his skin.

Pyotr jumped off the stone slab, his arms full of socks, and hesitantly sniffed Laurent. "Is Banim Shovavim."

I sat back on my calves, my head bowed, taking deep breaths to calm my racing heart down. Twice I swallowed against the bile that surged up my throat, because I'd never seen anything so violent or painful. I reached out to place my hand on Laurent's chest, but he was shaking, and I pulled away, terrified of adding to his pain with even a simple caress.

"See? No more Ohrist." I made sure to sound unconcerned. "He's unsullied."

Not for long. Unlike Emmett, where magic was a one-shot-and-done deal, Laurent was not an inanimate object. He was human with the ability to tap into the ohr, and while I may have suspended his powers, they'd be back.

We had to get out of here before then.

The skeleton jabbed its hand from its eyes to mine and disappeared, while the neon sign face got a thoughtful look. It didn't comment—and the green door appeared—which was all I cared about.

I tugged on Laurent's arm. "Get up, we've got to go."

His eyes were glassy, his pupils enormous, and his body had the consistency of gluey spaghetti. He tried to obey but his legs kept buckling.

The gargoyle, as usual, refused to get involved, leaving me sweating and cursing as I got my shoulder under Laurent's arm and hoisted him to his feet.

Laurent was mumbling in French, half-delirious. The vial or this place or both were doing a number on him.

"At least get the door," I ordered Pyotr.

He hesitated, then did the bare minimum, holding it open for me and tucking a couple of socks into the collar of my shirt as we left.

The smart thing would be to visualize a door back to Hotel Terminus so Laurent could recuperate, but there was no time to waste. Even if the Wise Brothers handed over the name and address of the woman, and no one else was involved in this fiasco, how long would it take to find her?

The clock was ticking down.

I lightly slapped Laurent's cheek, hauling him forward. "Stay with me, Huff 'n' Puff."

It would have been easier to drag an anchor through the cave. Laurent stumbled over every dip and bump, while I muttered "Come on" repeatedly like a mantra, the Los Angeles address firmly fixed in my head.

An orange door shimmered into existence less than twenty feet away. With the knowledge that Laurent's Ohrist magic could roar back into life at any second and doom us, I pushed past the burn in my lungs and the sharp pain from where I'd pulled something in my lower back getting him upright and hauled us through the door into the searing sunshine.

We crashed onto the sidewalk in front of a sign reading "Wise Brothers' Lair of Lore and Learning." The bookstore occupied the ground floor of an older three-story apartment building, its cedar shingles painted a faded purple.

I took a moment to recover, breathing deeply with one hand on my belly and grateful that I'd brought the vial along, even if Laurent was still rambling from the divination sauce. Leaving him propped up against the outside wall, I peered in the window and my librarian side recoiled.

Books were piled three-quarters of the way up the glass with absolutely no rhyme or reason to their grouping. The ones stacked at eye level in front of me consisted of a biography of Burt Reynolds with a sun-bleached and broken spine, a leather-bound copy of *The Velveteen Rabbit* with gold-leaf printing, and *Daddy-O's Guide to the BBQ Good Life*. Cracks snaked between the uneven books like ant trails, affording a glimpse into an equally crowded and haphazard interior.

And yet, I inhaled, imagining the scent of old glue and parchment mixed with dust motes floating in the air, all subtly amplified by the warm sun blanketing the inside. It was the smell of the small library where I hung out as a kid, or those upper floors of the university libraries rarely breached by students, where I spent many an hour.

Laurent flexed his hands, staring at his fingers, his eyebrows pinched together. "I can't shift." His voice reminded me of a wolf's pained howl. He grabbed my calf and I flinched. "Tell me you can fix this," he said. "Please."

The last time he'd touched me there, the tension that had crackled between us was ripe with promise, not despair. It seemed like an impossibly long time ago.

I rubbed my hand over my aching stomach. "It will wear off soon."

Laurent was an Ohrist. His magic *would* come back.

There were no pedestrians to complain about us blocking the sidewalk and we didn't rate a second glance from any of the passing motorists. In this town, Laurent might be an extra in a zombie film, blood and all.

He rested his head against the wall, his hand curled around my leg as if for support, seizing on my assurance with a shining face. "Yes. This is only temporary." He licked his lips in cautious hope, then locked wide green eyes on me. "I'll be back in no time."

I nodded but drew my eyebrows together. He hadn't said "back to normal." Or that his magic would be back. He'd be back. I'd wondered more than once how tied Laurent was to his ability to kill dybbuks in his wolf form. Whether it was a calling or a curse. I still wasn't sure, but where I'd be devastated if I lost my magic, Laurent sounded desperate.

And if I was responsible, even inadvertently? I braced a hand against the bricks, seeking their warmth. Could he even survive having Banim Shovavim magic without his own Ohrist powers to anchor them?

I sat down next to him. "I swear I didn't know this would happen. Emmett went into the Kefitzat Haderech without any..." I bit my lip. Pyotr had made a comment about Laurent not being a pet because he had a heartbeat. Had that saved Emmett from hitting the KH's radar? "I'm sorry," I said.

Laurent leaned forward, his hands draped limply over his knees.

"The great French poet Jacques Prévert once met a blind beggar." The man standing in the doorway to the bookstore had a slight stoop, his thinning hair carefully brushed to one side, and his chest no longer as broad as when he'd bought his yellow suit with the wide lapels, yet his hazel eyes twinkled. "In front of him, the beggar had placed a sign reading

'Blind man without a pension.' But when he confessed that people weren't giving him money, Prévert flipped the sign over and wrote a new one."

Poet. Beggar. Blind. I quickly assembled a list in my head in case this story was our first test.

Laurent hadn't moved but he held himself with the stillness of a deadly predator, his hard eyes assessing.

"A few days later," the man continued, "the poet stopped by and asked how things were going. The beggar exclaimed that his cup had been filled with coins every day and asked what he'd done. Prévert replied that he'd changed the sign. It now said—

"Le printemps arrive mais je ne le verrai pas." Laurent made it sound like "Fuck you."

Now was probably not the time for me to make a crack about the wolf being book learned.

The man made a snarky face but translated from my benefit. "'Spring is coming but I won't see it.'"

"Your point?" Laurent barely looked at the man.

"If you're going to loiter pathetically outside my store, at least get a catchy campaign, kid."

I scrambled to my feet. "Are you Mr. Wise?"

"One of them."

"We were sent here to see you. We have questions."

"Questions?" A Black man exited behind the first proprietor. His neat mustache was as silver as the hair visible around the edges of his white fedora, and his lightweight blue suit matched the cane that he rested his gnarled hands on. "What luck. We have answers."

"Not so fast, Hiram," the first man said and jerked his chin at me. "Who sent you?"

Hiram rolled his eyes. "Stop being so suspicious, Ephraim. You grew up in Beverly Hills, not a fascist dictatorship."

Laurent still hadn't stood up—or shown any ability to

shift, though his hostility was in fine form—but I smiled at Hiram and Ephraim.

I liked these two eccentrics. "Zev BatKian told us to come see you, but we're not working for him. We're actually working for—"

"Ourselves," my partner said.

Hiram prodded Laurent's foot with his cane. "Didn't anyone teach you manners? Stand in the presence of your elders."

I bent down to help my partner, but he knocked my hand away.

For a moment no one moved, and I gave a strangled laugh, half expecting Laurent to bust out Westley's speech in *The Princess Bride* when he's on the bed after a day of being mostly dead, and we're not sure if he can stand up or not on his own, but like Westley, Laurent pushed to his feet steadily enough.

The Wise Brothers exchanged amused looks, which I was grateful for because they missed the momentary tightening of my friend's features.

"This way," Ephraim said.

I shot Laurent a thumbs-up. Things were back on track, and we could hash out what had happened in the Kefitzat Haderech after we learned more about the dybbuk-possessed woman.

"I told you to trust me," I said and sailed confidently into the bookstore.

12

I EXPERIENCED A MOMENT OF BLINDNESS WHEN I stepped inside after the relentless California summer sunshine, then lights came on with a loud, deep click and I threw up my arm against this new glare, blinking through the disorientation.

There was no sign of any bookstore.

A bouncy theme song with a rocking trumpet line played and Hiram, cane in hand, danced a soft shoe number onto a cheesy game show set that was decorated in bold blues and golds like a 1970s throwback. Next to the host's podium was a love seat facing a gameboard that took up most of one wall. It was a low-tech wonder lined with blank-faced gold slats. *Jeopardy!* this wasn't.

I sighed. Fucking hidden spaces.

"Welcome to *The Naked Truth*," Ephraim boomed over a microphone somewhere. "A Wise Brothers Production of facts and quid pro quo."

"I am not undressing," Laurent said.

A loud "oooooh" and laughter boomed out of the darkness, as if we were being filmed live in front of a studio audience.

"What. The. Fuck," I whispered.

Laurent stormed off, but Hiram grabbed his arm and spun him onto the love seat, not even pausing his shuffling dance.

That old man should not have been able to overpower Laurent. Was that another side effect of his suppressed —*please be suppressed*—powers?

Our host raised his eyebrows at me, and I hurried to sit beside Laurent. An invisible seat belt cinched over my lap.

"Let's meet this week's contestants, Hiram." Ephraim's disembodied voice seemed to come from everywhere.

I glanced around, trying to spot him, but lights were too hot and strong to see anything beyond the edge of the set. How alone were we? Were there people sitting out there eagerly waiting for the show to start? Was this being broadcast on some magic TV station? I shook my head. No, Tatiana would have known if that was the case and forbidden us from publicly asking questions about anything that could be traced back to her as a weakness.

So, what was their deal?

Hiram raised his hands to curtail the applause from the invisible audience, then removed the microphone from its stand and limped around the front of the podium. He thrust the mic in Laurent's face. "Tell us a bit about yourself."

The disparity between the genial host and his reluctant contestant with the torn clothing and bloody gashes was completely ludicrous.

The shifter stared stonily ahead, his arms crossed, and while the hairs on the back of my neck prickled from our situation, I almost hugged him, seeing that grumpy, suspicious look on his face. At least one thing was normal.

I nudged his leg. "Remember, we're doing this for Tatiana."

"Your name?" Hiram prompted.

"Laurent," he ground out.

"Stoic fellow, isn't he?" Hiram mugged at where the audience would be and received laughter and applause.

I squinted into the darkness but try as I might, failed to see anyone else here with us.

"And you?" Our host swished the black mic cord out of his way as he moved over to me.

I was on edge from the unfinished discussion with Laurent, disoriented by the bright lights, and panicked by whatever this stint was going to cost us.

I word-vomited.

It started okay with my name and hometown, but Hiram just stood there with the damn microphone extended, and worried that this was a test, I kept babbling. I'd offered up my academic background (BA English Lit, Masters of Library and Information Science), favorite books (mysteries), name of my first best friend (Mia Filippelli,) and was trying to remember my blood type when Laurent's gaping shut me up.

I grabbed the mic and leaned in with a big smile. "Glad to be here."

That earned me a "what is wrong with you" stare from Laurent, and flustered, I shrugged.

"All right," Hiram said jovially, replacing the mic in its stand on the podium. "Well, this promises to be interesting."

More applause.

Laurent briefly closed his eyes like he was being punched but had resigned himself to the beating.

The top row of slats on the board flipped around with a series of ka-thunks and I leaned forward, reading them: Nighttime Haunts of Paris, Libraries, British Crime Shows, Wolves, and Days of the Week.

"What the hell?" Laurent muttered.

Apart from that last category, it was as if they'd been tailor-made for us. Had Zev given them a heads-up that we were coming, allowing these two men to gather some cursory information on us? If not, then why these particular categories? If I ground my teeth any harder, I was going to require reconstructive dental surgery.

"Ephraim," our host said, "tell our contestants the rules."

"Sure thing, Hiram," the other man boomed. "Each round on *The Naked Truth* consists of three questions. Get all three right and our contestants may ask a question of their choosing, which we will answer honestly, should we know it. Lose a round and they forfeit their question. Goooooood luck!"

"Miriam, we'll start with you." Hiram gestured at the board. "Pick a category."

Wolves and Nighttime Haunts of Paris were out, unless the point was to find out how much Laurent and I knew about each other like on *The Newlywed Game*. But no. Because not married. So, then I didn't have to choose those ones, right? I tapped my foot, practically vibrating. How was I supposed to decide when any choice could lead us into a minefield in this creepy-ass game show and there was so much at stake?

"Miriam," Hiram said impatiently.

All right. I would stick with familiar subjects. Less chance for error. "Libraries, please."

Hiram read the question off one of the cards stacked on his podium. "What was the Dewey decimal numbering..." He paused for dramatic effect.

I preened. This first question was in the bag.

"The Dewey decimal numbering in the stack where you gave Dex Lassiter a blow job shortly before that relationship ended?"

My face drained of all color.

Laurent broke into a belly laugh, and when I failed to answer, he nudged my leg. "We're doing this for Tatiana."

There weren't a lot of actions in my life that I regretted, but that one was in the top two. Dex was the first man I dated after my divorce and even that would never have happened if my self-esteem hadn't been at an all-time low.

We had very little in common, but I didn't want to be alone again, and after a lot of badgering, I gave in to his request that we play sexy librarian. It was all kinds of stupid and I'd never told anyone, not even Jude.

"H-how do you...?" I stammered. "I mean, I never—"

Hiram's jovial expression took on a hard glint. "Audience, remind our contestants of the name of this show?"

"The Naked Truth!"

I dug my nails into my thighs. "Who are you people? Where did you learn this? What's going on here?" I struggled to stand up, but the invisible seat belt had me pinned.

"Your awkward adorableness reminds me of my younger self, Miriam," Hiram said, "so I'll answer you free of charge. Long ago, Ephraim and I discovered that if we teamed my Banim Shovavim divination magic with his Ohrist abilities to suss out a lie, we had a very effective information gathering tool."

My anger outweighed my amazement that Hiram was Banim Shovavim. "You can dress it up all you like." I flung a hand toward the board. "It's no better than hot lights and thumbscrews interrogation."

"That's so trite." Ephraim made a scoffing noise from wherever he was. "Give 'em the old Razzle Dazzle."

"You're a *Chicago* fan?" Somehow sharing a love of Broadway musicals was incredibly surreal. And dangerous. Magic plus love of artifice. God help us if there was chore- ography.

"We met doing a production," he replied. "Hiram was Roxie. I was Velma."

Sure, why not?

"Why this bullshit show at all if you already know every- thing about us?" Laurent narrowed his eyes. "And who else is watching?"

"Why would we share what we learn?" Ephraim paused. "Until we have to."

"Are we trading threats now?" Laurent draped his arm along the back of the love seat, but his expression made me shiver and try to move over to put more space between us. A pointless endeavor given the magic seat belt.

"Stop it," Hiram chastised. "We don't actually know anything until the question is revealed. Divination magic isn't a precise science." That much was true.

"Then how does it work?" I said.

He pressed his lips together.

"I'll give you a fact for free." Laurent shook his head at my words, but I ignored him.

Hiram blinked at my offer. "All right."

"I'm Banim Shovavim too."

"Interesting." Hiram tapped his chin. "Okay. My magic pinpoints the categories, which mean nothing to us at the start of the game. The questions appear on these cards only once the slat has flipped." He held up some of the cards, fanning them out to show that only one had printing on it. "Until the board, via Ephraim's powers, verifies the answer as correct, we aren't certain we even got the question right." He stroked his mustache. "Though after so many years, we've hit a ninety-nine percent success rate."

My lips pulled back in disgust. "And the point?"

"Answers for answers. Quid pro quo is only fair."

"Yeah, right," I said. "What is it really? Curiosity? Black-mail material?"

He shrugged. "Since the magic rooted out a question about the Dewey decimal system for you, then I'd guess you have more than your fair love of knowledge. How would you respond?"

"Knowledge is power." Laurent's words echoed the thought in my head. "And the devil is in the details," he added darkly.

Hiram shook his head. "The actual quote is 'God is in the details.'"

Laurent looked ready to rip the man's head off.

I briefly buried my head in my hands.

"Now back to the game." Hiram was once again the upbeat host, but I blinked because he'd appeared in a close-up with the light glinting off his perfect white teeth even though he hadn't moved from behind the podium. "Do you have an answer or is this round forfeit?"

I cast my mind back to that day. There'd been this one book I'd been eye level with while on my knees, its subject matter at such comic odds with my actions, that I'd screwed my lids tight. Luckily, Dex hadn't been one for procrastinating and the entire thing was over quickly.

"The Dewey decimal numbering was 440–449," I said tightly.

A slat under the category title flipped around with a bing, revealing the answer.

"That is correct!" Hiram grabbed his cane and banged it twice against the ground.

Loud applause burst out. I imagined taking a machine gun to whatever supplied the audience reactions.

Hiram touched his ear like a director was communicating with him. "We have ourselves a two-parter, people. For a follow-up question, and the second right answer in this round, what was the subject matter of that classification?"

I sighed, my eyes on my lap. "Christianity and Christian theology."

Another slat turned around with a binging sound.

"The milk of human kindness," Laurent said with a bland smile.

My hands clenched into fists.

"Laurent," Hiram said. "Your turn to pick the third question of round one."

"Libraries," he said cockily.

"Bastard," I muttered.

"Great topic." Hiram tapped a new card against the

podium. "Laurent, what book ended up being overdue by a year because you read it over and over again, crying every time?"

"Great topic!" I enthused.

"I was seven," Laurent said. "And I didn't cr—" He glanced at Hiram's expression and swallowed the rest of that sentence. "*Charlotte's Web*," he said sulkily.

The final slat in that category turned over with a bing.

"A successful round," Hiram said. "Ask us your first question."

We hadn't prepared a list beforehand, and Laurent jumped in before I could.

"Can a Pulsa diNura be broken?" he said. A reasonable place to start.

"Yes," Ephraim said enthusiastically.

When Laurent realized the catch—that the questions were like legal contracts where the Wise Brothers would answer extremely literally—his growl made both Hiram and me jump.

At least the Wise Brothers couldn't tell he'd lost his magic.

"Round two." Hiram turned to the board. "Laurent will start."

"Wait." I held up a hand. "Can we have a moment to huddle up before he selects his category?"

Hiram shrugged. "I don't see why not."

I leaned over to Laurent. "We have four more categories and four more chances to get answers."

"If we get them right. What if one of us doesn't remember some ridiculous fact from our past?"

"Given what they've already asked, I doubt these are moments easily forgotten. They're stripping our dignity, not our clothing. Let's make a list of what we need answered," I said with resolve.

Our next two questions to ask the Wise Brothers were

easy enough to compile, but we disagreed on the final ones. "How about we wait and see if our other inquires take us in the direction we suspect?" I said. "We can choose from our list then."

"Great," Laurent said tonelessly.

The cost of this information was totally shitty, but our chances of success were high. Still, I clutched the domino for an extra bit of luck.

Hiram arched his eyebrow. "Ready to choose your category?"

"Wolves," Laurent said with that same lack of inflection.

We won the second round thanks to Laurent divulging his panic attacks as a kid, and my clear recollection of the bullying I'd faced in elementary school for my weight. There was nothing about either of these revelations that we should have felt ashamed of, but of course we both did. The Wise Brothers were homing in on the memories that we still carried humiliation or regret for, and I dreaded where the game would go from here.

Or what they planned to do with this information.

It was impossible to tell where Laurent's head was at, so I asked the Wise Brothers our second question. "How do we defeat the death curse?"

Ephraim informed us we either comply with the curser's demands or kill them. Since we couldn't get our hands on the gloves, we were looking at murder. Fan-fucking-tastic. Though I was open to the idea, just not for the Ohrist woman.

The game show cut out for a "word from our sponsor" with some retro-sounding jingle about toothpaste. It was catchy in a batshit insane way.

"There has to be some other means to break the curse," I said to my partner.

"There isn't. You heard them." He scratched at some dried blood on his arm.

"I know, but—"

"Had you given the golem the vial, like I wanted to, we would not be in this position," Laurent said.

"So, it was okay to let Emmett lose his magic and possibly die, but you're pissed that you—" A muscle ticked in his jaw, and I revised the rest of that sentence. "That yours has been temporarily suspended?"

"It's not the same thing at all," he hissed.

The jingle ended with the reminder to kick plaque in the teeth.

"Round three!" Hiram once more banged his cane on the ground.

This round delved into Laurent's nonexistent relationship with his father and the highlights of my worst parenting moments. British crime shows, my ass. The questions had only the most tangential relationship with the category.

My partner's voice grew quieter and quieter with each answer, while I got perkier and perkier until I sounded like a squirrel who'd mainlined too much cocaine.

When we won that third round, I waved my hand like the teacher's pet. "How did that woman cast the Pulsa diNura?"

"Pretty easy to make a letter appear," Hiram said.

"That's not what she asked," Laurent said.

"The curse is an urban legend." Ephraim's disembodied voice brooked no argument.

"Then why say it could only be broken by compliance or murder?" I fired back.

"Because there would still be a hit on the target regardless of whether the curse exists," he retorted. "How else would you get the curser to back down?"

"You're wrong," I said. "It exists. A man who received the letter was killed via a dybbuk attack. He was a powerful Ohrist, but his magic did nothing."

"Ohrists can't see dybbuks," Ephraim said impatiently from wherever he was. "That's why he couldn't kill it."

"There you go," Hiram said, fidgeting with the question cards. "No curse."

"But—" I said.

Ephraim made a raspberry noise.

I shook my fist, the domino falling to the seat beside me. "Listen, old man—"

Laurent tilted his head, all his focus on Hiram. "The latest curse victim was marked by a burn that looked like lashes of fire."

"Smoke and mirrors," Hiram replied.

"Is she Banim Shovavim?" Laurent said.

I blinked. "You said it wasn't possible."

"Not specifically." Laurent didn't even hedge his answer, though he wouldn't look at me. "You drew that conclusion."

"Like you let Naveen do about your magic?" I put my hands on my rib cage, breathing through my anger.

"Miriam was attacked by a dybbuk the other day," Laurent said, ignoring me. "The fight lasted a long time and she doesn't believe she killed it. She couldn't sense it and when she'd seen this supposedly possessed host previously, there was nothing wrong with that woman's shadow."

"Dear God," Hiram whispered, startling. His elbow jostled the mic and feedback screeched through the room.

Worse than that noise was the earthquake that rolled under the house of cards in my head. I mentally willed the structure to stay intact.

"So, it was *your* kind. All of it? The curse and that dybbuk?" Laurent's voice was ice, turbulence swirling in his eyes.

A distant part of me noted he'd disassociated himself from the other half of his magic, but mostly I was in shock.

We'd have to kill a Banim Shovavim.

13

———

Ephraim's voice surrounded us. "You had your question. Moving on."

"Answer me." Laurent had gone to some cold place that reminded me of Zev and it was terrifying. This wasn't him. He was the supernova always on the verge of self-destructing. This... I didn't know what this was.

I shied away from him, unable to go anywhere because of these invisible seat belts imprisoning us, but I longed to clap my hands over my ears and run as far as I could.

If Banim Shovavim could place actual curses and somehow pilot dybbuks, Laurent would become a one-man crusade to destroy every last one. And I'd have to stop him, because as dangerous as that magic was, these were my people.

Battle lines appeared around my internal house of cards. Was Poe's game of Memory, with the card faces flipping violently between darkness and light, predicting this ultimate clash between Laurent and me? I'd speared one of Poe's cards to end that mad game, but was the sunlight that appeared in the wake of that action because I'd win this war?

Or lose it?

I shot an anguished look at Laurent.

A stranger looked back.

"I'll answer the original question. Properly." Hiram gripped the podium with trembling fingers.

Laurent tensed like he was going to argue, then nodded.

"Only a Banim Shovavim can place a real Pulsa diNura," Hiram said. "That burn is the proof. Think of it like marking someone for death, be it in a day, a year, or twenty years."

"Dealer's choice," Laurent said snidely.

Hiram bowed his head, then gave a weary shrug. "Dealer's discretion."

This was bad, but still I eagerly drank in this new information. Any fact at this point would help.

"But the mark is only part of the magic." He paused.

Laurent crossed his arms, his raised eyebrow conveying more aggressive menace than a loaded gun.

Hiram wasn't a fool and he kept talking. "The Banim Shovavim with that ability acquire a familiar soon after they're born."

"Like a cat or an owl or..." I grabbed the domino off the seat, its edges cutting into my flesh. "A dybbuk."

"Then she is controlling it," Laurent said, his eyes dark with fury.

"Not exactly," Hiram said. "It's more like she exists in a state of permanent enthrallment."

"With each of them gaining control at different times?" I said.

He nodded.

Talk about a house divided. I'd chosen to first suppress my magic and then reclaim it, but she'd constantly been at the mercy of hers. I rubbed my finger over the domino tile. What a horrific fate. "How is she not insane from a lifetime of that?"

"How do you know she isn't?" Laurent retorted. Our camaraderie felt as impossible as him having an ounce of sympathy for this woman's plight. "Why have I never heard of this before?"

Hiram jutted his chin up, his own anger flaring in his eyes. "Everyone with that power was killed long ago. Or so I thought," he added quietly.

"Hiram, don't upset yourself with this," Ephraim said.

Our host held up a hand. "It used to be a fairly common ability of ours, and a deadly one because unless the curse was removed by the curser, nothing short of compliance or the curser's death would stop it."

My head reeled. "What about wards?"

"They're powerless against the curse." Hiram swept off his hat and wiped his brow, looking frail. "The Banim Shovavim who can curse people with the Pulsa diNura are the ones who have familiars. But since Ohrists couldn't see the dybbuk familiar to kill it and were especially vulnerable to this curse, they didn't like that we had this edge on them. They came up with a solution to remove these Banim Shovavim from the playing field."

"Hunters," Laurent said grimly.

Hiram nodded. No wonder he gathered all the information he could. Forewarned was forearmed. I understood it, though I didn't forgive it.

I grabbed the arm of the love seat. "That's why we were killed? Because Ohrists couldn't stand us being more powerful?"

"What did you expect?" Ephraim's weary voice swirled around us. "You arm one side with a nuclear bomb, the other will find a way to defuse it. By whatever means necessary. It's not right but it's human history."

He wasn't Banim Shovavim, and this genocide wasn't part of his past, so why did he sound so resigned to that facet of humanity? What was he arming himself against that he'd partnered with Hiram and gone to all this effort?

Or what was he atoning for?

"Ephraim, were your people hunters?"

"Did you just win a round and I missed it?" he snarked.

"I'm old enough to remember the tail end of the slaughters," Hiram said. "They'd kill any Banim Shovavim, just in case. Until the slaughter became too much for even the Lonestars to cover up and they put a stop to it. Too little too late."

Any shadow of a doubt about who'd attacked me in Gargoyle Gardens vanished. This ability was so rare nowadays that the person who'd killed Torres, gone after me, and placed the curse on Tatiana were one and the same: the woman from the island. If her victims piled up, would she unleash a new wave of hunters determined to end those of us left?

I shot a sideways glance at Laurent, my heartbeat stuttering. Had it already?

Was death the only possible outcome regardless, be it hers or all Banim Shovavim? Tatiana's? Laurent's? Mine? My anxious thumb rubbing should have worn a new groove in the domino.

More than anything I longed to ask Laurent what was going through his mind, because I couldn't read his expression and he'd grown stiller and stiller.

At that moment, the theme song blared, its jauntiness jarring and unwelcome. Ephraim ordered us to resume the game.

We won the fourth round and the category of Nighttime Haunts of Paris, but I couldn't tell you what questions Hiram had asked. Our host clearly had no heart for this anymore, and even Ephraim's joviality had a forced determination to it, but for whatever reason, we were stuck on this ride until its final destination.

My question to the Wise Brothers landed a second before Laurent's inquiry about the woman's name.

"Did that Banim Shovavim put a curse on me? I didn't get

a letter, but she sent her dybbuk after me." Its behavior made sense now that I knew it was the woman's familiar.

The shifter turned his head to look at me for the first time since the Banim Shovavim had been confirmed. His expression softened for a moment, and he reached out a hand but curled it into a fist and dropped it in his lap before making contact. "That wasn't our final question."

"I deviated from the script. Sue me." We'd have to make sure we won the last round to ask that all-important final query about her name, but I had to know if I had a target on my back. Or would soon.

Hiram replied that only one Pulsa diNura could be placed at a time, but she could send the dybbuk after me at any point. It just didn't ensure my death, especially since I saw the familiar and could fight back.

The woman hadn't let the dybbuk kill me, but she'd been in Blood Alley. She'd watched the battle and known I was like her. Was that why I was alive? The thought of meeting another woman like me was like seeing the sun after a long, dreary winter, but my excitement shattered under the ugly truth.

This wasn't the beginning of a beautiful friendship. I swayed closer to Laurent, despite his hostility, and crossed my fingers that it wasn't the end of one either.

At long last, we came to the final round. My stomach was a hard knot and Laurent was practically MIA even though he sat right beside me.

The only remaining category was Days of the Week, all the questions unasked.

Hiram picked up a card and widened his eyes theatrically. "It's an all or nothing question!"

There were big whoops and claps from the audience or whatever annoying magic or sound effects program Ephraim was fucking around with.

"In our final round, one of you must answer a single question worth the usual three," our host said. "Get it right and you receive your final answer. Get it wrong and you walk out of here with your memories wiped clean of everything you've learned."

I rose in objection like a TV trial lawyer, but barely got my butt a half inch off the love seat before I was hoisted back down by the magic invisible seat belt. "That's not fair. You said if we won each round, we'd get answers."

"And you did," Hiram said.

"We never promised you'd remember them," Ephraim added to audience laughter.

I'd done a phenomenal job of keeping my powers under wraps thus far, but Delilah exploded out of me, tearing around the set like a tornado, scattering cards and rattling the wooden slats.

"Stop." Laurent spoke the one word softly but with a wealth of power and Delilah froze.

I sank my head into the palms of my hands, pressing so hard that I saw stars. Everything in this world was games and manipulations and reading between the lines, designed to test every single moral code and relationship.

So be it. I refused to lose now.

I raised my head. "I'll—"

"Days of the Week," Laurent said clearly.

"You don't have to do this," I said.

He gave a bitter laugh. "What else do I have to lose?"

"You really want to taunt the universe like that?"

The shifter held my gaze, the wolf in him peering out, unblinking, unflinching, even without his Ohrist magic.

"All or nothing," he said.

I looked away first.

Hiram plucked a card out of his dwindling stack. "This event shares the date of March 15 with another famous betrayal."

Laurent tensed.

173

I hunched back against the sofa, fear pricking me with icy hooks. The shifter had many failings, including his failure to see any shades of gray where dybbuk killing was involved, but betrayal? I couldn't reconcile that idea with the man I knew, and yet it was worse if someone had betrayed him, stabbing him in the back like Brutus had to Caesar. Even now, with this impossible gulf between us, I'd want to destroy that person.

"On what day of the week—" I expected Hiram to pause theatrically again to draw out the suspense, but he gaped at the card for a moment before he cleared his throat a couple times and composed himself.

Hiram hadn't broken character as the host for any other question. What had his divination magic just revealed to him on that card that was so shocking?

Laurent's chest rose and fell raggedly as if he'd run a marathon and his pulse fluttered in his throat.

I clenched my hands into fists, willing Hiram to end my friend's torment.

Hiram didn't appear to notice our distress, tapping the cards into a neat pile and schooling his expression back to that of a pleasant host. "On what day of the week did you betray your alpha oath to protect your pack and walk away from them, leaving chaos and bloodshed as others attempted to seize the power vacuum you'd left?"

No. He'd never. Shaking my head, I turned to Laurent to implore him to speak up and clear his name.

His pupils were fully dilated, almost crowding out the whites of his eyes entirely. "Saturday," he whispered hoarsely.

The slat flipped over, but its bright sound came off like a death knell.

"Saturday it is!" Hiram exclaimed.

I sat there, numb.

Laurent was lost to his pain, his fingers in claw formation without becoming claws, though he shook from the effort of trying to transform. He couldn't even get up because we were pinned in place. He scrabbled frantically at the magic seat belt, his breathing labored.

"Let him out!" I demanded.

"Ask your final question," Ephraim said. "The big prize," he added sarcastically.

When Laurent and I were in our huddle earlier, I'd suggested asking where to find the Banim Shovavim, pointing out that if we got her name, we'd still need to narrow her location down from the entire world, but my partner had pressed for the reverse. He'd stated that if we asked where to find her, they could very well say "behind the blue door in Timbuktu," at which point we'd still have to hunt her down and we wouldn't have anything to go by.

I went with Laurent's question, asking, since he was in no state to. "What's her name?"

"We don't know," Hiram said.

It was like one of those record scratch moments. I shook my head because it wasn't possible. "No." My voice cracked, and I pounded the armrest. "Tell us!"

At Hiram's answer, Laurent had frozen, but he began laughing, a demented sound free of any amusement.

"We said we'd answer honestly if we knew it." Ephraim walked onto the stage. "I'm sorry, kid."

Laurent didn't stop laughing. It racked his entire body, agonizing to watch, and horrific to hear.

Our seat belts fell away.

The shifter curled into a ball, his laughter now silent, and yet more chilling because he rocked back and forth.

Afraid he'd cracked, I placed a tentative hand on his back. "Laurent. Please stop."

He flinched away from my touch.

The red exit sign lit up with a bing and Laurent bolted.

At some point I'd feel sick about all this, but right now I remained numb to everything except the haunted look in

Laurent's eyes before he'd raced out of here. I shoved the blank domino in my purse, my belief in good luck talismans shattered. "This isn't a game anymore. If we don't stop this person, it could unleash an entirely new wave of hunters."

"I know," Hiram said softly.

"Then why would a Banim Shovavim who has this magic care about the Torquemada Gloves?"

The two old men didn't even bother arguing about whether to answer. Ephraim dropped onto the love seat next to me.

"You know what the gloves do?" he said, rubbing his knee with arthritic hands.

"A person puts them on and becomes convinced that they no longer wear their own skin. They go mad and eventually die by clawing their skin off."

"Exactly. But the key word is 'person.' Do you know what they do if a demon puts them on?" Ephraim took a deep breath, steadying himself to continue. "The reverse. The gloves become a second skin, giving them a physical form that they can hold indefinitely. They can look human forever if they wish so long as they wear the gloves." His eyes bored into me with a flintiness that I couldn't look away from.

I clutched my purse to my chest like a shield. "A dybbuk isn't a demon."

"It's an evil spirit," Hiram said, leaning heavily on his cane as he came out from behind the podium. "It qualifies."

I shook my head, grasping at straws. "Dybbuks don't have a solid form."

"The gloves would give them one." Hiram sat on the armrest next to Ephraim, leaning against the other man's shoulder. "It would look human and never have to worry about its Banim Shovavim dying. It wouldn't even be tied to that person anymore. It would be a mindless killing machine in physical form, existing forever."

No wonder both the dybbuk and the woman were after it.

I dropped my head in my hands. This female Banim Shovavim had threatened Tatiana, and Laurent would hunt her down for her magic abilities alone.

That was his line; what was mine?

When Tatiana failed to produce the gloves, the curse would kill her, and this woman would go after Zev next. He had to be convinced to see reason. And if not? Perhaps there was a way to neutralize her magic? If dybbuks qualified as demons, then would Naveen have a way to find out?

I slung my bag across my chest. "I'm leaving and I better remember everything I just learned."

Hiram nodded tiredly. "You will. You won."

Had we?

Ephraim sighed and rested his hand on the back of Hiram's neck. "Good game."

The words reminded me of Zev at his fight and I shivered. This too smacked of ritual, though there was no threat in it.

There were a lot of things on the tip of my tongue: "You should be ashamed," "I hope it was worth it," an unending scream, but in the end, I said nothing, leaving the cold emptiness of the studio for the bright light of day.

Only to find it just as desolate because Laurent was gone.

14

LAURENT DIDN'T RESPOND TO MY TEXTS. I LET HIM know that I'd wait for an hour at a café across from the bookstore, then I was leaving. My tea and sandwich sat untouched, but my phone got a workout as I checked every few minutes to make sure I was receiving a signal.

He never showed.

I assured myself that this was a good thing. It meant that he'd regained his shifting abilities and couldn't travel via the Kefitzat Haderech, and not that he'd rather spend four hours "in a cage" on a plane than see me.

I waited another fifteen minutes, just in case. Also, I was kind of nervous of my reception in the KH. Best case, Pyotr would glare balefully. Worst case... I shot back my cold tea and threw down a tip.

I was walking around the neighborhood, willing the sun to thaw me out, when Ryann called, asking whether I'd reconsidered my stance on having Elizabeta ward my place up. Despite the fact it would alleviate Eli's fears, I once more declined the offer. Pissing off Zev would be bad enough; I certainly wasn't going to trust another Lonestar when I barely trusted Ryann.

She pressed her case, unhappy about putting my family's well-being in the vamp's hands. I wasn't exactly jumping for joy over the prospect, but the lesser of two evils at this point.

I stood firm on my decision.

The call over, I stepped into the shadows, a litany of apologies at the ready, but Pyotr was nowhere to be found. Instead, an expressionless golem stood in the center of the gloomy cave between me and the pile of socks. While they weren't necessary for travel, it was still obligatory to take one.

"Where's Pyotr?" I said, my stomachache flaring up. Was there some kind of shadowland gulag that he'd been banished to after my mishap?

If something had happened to that sweet hapless gargoyle, I'd lose my shit.

"Your privileges have been temporarily suspended," the freakishly tall golem intoned in a deep voice. Its head almost brushed the top of the cave.

"Say what?"

"Your privileges have been temporarily suspended due to you bringing an Ohrist into the Kefitzat Haderech," it repeated. Roughly fashioned, with features barely a step up from a stick figure's and not a scrap of clothing on, it had zero personality, giving me a new appreciation for Emmett.

"Laurent was Banim Shovavim." I balled my hands into fists. "He'd have been killed otherwise."

"He became Banim Shovavim and was allowed to live." The golem spoke in a mechanical voice, as if reciting a regulation from memory. "However, when you brought him here, he was an Ohrist, and thus you must suffer the consequences."

It stared at me with cold, button-like eyes, giving the sense that I should be grateful this punishment was as bad as it got.

"I understand. I'm guessing the suspension starts once I return home?" I went for a sock, but the golem blocked me.

Immovable, expressionless, and intent on ejecting me.

I kicked a rock against the wall. Laurent had gone AWOL, and we still didn't have the name of the Banim Shovavim who'd placed the death curse on Tatiana. I was hanging on by my fingernails and if this golem stopped me from getting home, I wouldn't be responsible for my actions.

It shifted its weight as if in anticipation of me losing it.

I took a deep breath and tamped down my anger, instead snapping my fingers twice. "I want to speak to your manager. Sign. Whatever."

"You are not welcome here. Leave."

I sat down on the uneven ground. "Make me."

The golem bent down and picked me up under the armpits, giving me access to its forehead—and the word "emet" for truth carved into it.

While I didn't know Hebrew, the language was read from right to left, so I jabbed my fingernails into the first letter to scratch it out. The nail on my index finger broke, but I didn't leave a mark because its forehead, like the rest of the golem, had been fired to a hard consistency.

A door appeared in the rocks with the image of the skeleton face carved into it. Oh, hell no.

I thrashed in the golem's hold, but my struggles failed to make its arms tremble, never mind slow it down.

Delilah grabbed a large rock and bashed the golem across the back of its head.

No reaction. As the good little minion programmed to finish a task no matter what, it continued to the door.

Delilah amped up her attack, hitting him again and again.

Specks of clay flew, and still the golem kept going, its skull barely dented.

The door creaked open, an icy wind gusting out and covering my skin in goosebumps. I threw my hands over my face as the golem heaved me into that void and the door slammed shut.

I landed in a dumpy office with cheap furniture and a lone poster of a cat dangling from a branch with the words "hang in there" written under the animal. One corner had come loose. A Muzak version of that "Between the Moon and New York City" song played, while the cold air was nothing more than an air conditioner with poor temperature control.

"Hello?" I sat down uncertainly in a dingy plastic chair next to a drooping potted plant.

Stacks of paper were piled high on the desk and along the wall. A small plaque reading "Customer Service" in brass letters was displayed on the desk.

The black leather chair behind the desk swiveled around so its occupant faced me.

Pyotr looked more miserable than usual, his wings crammed into the seat. He held a pencil whose tip had been ground down to a dull nub, his middle finger bearing an enormous callus. "Customer service. How I help you?" he said morosely.

"Pyotr!" Relieved to see him, I rose out of my chair, but he tapped the plaque and I sat back down. "I want my travel privileges back to get home."

The gargoyle laboriously took a stapled packet off a large pile, leafed through to the third page, inked up his stamp, and stamped it. "No."

I calculated how much time this punishment would cost me in terms of our three-day deadline and finding this Banim Shovavim. "How long is this ban going to last?"

He heaved a sigh and turned the chair around. There was a creaking sound and a groan, then he dumped a huge, fat, dog-eared book on the desk. Muttering in Russian under his breath, he thumbed through the pages. "Two weeks."

"No problem. Return me home now, please, and I won't cause any trouble."

"Must go back to start."

"Los Angeles? Oh, come on." I placed a hand on his stone arm. "I'm sure you can deposit me at my place."

"This your fault." He slammed his hand on a stack of paperwork. "Report. About you." Then he grabbed a thick file and shook it at me. "Paperwork required to change exit."

He held up his middle finger and I raised an eyebrow, but he was showing me his callus. "Hard like stone," he said.

"To be fair, all of you is—"

He snapped the nubby pencil in half, and I backpedaled. Hard. "There's a new *Fast and Furious* movie coming out."

His lip trembled for a moment. "No."

"Plus, there are all the Jason Statham action movies you haven't seen." I threw him an encouraging smile.

He clapped his hands over his ears, whimpering "No." The pencil halves bounced to the floor.

I went around the desk and pried one chunky finger off his ear, allowing me to whisper, "*The Transporter* franchise."

He banged his head on the desk. "You are horrible person."

"Deal?"

He sighed and opened a drawer. "Give me wrist."

"Why?"

"Part of deal. No coming back until ban over." When I didn't comply, he grabbed my arm, but not hard, and slapped something against it.

There was a quick sting and then the skin became warm. He'd stuck one of those kids' tattoos on me depicting the neon sign doing its sad face.

"Is this a joke?" I scratched at it, but Pyotr brushed my hand away.

"No coming back until this disappears." He crossed his arms.

"I said I wouldn't. You didn't need to give me this thing."

"I trust you like happy little beet trusts babushka."

I scratched my head. "Does that mean it does or it doesn't? Is that some Russian proverb that doesn't translate well?"

A door appeared in the wall next to the plant and he pointed at it. "Go."

I grabbed the knob but before I could leave, Pyotr barked for me to wait.

"Make up your mind. Now what?"

He pulled a garbage bag full of socks out from under his desk and shoved it at me.

"What am I supposed to do with these?" Sighing, I took it, the black plastic crinkling.

"Make kite, build fort, bake cake. Use imagination," the golem said impatiently. Yeah, sock cakes were all the rage. "We have too many. And come back with new movies. Or else."

Eyes narrowed, I jabbed a finger at Pyotr. "I've suffered threats at the hands of head vampires, manipulative game show hosts, and Lonestars. You, on the other hand, will say please."

Impressive how a stone gargoyle could seem to melt into a puddle of sadness. "Please."

"We'll see." I marched out, stumbling almost immediately through another door and out under the cherry tree on my property, single socks spilling out.

I stepped back into the shadows to test the ban, but an electric shock sparked through me, emanating from the tattoo and barring my entry into the KH. Swearing, I shook out my hand and lugged the bag up my front walk.

Eli opened the door. "Something wrong with your washing machine?"

"Long story." I stuffed the fallen socks back in the bag and deposited it on the porch.

"O-kay. Sadie's here."

Awesome. I'd totally forgotten about my kid. Way to suck as a mother.

He motioned for me to come into his townhouse. "She's in the yard having a snack."

"Have you spoken to her more about magic?" The layout of Eli's place was identical to mine, but our furnishings couldn't have been more different. My ex had no design aesthetic and his first attempt at furnishing this place had been two leather recliners, a giant television, and a framed hockey jersey bearing Henrik Sedin's number "33." It was autographed by both the player himself, arguably the greatest Canuck of all time, and Henrik's twin brother, Daniel, who ranked as second-best.

After I'd told Eli that he had to do better if our daughter was going to live with him part-time, he'd gone to the other extreme and hired a designer who had made the place look like it was staged for an open house with sleek, high-end furniture. Years later, the furniture was scuffed and there was a lot more clutter, but it had settled into a homey place that suited him and Sadie. Though the hockey jersey still occupied a place of honor and the original television had been replaced by a much larger screen.

We headed into the yard where Sadie was slumped in a chair shoveling cereal into her mouth. Her choice of snack hadn't changed since she was three. She glanced at me but didn't say hello.

Eli tapped the metal bowl of fruit salad in the middle of the table. "Don't fill up on carbs."

"Fruit is carbs," Sadie said. "The more you know, Dad."

"Dazzling me with smartass facts?" He pointed to me before pushing the bowl to our kid. "I blame you."

I shrugged.

"There's cantaloupe in it." Sadie made a face. "It's gross."

"Cantaloupe is delicious." He ate a piece.

I took the fork away from him and fished out a piece of

pineapple. "Cantaloupe is the drugstore chrysanthemum of the fruit world," I said. "What kind of monster are you?"

Sadie snorted, then shoved another spoonful of cereal into her mouth and chewed like she was out for revenge.

"Did you have a good talk with Aunt Jude?" I sat down beside her, Eli taking the seat on Sadie's other side.

"I want to be there when the vampire wards up our house," she said. "Jude said that the more I see magic first-hand, the less it'll feel weird or scary."

"That makes a lot of sense," Eli said.

I kept my smile on my face, but under the table, I dug my nails into my thighs. Jude got to be the voice of reason when all I got was pushback and animosity? "No problem. What else did Jude tell you? Did she explain the work I do for Tatiana?" I was torn between hoping she had since Sadie was accepting this new reality easier from Jude and praying she hadn't because I could spin it much better.

Sadie shrugged. "Not really. She said you had to tell me. Dad, do you know?"

"Not everything." Eli mirrored his daughter's body language, the two of them angled toward each other and away from me.

Thank you so much for the support and backup, coparent of mine. "Tatiana's a fixer for the magic community," I said.

Sadie screwed up her face. "What's that?"

"It's someone who takes care of problems for people who don't want to go to the police," Eli said.

"Criminals," Sadie said, crossing her arms.

Eli shot me a "she said it, not me" smirk.

"Not necessarily," I said. "Some clients have specialized needs that they trust us to carry out."

"Is the part about Tatiana writing her memoirs even true?" Sadie said.

"It is. And I am doing all the documentation for that as well." I ignored the texts lighting up my phone to stay focused on Sadie, but when it began ringing, my daughter rolled her eyes and told me to answer it.

"Emmett?" I said. "What's wrong? Is Tatiana okay?"

"Emmett's a golem that Aunt Jude made." My daughter drank the rest of the milk directly out of the bowl.

"Uh-huh." Eli sighed, then picked up another fork and more cantaloupe.

"We got a call," Emmett said. "On the enthrallment hotline. Our first."

"Text me the details."

"Will do. Later, gator." He hung up.

Sadie put the cereal bowl down. "The details of what?"

I appreciated her wanting all the facts, but I also wanted to wrap this conversation up and go check out that situation. If a person had been inhabited by a dybbuk, the sooner I got it out of them, the better for all concerned.

"Hang on," Eli said. "Miriam, you told me that your other jobs had been small caliber stuff. Driving people, retrieving belongings. I assumed the murder was a one-off—"

"Murder?" my daughter squeaked. "You were in that case that Dad worked?"

"Great job keeping things under wraps, Eli," I muttered. "Someone impersonated a client, and he got killed. I was in no danger..."

Two sets of eyes stared accusatorily at me.

"You don't demand that your father tell you every detail of his cases." I threw down my fork. "Why am I expected to?"

"Dad is a trained cop with a whole police force behind him." Sadie hugged her knees to her chest. "You're just some mom with...I don't even know what."

I stood up, shadowy tattoos swirling over my skin, too angry to feel guilty at my daughter's flinch. "Guess what? I have an entire identity that doesn't involve being your mother. I've had magic since I was fourteen, but I cut it off.

186

Now I've let it back into my life. I work with powerful people and I'm not an idiot."

Sadie stared at me wide-eyed, like I'd grown a second head.

I gentled my tone, doing my best to recall my magic. "I'm sorry that I didn't raise you with this knowledge and that you had to find out this way, Sadie, but I'm not helpless or useless. This is how things are. I love you more than anything, kid, but you're growing up. You have a boyfriend, and in a couple years you'll be off to university. You'll be living your own life, which is exactly how it should be, but I want to live mine." I shrugged. "Yes, it's a bit unusual, but some would say our family unit is unusual."

Eli got interested in the fruit salad bowl, pushing food around.

"You have to believe that ultimately, I'm trying to do good in the world," I said. "If it hadn't been for me, that murder victim would never have gotten justice. I can make a difference. I *want* to make a difference. And I hope you both can live with that, but I can't make that decision for you." I fished my keys out of my pocket.

"Where are you going?" Sadie said warily.

"To save someone from being possessed by an evil ghost." Killing dybbuks wasn't exactly a spectator sport, but if I left my daughter now, her imagination would go into overdrive. My family was Sapien and couldn't be possessed, plus there was no moral gray zone here. I'd be saving someone. "Want to come? See what I do for yourself?"

"I'm not sure that's a good idea," Eli said.

"Think of it as community outreach," I said. "The police do it all the time."

"Touché," he murmured. He was a big fan of community events to forge better relationships with cops and make them less scary to the average citizen. "All right. I'm in."

Sadie agreed as well, getting ready in record time.

The directions I'd gotten from Emmett led us to a long-term care home in a quiet suburban neighborhood.

A balding man in scrubs paced nervously outside the front doors, glancing over hopefully when we got out of the car. "Are you here about Mrs. Krantz?"

"Yes. I'm Miriam Feldman and these are..." I scratched my head. Sadie wore a T-shirt bearing the logo of the theater camp she worked at and Eli had on shorts and flip-flops. "My associates."

He barely spared them a glance, hurrying into the facility. "I'm Edgar. Normally, Mrs. Krantz is the sweetest person, but..." He sighed. "You tell me."

With that, he opened the blue doors leading to the large lounge area.

Two elderly women, one of whom was in a wheelchair, sat at a table, crying. A tired-looking nurse attempted to console them, while a man sitting on the seat of his walker yelled "Cheater!" at the dealer seated with the trio.

The plump woman in a lurid floral shirt and plastic visor from a long-ago cruise collected the ante of pennies and Hershey's Kisses. "I don't need to cheat when I'm playing morons!"

The man grabbed the plastic spoon out from his pudding cup and flung chocolate goop at her.

She slammed her hands on the table. "I'm going to kill you."

"Yikes," Sadie said.

Two male nurses moved in, and I called out, "Wait! Don't get close."

Edgar shook his head. "Not them. They do this a couple times a month. Mrs. Krantz is outside." He led us to the French doors, which opened to the courtyard.

A sweet-faced woman in a pharmacist's coat who wouldn't have been out of place in a kindergarten classroom sat at a table littered with small glass bottles. Several were smashed at her feet, the flagstones stained dark. She was in a standoff with a burly attendant, who held a loaded syringe.

"Damn it," Edgar muttered. "I told him not to get involved. Roger is a Sap."

"Put the medication down and no one gets hurt," Roger said.

The woman's shadow looked normal, so she wasn't fully possessed yet.

Mrs. Krantz threw a bottle up, almost missing catching it. Both the attendant and Edgar flinched.

"That medication is in extremely short supply globally right now," Edgar said quietly. "Several of our residents will die without it."

Sadie started to say something, but I put my finger to my lips, probing deeper into Mrs. Krantz's shadow.

Eli watched it all with his cop face on.

I exhaled. Ah, there it was. That faint violent cry inside her. At least this dybbuk was behaving normally.

"Day in, day out," Mrs. Krantz said, "I feed the sheep pills to make their piteous lives go on a little longer. I'm doing them a courtesy by putting them out of their misery." She rounded on me. "Who are you?"

Taking advantage of her momentary lapse in attention, the burly attendant lunged for her, glass crunching underfoot, but the woman swept a hand across the table.

The bottles flew.

Roger spun away so as not to get hit.

Edgar gasped and Sadie yelped, but I'd already shot Delilah out.

She extended over the ground like a net before the vials landed. My shadow softened the impact and they rolled harmlessly off her. All except one that overshot my shadow and shattered.

"What have we here?" A cruel smile flitted over Mrs.

Krantz's lips, and she pushed the chair away from the table, with a scrape like nails on a chalkboard.

"Get Roger out of here," I said, not taking my focus off the woman. I'd intended my directive for Edgar, but Eli stepped forward, pulling his badge out of his pocket.

"Detective Eli Chu, VPD," he said, approaching Roger. "Could I get you to come with me and give me a statement?"

Roger looked uncertainly at Edgar, who nodded. "Yes, we'll both come. It's okay," Edgar told the attendant and motioned at me. "She's from corporate. Trained in these situations."

Eli ushered the men back inside to question them, which was good. I wouldn't have to worry about Roger's Sapien status or Eli jumping into the action.

Just keeping Sadie out of it.

I ordered her to stay out of the way, no matter what. When she gave me a nervous nod, I strode over to Mrs. Krantz, Delilah turning into a wreath of smoke that flowed up my body and down my left arm into a scythe.

Mrs. Krantz grabbed the chair and jabbed it at me like a toreador waving a flag at a bull.

"Mom?" Sadie squeaked, backing up closer to the French doors.

"It's okay." I circled the enthralled woman, my weapon raised.

The woman threw the chair at me, winging me in the shoulder.

I grunted and jerked back, and she overturned the table, almost hitting me before fleeing. I raced after her, weaving around the other small tables in the courtyard to catch her before she made it to the door at the far side leading into another section of the building.

"She's getting away!" Sadie cried.

Yeah, but her shadow was still close enough to hit. I slammed the scythe down into it, severing it from her body.

"Holy fuck!" Sadie said, ducking down behind a table.

I had a second of relief that we were all safe, then Mrs. Krantz collapsed, and I swore under my breath. We hadn't worked out how to keep that from happening, though I'd really hoped it had been an anomaly when I'd done this to Jude.

My daughter ran toward the woman right as the dybbuk tore loose, pulsing and swirling in a furious crimson mass. "Mom!"

Shoving Sadie behind me with a sharp "Stay!" I righted my hold on the scythe. "Mut!" The Hebrew letters appeared on the blade. "Batter up!" I drove the scythe into its center and leaching of all color, the spirit imploded and vanished.

I dropped to the ground next to Mrs. Krantz, my weapon disappearing, and began chest compressions. I wasn't sure if this made a difference, or if her survival was based on some magic criteria, but it couldn't hurt.

"She's not breathing," Sadie said urgently, kneeling beside me. "Should I call 911?"

I shook my head.

"Give her room to work, hon." Eli had joined us, placing a reassuring hand on our daughter's shoulder.

Mrs. Krantz came to groggily—recovering much faster than Jude had. I sat back on my calves. Could her recuperation be tied to how fast I'd dispatched this dybbuk versus when I'd saved my best friend?

"Are you all right?" I said gently.

She gripped my hand. "Is it out?" Her voice shook.

I smiled. "Yes."

She burst into tears, covering her face with her hands. Eli and I helped her sit up, leading her to a chair.

I hugged her while she sobbed, telling me through her tears that she thought her baby would grow up without her. She'd been so tired, up all the time feeding her son.

Edgar rejoined us and his face drained of all color. "Wh- where's her shadow?"

Mrs. Krantz's head snapped up, her eyes wide.

"Don't panic," I said. "It's temporary. As is your magic loss." I told them what to expect based on Jude's regeneration, and was about to leave Mrs. Krantz in Edgar's care when I noticed a bunch of residents staring at us out the lounge windows.

"Sapiens or Ohrists?" I asked.

"Mostly Saps," Edgar said, pulling a juice box out of his scrubs pocket and punching the straw in for Mrs. Krantz.

"Oh no," the woman moaned. "What will they think?"

"That you had a bad reaction to some new medication," Edgar said. "Just like I told them. They'll believe that you fainted and need to take time off."

Assuring myself that all was well, and I could leave Mrs. Krantz in Edgar's care, Eli, Sadie, and I walked back to my sedan.

My family was quiet. Too quiet.

I unlocked the doors. Had this backfired horribly and they were even warier of magic than before? Where had I gone wrong? Was it the scythe, Mrs. Krantz losing her shadow, falling unconscious, or—

Sadie's arms came around me in an attack hug.

"That was badass, Mom!"

Beaming, I squeezed her hands. "Told you."

She scrambled into the back seat. "If you hadn't helped her, she would have died, right? Like Aunt Jude?"

"Yup."

On the passenger side, Eli clicked the seat belt in. "I saw it through the window. It was pretty incredible."

Yaas, queen.

"You had your badge on you?" I pulled the sun shade down and backed out of the parking spot.

"Figured it might come in handy," he said.

Sadie requested the right to DJ. When we were partway home, she put on "Fuck You" by Lily Allen. Usually, I rolled my eyes at the peppy, yet expletive-laden tune, but today I turned it up, jumping in on the chorus.

Laughing, Eli joined in, adding his bass to our voices. We sang at the top of our lungs, the windows down, and the summer breeze streaming in. Our fuck yous weren't about the song. They were about magic, and dybbuks, and all the strife we'd experienced, but in the end, we'd come together, because we were a family and that's what families did.

Fuck you, house divided. We had this.

How wrong I was.

15

EVEN THE KNOWLEDGE THAT ZEV WAS COMING OVER
to ward up our house didn't dim our upbeat mood. Team
Feldman-Chu was standing strong and ready for any games
the vampire attempted to pull on us.

Eli had gone inside his place, promising to return at
sunset.

Laurent wasn't responding to my texts, so I called Emmett
and Tatiana, who put me on speaker.

"She sent the details of the handover," Tatiana said.
"We're meeting at the Bear's Den on Thursday morning at
eleven." The speakeasy was a known neutral meeting place.
This woman was familiar with our city.

Frowning, I stripped the sheets off my bed to throw in the
wash. It was already late afternoon on Tuesday. "Then that's
our deadline to find her."

Was it still "our" or was it now "my" deadline if Laurent
didn't resurface? Hoping for the best, I told my employer
everything that we'd learned at the Wise Brothers', minus the
revelation about the alpha abandoning his pack. This likely
wasn't news to Tatiana and I wasn't giving Emmett any
ammunition to throw in Laurent's face.

My update was accompanied by an irritating popping noise. "What's that?"

"He's supposed to be unpacking art supplies, not playing with bubble wrap." Tatiana tsked. "They sent the wrong color. We'll have to go to the art supply store."

"Field trip!" Emmett crowed.

"You should stick close to home." I shook the pillows free from their cases.

"Why?" Tatiana said. "You just said the wards won't protect me."

"It's a known environment and easier to protect you."

"This woman won't come after me before our meeting, meaning I can finish this one piece with the precious little time I have left." Tatiana sighed dramatically. "There was still so much I wanted to accomplish before my untimely end."

I rolled the sheets into a ball for easier carrying. "No one is going to kill you. You'll live to a hundred."

"Fun dayn moyl in gots oyern." From your mouth to God's ears.

"Look, if we can neutralize her familiar, she has no way to attack. I'm looking into some things." I didn't add anything about Laurent. No point in worrying her that her beloved nephew was loose somewhere in the world and might not have any ability to shift.

"Keep me posted," she said and hung up as usual, without saying goodbye.

I'd lied to Tatiana. I had only one idea to stop our foe. Dybbuks were considered demons where the gloves were concerned so why not ask a demon directly if there was a way to kill the woman's familiar?

I fired off a text to Naveen asking him to call me, then I sat on my stripped mattress, my finger hovering over Laurent's number, debating whether I should text or call.

He'd ignored my previous texts, so I phoned him, but it went straight to voice mail. "Laurent..." I licked my lips

195

nervously. "Where are you? Please let me know you're okay. If you don't want to speak to me, well, I get that. You could call Naveen or Tatiana. Just check in. And if you are back home and want to come over tonight, Zev is setting up the ward. You wanted to know so..." I sighed. "I never meant to hurt you. Call me."

Shoving the phone in my pocket, I gathered up the sheets and carried them downstairs.

"Here." Sadie added her sheets to mine in the washing machine. "Do you know where my wooden stake is?"

"Hmmm." I poured detergent in and hit the correct settings. "Right. It got damaged in a vampire attack."

"You killed a vamp with my stake? I had to special order that thing."

I shut the closet doors hiding the machine in the kitchen. "I'll get you another one. Also, they don't work as advertised. Do not try and stake an undead with one." I grimaced, recalling how it had stuck in Lindsey's ribs. "They don't like it."

She planted her hands on her hips. "That's it. My cosplay stuff is off-limits. Get your own weapons."

"Baby girl." I ruffled her hair, then opened the fridge to figure out dinner. "I am a weapon."

So was the woman with the familiar. How thin was the line between her dybbuk and Delilah? Could my shadow ever gain enough sentience to act independently of me? Would I become the hunted one day? That thought led me back to Laurent and our dividing lines.

"God, you're going to be so annoying now, aren't you?" Sadie said.

"Yup." I shook off my morbidity. "Welcome to the new world order."

She retrieved a bag of chips from the cupboard and tore them open. "Why don't I have magic?"

"Blame your dad. His Sapien genes were too strong." I

snatched the bag away, grateful she hadn't found my hidden PMS emergency stash. "That's not dinner."

"It could totally be a side dish with hot dogs. There's stuff in the freezer."

I debated making something healthier—for about thirty seconds—but dealing with Zev and Eli in the same place would require all my energy. Plus, even though my period had slowed down considerably, I was majorly craving salt. "Fine."

"Whoo-hoo!" Sadie crammed a handful of ripple chips in her mouth.

"Put them in a bowl and let me have some."

Once I'd helped myself, my child leaned over the counter making puppy dog eyes. "Can I have a weapon tonight?"

Had she only been trying to be cute, I would have turned her down, but there was a note of anxiety in her voice and she gnawed on her bottom lip.

What happened to the good old days and worrying about sex, drugs, and the evils of rock and roll with kids? Was I honestly debating whether my daughter was old enough to arm herself? It would have been so much easier if she had been born with magic. "I may have a mini flamethrower that—"

"No way!"

"That you can hold on to." I gave her my sternest warning look. "No actual usage. And if I say it goes away, then you obey immediately, got it?" Could I spin it to Zev as a security blanket kind of thing?

She bounced up and down on her toes. "Let me see it."

I sighed. If the vamp didn't kill me, her dad would.

Eli and I met on the porch after dark. I'd gotten a text from Zev, or someone on his behalf, because as always with his messages, it came from a blocked number, saying he was on his way, so we sat down on the stairs to wait for the vampire while our child finished dressing in the perfect outfit.

I decided to wait until she arrived to explain about the

flamethrower, though I did check for Eli's religious artifacts necklace. Happily, he'd removed it.

My ex wore a thoughtful look on his face.

Oh dear. Was he getting lost in a spiral of paranoia? I nudged him. "Care to share?"

He pointed at the spindly trees lining the sidewalk on our block. "Ever get the feeling that we got the reject trees from the rich side of town?"

"Right? Who do you have to bribe at City Planning to get the ones they have over on sixth?" Those old growth elms provided a majestic canopy spanning blocks and blocks. "Ours are ugly and they blow sticky sap all over any cars parked out front."

"The Ron Jeremy of trees," he said.

A snort-laugh burst out of me, and he winked.

"We've got this," he said.

Sadie stepped outside, throwing a slash of light onto us from my foyer. "I'm ready." She'd opted to go full Victorian steampunk with a lace-up corset, a ruffled skirt, and a pair of thick steampunk goggles shoved in her hair.

Eli squinted at the flamethrower. "I don't get the wand."

"It's a mini flamethrower." She merrily waved the weapon. "Her name is Phoebe."

To Eli's credit, I only got a single pained stare. "Of course it is," he said.

I patted his shoulder. "She's not allowed to actually use it. Prop purposes only. Now, flamethrower aside, we need to keep our guards up. BatKian is incredibly dangerous. Do not cross him."

"We won't." Eli held out his fists and we all bumped. "We're in this together."

It was such a relief to have these two firmly on my side and know that my family was no longer divided.

Eli slid a sideways glance at the flamethrower. "That works, huh?"

"It does," I said.

His eyes lit up and Sadie stepped away from him. "This is mine," she said, cradling the weapon.

"Let the child have her fire."

"But Mir," he whined. "You didn't let me bring my gun or anything…" His mouth fell open and he sat up straight. "Oh, baby."

A low-slung red car prowled to the curb. Its engine revved once loudly, then it fell silent, the two doors opening upward like dragon wings extending.

Eli had gotten to his feet. "LaFerrari." He whispered it like a prayer.

For a moment I expected Laurent to step out because the sports car had the same predatory feel that he did, and I stood up, watching the driver smoothly disengage from the vehicle.

"Good evening, Ms. Feldman." Zev BatKian wore dark jeans and a light sweater instead of a suit. He could have been any tech billionaire, which compared to the vibe he usually gave off made him basically look like a commoner.

Eli prodded me in the back, and I stopped gaping, the two of us descending the porch stairs to greet the vampire. "Mr. BatKian. Welcome to my home."

"Thank you." Zev smiled at Eli, whose face lit up like a kid seeing fireworks for the first time at the sight of the car doors folding down to resemble a beast at rest. "A fellow Ferrari aficionado, Detective Chu?"

"No shit, considering this is the ultimate Ferrari," Eli blurted out. I elbowed him and he blinked, recalling who he was speaking to. "Sorry. May I get closer?"

"By all means." The vampire waved a hand at the sports car and Eli bounded over to it, though he stopped short of touching the fancy vehicle.

Good man. Proceed with caution. I released my breath.

Eli circled the Ferrari, speaking in tongues—okay, muttering car words, which made about as much sense. The only thing I caught was that the price tag was well over a million dollars.

I swallowed, silently willing him to back up.

Sadie had remained on the porch, but now she sidled up behind me. "Hello." Her voice was steady, however, she white-knuckled the flame thrower.

Zev's eyes darted to the weapon and his lips quirked up. "You must be Sadie. Your mom talks about you all the time." He held out his hand to shake.

Sadie barely hesitated before she took it. "You feel way warmer than I thought you would."

"Sadie!" I hissed.

Zev laughed. "I detest being cold."

"Me too." My daughter nodded enthusiastically.

That was nice, I guess. He was trying to put her at ease. I wouldn't have expected that from him.

Zev leaned in conspiratorially. "Do you have fuzzy sleep socks? Mine have stripes."

"Mine have hearts," Sadie said. "But I always get too hot in the middle of the night and kick them off."

Zev nodded sagely. "I hear you."

All right. That was enough of that. "We don't want to take up too much of your time," I said, stepping forward with a polite smile. "Tell me what you need for—"

"I bet this is all pretty scary," Zev said. "Magic, vampires. Shifters."

"Shifters?" Sadie's hand went to the lid of the flamethrower, and I shook my head at her.

Zev gave me an innocent look. "Oh, you didn't mention your friend Laurent is a wolf?"

"It hadn't come up yet," I said tightly.

Sadie glared at me. "It's a lot to take in."

You sneaky bastard. No bonding with my child and no turning her against me when I'd just gotten her on board. I motioned at Eli for some support for Team Feldman-Chu, but he was busy drooling over the damn car and all I got was a vague head bob before he crouched down to examine the tires.

"Perhaps there's something I can do to make it less overwhelming." Zev stroked his goatee. "Give me the names of your closest friends and I'll make sure that none of my people cause them any harm."

Sadie gave him the same look of adoration that I'd gotten the year I gave her the Barbie Dream House for Hannukah. "You will?"

I checked myself for waves of steam. I expected this manipulation from Zev, but I thought my family wasn't that easy. They weren't supposed to roll over like puppies wanting their bellies scratched.

Zev's promise was pointless since he wouldn't target Sadie's friends and stir up the cops. Please. I could have told her that. Oh wait, I had.

As for the walking midlife crisis still checking out the car? Jeez, Eli, normal people didn't look at headlights that way, even fancy-ass ones. Get a room already. And get real. If someone handed you a Ferrari, you wouldn't drive it over the speed limit and you'd be paranoid about bird shit marring the finish.

"Give me a fucking break, both of you."

"I beg your pardon?" Zev looked askance at me.

Whoops. I'd said that out loud. "Nothing."

"Do you really promise?" Sadie said.

"You have my word." The vampire pulled out a phone, allowing her to type in her friends' names and addresses, while he smiled at me over the top of my daughter's bent head.

I motioned at him to move out of Sadie's earshot with me. "Are you compelling my family?"

Zev placed his hand on his heart. "I can't be liked for myself?"

I planted my hands on my hips. "Then what's with the full-on charm offensive? Are you out to divide and conquer or is your strategy more a show of strength? Proving to me that you can get to my family in other ways than direct harm?"

"I'm simply concerned with making a good first impression."

Sadie joined us to return his phone. "Thank you."

I silently fumed, grinding my teeth. If he'd compelled my family, I could have busted Delilah out as a violation of his promise, but this was straight up moving pawns on his chess board.

"How's the HY-KERS system?" Eli asked. "Is the hybrid really better than the classic V12?"

I kicked a twig halfway across the yard. This family was rubbish.

"Instant throttle response," the vampire said. "But to truly experience it, you have to open her up on a stretch of road." He got a dreamy look on his face and my heart sank. Whether or not the look was an act, it humanized him, and given the expressions on my family's faces, they'd met the coolest person ever. "Imagine steering the Space Shuttle," Zev said, "but wrapped in velvet, and bending the fabric of space and time."

Eli gazed at the vehicle reverentially.

"Want to drive her sometime?" Zev asked.

"No!" I squeaked. Everyone looked at me—Zev amused, Eli hurt, and Sadie puzzled—and I frantically backpedaled. "Insurance issues, am I right? Can't have just anyone driving this expensive car."

One stray rock, one tiny ding, and Zev would pulverize Eli's head.

"I'd be careful," the father of my child said in a sulky voice.

"It's never good to anger the women in our lives." The

202

vampire gave him a conspiratorial wink. "Perhaps I could sponsor you to go through Corsa Pilota."

"Ferrari's racing school?" Eli made a noise no dignified human should and swayed in toward the sports car like a flower to the sun. He puffed out his chest, speaking in a gruff and lower voice than normal. "I do have time off that I could take."

Five more minutes and Eli would be weaving him a friendship bracelet.

"Then it's settled. Shall we proceed with the ward?" Zev headed into my backyard, Eli right behind him. Zev looked around our age, but he had the air of someone much older, and Eli was treating him with the hero worship of an elder brother.

I rolled my eyes. That was all I needed.

"I don't know what you were so worried about, Mom," Sadie said, handing me the flamethrower. "He's nice."

Said no one about that vampire ever.

16

Zev strode around the perimeter of the property, casing it for something only he understood, when the gate squeaked open and someone else joined us.

My head shot up, but it wasn't Laurent. "You've got to be kidding," I muttered as Naveen strode toward us.

Zev looked at the newcomer with narrowed eyes. In the moonlight, the vamp was pale enough to seem carved from marble, untouchable, forbidding. "What are you doing here?"

I shivered at the icy tone, but if that got my family back on board with my opinion of him, then I'd never say an unkind thing about Naveen again.

"I'm the proxy," Naveen said in his posh British accent. "Laurent sends his wishes."

Eli rolled his eyes at Laurent's name and Sadie scowled at me. Great.

Zev gave Naveen a snarky smile. "Shame he couldn't join us."

Why couldn't he? My gut tied itself into knots and I hurried over to Naveen to ask.

"I'm Detective Chu," Eli said. "Who might you be?" He

moved closer to the vampire, aligning himself more firmly with the bloodsucker.

"Eli," I said, "you remember Dr. Kumar? Daya?"

"Sure."

"This is her brother, Naveen." I shot my ex a "quit being a dick" look. "Come say hello."

"The doctor who delivered me?" Sadie said. "Cool. Hi." She waved, but stayed next to Zev, watching as he crouched and ran a handful of dirt through his fingers.

I wrestled my soaring blood pressure under control with the sole uplifting thought that Laurent was safe or Naveen wouldn't be here.

As Eli strode closer, clearly unhappy at leaving his new bestie, I tabled my questions in favor of making sure the warding proceeded smoothly.

"Talk some sense into him, please," I said quietly to Naveen. "Zev has my family snowed."

Naveen made a disparaging noise, his expression hard as he watched the vampire, which cheered me up. Finally, an ally. Vampirism made strange bedfellows.

The two men shook hands for a moment longer than necessary and I tensed, ready to shut down some alpha bullshit, but their body language was relaxed.

I let out a sigh of relief before seeing Eli rake a slow gaze over Naveen and I clued into what was really happening. They weren't establishing dominance; they were eye-fucking each other.

Are you freaking kidding me, universe? One little proverb mentioning bedfellows, and this is what you come back with?

"Shame we never crossed paths before." Eli rubbed a hand over his head, his biceps flexing.

Remember your hard-on for the Ferrari? Go back to those good times.

"Isn't it just," the younger man said, smoothing his shirt down over his rock-hard abs.

Shoot me now. I muscled between them. "Can we get on with this, please?"

The sooner we got the ward dealt with, the sooner I could question Naveen about Laurent.

"Yes." Zev beckoned me over to the fig tree growing along the fence between Eli's yard and mine that taunted us every year with a paltry couple of figs that we fought with the ants to eat first. It did have lovely broad leaves though. "This will be the anchor point. The ward requires blood, yours and mine."

I clapped a hand over my neck. "Maybe my family shouldn't be here for this."

He gave me an exasperated look. "I don't drink human blood, remember?"

"You don't?" Sadie was listening to our conversation, but for all of Eli's bitching about never letting the undead serial killer do his magic mumbo jumbo to protect our property, he was perfectly content to hang back and flirt with Naveen.

"No," BatKian said. "It's prohibited in the Jewish religion and I used to be a rabbi. With the advancements in synthetic blood, there's no need to break that forbiddance."

My daughter hung off his every word. "That's amazing."

Yay. Gold star vampire for not feeding off humans. I snorted. In my head. Where Zev couldn't hear. Hopefully.

"Where do you want to take the blood from?" I said. "Neck? Wrist?"

"Would you like to remove the intruder first?" Zev asked.

If I didn't, then Naveen would be able to get through the ward, but I doubted he'd hurt me anymore. Well, not until he'd gotten it on with Eli. I shuddered. Laurent's best friend and the brother of the doctor who'd delivered my child hooking up with my ex. This was getting incestuous.

"No," I said. "He can stay."

"As you wish." Zev held out his hand and I placed mine in it. Sadie was right. He was warmer than expected.

I blushed, remembering being pressed up against his body, craving him. Yeah, no. That wasn't happening ever again.

The vampire pulled a tongue depressor out of his pocket and handed it to Sadie. "Hold this please." He sliced his fingernail across a vein on my inner forearm and I jerked. His nail hadn't looked long enough to inflict damage, yet a fat drop of blood welled up. He cut his own skin, then took the tongue depressor, squeezing his blood onto it.

"This might hurt," he said.

I nodded and he squeezed my arm hard to get more out. Once the stick had a good amount of our mingled blood, he licked his finger, running his saliva over my wound, which immediately healed up.

"Whoa," Sadie whispered.

Zev dabbed some blood into the dirt under the fig tree, then Sadie and I accompanied him as he circled both my house and Eli's.

Naveen and Eli trailed behind, bonding over a Canucks' home game they'd both recently attended. A mutual love of stick handling. Spare me.

When Zev returned to the fig tree, he wiped the rest of the blood on the ground. "Kinehora!" he cried, following it up with *ptu ptu ptu*, mimicking spitting three times.

I stared at him gobsmacked.

Sadie nudged me. "Is he messing with us?"

Zev brushed his hands off on his jeans and stood up, handing me the tongue depressor.

Yum. Just what I always wanted.

"I could have made up something complicated," he explained to her, "but simpler is better. The Jewish expression 'kinehora' is a bastardization of 'kayn' for not, 'hara' meaning the evil, and 'ayin,' eye. It's a protective folk action intended to avoid, fool, or attack evil spirits and perfect for our needs. Give it a second to cohere and—" He seized up, his body stiffening out, and was blown backward into my fence.

Sadie screamed.

I pushed her behind me. "Mr. BatKian?"

A flash of light out of the corner of my eye showed Naveen had unleashed his staff.

Eli sprinted across the grass to grab our daughter, snatching the flamethrower away from me.

The vampire rose up hissing, his eyes red, and his fangs descended. "What did you do?"

"No-nothing." I stumbled back, shrieking when a hand came down on my shoulder.

"Steady on," Naveen murmured.

Nodding, I held out a beseeching hand to BatKian. "I wouldn't ever screw you over. I swear. Especially not with my daughter here."

He glanced at Sadie, who'd buried her face in her dad's chest, her foot tapping rapidly. She was in full panic mode and there was nothing I could do to help her because I had to appease the vampire.

I channeled every ounce of sincerity into my voice. "Please believe me."

His rage drained away, his eyes and teeth returning to normal before giving me a brusque nod. "Don't be afraid, child. I'm not going to hurt anyone."

Sadie nodded silently at him, but she wouldn't look at me, grasping her father tighter, the dividing lines clear. Sapiens on one side, supernaturals on the other.

I lay my palm on my racing heart, breathing slowly, my body dull and heavy. "What happened?"

"There was some kind of static interference." The vampire squatted down to examine the ward. I couldn't see or feel anything, but when he touched the dirt, he frowned. "Is your magic working or have you gone blank?"

I paled. Blank. As in the domino tile and Emmett's prophecy? No. I scrubbed a hand over my face. "I saved an enthralled. My magic worked fine this afternoon."

"It's true," Eli said. "Sadie and I both saw it." He'd flicked the lid off the flamethrower, but at Zev's calmer tone, deposited the weapon on the ground.

I gave thanks for all of Eli's training in not escalating a situation.

"What does this mean for the ward?" Naveen had lost the staff, but he sounded grim.

"We have to try again," I said.

Naveen shook his head. "It's not that simple, is it?"

"No." Zev stood up, brushing dirt off his hands. "This ward had unique requirements, thus necessitating my blood. But as it is only half-set, with my blood alone, it's not acting as a repellant but a beacon, if you will."

My heartbeat turned into the thunder of hooves in my chest. "For demons?"

"Yes. Until the ward is closed with Banim Shovavim blood, this entire property is compromised."

Eli swore and gave me a hard look, wrapping a protective arm around Sadie, who was practically vibrating. "So, we're in an even worse situation? How is this possible, Miriam?"

"I don't—" I spread my hands wide in a helpless gesture, catching sight of the sad face that Pyotr had put on me. "Oh shit."

Zev grabbed my arm, turning it up to view the tattoo.

"It's—"

"I know what it is, Ms. Feldman," he said coldly. "And I cannot believe your stupidity in not mentioning this beforehand."

"I didn't know," I said weakly.

"That is par for the course with you, isn't it?"

Eli snorted. *Oh, fuck you, Chu. It's not like you're some great font of knowledge about this shit.*

I massaged my temples. Everything had spun so badly out of control.

"How long is the ban?" Zev said.

"Two weeks." I hung my head. "I'm so sorry. Can you redo it then?"

"Absolutely not," he said. "My blood is active for twenty-four hours. Should you remove the tattoo or find some other Banim Shovavim before then, I'll return and complete the ward. This is your last chance." Inclining his head at the others, he strode out of the yard.

I sank into a crouch, poking at the dirt with the tongue depressor like I could decree the ward to work properly. Where was I going to find a Banim Shovavim in twenty-four hours? If the Wise Brothers had given me that killer's name, then at least...what? Like she'd give me her blood when she was determined to kill Tatiana if we couldn't produce the gloves?

"What did you show the vampire?" Eli said.

The last thing I wanted to do was to tell them about the Kefitzat Haderech, but if I didn't speak up now, I'd lose the one tiny shred of Eli's and Sadie's trust that might be left. I stood up, revealing it.

Sadie's eyebrows shot up and she stared at me like I had two heads. "You got a tattoo?"

"Not willingly and only temporarily. I'll explain, but this goes no further. I need everyone's word on this." I gave Naveen a pointed look.

"I promise," he said.

Eli nodded but Sadie reluctantly shrugged. I didn't push it.

Nobody said much as I told them about the KH and my ban. I didn't say why it had happened, but from Naveen's shrewd glance, I suspect he'd figured it out. Sadie and Eli looked shell-shocked at this new facet of the magic world— and yet another reveal about my abilities.

"First things first," I said briskly. "We all need to pack and move to a hotel temporarily."

Sadie looked at her father. "Dad?"

He put his arm around her. "We'll figure out where we stay." They looked like a self-contained duo, their bodies angled in together—and away from me.

"Come home with me," Naveen said. "We're warded up and no one will think to look there." At Sadie's doubtful look he added, "There's a guest room. It's my sister's house, but Daya would love to see you again. And Evani, my niece, she's three and having an older kid like you to play with would make her so happy."

Eli would never agree. It would take time and slow, careful steps to get him to trust anyone magic after tonight's shit show. Even me.

He looked down at Sadie, who nodded.

"Are you sure?" Eli said. "This is a huge imposition for people you've just met."

I flinched like I'd been punched, but none of them saw it. Naveen, a virtual stranger, was welcomed into their lives when I'd had to fight for every tiny grain of trust in this area? Case in point, tonight. They'd cozied up to Zev until he'd scared them, and even then, the "us" against "them" vibe had not been drawn along family lines.

"It's no imposition," Naveen said. "Laurent charged me with keeping you all safe." He smiled slowly at Eli. "I'm happy to do it."

Be logical, Feldman. Naveen had wards—I was dying to know how and why—and a hotel didn't. Obviously it was the better choice. This wasn't personal.

"Wonderful," I said.

"Then we'll gladly take you up on it," Eli said.

"Miriam?" Naveen raised an eyebrow.

I straightened, already planning out all the bags and things I'd need to take to Naveen and Daya's. Hopefully their refrigerator would be fixed by now, but if not, the Moka pot and a lot of takeout recommendations were in order. This might actually be a lot of fun. I could smooth things over in my family by showing them more of the secret world of magic and introducing my friends.

I noticed belatedly that Naveen was still waiting for me. "Yes, sorry?"

"I said," he repeated, "do you have a place you can stay? We only have one guest bedroom and I'm imagining you don't want to crash on the floor."

Oh.

I walked over to the trash can and threw out the tongue depressor, swiping at my damp eyes. "Tatiana's," I said once I returned.

Sadie bit her lip. "Did he mean what he said about not hurting my friends? Or any of us?"

"Yes. If nothing else, Zev stands by his word."

"Okay." My daughter had been pushed past meltdown into a weird calm, like being in the eye of a hurricane, and I couldn't imagine what would happen on the other side, but I shoved those worries down for now. Getting us all to safety was more important.

Eli prodded her gently. "Go on. We should pack quickly."

"I'll wait for you out here," Naveen said.

Sadie went into my place and Eli disappeared through the door in our shared fence.

Naveen eased himself into one of the patio chairs. "They'll come around."

"Sure." I draped a leg over the arm of mine. "Hey, you never called me back."

"Right. What did you want?"

"Could you hook me up with a demon?" I said. "You must have some informant in your network."

"Is this about the curse? Tell me what you want to know, and I'll ask around."

What I want is to not be sidelined on my own case. Saying that would lead to another fight, though, so I moderated my tone. "The woman from the island is definitely behind all this and she's Banim Shovavim. I'd like to go along if I may."

He pursed his lips. "I'm not sure that's a good idea."

"Because I'm"—I made the quotes—"a 'BS'?"

"Don't let Daya hear you use that term," he joked weakly and rubbed his arm.

His lame teasing made me sad. I plucked a long stalk of grass from the lawn and tore it into strips. "Losing Rishi like that must have been awful, but I never deserved to be painted with the same brush as a murderer. You liked me when we met, but the second you found out what I was, that was it. I never stood a chance."

Naveen bowed his head, his face in shadow and his expression unreadable.

I brushed the pile of decimated grass off my lap. "You really hurt me."

He gave me a rueful smile. "I didn't much like myself either."

"Then why?"

He rubbed at a patchy spot with his shoe. "Rishi died trying to break up an altercation between two big guys outside a club. That's who he was. A peacekeeper."

"One of them was the Banim Shovavim?"

Naveen nodded. "The Ohrist in the fight had been stabbed so Rishi used his healer magic to help him. But the other guy wasn't happy about that and followed Rishi to his car. He attacked my brother-in-law, punching him again and again, forcing Rishi to use his magic to keep from bleeding out. Someone saw and tried to intervene but they were injured too." His jaw hardened. "The witness said that the Banim Shovavim toyed with Rishi like a cat with a mouse until Rishi used his magic one too many times."

I pressed my hand to my mouth. "Ohr got him?"

"Yeah. The bloody bastard had the nerve to spit on the ground where Rishi had stood, then he walked away." Naveen

213

tipped his head back to stare at the sky. "Daya was destroyed and my niece would never know her father."

After hearing that, I didn't have the heart to bug him about a demon informant. Laurent might not want to talk to me, but he wouldn't hang up if it was about helping Tatiana.

Speaking of our absent friend... "Where's Laurent? Is his... Can he...?"

Naveen shook his head. "Not yet. He's booked on some nightmare red-eye from Los Angeles involving two stops. It's a three-hour flight that they've turned into six. I swear, demons run that airline."

"He can't stay in a plane that long. Is it a question of money?" I calculated the balance on my credit card. "I'll pay for him to upgrade to a direct flight. Business class even."

Naveen stared at me like he was weighing something out in his head. "He can afford it. There was no other availability." He shifted his weight uneasily in his seat. "You know he's Banim Shovavim."

"Yes." I pulled my cardigan tight, not up for a fight about having learned about Laurent's magic before Naveen had, but he watched me expectantly. "Oh! You mean, could he use the Kefitzat Haderech? He could try. If his shifter magic hasn't come back, he should be fine." I could even meet him there. I sagged. No. I couldn't. "Call him."

"I'm sure if that was an option over flying, he'd have taken it," Naveen said.

"You're right." Sighing, I plucked another stalk, wrapping it around my finger. "Laurent isn't a true Banim Shovavim. His magic must be restricted to scenting and dispatching dybbuks, since he can't put them down for good, like I do. Damn it."

Naveen looked at me oddly. "That's where your head went?"

I frowned and flicked away the piece of grass. "Where should it have gone?"

"Laurent is the solution to your problem."

"I hadn't thought of that," I said slowly.

"You hadn't, had you?" he murmured. "Well, would you like to come see a demon with me tomorrow?"

"Really?" I clapped my hands. "Yes. But..." I lost my smile. "What about Laurent?"

Naveen stroked his chin. "Like I said, he's your solution but he's also really angry. He'd do it for you but pushing him to work with BatKian might be the final straw for him."

"I meant him flying."

"He's tough. He'll be okay."

"And if not tough, stubborn as hell, right?"

"Right," he said.

There was a scrambling in the bushes on one side of my garden and I jumped, but it was a raccoon darting across the lawn.

I drew my knees into my chest, my heels resting on the edge of my chair. "So, unless I miraculously produce another willing Banim Shovavim, I risk my friendship with Laurent, and demons invade my place for the next twenty-four hours?"

Naveen gave me an odd look, which softened into pity. "BatKian's blood is only good to complete the ward for that long. The beacon, however, will remain. Indefinitely. Your home will be a permanent ground zero for the supernatural."

In my head, my house of cards collapsed.

17

Naveen and I agreed to meet at his place in the morning and go see his contact for further information about how to kill the dybbuk familiar and hopefully learn the Banim Shovavim's name. That would give us just over twenty-four hours to stop the curse.

I helped load my family's stuff into his sports car, Sadie squishing in next to the car seat, with Eli up front, and waved them off with a heavy heart.

My home, my sanctuary, was a siren's call for demons. The late-night hush that often comforted me now menaced like an ominous fog hiding a deadly foe.

Throwing random shit into a suitcase, I drove to Tatiana's place on autopilot, formulating plans to shore up my relationships and set that house of cards to right, but in my head, the deck remained maddeningly scattered.

The universe cut me a small break and I got a steady row of green lights all the way up Main Street to East 41st Avenue, leaving me free to go on autopilot.

If I didn't ask Laurent for his blood to complete the ward, then my family's duplex was compromised for good. I let out a bitter snort. If I hadn't taken him through the Kefitzat Haderech in the first place, we'd never be in this position.

Damn, I was tired. Making up for a lifetime of living within the magic community and learning its mores was like playing a game of Whac-A-Mole. I'd nail one situation, only to have four more spring up.

I was swinging blind, and right now it was of little consolation that thanks to the experience I'd already amassed, these obstacles weren't coming as quickly as they first had. It wasn't quantity, it was quality. The deeper my road into this world led, the more dangerous the hurdles to overcome.

I cut across to the west side of town, past rows of houses put up for sale together in hopes of getting a huge buyout from a real estate developer, a large upscale mall, and cranes parked in front of half-finished condo complexes, silent and still against the night sky.

Putting aside the practicalities of finding another duplex in the same area given Vancouver's insane housing prices, the emotional fallout of this on Eli and Sadie would be monumental. To make matters worse, any plea to Zev to reconsider giving us the Torquemada Gloves was off the table after what had transpired tonight.

Frustrated, I hit the wheel. As mad as he was, Laurent would donate his blood to protect me but that fact failed to cheer me up. I didn't blame him for his anger. His loss of powers aside, the shifter was intensely private and a closely guarded secret about his pack and his past had been pointlessly pried out of him.

The cruel irony was that even if our friendship was miraculously preserved in the face of my request, would it be over the moment Laurent killed the Banim Shovavim?

The houses grew larger here in Shaughnessy, the silence more pronounced.

I yawned loudly and cracked my neck, running on fumes

and grateful to finally turn onto Tatiana's street. This day couldn't end quickly enough.

Hauling my small suitcase out of my trunk, I raced up to the front door, sparing a guilty glance at the darkened windows before rapping loudly.

Emmett cracked the door open, wearing a pair of lurid orange leggings. He scratched his hairless red clay chest. "'Sup?"

"Is Tatiana awake?" I lugged my suitcase inside.

"That or she's dead."

I almost knocked my suitcase over. "Was she attacked? Why didn't you call?!"

Emmett grabbed me before I could tear through the mansion looking for her. "Calm your tits. Nothing like that. The wolf phoned earlier."

He'd checked in with his aunt like I'd requested. Tiny bubbles of hope fizzed in my chest. "Was it a good conversation?"

"Get real. They had a huge fight and she pounded back the gin and tonic big time afterward until she passed out. Probably."

"Emmett!" The bubbles inside me popped as if someone had stomped on my chest.

"You have no sense of humor. I checked her breathing. She didn't pull a rock star move and drown in her own vomit. The woman's fine. Snores like a buzz saw, though."

I scratched my arm, my magic itching at me. Laurent and his aunt were constantly sniping at each other so this fight didn't necessarily involve Laurent's reveal of his Banim Shovavim magic and the existence of the Kefitzat Haderech. Angry red lines marred my skin, and I dropped my hand.

The golem poked my suitcase, a sulky expression on his face. "Don't trust me to do my job and take care of Tatiana? You moving in to check up on me?"

"I'm moving in because my home just became the Hellmouth."

"Huh?"

I gave him the Buffy synopsis version of what had transpired with Zev. "So, yeah, demons, basically."

"Shitty. Hope they don't eat the neighbors."

Thank you for that. Now all I pictured was poor Luka, disemboweled, his blood splashed across his newspaper. My head throbbed, a tight ache that pinched down into the base of my neck. "Is there a guest room I can sleep in?"

Emmett led me upstairs to a small but lovely bedroom decorated in soft shades of cream and sky blue. While the furniture had clean, simple lines, everywhere the eye landed offered a visual treat in terms of a pop of color or a textured fabric. I wrangled my suitcase into the closet. "This is great, thanks. If I'm not up when Tatiana awakens, come get me, please."

"Sure. Night, toots." Emmett closed the door behind him.

I fell back onto the foam mattress with its extra cushioning and soft blanket with a sigh, my body exhausted but my brain unable to stop whirring.

Laurent was probably on his red-eye flight.

I curled into a tight ball, closing my eyes to lessen the headache. How messed up would this trip make him? I gasped. What if his magic returned while he was on the plane? Would I wake up to news of a slaughter and the exposure of magic? This summer's next blockbuster: *Wolf on a Plane*. I pulled a pillow over my head. In giving Laurent the potion in the vial, I'd fucked up both his Ohrist magic and my own. Loath as I was to admit it, Zev was right. There was still so much I didn't know about magic, and despite my good intentions, there were times I made things worse.

When I was in university, I'd discovered jigsaw puzzles as a stress buster, progressing through harder and harder ones over the years. My approach hadn't changed though. First I laid down the corners, building a framework before moving on to large set pieces. Eventually I'd end up in the weeds cursing at some blobby color that didn't seem to fit anywhere, but all it took was two pieces connecting and suddenly an entire section could fall into place.

If only life worked the same way. Instead, the pieces of my life were disjointed. I gave a resolved nod. I'd asked Naveen for help tonight and difficult as that conversation had been, I'd gotten it. Next time I'd remember that I had people in my life to turn to when I was lost, like Jude and Ava.

And Laurent? The one person who'd been by my side through all the crazy twists and turns since I'd reclaimed my magic? I sighed. Not having the energy to change or even brush my teeth, I wrapped myself in the blanket like a burrito, grabbing my phone so I didn't end up sleeping on it.

My email showed one notification. It was from the Oxford librarian asking me to call her at my earliest convenience. While it was the middle of the night here, it was late morning over in the United Kingdom. I dialed the number she'd provided, nervous about what she might tell me about the Torquemada Gloves. Or worse, that she'd never heard of them. But she wouldn't ask me to phone in that case, would she?

The woman who answered had a pleasant voice and an upper-crust accent similar to Daya's.

"Hi. I'm phoning for Veronica Taylor. My name is Miriam Feldman."

"Miriam, hello. This is Veronica. Let me just..." A door closed. "There. Now we have some privacy. I was very intrigued by the email I received from Franklin."

"Had you heard of the Torquemada Gloves, then?" I crossed my fingers.

"No, but the idea that someone had either named a pair after the Grand Inquisitor or perhaps skinned him postmortem in retribution was a terribly exciting prospect. Historically, this could have great significance."

I thunked my head against the pillow. Could I be more of an idiot? Of course these gloves would make people take notice—and have Sapiens poking into things they shouldn't.

"Franklin mentioned you said the gloves were old," she said. "Did you have them dated?"

"No, and they aren't in my possession. They might also have been given that name to make them sound evil."

"Branding is important." She laughed. "I put a few interested friends on the hunt with me."

I smothered my groan with the pillow.

Keys clacked on a keyboard. "Sadly, none of us unearthed anything by that name despite our various resources covering theology and history."

"Shame." I modified my tone to sound genuinely upset. "I'm sorry to have wasted your time."

"That's the brilliant news. The name didn't yield anything, but that mark you described?" She rustled some papers. "Right. The half circle. That turned up something fascinating."

Nonono! That was a demon mark and I recognized that breathy excitement. She had caught the tail of something big and there would be no letting go. Not until, in this case, it swallowed her.

Visions of orange corrosive smoke belching in the sky over Deadman's Island taunted me. Would I be penalized here in Vancouver for violating the Lonestars' prime directive that magic must remain hidden, or was there some special hidden space in the Tower of London reserved for criminals like me?

I eyed the car keys I'd tossed on the dresser, considering driving home, lying down in the middle of my lawn, and letting the demons get me. I was so distraught that I almost missed what Veronica said next.

"...blood libel?"

I sat up, braced on an elbow. "Sorry, could you repeat that?"

"I asked if you'd ever heard of blood libel?"

"I'm familiar with the term." An antisemitic conspiracy theory whereby Jews were accused of killing Christian children and using their blood for religious rituals, most notably, to make matzoh. Jews were tortured and murdered in retaliation, often after a sham of a trial, the charges at their height in the Middle Ages. "Torquemada. Was he involved in some cases?"

"Oh yes. There was one in particular where a number of Jews were charged with blood libel, confessing under torture, and placed on trial by Torquemada's inquisitors. Later, they were burned at the stake in Avila, Spain. The murdered child, whose body was never found, became canonized, as many of these alleged victims were, and known as the Holy Child of La Guardia."

I sat up, the blanket falling in a pool to my waist. "How do the gloves fit into it?" I couldn't help the excitement in my voice. I'd found a previously unknown puzzle piece and these librarians had slotted it into the larger context of history.

She chuckled, appreciating my curiosity, and there were more typing sounds. "Torquemada was supposed to preside over this trial but it was moved, and instead, he personally appointed the judges. The entire purpose was to create a conspiracy that Jews and Conversos intended to destroy Christianity and the Inquisition itself."

Conversos were those Jews who had been forced into conversion. To the public at that time, they'd still been seen as Jews. I sorted through my shaky historical data of that era. "Was this trial before or after the expulsion of the Jews from Spain?"

"Before. It was, in essence, the PR campaign designed to get public opinion on the Inquisition's side for that very expulsion."

I sagged back against the plush velvet headboard. "Holy crap. And the gloves?"

She clapped her hands, sounding positively giddy. "Some of Torquemada's torture methods involved skinning both suspects and their families. While we didn't find any specific mention of gloves, we did learn of a book bound in human skin with a half-circle mark, which turned out to be a fingerprint of the victim. Now, if that's the case here?"

I sat forward, my words rushed and my eyes wide. "Then the gloves are physical proof of that witch hunt. An actual relic documenting a terrible chapter in history."

"Is there any way you can get hold of them and send them to us?"

My bubble burst because I knew something that she didn't.

That she could never learn.

The half circle wasn't a fingerprint. Or, rather, if it was, it wasn't a human one. Naveen wouldn't have gotten that detail wrong, Santiago wouldn't have hidden the gloves behind deadly booby traps, and the female Banim Shovavim certainly wouldn't be killing people to get her hands on a pair that did nothing. Even Laurent, who'd debunked a ring known as Ghost Minder as nothing more than a story, accepted the demonic nature of these gloves.

The rest of the tale could all be true, but at some point, a demon had gotten hold of the Torquemada Gloves and cursed them.

"I'm afraid they're owned by a private collector," I said, "and he won't part with them. Is there any way to do further research without them?"

She sighed. "Not really. Even if we did have them, the chances of revealing anything further, or authenticating them, would be slim, but it was worth asking."

"I'm sorry." And I was. It would have been a big deal to share this hypothesis with the academic world. What other puzzles could this piece have unlocked, giving us a glimpse into our past and into the human condition? But, like so much else, it would remain a secret, known only to a few. "I hope I didn't waste your time."

"Not at all. It was a delightful pursuit. But if you do learn anything more, please let me know."

I assured her I would and hung up. As intriguing as it all was, it didn't illuminate Zev's motives for hanging on to them.

With everything still in limbo, I crashed, awoken what felt like minutes later by Emmett.

"She's up," he said. "And in a mood."

Yawning, I pushed my hair out of my face and wiped away my eye granola. Telling Emmett that I'd be down shortly, I dragged myself into the bathroom. My period was finished—huzzah!—but I looked like shit, with deep bags under my dull eyes.

Showering, I put myself together as best as I could, given I hadn't packed conditioner, hair product, or decent clothing. The best I could do was throw my hair in a ponytail and hope my denim swing skirt with the ratty hem and the yellow blouse with the tiny buttons that gaped, straining across my chest, didn't elicit snide comments. Apparently, in my haste and distress last night, I'd grabbed the clothes intended for the second-hand store.

No matter. Be it a designer gown or a burlap sack, it was time to face the dragon.

18

ANY HOPE THAT TATIANA'S FIGHT WITH LAURENT
hadn't been about her discovery of her nephew's Banim
Shovavim magic and the existence of the Kefitzat Haderech
was dashed by the cobra smile Tatiana gave me as I poured
coffee into a large mug.

She motioned at the croissants, still warm from the oven,
that were set out on a platter, along with butter and jam.
"Eat, bubeleh." Her false smile added to the sting in her tone.
"Such a busy woman like yourself needs to keep her strength
up."

I slid a pastry onto a plate and sat across from her. "Laurent's secret wasn't mine to share."

Tatiana blinked then frowned. "He told you *before* all this
happened?"

I crammed a massive piece of croissant in my mouth and
mumbled something unintelligible and noncommittal. I'd
always joked that give Sadie silence and she'd crack and start
talking in no time at all. Apparently that gene came from me
because I lasted all of five seconds under Tatiana's weighted
stare before I caved and told her everything, starting with my
own discovery of the Kefitzat Haderech, Laurent's magic

reveal when we'd arrested the corrupt Lonestar, and right through to giving him the vial and my fear that demons would turn my place into an evil frat house.

The cat was out of the bag and there was no point in holding back now.

Tatiana's croissant shredded itself into smaller and smaller pieces, until it was nothing more than a desiccated heap. There was no sign that she used magic, but unless the pastry had suddenly gotten suicidal and self-destructed, my boss was super pissed.

I pushed my plate away, the food sticking in my throat like lumps of cardboard. "How did he sound?"

Regarding me a moment longer with narrow eyes, she grabbed another croissant, ignoring the wreckage on her plate to slather it with butter. "Like he's ready to gnaw off his own paw. If he could."

I winced. "His Ohrist magic will come back." My voice didn't attain quite the hopeful note I'd intended.

Tatiana didn't follow up with a platitude. "What are you going to do now?"

"Talk to a demon for ways to neutralize this Banim Shovavim. After that?" I twisted my napkin into a pretzel. "Depends on whether I'm fired or not."

She daintily took a bite, wiping a blob of butter off her lip with a manicured finger. "You're not getting off that easily, Miriam. Not when I can once more expand my business dealings out of my home base, thanks to your traveling abilities."

I dropped the napkin onto my plate. "What?"

"What if a demon does give you a solution?" Tatiana added jam to her croissant, uninterested in my input on her business plan. "You'd strip another woman, another Banim Shovavim, of her powers?"

"It beats the alternative where Laurent kills her." Although it didn't negate the possibility of a new wave of hunters destroying all Banim Shovavim, including me.

"Then go. And find somewhere else to stay tonight. I don't want to deal with you before the meeting."

I turned stricken eyes to her, but she dismissed me with a wave of her hand.

Emmett met me in the hallway, accompanying me upstairs. "You really screwed the pooch, huh?"

I was ready to lash out with some sarcastic retort, but he looked worried. "Yeah. I did."

The golem patted me awkwardly on the shoulder. "I've got things here," he said, leaving me at the bedroom doorway.

It was nice having one person involved in this mess on my side.

I shoved the few things I'd unpacked back into the suitcase, lugged it out to my car, and drove over to Naveen and Daya's place. My family could suck it up and see me.

Daya answered the door with a big grin. "I'm keeping your daughter."

I shrugged. "Fair enough."

"Can you stay for coffee?"

"Not really, but thanks."

Everyone was cozily ensconced in kitchen, signs of one of Eli's giant pancake cook-ups evident in the smear of batter on the apron he wore over his dress shirt, the lone pancake on a platter on the table, and Evani's blueberry-stained face.

The toddler followed Sadie around, carefully holding a Play-Doh penguin that was a signature Sades creation, while my daughter made lunch for work. Evani grabbed a juice box from a low pantry shelf and gave it to Sadie, who rewarded her with a fond pat on the head.

"Hi," I said, scratching the itch of magic under my arm.

Sadie nodded at me and Eli waved, laughing in horror at Naveen's insistence that the fish heads baked into the crust of Stargazy Pie, so they "gazed" up at you, was perfectly normal.

Shaking her head, Daya groused that anyone who thought that was better than Marmite on toast was clearly wrong.

No need to worry about how they were doing, they'd settled in just fine. I mustered up a smile. That wasn't fair to Daya and Naveen. I was grateful to them for their kindness and hospitality. Daya, in particular, since she'd model treating magic as perfectly ordinary. If she could help guide them, they'd be in good hands.

Still, I felt shut out, watching someone else raise my kid, and fair or not, I wanted to stamp my foot. Daya had been my doctor, my friend. I was the one who'd had to weather Naveen's jeers and slurs, and yet, Eli and Sadie had slotted right in.

Almost like they'd reformed as a new family.

I rubbed my palm against my chest, swallowing the thickness in my throat. "Ready to go?"

"Interesting outfit." Naveen stood up. "I'll grab my keys."

Holding my shirt closed with one hand, I gave Sadie a one-shouldered hug. "Anything special happening at work today, sweetie?"

"Not really."

There was a honk and Sadie grabbed her lunch, shoving it in the backpack on the counter. "That's Asha. Gotta run." She picked up Evani, spinning the child around. "We'll play Candyland later, okay?"

Evani nodded, hearts practically floating in her eyes.

Sadie slung the backpack over her shoulder. "Bye, parents."

"Bye, spawn," Eli said.

"Bye, kiddo. Love you."

"Yup." She jogged out of the kitchen.

Evani followed, but Daya scooped her daughter up by the waist, passing me with a sympathetic squeeze of my shoulder.

"Let's get you dressed, monster." She blew a raspberry on her daughter's stomach and sailed out of the room.

I leaned onto the counter, blinking quickly to dispel the moisture in my eyes.

"Sades needs to blow off steam," Eli said. "Last night was a lot to deal with. She saw firsthand what an angry vampire looks like, she found out you can travel through some alternate dimension, and then she had to leave her home because of potential demons."

I sighed. "I know."

"But our kid is resilient. All will be normal soon enough."

"You certainly seem well." I forced a lecherous smile onto my face.

"Get your mind out of the gutter. He's a good guy." Eli removed the apron, picked his police shield up off the table, and clipped it to his belt. "Nav said he'd have some of his people watch our house in case any demons showed."

Eli got to call him Nav?! I mean, Naveen had people? And why was Eli fiddling with his empty coffee mug? He was always Mr. Confidence when it came to potential fuckbuddies. He couldn't *like* like him, could he? There wasn't someone nicer like a cocaine-sniffing stockbroker or a sleezy used car salesman he could be attracted to?

I didn't get a chance to pry further because Eli caught sight of the time and hurried off to work.

I had to face facts.

Fact: Eli and Sadie had gotten cozy with the Kumars in the space of one night. Fact: I was jealous. Fact: I had until tonight to find Banim Shovavim blood for Zev to complete the ward or our home was a write-off. Fact: Laurent wasn't speaking to me.

With a heavy heart, I called Ryann and asked to speak with Elizabeta. Given the current complication with my blood, even she might not be able to help, but if she could, it was the least horrible of all my current options.

There was a long silence.

I checked my signal. "Hello?"

229

"It's not a possibility anymore," Ryann said curtly.

A slither of unease snaked down my spine. "Why not? Because I said no before?"

"One moment," she said. There was the sound of footsteps and voices getting fainter. Then I heard birds and the heavy slam of a door.

"You don't have a car," I said, totally confused.

"It belongs to the department. I came out here because I didn't want to be overheard. You're playing a dangerous game, Miriam."

I blinked. "What are you talking about?"

Upstairs, Evani yelled about wanting to wear blue shorts, exactly like Sadie. Oh, dear.

"Contacting Saps about the Torquemada Gloves? You're skirting the line of violating the prime directive." Ryann had taken a lot of tones with me: ditzy, sad, supportive, but never stern.

I sat down hard. "You're right and I'm sorry. That honestly didn't occur to me at the time. I was trying to get information about a relic."

"A demon-cursed one," Ryann said.

"How did you even know?"

"We have people who scan all digital mediums for certain keywords."

I smacked the table, sending pancake crumbs flying. "You spied on my private correspondence?"

"I did my job and made sure that magic remained hidden. Do you know how hard it was to get Lonestars in a foreign country to take care of this without revealing your name?"

Upstairs, Daya's soothing tone turned more heated. "For the last time, Evani, those shorts are in the wash. You can wear the green ones or a dress."

I'd have gone up to offer my sympathy if my head wasn't reeling about this new development. "What did you do to them?"

Ryann made a sound of impatience. "Erased their memories about the gloves."

Hitting the button for the speaker, I scrambled to check my emails. All correspondence on the matter was gone. I'd spoken to Veronica only a few hours ago. How was this even possible?

"Pink shirt!" Evani wailed.

I glanced at the ceiling. Good lungs on that kid. And no soundproofing between floors.

Naveen told Evani to take a breath and use her words, which resulted in the three-year-old screeching.

Plugging my ear, I jacked the volume up on the phone to better hear Ryann.

"Elizabeta knows someone requested assistance with a ward against demons," she said. "There's no reason this gloves incident should get on her radar, but if we push forward with the ward, it increases the likelihood of her finding out what you did. You don't want her getting involved."

"Which was exactly what I said from the beginning." Pacing the length of the kitchen, I gestured in short jabs even though Ryann couldn't see me. "You and Eli were the ones pushing for her when I explicitly told you that Zev would take care of it. I keep being accused of not knowing what I'm doing, but I was right in this case. I just wasn't believed." It was bad enough I was playing catch-up, but how was I supposed to fight against people's preconceptions that I was clueless?

Ryann was silent.

Naveen marched into the kitchen, a screaming Evani in green shorts and nothing else tucked under his arm like a football. He plopped her down at the plastic kids' table. "Time out."

Her tantrum almost drowned out Ryann's words.

"You still brought those Sapiens into this matter," the

Lonestar said.

"I understand not wanting to start a witch hunt by revealing magic," I said, moving out onto the porch, "but fuck, Ryann, we live in the real world and lines get messy. The gloves are a real item that were named after a historical figure and Torquemada skinned other victims. Are you positive there were no other resulting demon relics?"

"No," she said tightly.

"And yet you haven't scrubbed all the academic journals or the memories of Sapien professors who teach about his torture methods. It seems to me that there's a lot of playing fast and loose with when the prime directive is implemented, and I resent being slapped down for something that has no clear rules." I leaned against the railing, exhausted by the impossibility of my situation.

"I appreciate that it feels that way to you."

I rolled my eyes. Of all the passive-aggressive bullshit. "You know how you had leeway to tell your dad about magic without any blowback and you would have done the same with Eli if I hadn't beat you to it? Well, consider this my leeway. I'm asking questions about the relic to save a Ohrist's life."

"Whose?"

"Client confidentiality." No way was I giving up Tatiana. "I'll get you the attacker, you keep me off the radar of any higher-ups. Deal?"

"Deal," she said after a pause.

I hung up and shoved my phone in my pocket, rolling my eyes at Naveen staring at me through the open door. "What?" I stomped back into the kitchen.

"You lasted longer than I do talking to her. I generally have about ten seconds before I want to throttle her."

Evani wailed, making sure we both saw her, and even mad, I laughed because that had been a total ploy for attention.

"Trade you children?" Daya had returned, watching her brother stand guard over the toddler. She looked worn down.

I hugged her. "Nah. I've sunk too much money into mine."

She sighed, resting her head on my shoulder briefly, before waving a pink shirt at her daughter. "You want to wear this? Go ahead. I'll just look like a shit parent for sending my kid to preschool in the same dirty shirt for a second day in a row," she added in a mutter.

"Aw, sweetie." I made a tsk sound. "You'll be judged for so much more than that. Are you going to brush her hair?"

"I hate you."

"Love you too. And thank you for taking care of my family. I mean it."

"I'm the one who invited them," Naveen said.

"Yes, you're brilliant," Daya said airily. "Evani, enough. Pink shirt?"

The toddler's cries calmed down to shuddery breaths. "Juice box."

Naveen rolled his eyes but got her a drink and she allowed herself to be dressed. I wished my problems could be solved with fruit concentrate.

After bidding Daya and Evani goodbye, Naveen and I got into his Porsche, though when I slammed the door a little too hard, he glared at me.

"Sorry." I hit the speed dial for Eli's cell.

"Detective Chu," he said.

"You owe me an apology."

"For what?"

"Call Ryann. And next time listen to me." I hung up. Not saying goodbye was a fun power move. Fine, Tatiana. I'd go along with your plans, but I'd also study and learn until the pupil became the master.

"Kicking butt and taking names," Naveen said.

For a second, I thought he meant Tatiana, then I realized he was talking about Eli. "He deserved it."

Naveen signaled, checking not only the rearview, but both side mirrors before he smoothly merged into the next lane.

I'd never examined driving as a means of psychological insight, but if I did, the way that I stayed at the speed limit while often invoking a slew of curses for my fellow drivers made me shake my head. The rule follower with underlying rage.

Tatiana was a nightmare on the road, totally confident in her abilities, while causing deep fear in everyone unlucky enough to be in her path—or her car.

I leaned my cheek against the cool glass. No rolling down windows in this vehicle. Naveen had adjusted the air conditioning immediately after starting the engine.

He drove like a man with a goal. His movements, be they changing gears with his manual transmission, changing lanes, or turning, were done with ease, calm, and absolute focus.

Unlike me, he didn't screech to a halt at red lights, sending passengers rebounding into their seat belts. He had this uncanny knack for assessing the perfect distance at which he should begin braking, coming to an even halt every time.

Nor did he possess Laurent's style of absolute control that was a breath away from smashing into a guard rail, should some button in his head flip.

"Stop watching me. I'm a good driver." Naveen drummed his fingers on the steering wheel, waiting for the red light to change.

"Why do you have people? What exactly do you do?"

"I kill demons and demon accessories." He drawled it in the Texan voice of Hank Hill, the cartoon character, and I laughed. "Did you think I was a lone wolf?"

I snapped a loose thread off the hem of my skirt. "No, there can only be one of those. Speaking of which," I feigned a casual interest, "did his plane arrive on time?"

"Haven't spoken to him. As for my people or further information on what I do, it's classified."

Intrigued, I half turned toward him. "Like Black Ops, classified? Do you work for some shadowy government organization who'd deny your existence should you botch a job? Do the Lonestars know?"

He ignored me, powering on the stereo. The smooth crooning of Robbie Williams's "Millennium" flowed through the speakers.

"Not what I expected." I grinned evilly. "You had frosted tips in your late teens, didn't you?"

"Coming from a woman dressed like a..." He raked a glance over me. "I don't even have words for that outfit. Stones and glass houses, darling."

"I was rush-packing to avoid demon hordes and I grabbed the wrong things."

"Mmm." He didn't sound convinced. He also didn't answer any further questions about his work or his best friend's travel itinerary, so I changed tactics while enjoying Robbie Williams's greatest hits.

"How does a person go to the demon realm?"

"They don't." He shifted gears, his biceps flexing. He was broader across the shoulders than Laurent, and his insouciance only added to his overall handsomeness. Combine that with the intelligence gleaming out of his eyes, his posh accent, and his warrior's alertness and I understood Eli's attraction.

"At least one did," I said. "The man disappeared for three weeks and when he returned, he'd been cured of a terminal cancer diagnosis thanks to a demon parasite who spent the next thirty years puppeteering his shadow."

Naveen cut in front of the car in the lane to our right. There was a screech of tires and a blaring horn behind us.

I yelped, digging my fingers into the sides of my seat and pumping imaginary brakes.

He jammed the sports car into a parking spot at the curb and wrenched up the emergency brake with a wildness that had me reaching behind my back for the door handle. "You're lying."

"I'm not. I swear. It was the Lonestar who covered up my parents' murders when I was a teen."

"Where is he now?"

"Dead." I flinched at his furious expression, Robbie Williams's "Rock DJ," providing a discordant soundtrack. "Don't look at me like that. I didn't do it. I went to talk to him about what had happened and someone or something broke his neck and set his house on fire. Exactly like with my parents."

Naveen slammed his hand on the wheel, then pulled out his phone and punched in a number. "It's me. Find out every-thing you can about—" He snapped his fingers at me.

"Not a dog." I crossed my arms.

Naveen shot me a smile with too many teeth. "His name. Please."

"Fred McMurtry. Tatiana compiled a dossier..." I trailed off under his withering look.

Naveen pressed me for a few more details, growing grimmer and grimmer as I filled him in on Fred's memory loss and rote recitation of answers pertaining to the missing three weeks of his life and the fire set in my family home. But he relayed it all to the other person, issuing further details to look into. "Was he kidnapped? Did he go willingly? If we have crossover happening..." He pressed his lips together, shaking his head at whatever the other person was saying. "Yes, thank you, Clea. I understand that."

I couldn't make out Clea's words, but she spoke in a monotone. Naveen watched me while he listened.

"Any movement on Miriam's place, I want to know about it," he said. "Thanks." He shoved the phone in his pocket. "Is this why you wanted the ward?"

I moistened my dry lips. "Yes." When he didn't stop staring at me, I nervously tucked a strand of hair behind my ear. "What?"

"Laurent's magic, my hunt for the gloves, a human in the demon realm, why is it you're connected to all these disparate things?"

While he sounded more resigned than suspicious, a flash of rage flared up, tightening my chest. But it just as quickly vanished, replaced by a deep fatigue.

"I wish I knew," I said softly, absently touching the domino tile that I'd slid into my pocket when packing at Tatiana's.

"You have to ask Laurent for his blood," Naveen said.

I turned startled eyes to his because that was the last thing I expected to hear.

"If you don't complete the ward while the vampire is on board..." He sighed, merging back into traffic with calm purpose and no trace of the urgency he'd exhibited moments earlier.

"Right?" I said blithely. "I have enough friends." After a sympathetic look from Naveen, the one person who appreciated how much losing Laurent would hurt, I stared resolutely out the window at the passing city. It didn't help me come to terms with the fact that the shifter was my sole option. I sighed. I'd go see him once we'd visited the demon.

However, when Robbie Williams started in on a darker haunting tune, singing about how he didn't understand his role, about all the life running through his veins, and not wanting to die, I punched the music off.

Naveen pulled up in front of a store on a sharply angled corner at the edge of Gastown, outside the gentrified zone. It had bars over the windows and a bright red door; I'd driven past this place dozens of times, but never gone in.

Frowning, I unclipped my seat belt. "This is where your contact is?"

Naveen turned the engine off. "Give me the quick rundown."

I told him everything I'd learned about the dybbuk familiar and her host, finishing up with the Wise Brothers' fact that the only way to stop the curse was to comply or kill the woman.

"But I disagree," I said. "If we can null her dybbuk, then the curse can't be carried out. Find out whether the demon knows how to neutralize the magic. We also need her name and location to get the jump on her before the deadline."

"Got it. Now remember," Naveen said, "Chester looks harmless, but he's not."

We exited the car and my nerves at this encounter twisted into a different kind of anxiety at the sight of Laurent, farther down the block, pulling off his motorcycle helmet.

My heart sped up.

The shifter stilled, then looked directly at me.

I lifted a hand in a tentative greeting.

He gave me a single curt nod then busied himself locking up his bike.

Naveen took long, purposeful strides over to him, a scowl on his face, with me hurrying behind him. "Why must you make everything seven times harder?" he said. "Chester hates you."

"The feeling is mutual." Laurent's voice was rough, raspier than usual. His olive skin had a wan pallor and there were faint purple bruises under eyes devoid of all their usual luster.

I drifted closer to him, trying to wrap myself in his scent.

"Then why are you here?" Naveen said. "I've got this."

"Because it doesn't just involve you but my—"

Naveen raised a pointed eyebrow and damn it, my breath caught waiting for his answer.

"Aunt," Laurent said. "I'm not letting the fucker wiggle

238

out of answers." He glared at me, baring his teeth. "Stop sniffing me, Miriam."

My mouth fell open, a fiery blush hitting my cheeks, and I stumbled back, allowing him to stomp past me.

Naveen's eyebrow shot higher, so I flipped him off and followed Laurent, intent on getting through this interrogation as quickly as possible and making the shifter talk to me.

The sign over the door had a quaint nostalgic feel to it that I would never attribute to a demon proprietor. Black filigree decorated the edges of a cream oval, much like a cameo brooch. In it was a painting of a curvy woman with dark hair tumbling out of her updo, her white Victorian nightgown spilling off one shoulder. She sat at an antique makeup table under the word "Curios" written in script.

I smiled at its vintage charm, but as I crossed under the sign, "ity killed the cat" flashed in black next to "Curios," and the woman disappeared, replaced by glowing red eyes and an evil floating Cheshire-cat grin.

Shivering, I froze, but Naveen clamped a hand on my shoulder.

"Show no fear," he murmured and nudged me inside.

I wasn't sure if he meant the demon or Laurent.

19

THE CURIO STORE REEKED OF PATCHOULI, COURTESY of an incense cone blazing away on a holder. Given that's what dybbuks smelled like to Laurent, it was no surprise he was already bristling.

Chester, the proprietor, smirked, knowing exactly the discomfort this induced in the shifter. For a demon, even wearing a human glamor, he was surprisingly dapper. I expected some burly douchebag, but he was slender, in a gray pinstriped vest, a white shirt with the sleeves rolled up, and a gray tie. He looked about thirty, with blue hair falling into his eyes of the same shade. I wasn't sure the hair was a dye job.

He had a patch of rashy skin on the crook of his right elbow that I took for eczema, but upon a closer look, saw it had the texture of lizard's skin.

The store was a cross between a hoarder's lair and a magician's trove of wonders, goods spilling off every surface: glass candelabras, stuffed birds, old clocks all displaying different times, and tiny framed vintage postcards.

I spun slowly, taking in the old palmistry guides tacked to the walls next to out-of-date maps. A metal bird cage with a mannequin head inside it shared window space with a replica dinosaur skeleton holding a baton in its mouth, while the long glass counter that Chester stood behind was crammed with mini faery figurines under glass, bells, and baby doll heads. I shuddered. Too many eyes.

Every wall was papered in strips of exquisite vintage wrapping paper from white lacy flowers to red poppies almost cartoonishly large, while a dizzying chandelier hung over the counter, the rest of the ceiling dotted with paper parasols.

A narrow staircase led to a basement, the dragon mounted on the wall along the railing beckoning patrons to enter its cave.

Overall, the store had a kind of kooky appeal.

We were the only ones here, plus Naveen had locked the door, so he spoke freely, explaining about the Banim Shovavim magic and asking if there was a way to stop the dybbuk without harming the woman.

Chester sprayed the top of the counter with cleaner, vinegar cutting through the patchouli smell. Not an improvement. "A dybbuk familiar is unkillable."

"But isn't her condition similar to someone who's enthralled?" I said. "Those dybbuks can be dispatched."

The demon vigorously rubbed a smudge with paper towel. "It's similar only in the most superficial way," he said primly. He barely made eye contact with me, like I was some groupie brought along by the rock stars.

"What if we took out the Banim Shovavim?" Laurent said, voicing my fear about our sole option.

"The dybbuk wouldn't survive." Chester tossed the paper in a small trashcan, stowing the cleaner behind the counter.

Laurent nodded. "That's it, then."

"There has to be another way," I said, ignoring Naveen's slashing motion across his throat. "One that allows her to live while handing her over to the Lonestars for justice."

Chester laughed. "Justice like Deadman's Island? Better to knock the wily bitch off."

Laurent propped an elbow on the counter. "Sounds to me like you know her."

"It's hardly a stretch what the Lonestars would do, given her magic." The demon knocked his elbow away.

Laurent's hand shot out, sliding Chester's tie around his own fist. "Who is she?" He wrapped the demon's tie tighter and tighter, forcing the creature to rise onto tiptoe and lean forward practically bent double in order not to be strangled. The shifter might as well have been putting on a pair of shoes for all the emotion he displayed.

Was this cold anger all that was left of Laurent without his Ohrist magic? I stepped farther away from him.

"I don't know." Spikes glistening with iridescent tips burst out from the demon's palms, but Laurent grabbed Chester's arm and torqued it, snapping the humerus.

I took a steadying breath and Naveen sighed.

The demon cradled his arm to his chest. "You're insane."

Laurent leaned over the counter. "You haven't seen the half of it." His tone was almost conversational. "Now give me her name."

Blood leaked from the demon's tear ducts. "I'll never help you. And you'll never find her on your own."

"Well done, mate." Naveen elbowed Laurent in the back, hard, then muscled in between his friend and Chester. "Need I remind you that you stay in Vancouver at my pleasure?" He gestured around the store. "You want to keep this message drop and neutral meeting space for your kind open? Don't get on my bad side."

Who was Naveen? The godfather of the demon world?

"You talk a big game, Kumar," the demon said. "But without this place, you'd be even more hard-pressed to keep a lid on us."

"Wow, I think he's got you there," Laurent said.

Naveen glanced over his shoulder. "Do shut up."

The two of them were making things worse. Men.

I rapped on the counter. "Is Torquemada a demon? You know, the Grand Inquisitor in Spain in the 1400s? These two idiots can't tell me anything, but you look like you have the skinny on a lot of intel."

Chester sniffed and shook out his now-healed arm. "No. He was one of yours."

"And the Torquemada Gloves? Who was the demon who cursed them?" It didn't matter whose skin they were made of, but maybe finding that demon could help us save both Tatiana and the Banim Shovavim?

"You're wasting time with a long shot," Laurent sneered.

I planted my legs wide, my chin up, and my hands on my hips. "But choking him was a brilliant idea?" I nodded at Chester. "I apologize for him." The saying "you could catch more flies with honey than vinegar" applied even to demons. "Do you know who the demon was?"

"No one does."

"But the gloves were part of the blood libel in Avila in 1491?" I said.

"Yes. The demon was attracted by the evil done in the name of the Inquisition. It is said that he rampaged through the inquisitors, his pleasure and his power magnified in torturing the torturers," Chester said. "It is said that those men ended up shredded like they'd been torn apart by a ravening wolf." The demon flicked his gaze to Laurent.

"Bit before my time," he drawled.

"Then our business is done." Chester headed for the door to unlock it, but Naveen stabbed the light staff through the demon's hands, wrenching them above Chester's head.

"Finally," Laurent said.

Naveen chucked the demon under the chin with his free hand. "Give us the woman's name, Chester. You're wasting my time."

The demon's skin sizzled, black bits flaking off. The staff hummed, its light growing darker and darker as the demon's

243

features grew more and more pinched, and his breath hitched. "Stop."

Patches of green skin bloomed over the demon's body, his hands mangled blobs of charred flesh.

"Give me a reason to," Naveen said.

"I'll make you a deal." The demon's voice had turned guttural, reminding me of a Klingon.

"Let's hear it," I said. "Take out the staff so Chester can speak."

Naveen glared at me, but he yanked the weapon free.

Chester sagged against the counter. His hands were gone, his forearms withered to burned stumps covered in pus-filled welts.

"State the deal." Naveen made the staff vanish.

"There's an item I'd like retrieved from a colleague of mine." Chester sat down on a tall stool, his breathing shallow. Green skin incrementally knit together. "I'll give you the woman's name and location once it's in my possession."

"A demon artifact, I presume." Naveen's lips pressed into a thin line of displeasure.

"Done," Laurent said.

There was no doubt in my mind that the second Laurent had that information he'd go directly there and kill the Banim Shovavim. I had to reason with him not to do anything hasty.

Naveen's jaw clenched but he didn't contradict his friend. "What is it?"

The demon took a labored breath. "His eye."

With his wound healed, a glamor once more spread over the demon's actual skin like a pebble rippling a lake until he looked human again. There was the tiny matter that he now had six fingers on his left hand, but hey, the eczema was gone.

"You had his eye previously?" I scratched my chin. "How does that work?"

"It's detachable," Chester said, like that answered the

244

question. "Give me a moment to complete regeneration and I'll tell you where to find him."

"Are we going into the demon realm?" I asked.

Chester fixed me with a cold stare. "Humans do not go into the demon realm."

Wrong. Thanks for playing. "My mistake. Naveen, you get the directions. Laurent and I will wait for you downstairs." We were hashing all of this out right now.

I marched into the basement, expecting Laurent to follow. Arguments crowded my brain, but then I hit the bottom of the stairs and saw the sole item in the small room: a huge wooden cabinet with dozens of small drawers.

Ignoring the heavy glass head with creepy marble eyes on top of the cabinet, I opened the drawers.

One held nothing but unused fuses, another dozens of felt finger puppets. A third drawer yielded tiny Etch A Sketch sets. Decks of tarot cards, toy magnifying glasses, ceramic knobs, packages to grow your own crystals—for a moment, all my anger fell away, replaced by the delight of unearthing treasure.

Though I kept glancing at the stairs.

By the time Laurent finally deigned to join me, I didn't want an argument. I wanted us to be us again. Feel like a team.

"This reminds me of old library card catalogues," I said. The next drawer held a stash of tiny makeup kits with fake beards. "You're probably too young to remember those."

"Les catalogues de bibliothèques. I'm not that much younger than you." Laurent peeked into a drawer with stickers of 1950s pinup girls. "They had…" He made the shape of a rectangle.

"Index cards, yeah." I pulled out an oblong glass item, tapping a finger against it before recognizing the old-fashioned vacuum tube. "Going through these drawers reminds me of all the hours I spent searching through index cards for weird and wonderful book treasures when I was younger. Losing all sense of time as I chased down different topics from one drawer to the next." I smiled wistfully as I closed a drawer of plastic scorpions. "Flipping through card catalogues definitely wasn't everyone's idea of fun, but for someone who'd always memorized her library card number, it was mine."

Digital catalogues may have been faster and easier to use, but I'd mourned the loss of those cabinets, every drawer its own map to new and wondrous secrets. Just like the ones here.

Laurent poked around in the cabinet as well, but the silence between us didn't regain any more companionability.

My palms clammy, I focused on a trove of silly mustaches like they held all the answers. Or any at all. "We need to talk about what happened. Find a solution."

He stepped closer, and no matter how hard my gaze burrowed into the three-inch gap of the drawer, it wasn't enough to hide the ragged rise and fall of his chest.

Between the Kefitzat Haderech and the Wise Brothers, Laurent had been ripped apart into painful shards, and without his Ohrist magic he was fusing back together wrong, like a bone that was never set properly.

"Bien. Let's write a list." He braced an elbow on the top of the cabinet, propping his head on his hands and wearing a lazy half-lidded stare.

"That's not what I meant." I untangled two Slinky toys in one of the drawers, almost preferring outright anger to sarcasm, though it was justified.

After all my concern about what might happen to Emmett if he took the potion, how could I have forced that vial on Laurent? Was there really no other way at that moment or had I blindly charged in, believing I knew best? I could tell myself that I didn't think that it would take his shifting away forever, but Zev had warned me that magic was unpredictable.

I'd had that fact, but I didn't take it into consideration. Did my problems stem not from a lack of information, but from a surfeit? Because I'd been picking and choosing which facts mattered, which I needed to act on? Not to mention, for all my piercing character assessments, I'd failed to realize how important and necessary Laurent's Ohrist magic was to how he viewed himself as a person. I'd focused on the thing we had in common, his Banim Shovavim magic, and dismissed the rest of it.

"You're right," he said. "There are no solutions. Only outcomes. Ohrist magic returns." He ticked off his index finger. "Or not." He ticked off his middle finger then held the two fingers up. "We won't be overwhelmed by possibility."

I opened one last drawer buying time to calm down. It was filled with glow-in-the-dark stars. "The sun's rim dips; the stars rush out; at one stride comes the dark," I murmured.

"Instead of the cross, the albatross around my neck was hung," Laurent parried back glibly.

He knew "Rime of the Ancient Mariner," but of all the lines he could quote, he chose that one? My jaw tensed. I wasn't an albatross weighing him down.

"We'll get this eye Chester wants," I said tersely, "and he'll hand over the woman's name and location. Then—"

"I'll kill her." Laurent's eyes were no longer the deep verdant of a rolling meadow but the cold depth of a glacier. "But you go on playing Nancy Drew and getting your little facts about ancient history. So helpful."

"You sure you can take her?" I regretted the words as soon as I said them.

"Even without my shifter powers, I'm good for one or two things." He widened his eyes in mock sympathy. "Too bad you can't say the same about your magic and that ward."

My head throbbed. "Who told you?"

247

"Tatiana." Laurent smiled coldly, a smug satisfaction in his expression. "What a relief that I can bail you out though." He paused. "Like always."

Laurent had refused to fight Naveen over the revelation of the shifter's Banim Shovavim magic, allowing the man to physically harm him, but he battered me with his contempt. He'd never unleashed his cruel side like this, and while he was certainly entitled to his anger, he hadn't said word one to Naveen whereas with me he methodically landed these barbs for maximum bruising.

"*Always?*" I slammed the drawer with the stars shut. "Like when I saved you from BatKian's compulsion? When I got you out of the cage that the Lonestars had thrown you in? Cages, which you hate, remember?"

"You forgot when I was caged in the air with hundreds of people, not knowing whether my shifter magic might hit because of you." His saccharine voice stung worse than yelling would have. "You've been cleaning up the messes from situations you got me into."

"Here we go again, the reconstructionist history according to Laurent Amar!" I ticked off items on my fingers. "You tangled with Zev because you took on a paying job. A job, I might add, that wasn't even about helping me, but finding Mei Lin. And if it hadn't been for me, you'd be on Deadman's Island, accused of killing Raj Jalota." I jabbed him in the chest. "Every single time, I've been trying to save *you*, so don't worry about me asking for a damn thing."

Laurent kicked the heavy curio cabinet hard enough to rattle it, but there was nothing left of me for him to shred.

"How lucky for you that you don't have anything to be at fault for," I said. "Even Naveen not jumping to conclusions about your magic was on him. How delightful to be so blameless." I snapped my fingers. "Hang on, you have Banim Shovavim magic too. But I bet that I'm the one who should

248

have known that taking you into the KH would anger it, right?"

"You were supposed to know not to risk me in the first place!" He swept his arm along the top of the cabinet, and I ducked as a glass head flew across the room and shattered into jagged shards. Even with a vat of glue, it could never be put right.

The crash had been shockingly loud, the violence of it hitting me like a bucket of cold water.

Laurent had spun away, clenching and unclenching his fists, but I went numb.

I laughed. "Real rich that the man who makes a point of never asking for support, who's the first one into the fire, is also furious that I put him in harm's way."

He sucked in a raspy breath, his eyes glassy and his defined jaw clenched so tight, I worried he'd start spitting teeth.

"Laurent?" I reached out, but he hunched over like an archer's bow, his hair sweeping the floor, and he shuddered violently.

His shirt exploded into tatters with a percussion of loud snapping sounds and his muzzle shot out from his face with a shocking suddenness. He was shifting, which should have been cause for celebration, but it wasn't happening in stages. More like his magic had been jammed and something had shoved it free with brutal force.

His shoes were flung off and his hindlegs got stuck in his jeans for a moment, which would have been comic were it not for how his skin flayed off his body, replaced by wild tufts of white fur bursting out over the animal's torso.

His entire transformation took less than a minute.

The wolf plowed repeatedly headfirst into the wall, the pinched noises he made having a choked quality to them. The plaster cracked, dusting his fur with white powder.

"Stop! You'll hurt yourself."

The wolf stood there for a second, his flanks heaving, then he raised his head and let out a deafening howl of rage and pain.

Laurent had gone over the brink.

I could bring him back. I had to.

Even if he hated me for it.

20

I DIDN'T GET A CHANCE TO DO ANYTHING MORE
beyond flatten myself against a wall, the wolf knocking into
me as he bounded past the card catalogue and up the rickety
stairs.

Naveen gave a confused cry, then there was the sound of
breaking glass, the Brit swearing and the demon laughing.

I went after Laurent on rubbery legs, almost crawling up
the stairs.

The wolf pulled his head free of the hole he'd bashed in
the glass door, blood oozing out from a nasty gash on one
side.

"You'll pay for that," Chester sniffed, now fully healed.

Naveen fumbled with the lock, imploring Laurent to calm
the fuck down. He'd barely gotten the door open before the
wolf practically tripped him in his haste to escape.

"Arse!" Naveen shook a fist at the wolf's back.

"Concerned, are we?" Chester smirked at me, twisting my
ring around my finger.

I clasped my hands behind my back with a shrug. "Just
annoyed at him being a prick."

I marched back downstairs, my heart racing. I'd messed

up, but I hadn't realized how badly. Laurent's anger wasn't about his suspended powers; it was about him. Had I committed the grievous sin that our friendship couldn't come back from?

Naveen stomped down the stairs, crunched over broken glass, and stopped. "What'd I miss?" he said lightly.

I lowered my voice so the demon wouldn't hear. "Is Laurent..." *All right? Sane?*

Naveen's expression turned bleak. "I don't know."

"It's broad daylight," I said worriedly. "Someone will see him and call animal services."

"They won't catch him before he gets to the Park."

"How can you be sure?" I kicked one of the creepy marble eyes from the broken glass head out of my way.

"I'm sure. But just in case." He dictated a voice text. "Clea, call the Lonestars and give them the heads-up. Laurent may not be capable of shifting right now, so leave him alone."

Naveen jammed the end of his staff into the wall across from the cabinet. The magic weapon shivered, and the plaster rippled, revealing a pink, fleshy portal. Glistening jellylike strands coated the tubular folds ringing the slitted entrance. "The demon is through here."

I clenched my pelvic muscles in horror. "You want me to step into a lubed-up demon vagina?"

"Absolutely not. I want you to wait for me. And keep your distance from Chester until I get back because he's in a right mood and you don't look capable of diplomacy right now." Naveen pulled his still-vibrating weapon free.

Aaannd now all I could think of was Naveen, quivering staffs, and my ex. Ew. Ew. Ew.

"I'm going with you."

"Guess again. I'm in charge here and you're staying. You're not in the right headspace for this. Not that I blame you," he added.

"I'll be fine." I grabbed one of the tubular folds and shuddered.

Naveen raised an eyebrow.

"I don't trust you"—I batted an errant goo-strand away from my face—"to exchange that eye for that woman's name, all right?" A glop of mucus dripped into my hair. "Ugh! So I'm coming along to make sure you don't destroy it. How about that?"

His eyes widened for a second, his brows furrowed, but he schooled his features into an insouciant expression. "By all means."

Feeling guilty, angry, and hating every single thing about my life, I shoved past Naveen and into the darkness of Pussy Galore, whimpering when the squelchy portal made a wet, sucking noise at my entrance and slime slithered down the side of my neck.

The entrance was tight. "You couldn't have fingered it first and loosened it up?" I spat out the taste of vinegar, trying not to breathe.

My attempt to lighten the mood was met with silence.

Finally, I broke through the mucous membrane into a tunnel made of the same pink fleshy material. But where the entrance had the drop-of-a-hat wetness of a young woman, this section was dry, its folds withered. Avoiding a telltale glance at my own perimenopausal lady parts, I raked slime out of my hair, wiping it on a tunnel wall that was tepid to the touch. Every inhale was like breathing in a sauna, the air a sharp burn in my lungs.

Naveen held his staff aloft, providing a warm glow of light to navigate by. "It's perfectly pleasant once you get inside."

I fell in step behind him. "If this isn't the demon realm," I said, "where are we?"

"A lair or a burrow," Naveen said. "Certain demons carve them out to stay in when they come to earth."

We hit a dead end and turned around, retracing our footsteps.

"Too cheap to stay in a hotel, huh?" I licked my lips, which were drying out in the heat. "And this lair isn't warded?"

"Demons would never lower themselves to bother with wards," Naveen said. "Might as well put out a neon sign saying, 'Come and get me, I'm easy prey.'"

"But it's a hidden space?" My foot caught in a crack and I stumbled, narrowly catching myself before I fell. "Like Ohrists build?"

"It's hidden, but you've got it backward." Naveen raised the staff high at a junction, peering into the gloom before choosing the right-hand branch. "We got the idea from demons."

It was slow going with all the twists, turns, and dead ends, the lair made creepier by the occasional reflective surfaces in the same slit shape as the portal entrance, which Naveen forbade me from looking at on pain of death.

I kept my eyes on the uneven ground. "Why can't I look?"

"Same reason Jews cover mirrors when they sit shiva," he said.

"So, we don't check our hair while in a period of mourning?"

"No." His voice was laced with forced patience. "Demons and evil spirits are attracted to grief, to an emptiness in the soul. We don't want them coming in and tormenting us when we're so raw and vulnerable."

If mourning was emptiness, then what was this emotion filling me up to the point of bursting, this hurt that I was choking on? "I'm not grieving."

"Of course not."

My shoulders crept higher and higher. It was hard not to read these reflective ovals as dozens of eyes about to snap to life, and that once seen, we would forever be on their radar. Whoever "they" were.

A growling noise poured out of one such surface, startling me, and I jerked my head toward it, but before I could make eye contact, Naveen shoved me toward the opposite wall. I sucked in a breath, clipping my elbow on the tunnel wall.

"Thanks," I said quietly, shaking out my arm.

"Don't be that way."

"What way?"

"Mopey." He poked my shoulder. "Buck up or I'll feed you to the demon."

I made a snarky face.

Just around the next corner, we found ourselves in the middle of a high conical chamber dotted with stalactites.

"We're here." Naveen flipped his light staff to his other shoulder.

At the very back sat a giant gray slug demon with chubby rolls for arms and a bump of a head that looked like an afterthought drawn on by a child. The demon shoved a human arm dripping with slime into its gaping maw—the only feature on its face—convulsing as it swallowed it whole.

Hundreds of yellow blobby maggots excreted from the slug's rubbery skin, plopping to the floor in wriggling heaps that immediately rippled out across the cavern ground.

"It can't digest human fat," Naveen explained. "So it converts that into sentient scouts looking for more food."

My stomach lurched and I skittered back.

Human bones were scattered carelessly in the dirt: a tangle of femurs here, a pyramid of rib cages over there, a scalp with some hair close enough to kick. They crunched underfoot, the noise only muffled by the demon's slurping as it sucked down another piece of its poor victim.

"The many men, so beautiful! And they all dead did lie," I murmured, reciting another passage from "Rime of the

Ancient Mariner" while tracking the maggot scouts' progress. "Where's this eyeball?"

"Not sure."

A quivering ball of maggots rolled close to Naveen's foot and he knocked them away with his staff. They ricocheted into the wall with a wet splat, turning into the same translucent slime that the human arm had been coated in. Oh, gross.

The demon stilled, the air charging with a wild electricity that lifted the tiny hairs on my body.

I swallowed and raised my scythe.

Naveen readied his weapon.

The slug demon swelled, black lines mottling over its body, and the top of its head flipped open, revealing an enormous reflective Cyclops's eye, which swiveled toward us.

We had our target. Now to get it.

The maggots rose like a cresting wave, hanging suspended in midair for a hot second, then exploded outward.

We were engulfed. The scouts leeched on to me with tiny stinging suckers, secreting a sticky slime that made it difficult to move. No matter how many I knocked off, more took their places.

The bones underfoot turned slimy and slippery, making each step treacherous. I was terrified that if I fell, I'd be wrapped in slime like a fly in a spider's web and never get up.

My mouth was tightly closed, my eyes barely open enough to see. I felt like I was in a recreation of the locust plague from Pharaoh's time, except not as friendly.

A knot of maggots wriggled against my scalp. I shuddered, smothering a scream and frantically brushing the sentient fat-bots off. A handful climbed over my shoes, attempting to glue my feet to the floor with their slimy secretion.

I lifted my legs high, prancing like a show horse, and skidded on the slime underfoot. Barely keeping my balance, I smacked the scythe against my leg to knock more maggots off as I fought another onslaught of tiny foes, my arms and shoulders aching. "Naveen!"

"Bit busy," came the strained answer.

Inch by hard-won inch, I slid over tiny corpses, making my way forward to the main demon. While Naveen was silent, the intermittent flashes of his staff slicing through the air assured me he was still in fighting form.

At long last, I finished the maggots off and hurried to help Naveen with the demon, the two of us attacking it in tandem.

My chest heaving and my calves screaming from standing on tiptoe, I hacked off one of the demon's arms, tossing the bloody chunk on the ground.

The demon whacked Naveen with its other arm, sending the man staggering.

In retaliation, I tore out a hefty piece from its upper half, and it tumbled over.

Naveen stabbed his staff through its middle, and while the demon convulsed, he worked his light staff like a lever to pry the eye out for Chester.

Finally, the slug demon fell still, but my relief was short-lived, because the second Naveen had extracted the foot-long eye, the cavern rumbled, bits of the ceiling crumbling to the ground.

The ground roiled and bucked, flinging both of us into a wall.

"Fuck!" Naveen rubbed his shoulder, his fallen staff zipping back into his hand like Thor's hammer. "That's it." He slammed the staff into a jagged crack.

Light shot out...

And the cavern exploded, expelling us back into the basement of Chester's store. My arm hung at a funny angle, my puffy eyes stung, and bits of rock were matted in my hair.

"What. The. Fuck!" I cradled my poor shoulder, wishing I could telekinetically make Naveen's head explode.

"You're not dead. You're welcome." Naveen leaned on his

light staff like a crutch, his ankle twisted at an angle that was painful to behold.

He limped toward the stairs, the miraculously intact eye tucked under his arm. "Let's get the damn name and location and get out of here before I kill that weasel, Chester."

Laurent's clothes were scattered around the basement of the curio shop. His shirt was toast, but I grabbed his shoes and jeans, careful to tuck the pockets with his keys and stuff inside the bundle so I didn't lose anything.

I hit the top step, bumping into Naveen's back when he stopped suddenly. Stepping out from behind him, I tracked the trail of blood to the green lizard body and dropped one of Laurent's shoes.

Chester was dead, his corpse crisscrossed with angry red lacerations. His demon form was much broader than his human one, studded with suckers like an octopus and a few unidentifiable protrusions.

"This can't have all been for nothing," I moaned. I ran forward but Naveen grabbed me by the back of my shirt.

"Look." Wincing, he crouched by the body, moving aside Chester's untucked and torn shirt to pull a piece of paper out from under one hip.

I peered over his shoulder to read the message, which was smeared with a bloody fingerprint. It glistened against the white paper.

Trusting a demon not to sell you out? Don't make me doubt your ability to hand over the gloves. It was signed Frances Rothstein.

The Banim Shovavim had struck again.

The other shoe dropped.

21

FRANCES ROTHSTEIN. A JEW, A BANIM SHOVAVIM, and ultimately our target. I reread the note memorizing the left slant of her handwriting—just like mine—and the flourish on the "R" of her last name, drinking in the details because I might never meet anyone else so much like me. She must have been keeping tabs on me since the dybbuk attack at Blood Alley, because even if Chester had contacted her, she'd made the connection between us and Tatiana.

For whatever reason, she wanted me alive, and vice versa. I walked around the crime scene, searching for any other clues, but there was nothing. We'd meet when she intended us to and not a moment before, because unless she'd gotten herself banned from the KH like I had, she could be anywhere in the world right now. Even if I could follow, I'd need a location, not just her name.

Naveen kicked Chester's corpse. "You idiot." He whipped out his phone, barking orders about a cleanup to that Clea person he'd texted previously, then nodded at me. "You want a ride back to my place to pick up your car? I have to stay here but I can arrange for someone to take you."

"No, thanks. I'll make my own way there." I couldn't

handle Naveen's people right now, even if they were perfectly nice. I needed some normalcy—like an anonymous Uber driver.

Unfortunately, I'd forgotten what I looked like, covered in dirt and demon portal vagina slickness. The poor driver was reluctant to have me in his car until I promised him a healthy tip. With an extra twenty percent if he didn't speak to me.

When I went to put on my seat belt, I realized that I was still clutching Laurent's clothes. I placed them in my lap, desperately seeking a silver lining.

Frances was hellbent on getting the gloves, so she wouldn't go after Tatiana before the meeting. That was something. And Laurent had his magic back, though its rather explosive return didn't bode well for any repair to our friendship. Zev said that he'd been stuck in wolf form before. Was that after Laurent left his pack? The reason he'd left them in the first place?

How many times could someone come back from that?

I hurried to my car, startling when Daya's front door opened and Sadie stuck her head out, already back from work. I'd lost track of time. I concealed the worst of my filth by hiding behind the car. "Hey, kiddo."

"What happened to you?" She slid her feet into flip-flops, now changed out of her camp T-shirt into a pink crop top, and came outside.

I wasn't going to lie, but damn did I wish I could and have her believe me. "Demon. It's dead now," I assured her.

She paused. "Whatever. Caleb's on his way over and we're going to Metrotown," she said, naming a large mall nearby.

"Is anyone else home?" I said.

"No."

"Could we talk for a minute?"

Sadie crossed her arms. "Is this going to take long?"

I joined her on the stoop. "I don't know, Sades. Depends how snippy you're going to be."

260

She dropped her gaze to her feet.

I sighed, my shoulders slumping. Her entire reality had been upended in a very short amount of time and everything that had gone down at our house with Zev had only exacerbated that. "Look, everything I've dumped on you... It's a lot."

"You think?" she muttered.

"If you don't want to talk to me," I said through gritted teeth, "you've got Jude, and I'm going to get you, me, and your dad into therapy."

"With an Ohrist," she said flatly. "Not a regular person."

"Ohrists are regular people, but yes. Our therapist will have magic since I'd like them to believe what we're discussing. When your father and I got divorced, you were still so young that it wasn't as big an adjustment as if you'd been older. And even then, we did everything we could to make it easy for you, including living next door to each other. I don't expect this to be easy for you, but you have to find a way to deal with it because like it or not, it's not going away."

"So, suck it up?"

"Basically." I nudged her to get the frown off her face. "Come on. You're the kid who clapped her hands every night for a month because you believed in fairies. Are you really telling me there's not a tiny part of you that loves the fact that magic is real?"

"Obviously," she said in a huff.

"And yes, it's scary." I motioned at the demon gore painting my clothing.

"It's not even that. Mr. BatKian was mostly okay, and I'd have been way bitchier than he was if I'd been zapped into a fence. But I don't get to share magic with anyone. You have friends who have powers. Even Dad is getting to know Nav. But I have no one my age to talk about it to or share it with." She jammed her hands into her pockets. "It sucks."

"I felt that way for a long time with all my Sapien friends, so I understand." I tapped a finger against my lip. "Maybe I could help you find some magic friends."

Sadie shook her head, looking appalled. "No way. I'll deal."

"You sure? Because it's no trouble," I teased her, but she was in a tough and lonely position. Maybe Jude knew some kids that Sadie could meet.

Her phone buzzed with a text.

"Caleb just got off the bus. Go away." She gestured to my car.

I scraped some goo off my arm with my nail and held it up. "You don't want him to see me like this?"

"Mother! I'll go to therapy. I'll be nice. Now leave."

I kissed her head. "There. That wasn't so hard, was it?"

"I'm moving out with my sister," she grumbled.

Grinning, I got in my car and drove off, but my smile soon died because I wasn't sure where I was headed. How long did my employer hold grudges? Pulling over, I called Tatiana.

When she heard my voice on the phone, she grunted and handed it to Emmett, making a big production about how she'd been clear about not speaking to certain people before the meeting. Then she told Emmett to ask me if I'd tracked down the Banim Shovavim yet.

We were having the teen girl "I'm not talking to you, but I'm talking to you" talk? Bring it. I was much closer to adolescence than Tatiana was, and I had a teenager of my own. I knew these games all too well.

"Tell her that I sort of tracked the woman down," I said. "We have her name but not her location. Frances Rothstein."

"You tell her," Emmett said.

"I would if she was speaking to me."

Groaning, he relayed the message.

Tatiana's sniff of disapproval was worth a thousand words.

"We'll find her. You're not going to die."

"I'm not afraid of death," Tatiana said. Either Emmett had me on speaker or she'd wrested the cell away from him.

She'd been upset when she was first cursed and even Emmett had noticed a change in her behavior, resulting in him entertaining and distracting her. I'd assumed that because Tatiana was old, she must fear death, but she sounded peevish enough to be telling the truth. My first assumption had been wrong. I considered who she was and what she valued.

When I hit forty, I'd felt invisible and sidelined, but here was Tatiana still at the top of her game and celebrated globally as an artist. She kept mentioning her art, usually as part of a passive-aggressive comment, but just as I'd failed to recognize the importance of Laurent's shifter side, I hadn't fully comprehended what her painting meant to her.

Tatiana's fears weren't about dying.

"You're not finished living," I said.

"No kidding. I'm supposed to fly to New York soon and show my new pieces to my agent."

"Then ask Zev for the gloves."

"It's not his place to save me. It's your job and I suggest you do it," she said coolly and hung up.

Emmett texted me immediately after. *She asked. The vamp was a no go.*

I tapped the phone against my thigh, staring out the car window. If Tatiana was willing to eat crow and make herself look bad in front of Zev to try to get the gloves back, she was truly desperate, however unaffected she pretended to be.

Between Naveen, Laurent, and me, we had this. Anything else wasn't an option, but damn, did I wish there was. We were going into a worst-case scenario of Tatiana's life versus Frances's.

I tossed Laurent's clothes in my car. His keys, wallet, and phone were in his jeans, so the right thing to do would be to return them. If he'd shifted back to human, then we could discuss our plan for tomorrow since Naveen's phone went to voice mail. The Brit must have been busy with the aftermath of Chester's death.

However, driving to Hotel Terminus could wait a bit. I was gross, sticky, hungry, and had to pee, so I stopped quickly at home to address my needs. Even with Naveen's people standing guard, it wasn't an appealing prospect.

I let out a soft cry at the damage in my backyard. My patio furniture had been trashed, the rattan lay in ratty chunks on the ground, and the pillows were ripped open and bleeding foam. My beautiful rhodo bush looked like half of it had been eaten and then spat back out onto my lawn.

A young man wearing gardening gloves was raking up the debris. "Are you Miriam?"

He didn't even blink at my appearance.

"Yeah. Is... When...?" I shook my head blankly.

"Two of them showed up early this morning," he said, "but we got them."

"Did anyone see?" My neighbor Luka was already wound tight. The existence of demons would do nothing for neighborly relations.

"Nope. All good. No one was up yet and we told the guy who lives on that side?" The young man pointed at Luka's place. "That you're having extensive landscaping work done." He paused, then leaned on the rake with a grimace. "Maybe don't look in your kitchen?"

I immediately sprinted in through the back door. Food had been flung out of the cupboards and fridge, and plates were smashed on the ground. There was a steaming pile of... something in the middle of the room that stank of rotten eggs.

"I told you not to look," he said woefully from behind me.

I pointed to the lump with a shaking hand, my magic swirling around my feet. *Did it shit on my floor?*

"It was marking its territory." He stepped in front of it to block the offensive coil from my view, but then I caught sight of the scorch marks burned along my baseboards.

I let out a defeated whimper.

"Oh. Yeah, those too." He brightened. "But we'll set everything to rights."

"Uh-huh." Upstairs, Sadie's bed was its usual mess, with a heap of clothes piled on it, and my bedroom hadn't been disturbed either. It was a small comfort.

I threw my clothes in the trash and had cranked the shower to scalding when my phone rang. However, I wasn't up to polite conversation so I stepped under the spray.

Demon vaginas, evil fire piss, unholy shits, my poor garden—I screamed for a solid minute. Then I slid down the shower wall, curled into a ball under the water until it ran cold. Once I was clean and clothed in yoga pants and a T-shirt, I checked my voice mail.

Eli had apologized, admitting that he should have listened to me about Zev and the ward and never brought Ryann into it. I appreciated that, but not enough to phone him back. I swallowed the last couple of painkillers in my medicine cabinet and left by my front door so as not to see the demon damage again.

The second I drove off with a screech of tires, my stomach growled so I stopped for a triple shot iced latte and snacks. Lots of snacks. I consumed two chocolate bars before I got to Hotel Terminus.

There was nowhere safe to leave Laurent's stuff, so I waited for him, running down the battery on my phone with endless games of *Tetris*.

He didn't return until later that evening, still in wolf form.

The soft golds and peaches of dusk's light caressed him, catching the wolf tossing his muzzle, his muscles rippling as he drove forward. He was an explosion of motion yet fluid, like a powerful plume of water had been captured, quicksilver and beautiful in its violence. He was magnificent.

I warily got out, keeping the car door between us.

The wolf's ears flattened out and to the side. His eyes hadn't lost their wildness.

"I've got your keys," I said hesitantly. "Want me to let you in?" I wasn't sure how he usually handled this feat, but maybe he always shifted before returning home. Unless he could clear his eight-foot-high back wall and get himself in that way.

He leveled me with the full focus of that animal stare while I held on to my door, prepared to lock myself inside the car. Then he stepped all of two feet to the left.

"Thanks so much for allowing me to help you." Grabbing his clothes, I slammed the door and marched toward him. Once I'd unlocked the hotel, he snagged his pants between his teeth and raced off toward the back where his bedroom was.

I lined his shoes up in the small foyer area, hoping his run through the Park had helped burn off some of his anger.

"Did you want me to wait or what?" Toeing off my sandals, I dropped his keys on his dining room table and sat down on the sofa, all my energy seeping away. He'd shift, we'd have a quick talk about the meeting tomorrow, and I'd figure out where to sleep.

The couch was so big and comfy that even his frustrated growl and the sound of something heavy being knocked over didn't get me up. In fact, it made me more exhausted. First, I cost him his magic, now he couldn't shake it off and transform back to being human.

The wolf slunk back into the main room and his air of defeat broke my heart. He lay down on the floor, illuminated by the honey-rich glow of a single sconce, his head on his paws and his tail wrapped around his hind legs.

"A couple of demons ate my patio furniture," I said. "And a plant that I was really fond of. It might surprise you that I'm not much of a gardener and Eli mostly takes care of that for me. But Jude had given me this rhodo as a housewarming gift when I first moved and the hardy little thing survived me."

I sat cross-legged, something I could never do comfortably on my own sofa because it wasn't wide enough, and massaged my aching left hip. Laurent shimmied slightly closer, so I kept talking. "I always prided myself on being the responsible one. In my marriage, at work, even with Jude. But how do I stay that person when every time I think I have a handle on what I'm dealing with, the universe laughs and shows me otherwise?"

The wolf leapt onto the sofa, positioning himself at the other end.

With the return of Laurent's magic, all should have been right with the world, but seeing him still stuck in animal form, I felt my grief swell inside me. I was bobbing in a tiny boat, the distance between us an ocean, so I crossed it the only way I knew how.

Words gushed out of me. I jumped topics from my fears over my family and friendships, to demon poos in my kitchen, and circling back again. My throat became dry, but I kept talking, unable to stop.

"The more I try to make things right, the more it all feels like everything is careening out of control." I poked at a ragged cuticle. "The only solid relationship I have is with my best friend that I haven't had time for and a potty-mouthed golem. I wish you could speak and tell me if I've broken us."

I blinked out of the trance I'd fallen into as I mused aloud, realizing that Laurent had pushed his head into my lap, and I was slowly raking my fingers through his fur. I froze, but his breathing was deep and even, gently ruffling my shirt with each exhale. I resumed petting him, so that he'd keep sleeping, the long, dense fur bristly to the touch. I was mesmerized to be this close to him. Not even to a wolf, just to Laurent, who deplored physical contact.

Maybe, though, I had that wrong as well. Maybe it had

been so long since he'd been touched that it was too much for him and he couldn't deal with it.

The scent of cedar that always clung to him was deeper tonight, mixed with the tang of rich soil. I flicked away a pine needle that was caught in his fur and small silky hairs from his undercoat clung to my fingers.

"I'm sorry that I risked you," I murmured. "You mean a lot to me, and I took you for granted. I won't anymore."

I scratched behind his ear, and the wolf huffed softly, a sigh rippling through his body, but he didn't stir. My breathing fell into sync with his.

"What are we going to do? Zev won't give up the gloves and that's the only way to save Tatiana." I rested my head against the cushions, staring up at the ceiling as I stroked his fur. "I can't kill Frances, and when I really think about it, I'm not sure you can either. You talk a good game about dybbuks, but you're also adamant that you only kill the host after their consciousness is gone and the dybbuk is in control. Frances is very much alive." I sighed. "We won't have a choice though, will we? Tatiana is our priority."

Frances was Banim Shovavim; she knew our history and the danger that using her magic placed on all of us. I was the first one to call people out for using slurs or being prejudiced against my kind, a real champion of my people. But champions had to make sacrifices. Was me being Banim Shovavim precisely the reason I had to be the one to end this?

I buried my face against the top of his head. "I won't let you have all the blood on your hands. My actions started this and if Frances's death is our only hope, then I'll find a way to live with it." I paused. "I'll kill her myself."

We hadn't turned on lights when we'd come in, and night had fallen, filling the space beyond the circle of light with moonlight and indigo shadows. My magic sang in my blood, enjoying the calm before the horrible storm barreling down on us.

"I hope we're okay, Huff 'n' Puff." I yawned. "Five minutes, then I'll go, 'kay?" I rambled on for a bit longer, then things got fuzzy. I might have heard Laurent's voice, but perhaps that was only in my dreams. All I know is that suddenly sun streamed in through the front windows, and I lay on his sofa covered by a soft blanket.

Stretching out my stiff shoulders, I sat up. "Laurent?"

He wasn't in the main room and although I hesitated, not wanting to disturb him if he was sleeping, there was no sign of him in his room, and his bed was made.

I found my phone among the pillow cushions with a text from Laurent that he was picking up Juliette and would see me at the Bear's Den later.

Laurent was bringing a healer to this rendezvous. Not just any healer either, his niece, who he wanted kept far from all of Tatiana's business. Juliette couldn't revive the dead, so was he bringing her for one of us? All of us?

There was a second text to eat breakfast so I didn't get hangry and screw everything up. I pressed the phone to my chest, relieved that he'd shifted back to human, though I could have done without the snark in his text, because I had no clearer sense of how things stood between us than when he'd been in wolf form.

Laurent had set out bread, butter, and jam, which was thoughtful, because I would have felt weird helping myself to food from his fridge when he wasn't here.

I pulled my hair into a ponytail, already halfway through a cup of the coffee that Laurent had made earlier. The toast had popped when I remembered some of what I'd shared with him last night. The only thing that kept me from feeling completely embarrassed was that he'd been asleep. I paused, a glop of butter on my knife. I'd said I'd kill Frances.

I would if there was no other way, yet I couldn't shake the feeling that there was some argument that would sway Zev. Yes, he'd refused me once in no uncertain terms and again to

Tatiana, his Tanechka, but he was equally adamant that she survive.

Pushing aside any concerns about Lonestars tracking my internet searches, I typed in what Chester had said about the demon who'd cursed the gloves. It had stayed with me because the wording had been so oddly old-fashioned.

The curio proprietor had called this slaughter akin to a ravening wolf—not ravenous, the more colloquial and normal way of phrasing it. Unsurprisingly, there were a number of references to ravening wolves in the bible. I followed up on them over breakfast, but most were dead ends.

Wiping my buttery fingers on a napkin, I chased down one more reference. This one came from the Book of Genesis about the Tribe of Benjamin. "Benjamin shall ravin as a wolf: in the morning he shall devour the prey, and at night he shall divide the spoil." The quote itself didn't give me any epiphanies, so as with the others, I dug a bit deeper.

And dropped my phone like I'd been scalded.

I snatched it up again, rereading what I'd found. This latest biblical reference to the ravening wolf had given rise to the Hebrew name Ze'ev.

A ravening wolf tearing men apart. A vampire capable of incredible violence.

Zev was the demon who'd cursed the gloves.

22

HOW COULD SUCH A THING BE POSSIBLE? THE vampire didn't possess the ability to create an artifact that would cause people to go mad and rip their skin off, and yet, there was no way the name was a coincidence or belonged to some other Zev.

The more I thought about it, the more confused I got. Assuming he did have the ability to curse the gloves, why not go curse another pair? Why risk Tatiana dying? There was a major piece of this puzzle missing, but I couldn't figure it out. Nor could I call Zev, since I didn't have his direct number, if the vampire was even awake.

My phone rang, startling me, and I warily checked the screen as if I'd invoked the ravening wolf himself, but it was Emmett saying I was to pick up Tatiana and him for the meeting. *Such* fun.

After shooting back an extra cup of coffee for fortification, I texted Sadie that I hoped she was having a good day and that I loved her. She immediately sent me a heart emoji back and I almost kissed the screen.

I spent the drive to Tatiana's steeling myself to receive the cold shoulder from her, but she flung the door open at my knock with a shake of her head.

"You're not going to my death battle dressed like that." Her shirt, leather pants, and leather duster were all black. Only her stilettos and glasses were bright red.

"Listen, Bubbe McBadass, I can't fight in leather or heels."

She snorted, but I'd caught her smile.

"Told you she'd make some wussy excuse." Emmett joined us, wearing an old-fashioned pinstriped suit, a fedora dangling from his sturdy clay fingers. With the hat on, he'd probably pass for human at a quick glance.

If he kept the brim down low over his face.

And the viewer was a half-blind pirate with an eyepatch.

I peered at his feet. "Are you wearing spats?"

The golem extended a foot. "You bet your sweet patootie I am. Get changed. You're letting down the team."

"Have you two been planning your outfits for this?" I checked my phone. We had time until we had to be at the Bear's Den.

Tatiana gave a weary sigh. "Obviously. Now get in here and put on yours."

This woman refused to be cowed. She truly was my badass role model. Still, I voiced protests the entire way to the guest bedroom upstairs, since my wet-blanketness seemed to be expected.

I changed into the garment that lay on the bed. "It's comfy. Can we go now?"

"Oh good, Miriam. I'm delighted that this exquisite work of tailoring merits the same adjective as the rest of your unfortunate wardrobe." Tatiana applied lipstick to my mouth, cutting off my response. After a quick head-to-toe scan, she refastened my ponytail to sit high on my head and motioned to the mirror. "Voilà."

I gave my reflection a cursory glance. "Looks gre—" I tilted my head really looking.

The jumpsuit, like my lipstick, was the color of freshly spilled blood. The soft fabric fitted my torso perfectly, its deep V giving me a long neck and, frankly, fabulous cleavage, while the outfit nipped in at my waist before cascading out in wide legs that gave me plenty of room to move and fight. They also hid most of my sandals. I needed shoes that wouldn't cause me pain and I wasn't shoving my feet into heels, but my plain black ones looked better being paired with this jumpsuit.

This wasn't clothing made for bad period days or being a couch potato. There was something viciously glamorous about it, the cut and the material screaming money. I even held myself differently, my spine straighter, and a sparkle in my eyes.

Yaas, queen.

Tatiana nodded, pleased. "There's the woman I knew was inside you."

Even Emmett whistled. "Hello, MILF."

I boffed him across the top of his head, drinking down the sight of this take-no-prisoners woman. "Let's do this."

The three of us strutted downstairs like the weirdest Charlie's Angels trio ever, my high dented when I saw my sensible sedan and sighed.

Tatiana tossed me a set of keys, pointing at a red vintage convertible with chrome accents parked across the street. "We ride in style."

We left the top down, the car streaming through the sun and the warm breeze like a yacht sailing the Mediterranean. My passengers didn't even fight my choice of disco from an oldies radio station or my singing along to "I Love to Love."

Tatiana bobbed her head to the music while Emmett danced in place in the back seat with a surprising amount of groove.

We cruised along on a cloud of adrenaline and good spirits, reminding me of the year Jude talked me into doing the Polar Bear Swim. We'd waited on the beach with our fellow insane participants, my dread growing. But then someone started chanting and jumping up and down and soon we all crested on this artificial high, our blood pumping, and the dread dulled under us raring to go.

That's what this moment felt like. Tapping my fingers on the wheel and singing the chorus, I hoped that when all of this was over, I felt as alive as I had after the swim, the cold an invigorating shock.

Pulling into the parking garage, we took the elevator to the basement. The second the doors closed, our energy changed, pulled tight and sharp. For all I clung to my previous buoyancy, I couldn't help seeing an image of playing cards washed up on the shore, too damaged to ever be rebuilt into a house again.

I'd resolved to take a life to save one. I could justify it all I liked: Frances was a killer, she'd murder Tatiana, she was after the gloves so her dybbuk could inflict terrible harm on humanity, but right now, none of that mattered.

She was too close to a cautionary tale about what could happen to me if my magic became corrupt. There'd be no vindication in snuffing out her life and I wasn't sure how I'd cope with the aftermath.

I stood up straight.

I'd do it anyway.

Once we were in the foyer, Tatiana depressed the switch hook on the broken payphone twice and the wall swung away.

Stripped of Vikram's commanding presence and with all the tables and chairs pushed to the edges of the room, the silent speakeasy felt naked. The sconce lights and chandeliers were dark, the place lit with the harsh glare of house lights hidden among the tin ceiling tiles.

It was also empty save for Frances Rothstein, garbed in a cocktail dress with a poufy skirt that would have looked at home in a 1950s Hollywood gathering, her dark red hair falling Veronica Lake–style over one eye. She was younger than I expected, somewhere in her thirties, but that was still more than three decades of sharing her body with a dybbuk familiar. What kind of toll had that taken on her, both mentally and physically?

Frances and Tatiana assessed each other's outfits with approval. "I own one of your paintings," Frances said.

"Really?" Tatiana sounded as unruffled as the Banim Shovavim, simply two women making small talk at a fancy dress party. "Which one?"

"*Alice Wishes.*"

I didn't know that piece, but Tatiana's eyebrows rose. "I heard it had been destroyed."

"It was. Your '70s-era pieces were a lurid mess of color and misplaced nostalgia. I look forward to owning more."

Tatiana's lips tightened and a large floral arrangement on the bar withered, brown petals cascading to the floor.

Code red!

Frances's dybbuk stepped out of her body.

Emmett shoved Tatiana behind him, talking her down.

I wasn't even conscious of summoning my scythe, but the reverberations shivered through me when I slammed the weapon into Frances's shadow. Even though I hadn't expected to kill the dybbuk, I hoped to slow Frances down for a moment. Disorient her.

She simply laughed. "Nice try."

The dybbuk slithered back inside her.

I shook out my arm. We didn't have the gloves, and the others hadn't arrived, meaning it was on me to protect Tatiana.

With my only option: killing Frances.

The urge to rip my outfit off and scour myself of the blood color that I was draped in was so strong that I clenched my fists, certain the material burned my skin.

Footsteps grew closer; the men had arrived. Something

heady rushed through me. Being here was a result of some hard-won battles but the chips were down and all of us were together.

"Did you bring the gloves?" Frances asked.

Before I could reply in the negative and cross the line that there was no coming back from, Naveen's voice cut across the room.

"Right here." He held them aloft.

I did a double take. Say what? That wasn't part of the plan.

Laurent padded behind him, once again in wolf form.

My fingers twitched; I wanted to bury them in his fur again, even as my heart plummeted into my feet. BatKian would never have given them up. Something was very, very wrong.

Juliette hung back, throwing me a small wave, which I absently returned.

Had the men stolen the Torquemada Gloves from Zev to trade? The vamp would kill them. They wouldn't be that stupid, would they?

Tatiana paled, a trembling hand covering her mouth.

Oh fuck, they were.

Frances's eyes gleamed greedily and she rubbed her hands together like a B-movie villain. "Put them on the stage."

"No! You can't!" I sent Delilah flying to grab Naveen, who was already making his way to the spot Frances had indicated, but the wolf leapt in front of me, growling, his teeth bared.

Naveen summoned his staff. "Shut your shadow down, Miriam, or you won't like the consequences."

Delilah landed on the ground, crouched and ready to attack on command.

"You *know* what will happen if the dybbuk goes into those gloves," I said. My blood ran cold. "It'll have form. It's already unkillable. Why would you let it loose that way?"

Frances slow-clapped me. "Someone's done her home-work. Are you always this much of a know-it-all?"

Condescending and calculating with zero compassion for the consequences of her actions—Frances was a total cunt. It didn't make the inevitable easier, it just made it time.

Heavy footsteps clattered over the ceiling in a rush, but any emergencies outside this room weren't my problem.

I hoisted the scythe, my shoulders squared, braced to end this once and for all, but the wolf growled louder, blocking my path, his eyes cold and his lips bared back from his sharp canines. Had the animal who'd slept with his head in my lap been a dream? Was Laurent finally venting his rage toward me, ready to crush me if I got in his way?

Was that what we'd come to?

The dybbuk flew into one of the gloves, inflating the shriveled yellowed human skin like a balloon as it bumped around.

Laurent glanced at it, and I whacked the flat end of my scythe blade against his side like a hockey player going for the winning goal. He yowled and stumbled sideways, allowing me to slip past and run for Frances, crying "Mut!" to make the letter appear on the scythe.

To conserve energy, I dismissed Delilah.

The elevator doors in the foyer opened, and I cast a trepi-datious look back since no one else was expected.

"Please," Frances whispered and threw her head up to the ceiling, her eyes closed, a small smile dancing on her lips.

She was so clearly excited to be free of the dybbuk forever and I pitied her. But I ruthlessly squashed it, closing the distance between us as footsteps thundered into the speakeasy.

Naveen raised his weapon above his head, poised to strike both gloves.

There was a choked gasp behind me, where Zev, our new arrival, stumbled to a stop. His usually haughty and carefully schooled features were twisted into a look of pure devastation. Like a mother about to lose a child.

Naveen hesitated.

Frances's eyes snapped open. "The gloves aren't working!" Her face twisted in pain. "You betrayed me!"

The gloves hadn't given the dybbuk form and Frances believed we'd double-crossed her, which put Tatiana in danger.

Zev wasn't even supposed to be here. He'd made it clear he was keeping his distance, but given the look on his face, if Naveen destroyed the gloves, the vampire would rain Hell down on us all.

Save Tatiana or save everyone? It was both the easiest decision I'd ever made and the hardest.

The wolf caught the back of my outfit in his teeth and Naveen readjusted his grip.

Then in one fell movement, he swung.

Zev recoiled, then lurched forward in a single step like he yearned to put himself between the staff and the gloves except he'd been paralyzed by shock.

I tore free, jumping between Naveen's weapon and the stage. My scythe clanged against his weapon, but the momentum of his swing was too strong, and my magic fell apart.

Weaponless, I stumbled back under the impact. My tailbone banged into the edge of the stage, the light staff whistling past my face.

I grabbed the gloves with the dybbuk still knocking about inside and clutched them to my chest, aware of Zev tracking my motion, standing tensely on the balls of his feet as if barely holding himself back from charging me.

Emmett hustled Tatiana toward the speakeasy's exit while Laurent and Naveen went for Frances.

I ran over to the vampire and stuffed the gloves in his hands. "Here. Tatiana, Emmett, and I didn't know this was happening, but the men were desperate to save her. I'm sorry."

He clasped the gloves to his chest with a deep exhale, like a prisoner on death row who'd just received a pardon.

Grunting loudly, Naveen tripped forward, a knife sticking out of his right arm. The Brit whirled on Frances, flipped his hold on the staff so his left hand was dominant, and swung at her.

She spun sideways out of reach, another blade appearing in her palm.

"Are you okay?" I asked Zev.

The dybbuk familiar flew after Tatiana, driving the elderly artist to her knees with a cry.

Zev frowned at me, but if he planned on retribution, he could take a number. I sprinted over to help Laurent protect his aunt since he and I were the only two who could see the dybbuk. Maybe between us we could weaken it enough that it couldn't finish Tatiana off.

I rematerialized my weapon, cried "Mut!" once more, and hacked into the dybbuk. It split into two, Laurent catching one half in his mouth and tossing it away, buying us precious seconds before it reformed.

Frances screamed, and I spun in time to watch her fall, one hand on her burbling neck.

Zev wiped the blood from her torn-out throat on his suit, calmly inclined his head at me, and strode from the room.

I gaped at him until Laurent headbutted my hip since the dybbuk was still attacking.

Naveen sprinted after the vampire, his sleeve seeped with crimson.

Juliette had been checking Tatiana out, but she ran over to the Banim Shovavim, who was still alive—barely.

Laurent could handle the dybbuk who slowed its attack as Frances's strength ebbed; now it was up to me to handle Frances.

279

"Stop," I commanded the healer.

"I can save her," Juliette protested.

I hefted my scythe. "I said no."

I stuffed Frances's gasps for help into some coldly clinical part of me. A woman, a Jew, a Banim Shovavim—and a murderer.

Frances and I had more in common than I'd anticipated.

She twitched her fingers, a shudder running through her body, then she blinked slowly. The light faded from her eyes, and in that last millisecond of her life, I slashed my weapon through the dybbuk.

The familiar cleaved in half and imploded. Dead.

Just like Frances.

"Now!" I urged Juliette, yelling her name when she didn't instantly respond.

She jumped in to heal the damage to the woman's neck and defibrillate her heart.

My magic vanishing, I slid down along the front of the stage, spent, looking anywhere but Frances's lifeless stare. I kept telling myself that if she was truly dead, that was on Zev, but her pleas for help rang in my ears and I shoved my trembling hands under my butt.

I'd done what I had to. Tatiana would live. The dybbuk was no more.

Now it was on Juliette to save Frances.

Laurent pressed his nose into his aunt's hand.

She patted him. "I'm okay, Lolo."

"What about me?" Emmett still held Tatiana's arm from when he'd helped her up. "I protected her."

The wolf flicked his tail at the golem then trotted from the room.

"Ingrate," Emmett called out.

I flashed him a thumbs-up. "You were awesome."

Emmett ducked his head. "Thanks. Wasn't that hard."

Naveen's shadow fell over me, his face a mask of fury. He'd removed the knife from his arm and bound the wound.

"Didn't catch Zev?" I idly noted the new scuff marks on my sandals.

"You've now sided with the vamp twice. Butt in the next time I go after the gloves and you'll be sorry."

I craned my neck up at him, one hand shielding my eyes from the glare of the lights. "Did you see the part where they didn't work?"

"On the dybbuk. You don't know the same is true of humans."

"Reasonable guess."

He slammed his light staff into the ground, cracking the tile.

I winced. "Vikram is not going to be happy about that."

"You don't guess where demon artifacts are concerned," he snarled.

"As opposed to all the hard evidence you had?" I pushed shakily to my feet, one hip propped against the stage for support. "Zev was the demon of legend who tore the men apart. You know his magic. Still think the gloves are cursed?"

"Zev?" If his brows scrunched together any harder, they'd switch places. "No."

"Yes."

Juliette performed chest compressions on Frances, tiny bursts of soothing green light flashing under her palms. The Banim Shovavim's neck was once more intact, although a jagged scar ran across it.

Naveen swore, rubbing his arm because Tatiana had pinched him.

Old Jewish women and pinching, I tell ya.

He looked down at her haughtily. "What was that for?"

"That was because Miriam was right to give him back the gloves."

I blew on my knuckles, shining them on my jumpsuit.

Tatiana gave a barely tolerant shake of her head before pinching Naveen again. "What were you thinking, stealing from Zev?"

The Ohrist threw his hands up. "Saving your life?"

"A nice justification for doing what you'd wanted from the start," she countered. "Getting the artifact."

"What was your plan?" Since it would keep me eye level with Naveen, I hoisted myself up to sit on the stage. "Let the dybbuk into the gloves and then?"

"The dybbuk would take physical form," Naveen said, subdued from the news about Zev. "Since it was a separate entity from the Banim Shovavim at that point, Laurent would send it back to Gehenna while I destroyed the gloves, leaving that woman without her magic. But I guess you took care of that." He sounded surprised.

"A Banim Shovavim putting Ohrists first. Shocker," I said unkindly. We'd achieved the best possible outcome—I glanced at Juliette still working on Frances. Potentially achieved it, but it had been by the skin of our teeth and with no thanks to the men. I didn't have the energy or the inclination to play nice.

My boss leaned in practically nose to nose with him. "I don't care who you work for, Naveen, when I say no, you *will* listen to me, understood?"

His eyes turned flinty; his lips twisted. "Yes."

Dressed casually in shorts and a blue hoodie, Laurent strode into the room, slowing as he gauged the chilly emotional temperature.

Juliette sat back on her calves and ran a hand across her brow. "D'accord. She's alive. Barely. I did what I could, but this will take more than one healer."

"Call the Lonestars," I said. "Let them have her." I was still pissed off at Ryann since I hadn't heard back about ensuring Elizabeta didn't poke her nose into my business.

Tatiana skewered me with a sidelong glance. "I'll do it." She walked past Laurent, pinching his arm as she went.

"Ow! Why did you do that?"

"Ask him." Tatiana pointed at Naveen. "Miriam, meet me by the car when you're done. The guest room is readied for you." She sailed out of the room, Emmett walking behind her like the queen's consort.

Royalty, bitches.

"I'll go with her to describe the patient's condition," Juliette said, checking Frances's pulse. "She's stable, but I've suspended her in a temporary coma. Don't disturb her." After securing promises that we wouldn't, she left.

"The pinching?" Laurent said.

"Tatiana doesn't appreciate you two going behind her back when she expressly said otherwise." I rubbed at a cigarette burn on the stage floor, one leg crossed over the other, and my foot bouncing. I couldn't keep still, my anger needing to come out in a dozen tiny ways. "Did you consider what could have happened if you'd destroyed those gloves?"

Laurent shrugged. "Not like my relationship would be any different with the vamp."

I stared at him, incredulous. "You're as bad as Naveen. I almost died getting Zev the gloves in the first place. And whatever your feelings about me, he associates the two of us together. And you with Tatiana. You think he would have stopped to rationalize out who was and was not involved?"

"Excuse me?" he said in a low voice.

Get over yourself. I pointed at Naveen. "What about Daya and Evani?"

"Even BatKian has a line," he said stiffly. "He wouldn't have hurt them. Especially not Evani."

"Maybe not under normal circumstances, but these aren't. We still don't know what the gloves mean to him."

"How great that you've barely reclaimed your magic and yet you have all the answers." Naveen laughed bitterly. "Too

283

bad you don't listen to yourself. If he's the demon who created the artifact, it's obvious why he wanted them."

"You might want to rethink this tunnel vision of yours, Naveen, because it's not doing you any favors."

"Meaning?" His eyes narrowed.

"If you'd paid attention, you'd have seen Zev's reaction when you were about to destroy the gloves. Whatever was going on, it wasn't about losing a demon artifact, and if you'd been successful, he'd have gone ballistic."

Naveen frowned.

"I absolutely do not have all the answers, and I'm delighted about that fact." I looked up at the ceiling with a smile. "I have to constantly question everything from a dozen different angles, and my open mind gives me perspective none of you will ever have. Like what was really going on with Zev."

"Bully for you," he muttered.

I fought past my first reaction to let Delilah wail on Naveen, because his glowering and posturing had a hurt quality. God, he was as bad as my teenaged child. I silently counted to ten, the same as when Sadie made my head want to explode, until I could speak calmly. Okay, it took me to twenty-three. "What are you really mad about?"

"Nothing." Naveen crossed his arms.

Laurent was still pissy about something, so I continued to ignore him and finished my talk with Naveen.

"Good," I said, "because everything worked out. No one died, the dybbuk familiar is no more, we didn't make Zev go all Four Horsemen on us, and we even proved that those gloves have no magic powers." I spread my hands wide. "I'm not your enemy. In fact, if you'd let me, I'd be a pretty good ally."

He was silent for a bit, then he pinched the bridge of his nose and exhaled. "I'm pissed off that I spent all this time chasing something that wasn't a danger to anyone. And because I could have endangered my family. Badly."

I just nodded.

He looked up at the ceiling, then stuck out his hand. "Naveen. My friends call me Nav, and you just earned your way into that highly sought-after circle. Treasure your position."

I shook it, a giddy smile on my face at hearing the words he'd spoken when we first met. "Miriam. My friends call me Miri, and likewise."

Our moment was short-lived, Naveen already turning away to make a call and heading for the exit. "Clea? Where did we get the intel on the Torquemada Gloves?"

One day I intended to meet this Clea and see their Batcave.

I slid off the stage, headed for the parkade. No point keeping Tatiana waiting any longer, especially to hang around and beat my head against Laurent's anger.

Laurent grabbed my shoulder and spun me to face him. "What was that crack about 'despite my feelings'?"

I shrugged. "I've apologized, and I meant it, but I can't make you forgive me. Or not hate me."

He raked a hand through his hair, causing his hoodie to rise and expose a sliver of olive skin. "If I hated you, then what was last night about?"

"Huh?"

"Sharing your thoughts and fears. Being so concerned about me. You think I'd have stuck around for someone I hate?"

I turned beet red, gaping at him. "You were asleep."

A bitter huff escaped his lips. "Guess again."

"But our fight at Chester's? You were so angry."

"What did you expect? I was grieving. Killing dybbuks..." He made a frustrated noise. "It's given my life purpose."

"Since you left the pack?" I said carefully.

Laurent fidgeted with his hem. "Yes."

The seconds ticked by without him adding more.

"When did you and Naveen decide to steal the gloves?" I said, still reeling that he'd been awake. I would never have confided in him if I'd known he was listening. "Was it before last night?"

"No."

"Was it pity?" I clenched my teeth.

"Is that really what you think?" he said sadly.

Was it? I replayed our conversation at the hotel, biting on my bottom lip. Once again, Laurent had my back. He'd heard what I said about not letting him have Frances's death on his conscious and done what he could to keep it off mine.

Thank you seemed so inadequate.

Unable to stop myself, I rested my hand on his stomach, my thumb lying against that strip of naked skin.

Laurent flinched, his gaze equal parts hurt and longing, and I curled my fingers into my palm, ready to apologize for invading his personal space. He gave the tiniest shake of his head, reached out ever so slowly, giving me the chance to stop him, and brushed a feather-soft fingertip over my cheek. His touch was warm, but the intensity of his gaze scorched me everywhere it landed.

"You coming?" Emmett thumped into the room.

Laurent's expression shuttered and I pulled away, hurrying over to the golem.

"Miriam."

I froze, my back still turned, hating the sound of my full name on Laurent's lips instead of his nickname for me.

"We were always okay," he said softly. "If you didn't know that, then Nav wasn't the only one with tunnel vision."

286

23

My hands folded on my belly, I stared into the murky depths of Tatiana's small pond, the occasional flash of goldfish scales reflecting in the moonlight. Laurent and I couldn't go on as we were. The ball was in my court, but I didn't quite have the guts to pick it up and run with it.

I was forty-two years old and more nervous than the first time I'd ever had sex. Not that sex was some foregone conclusion. I mean, he seemed attracted to me but I'd believed that Alex had been as well so I might be zero for two. Zero for three if I counted Ben, my sweet suitor, who'd ended up dybbuk-possessed.

Who was I kidding? If I went to Hotel Terminus, we'd totally have sex. I stretched out my legs, cool grass slipping between my bare toes, and pulling out my phone, started a new list.

Pro: hot sweaty sex with a younger man.

Con: hot sweaty sex with a younger man.

Would I freeze up? Was I even programmed for hookups? I'd never done friends with benefits.

A cockroach scrabbled up out of the dirt. It stayed in one spot, its antennae twitching as if overwhelmed.

"I feel you, cockroach," I said.

Eli and I had had an amazing sex life and once we'd finally slept together, our lust had hit us both like an addiction. I'd ended up getting such a bad rash on my chin from his stubble due to making out with him for hours that my friends staged an intervention. Jude had ribbed me about that for years, but I had no regrets. Even now, I remembered that time *very* fondly, but I wasn't in my early twenties anymore and the tension between Laurent and me wasn't a precursor to him courting me with dates and flowers.

I resumed typing.

Pro: I didn't want a romantic relationship. With everything I had on my plate, that was a clear line for me. He wasn't offering that.

Con: he wasn't offering that? No. No con on this point.

Sex with Laurent would eclipse anything I'd ever experienced, a wild storm that would devour me. I squirmed, crossing my legs beneath my ankle-length sundress, a jolt of liquid heat shooting through my core. But I typed and deleted both pro and con multiple times on that one, eventually settling for a question mark.

Pro: if I simply wanted to be friends, Laurent would respect that.

Con: see above.

I clenched my phone, hating my tendency to overanalyze everything, but after forty-two years, the habit was hard to break.

A text came through but I didn't read it, scared it was Laurent asking me to come over. Equally afraid it was him telling me not to.

The message consisted of three words. *Blood Alley. Now.* Wow. Zev wasn't even couching his order as a request. I could be walking into a death sentence though I doubted it. I clearly wasn't a party to the theft, and I'd saved both the gloves and Tatiana like he'd decreed. Which left a minuscule glimmer of hope that he'd reward me by redoing the ward once the Kefitzat Haderech lifted the ban.

Rubbing the sign face tattoo on my arm, I buried that hope in seventeen layers of doubt and disbelief, then went to tell someone where I was going, in case body retrieval was necessary.

Tatiana had been subdued on the way home and through our Thai food dinner. She'd gone to bed early, claiming she wanted some alone time to read, but she was clearly shaken.

We all were. The burn mark on Tatiana's arm was gone and she was out of danger, but our anxiety and adrenaline required time to fade.

Even Ryann's text that I didn't have anything to worry about with Elizabeta barely registered with everything else on my mind.

Tatiana's bedroom door was closed with no light slipping out from the crack between the door and the carpet. My boss was a tough lady, but she was also eighty.

"She asleep?" Emmett whispered.

"I think so." I drew him away from the door, so we didn't wake her. "What are you going to do now that this assignment is over? Go back to Laurent's?"

I crossed my fingers even though I wasn't sure which answer I wanted.

"Not unless I'm forced at gunpoint." The golem glanced down at his feet, before bashfully raising his eyes to mine. "You think I could stay here? Tatiana's the only one who's ever wanted me around. I mean, I know it was for her safety and all, but..." He shrugged.

Jude had brought him to life but then couldn't wait to get rid of him. The vamps didn't want him and neither did Laurent. All the time I'd felt like a house divided, worrying about how to get all my relationships aligned, Emmett had felt alone.

"She's not the only one who wants you around," I said. "I

don't have the space for you to live with me, but I like working together."

"Really?" He sounded suspicious but his eyes were wide and shining with hope.

I hugged him. "Really."

The golem hugged me back tight enough to bruise my rib cage, then abruptly released me with an indifferent "Whatever."

"Zev wants to see me. If anything happens with Tatiana, text me, okay?"

"I'll take care of her," he said solemnly.

"I know you will."

I climbed into my car and headed out. At this time of night, there was little traffic to slow me down.

Yoshi met me inside the gates at Blood Alley, shooting me questioning glances all the way up the crooked lane past revelers streaming in and out of rooms, black doors closing and red light bulbs glowing.

"If you have something to ask, then ask it," I said.

"Not my place." We stopped in front of the sake bar and Yoshi motioned me inside. He didn't come with me this time, and like my first visit, Zev was the only patron.

"Is this your private bar?"

Zev swung around on his stool. One of the individually spotlit bottles of imported sake had been removed from its display and set on the polished bar top next to a small carafe and two sake cups. "It's for Yoshi and me."

I swallowed my boys' club comment and sat next to him.

The vampire poured the fragrant liquid into my cup, then I did the same for him. He clinked my glass. "Kanpai," he said.

"Kanpai." I sipped the warm sake, enjoying the light, smooth nutty flavor.

He'd changed out of his bloodstained suit from earlier, wearing his billionaire tech dude persona with dark slacks and a casual button-down shirt. The one other time I'd seen him dressed like this was when he came to make the wards. He'd intended to fuck with me that night, swaying Eli and Sadie to his side, at least initially, but I couldn't figure out what the outfit signified now when there was just the two of us.

"Did she live?" He rubbed a finger over the thin ridges of the small handleless cup, gazing across the bar.

"Tatiana? She's tired, but unhurt."

"That's not who I meant."

I set my cup down with a shaking hand. Was that why he'd brought me here? To "chastise" me for letting the Banim Shovavim live? He hadn't specified that she had to die, had he? I tried to remember our conversation when Zev had set out his conditions, but I couldn't get past the image of the vampire with the smashed-in face peeling off the wall.

"She did," I said, "but I killed her dybbuk familiar. Her magic is gone and the Lonestars have her." We'd hung around the parkade until a Lonestar showed up with another healer. After a quick debrief, they'd taken charge of Frances.

Zev splashed more sake into his cup and shot it back.

I leaned back on my stool, my eyebrows raised, but kept mum.

"Why did you give me the gloves?" he said, his blandly polite mask firmly in place.

How much honesty was a good thing? I hedged my answer. "The gloves didn't give the dybbuk form, and probably weren't cursed at all, and you'd gone to a lot of trouble to get—"

"The real reason." His smooth voice was tempered with steel.

I swallowed. "Because you looked at them the way I would have looked at Sadie if she was in danger."

The vampire returned his gaze to the cup, turning it around in his hands.

The adage *curiosity killed the cat* was the only thing keeping me silent. I sipped my drink slowly, waiting for his next cue.

"What did you figure out about them?"

"Nothing," I said hastily.

He quirked an eyebrow at me. "We both know that's not true."

"All right." I finished my sake and pulled up my notes before this shot of courage disappeared.

Zev poured himself more alcohol.

"The initial story I heard about the Torquemada Gloves was that they'd been cursed by a demon and that anyone who put them on would become convinced they no longer wore their own skin. They'd go mad and eventually die clawing their skin off."

The vampire snorted, the cup poised at his lip.

"But that didn't make a lot of sense given your reaction when I handed them to you after stealing them from Torres."

He startled. "What reaction?"

"You looked like you were praying."

Once again, he downed his drink. Could vamps get drunk?

However, Zev hadn't told me to shut up or torn out my throat, so I kept going, finding my place on the screen. "Supposedly the half circle on the gloves was the mark of the demon who'd cursed them, but then I learned of the blood libel in Avila in 1491 and Torquemada's torture methods of skinning people alive. He'd made a book out of human skin with the same mark, which turned out was a fingerprint, and—"

"*Enough.*" The word was wrung out of the vampire's deepest misery. His fingers tightened on the cup.

My magic curled into a shadowy cuff around my left wrist. I was braced for anything, even having to use my scythe against him. I didn't want to, I realized with surprise, but I didn't want to die even more.

"What did you learn of the demon?" he finally said.

"How he slaughtered people. The connection to a ravening wolf. The meaning of the Biblical name Ze'ev," I said gently.

The vampire raised his cup in a salute. "You've put almost all of it together. It's only fair that I fill in that final piece." There was something reckless about him tonight, an abandonment that crackled the air around him. It sat as wrong on this always-in-control supernatural creature as people believed the cursed gloves would, and I scratched at my skin as if I already wore them.

"That's okay. I don't need to know."

"Ah, Ms. Feldman, but what if I want you to?"

I'd had a friend who had shared all the details of her husband's infidelity with me, including all her anger and hostility toward him. I'd sat with her for hours while she sobbed and talked through her emotions, but when she and her husband reconciled, she'd cut me out of her life.

I felt used and abandoned, and although I told myself that she was probably embarrassed or simply didn't want me reminding her of the past, it took a long time for the hurt to fade.

I didn't want to suffer Zev's inevitable regret at baring his soul because it wouldn't be as simple as him blocking my number, but it's not like I had a choice. Inwardly sighing, I smiled. "I'd be honored to hear the tale."

"I was still a rabbi back then. Human." He paused. "Married."

I closed my eyes briefly, really not wanting to learn more.

"Torquemada." Zev rubbed his thumb over the rim of the sake cup. "Enough has been written of his evil, and if there is a God, then that monster is tortured a thousand times over every day for what he did to our people." He frowned, gazing off, then shook his head. "You must understand that a Jew's position was precarious at the best of times. My wife, Naomi?" He added the Jewish phrase "zikhronah livrakha." May her memory be a blessing.

My cousin Goldie had often said that when speaking of my mom.

Zev cleared his throat. "Naomi was a beautiful woman and she commanded unwanted attention."

I topped up my drink.

"But she stayed within our community, and we all made sure to keep her safe. However, when Torquemada unleashed his chosen inquisitors, it was a very different story. Both of us were rounded up and tortured, forced to confess that we'd seen the suspects commit blood libel. She..." He stared into his empty cup, then blinked. "Died. I was not so fortunate."

There was a long silence. Yet even with the dread looping around my neck like a noose, I had to know.

"The gloves...are they...were they..."

Zev nodded. "I was still clinging to life when I heard one of the inquisitors was boasting about how he'd finally broken the Jewess. He even had a trophy to prove it."

The gloves. I bowed my head, overcome by the sheer horror of what had been done to Naomi.

"You killed him, right?" I white-knuckled the counter.

"I prayed for the strength to," Zev said. "But God didn't answer me." He tilted his head, his expression distant, then pursed his lips. "Or perhaps he did. I'll never know."

"The estrie?" I guessed.

"Yes. She turned me and I gave her a feast."

I hung rapt off his grisly tale, waiting to hear the gory details about what Zev had done and slake my own desire for vengeance on his wife's behalf, but he sat up like he'd come back to himself. Scooping up both our cups, he set them with the carafe behind the bar.

Storytime was over.

Zev had spent more than six hundred years searching for this piece of his wife. The gloves were a desecration and yet precious because they were all he had left of her.

"Why did you tell me this?"

He rubbed a hand over his chin. "I wanted someone else to keep her alive."

I pressed my hand to my heart. "I won't tell anyone."

"I would kill you if you did." There was no heat in his words, but their matter-of-fact nature gave them weight. He grasped the door handle, then turned back. "I expect to hear from you in two weeks. Don't bother me before then."

I shook my head in disbelief, running my thumb over the KH tattoo. He was going to ward me up. I followed him out the door like an eager puppy. "Why? I mean, thank you. But why?"

"Because you saved the gloves. Not because you knew the story and pitied me, simply because you judged that they mattered." With that he strode into the night, until the shadows swallowed him.

Tatiana had forgiven me, while Nav and I had restored a tentative friendship. And now Zev had agreed to redo the ward, which would go a long way to smoothing things over with Eli and Sadie.

A house divided could stand, and in fact had been doing so for time immemorial. Families had been tolerating differences while still standing strong forever. Any parent of a teenager learned this. Relationships weren't based on total agreement. They required respect and empathy. What mattered most was not seeing eye to eye but seeing each other clearly.

These people I'd fought with had become my extended family. Okay, not Zev. But even he had stood with us, uniting at the crucial moment.

I mentally rebuilt my house of cards. No, my House of Bricks. But there was one important piece to secure before I could complete it. I smiled, hoping that surprising Laurent would go better than the last time.

24

The Billy Idol blasting from inside Hotel Terminus took me so aback that I almost didn't knock, and when I did, no one answered. I wasn't one for walking into someone's house unannounced, but Laurent never listened to anything other than jazz and classical. What if he'd been attacked and was bleeding out to '80s British New Wave?

"Laurent?" I pushed inside and came to a dead stop, my mouth hanging open.

He was jumping around to "Rebel Yell." He'd committed to it with the same absolute intensity that he gave everything, singing at the top of his lungs and headbanging, his chocolate curls flying. He punched the air with his fist, belting out the chorus, and the sheer carnality of the song and this man made me rock back on my heels.

I licked my lips.

Boo jumped and pounced along with him. He scooped her up, dancing with the kitten cradled against his bare chest.

I pressed back into the shadows so I could watch him without being caught. Yes, there was an unflattering word for that and I so didn't care.

The guitar solo kicked in, and Laurent whipped around, catching sight of me.

Boo pawed at him, but when Laurent didn't continue their game, she jumped out of his hold and ran off.

The melody fell away, cutting to percussion and Billy's sexy croon while Laurent prowled toward me, his eyes gleaming like green crystals from an undersea kingdom.

I backed up, hitting the wall.

He caught me around the waist with one hand, jamming his leg between mine. The fabric of my wrap dress slid sideways, my bare legs straddling his muscular denim-clad thigh, as he rocked us back and forth, dancing and singing about selling his soul for me.

Had he not been holding me down, I might have floated off the ground with only his eyes to tether me. His grip tightened, exerting enough pressure to pull me closer to him, the sundress getting twisted and making things slippery.

I swallowed and clutched his forearms, the drum beat vibrating inside me.

The music amped back up but Laurent fell silent. His hand still gripped my side, his leg between mine, but neither of us moved.

"Mitzi." The sound of my name in a breathless French accent wrapped around me and my guts twisted themselves into knots. This was the precipice and once jumped, it was free fall all the way.

I drank him in from his ripped abs to the dimples in his hips, his jeans slung low, for once in my life not wanting to think, just leap. "Yes."

He turned my wrist up and rasped his teeth against my skin, his tongue laving the mild sting.

My breath caught, a hot spear of arousal spiraling up from deep inside. It had been so long since someone desired me and never like this. It was intoxicating.

It was terrifying. I almost ran back to the comfort of my house and my sofa and the familiar confining box of my life.

New to-do list: Laurent.

I closed the gap between us and sucked on his lush bottom lip.

Laurent growled and clasped the back of my neck, his mouth claiming mine.

I grabbed his shoulders, falling dizzily against him and rising on tiptoe so we didn't break the kiss. I was lost to the friction of his tongue tangling with mine and the press of his fingertips against my belly as he found the ties that unwrapped my dress.

Without even thinking, I slammed my hands down, dislodging his and pulling the material taut.

Laurent stilled for the briefest second, but before I could stammer out an apology, he placed his hands on the wall to either side of me. He ducked his head, dragging open-mouthed kisses over my neck, pausing to suck on my fluttering pulse.

My head fell back and I clutched his belt loops with one hand to steady my rubbery legs, sinking the fingers of my other into his hair. His curls were as soft as I'd imagined and his lips as hot, branding me. I moaned.

When he lifted his head, his ragged breathing matched mine. "Are you nervous?"

I blinked, uncomprehending, and he pressed his hand to my racing heart. "I forgot you could hear that." I didn't dare think about what else his wolf senses were picking up about me because I was already so wet. "It's not nerves," I assured him. "Not anymore."

He regarded me through half-lidded eyes, fringed with those dark lashes that were a silky screen hiding all but the barest sliver of green, then his lips curled up in a gleeful smile. Keeping hold of my hand, he steered me through the main room and into his bedroom, teasing me with sweet kisses that left me light-headed.

We fell onto the cool mattress and Laurent rolled me on top of him. His hard cock pressed against me, and I couldn't resist.

"Is that a vorpal blade in your pocket, or are you glad to see me?"

Laurent groaned. "Non. C'est fini." He playfully pushed me away.

Laughing, I scrambled closer on my knees. "I'll be good."

"I don't want you to be good," he growled and, clutching my hips possessively, yanked me down beside him.

Desire smoldered deep and low inside me, catching in a fast blaze to spread like wildfire through my blood. "Touch me," I said, my breaths shallow. I was caught in that prickling feeling before going over the big hill on a coaster, or the drop in my stomach before jumping off a high diving board. Worth pushing through the nerves for the rush to come.

Laurent propped himself up on his elbow and slid his hand along my bare thigh, nudging the dress away to reach the outside curve of my waist. He reached for the ties, his eyes on mine, giving me ample opportunity to protest, and when I didn't, he unwrapped me with a careful and reverential awe.

He pressed his lips to my bare stomach for the barest caress, then lay his palm on my midriff, his fingers spread wide. I forced myself not to stiffen, instead giving thanks for my sexy underwear.

Laurent jackknifed up with a sure curl of his abs to slide my dress off my shoulders. Hungry emerald eyes devoured every inch of me, and I thrust out my chest, feeling a long-dormant sexual power. Laurent got my ivory lace bra off very adeptly, sucking one breast into his mouth.

I squirmed against the mattress, hot and tight and wanting more, trailing my fingertips along his spine.

He pulled back, his gaze fiery, then he crushed his lips to mine in a punishing kiss that I met in all its ferocity, our tongues tangling.

I was coming undone, arching my hips up and grinding against him.

His groan made my nipples harden almost as much as the tender caress he pressed to my cheek. "Attends."

"Really? Because now would be a great time to go for take—"

He kissed me to shut me up, and when he pulled away, I shrugged.

"You do you," I said.

"Not how this works," he said with a sly and impish grin, yanking my underwear off and tossing them into the corner. With a wicked grin, he pressed messy kisses up my legs, lightly biting the inside of one thigh.

"Laurent," I said in a thick voice.

"Dites-moi," he said. "Tell me what you want me to do to you. This?" He lazily licked my clit and I shivered.

"Not bad," I said.

"Not bad?" He pressed a hand to his chest with a look of mock hurt.

"Well, you only did it once. It might have been beginner's luck."

He flicked a dark curl out of his face, the intensity of his stare making me shiver in delight. "Is that a dare?"

I waved a hand at him. "Take it as you wish."

He slid me against his mouth and resumed licking me, all the while watching my reactions.

I was so turned on, I saw stars. "Fuuck," I breathed.

Laurent lifted his head, frowning. "You can still speak? Non." He pushed a finger deep inside me as he sucked on my clit and I came hard, screaming his name.

"Go for two," he said and kissed my inner thigh.

Squirming, I pushed him away. "Ticklish. Stop."

He crawled up my body and rested his forehead against mine. "That's a defeatist attitude."

"I never said we were finished." I trailed my fingers down his chest to his fly, unzipping his jeans and pressing the heel of my palm against his erection.

He hissed, covering my hand with his, his pupils dark and lust drunk.

I bit his earlobe. "Fuck me."

He grimaced. "I can't. No condom."

Because he'd run out from all the sexual activity in his life or because, like me, he hadn't needed them in a while? That couldn't be it. This beautiful man with that smile, his sculpted body, and expressive eyes could get anyone he pleased. Then I remembered how other Ohrists spoke of him and wondered if that was true.

Their loss. My very big gain.

"Take off your jeans." Wow. No one had ever listened to me so quickly. He'd shucked them off before I'd finished the sentence and oh my, he went commando.

"You're beautiful." My voice was husky. "A Greek statue come to life."

Laurent made a *pfft* noise. "Greeks are nothing special." He looked pleased when I laughed.

I didn't remember being this carefree during sex. It was heady. Just like being with him. I slid down Laurent's body, positioning myself so that my legs were pointed toward his pillow, and took him in my mouth, moaning at his salty, musky taste. I went slowly at first, reveling in this simple intimate act, but when his hips rolled in time with my movements, I sped up, the wash of his French murmurings and the feral gleam in his eyes, like he was holding tight to the shreds of his civilized nature, getting me wet again.

I squirmed, and Laurent nudged my legs open, finding my clit.

The sensation of having him in my mouth and his

301

fingering me was almost too much. I came again, a second before he did. He pulled out and caught his spill with the edge of his blanket.

I rolled onto my back, one hand on his calf, needing our connection.

Laurent repositioned himself to kiss me just as "Rebel Yell" started up again.

"Is this on repeat?" I said in a dazed voice once we drew breath.

"It's a good song." He gave that French shrug that was all kinds of charming right now and kissed my shoulder. "How old are you exactly?"

I sat up, pushing my hair off my shoulder and regarded him with narrowed eyes. "Is that really the question you want to ask me at this moment? Think carefully."

"You told me you were in your forties when we first met." He propped an arm behind his head. "I've always wanted to sleep with a woman in her sexual prime." He shot me that piratical smile of his. "It lives up to the hype."

"I'm forty-two, and you're welcome. How old are you?"

"Thirty-seven." He was silent a moment before he mused, "The wolf and the cougar."

I smacked him with a pillow, and laughing, he caught my wrists and pulled me to him. We made out like horny teenagers, our kisses eventually turning soft, and then easing into gentle caresses.

I laced our fingers together. "You lied."

"About what?" He flung his leg over mine, languidly kissing the crook of my neck.

"Us being okay the whole time. You were really mad at me. I don't blame you, but you were."

Laurent groaned. "Do we have to do this now?"

"Yes. Now that I've fucked you out of my system—"

He nipped my bottom lip. "Liar."

I rolled my eyes. "Fucked you out of my system for now."

"Liar." He laughed, rolling onto his side away from me when I slugged his arm.

"We will be adults and discuss this."

He sat up. "There's nothing to discuss. I was mad, yes, but we were still okay. Do you think your friendship with Jude is over if you fight?"

"If it's a big one like we had? Yes. I worry that it could be." I traced a finger through the dark hair dusting his chest, marveling at getting to touch him this intimately.

"I'm sorry about lashing out at you," he said. "I was scared and hurt. But people fight. Then they find solutions and move on." He shot me a wry smile. "Or so I've been told. Supposedly I have these lone wolf tendencies, but I'm trying to do better."

His admission elicited a small smile from me. "You say that, but—" I struggled to find words that wouldn't hurt him. "You don't let many people get close to you."

"That's why—" He cut his soft words off with a brisk head shake, his expression turning cocky. "You are correct. I am an arrogant, insufferable bastard who abandoned his pack when they needed him and still refuses all contact with them."

I raised myself up on one elbow, wishing he'd finished his first thought. "That's not what I meant."

He pressed a finger to my lips. "I hate most people." When I called him a liar, he clapped a hand over my mouth.

I licked it and his eyes gleamed.

"Do not distract me with your womanly ways, *Miriam*," he said.

I curled my toes under like a giddy fifteen-year-old.

"However, some people keep coming back and caring about me despite all my best efforts, so even if we fight, what am I to do?" He fell back in a long-controlled movement, the mattress bouncing. "There is no point being mad. I allow them to adore me."

"That's so magnanimous of you."

"You think I do not know that word." He tapped his head. "Book learned." He rolled over to face me, completely serious. "We are okay. Yes? You're not mad at me for stealing the gloves?"

"Would I have slept with you if I was?"

He scratched his stubble. "I don't know. I haven't discovered all your kinks yet. Hate sex could be one of them."

Even I could smell my arousal at that idea.

He smirked. "Time to start a new to-do list."

I buried my face in the pillow. But only briefly because I didn't want to miss a second of this playful Laurent. Was this the man he'd been before tragedy struck? He reminded me of a shy little kid who never really said much until they warmed up to you and then you couldn't get them to shut up. How starved had he been for company? How many conversations did he have stored up in his head, waiting for someone to stick around long enough to have them?

I hugged him tightly, burying my face in his chest.

"Are you sniffing me again? Another fetish?"

"You're impossible." I reached for my bra, hoping things didn't suddenly turn awkward because it was after midnight, and this wasn't a sleepover.

Laurent hopped back into his jeans. "Come. I'll feed you before you go back to Tatiana's."

It was the perfect thing to say. Also, the best thing about hanging out with a werewolf was that he made my portions look dainty in comparison.

He cooked me an omelet with tomato and cumin, the way his Moroccan parents made them. I played with Boo, watching Laurent whip up our food, telling him how Zev was going to ward me up, and about the enthralled woman that I'd saved. I kept Naomi's story to myself.

"It's nice hanging out and talking about normal stuff," I said.

Laurent flipped the omelet one more time before sliding it

onto a plate and setting it in front of me. "Yes. A vampire warding a house up against demons and severing ghosts from bodies is completely normal."

"It is now." The omelet was delicious, the cumin giving it a depth not found in a regular cheese omelet. I could get addicted to this.

He topped up my glass of chilled white wine. "You might want to reevaluate your life choices, Mitzi."

Just for that comment, I reminded him that I expected him to host the playdate between Evani and Boo. He bitched about that, but he also spent another five minutes kissing me before he walked me to my car.

I drove away, watching him in the mirror with his hand raised in goodbye until I could no longer see him. I was a grown woman who'd had mind-blowing, no-strings-attached sex. There was no regret or embarrassment or agonizing over my body being less than perfect. I was a modern, confident woman meeting her needs with a freakishly sexy younger man.

That said, I still texted Emmett to make sure Tatiana was asleep before I crept into her house. There was confidence and then there was my boss, Laurent's aunt. I could face a vampire, but I wasn't brave enough for her knowing looks. Baby steps.

25

Not trusting Laurent to arrange the playdate, I set it up for the next afternoon. Since it was Saturday, Daya didn't have patients, nor did she have any births scheduled, and Evani was home from preschool. The jubilant screaming in the background when Daya told her daughter made Laurent's complaints worth it.

Then I realized that I had to keep from either jumping him during the playdate or giving away the fact that we'd gotten naked and sweaty and almost canceled the entire thing.

Sadie wanted to come with me to see Evani, so I picked her up from her aunt Genevieve's house. Eli had moved the two of them in with his sister's family until the ward was set, blaming a burst pipe, but telling me privately he didn't want to intrude on the Kumars any longer.

Sadie had a different take on it as we drove over to Hotel Terminus. "He didn't want Nav to see all his bad habits. I think Dad really likes him."

"And you?"

She hummed the chorus of the pop song on the radio as she thought it over. "I do. He's a bit bitchy at times, but he's really sweet with Evani. And Daya is the best. So, I'll take him to keep her."

I chuckled. "Funny. That's how I feel."

After everything I'd gone through, I no longer saw Sadie's and Eli's relationships with the Kumars as a threat or any kind of aspersion on me. The more ties they build within the magic community, the better, and besides, I would never begrudge other people loving them as much as I did.

Provided I was always first in their hearts. I wasn't a saint.

"How have you been?" Sadie plugged her phone into the stereo. "It's weird skipping our week together."

"This will all be over soon." I squeezed her shoulder. "I've missed you. Work was a bit nuts there, but hopefully I'll have some quiet time now."

"That's good." She scrolled through a playlist.

If things weren't chatty between us, they weren't strained either. We'd fallen back into comfortable silence, which was golden.

When we got out of the car, Sadie grabbed me in a fierce hug. "I really missed you, too, Mom."

I savored it for the three deep breaths until my daughter saw the hotel and bounded over to the boarded-up front door.

"You sure he lives here?"

"Positive." I grabbed the bottle of wine that I'd bought for drinking after the Danger Zone had passed. It was hot out, and I didn't want to leave it in the car.

My knock on the side door was answered almost immediately by Emmett, who'd been shoehorned into the top half of a dragon costume.

He grabbed the bottle of wine with the desperation of a drowning man reaching for a lifeline. "You shining booze angel, you."

"That wasn't for... Okay. You keep that."

He'd already uncapped it, tipping the bottle back to take a

swig, before wiping his mouth off with his hand. "Yeah, planning to."

"Whoa." Sadie shook her head.

Emmett narrowed his eyes. "You the daughter?"

"Yes." She shot me a nervous glance and I smiled reassuringly, despite a flutter of anxiety that Emmett would get weirdly territorial.

"Call me Uncle Emmett." He slung an arm over her shoulder.

I waited for her to elbow him, but she allowed herself to be led inside with an enthusiastic "Cool!"

Oy vey.

Inside was chaos. Evani in her pirate costume and brandishing a plastic cutlass screamed my daughter's name then stabbed her in the stomach.

Sadie gave an Oscar-worthy performance of her death throes before crumpling to the ground.

"Again! Again!" Evani jumped up and down, smacked Emmett in the leg with the cutlass, and then zoomed after Boo, who immediately dashed behind the sofa.

Five seconds around the child and I was exhausted. I was not cut out for toddlers anymore.

My daughter ditched me to try to coax the kitten out.

Daya sat on the sofa chatting with Tatiana, both women drinking lemonade, with a charcuterie spread that could feed a small army set out on the ottoman in front of them.

Our host, on the other hand, hovered alone by the elevator, looking like he wanted to hide with the kitten.

I wandered over to Laurent in my best casual manner and slugged him in the shoulder. "Hey, you."

He looked at me like I was insane, shook his head, then disappeared into the back part of the hotel.

"Hey, you?" Jude said. She gasped. "You slept with the French wildcard!"

Even though she whispered it, I still glared at her. "Shut up. And why are you even here?"

She fiddled with the tab of her pop can. "I missed the asshole."

"Laurent?" Sure, they'd gotten to know each other when she'd been imprisoned here while enthralled, but a reunion seemed odd.

"Emmett." At my smirk, she held out her little finger. "I won't harass you, if you don't."

We pinkie swore.

"I do totally insist on all the details, however," she said.

I grinned and blushed.

Jude high-fived me and we went to join the women on the sofa.

It was a great, if noisy, afternoon, other than the fact that Laurent seemed to make himself scarce. I kept telling myself that this was a lot for him to handle. It was a lot for me—and I'd been through loads of playdates with rambunctious children.

But when I carried the empty charcuterie plate into the kitchen and found him alone, washing glasses, my stomach did a little flip, positive that I'd get a brush-off. "So."

"I bought condoms," he blurted out.

A smile lit up my face. "Okay."

"Okay." He nodded, his bottom lip caught between his teeth, then grinned.

"Uncle Wooooolllllf!" Evani bellowed.

"Her lungs are not Sapien," he groused, drying his hands on a tea towel.

I followed him back to the living room.

Evani pointed at the couch. "Make Mean Lou come out."

Sadie looked over at me. "Isn't the kitten's name Boo?"

Evani stomped her foot. "Mean Lou."

Laurent laughed and crouched down by the little girl, ruffling her hair. "Minou is 'kitty' in French. Not Mean Lou."

The rest of us cracked up, while Evani stared at us imperiously. "That's what I said."

"D'accords." He reached under the sofa and murmured to the kitten, who poked her head out. Laurent picked her up. "Gentle, Evani." He sat down on a chair, the animal in his lap so the child could pet her.

I was melting, my insides turning to goo. I looked away quickly, only to meet Jude's eye. She made a crude motion of her finger in and out of a hole and I snorted, drawing everyone's attention.

"Something caught in my throat," I said.

Jude stuck her tongue in her cheek like she was giving a blowjob.

"Water," I croaked out and ran for the kitchen, doubled over, laughing.

The party wrapped up soon after that highlight, but the rest of the two weeks until I could return home crawled by. Nav went out of town on some job and took Laurent with him, so I didn't get to see him, and since I was still staying with Tatiana, I couldn't even work out my frustrations with my vibrator, because there was no way I'd do that in her home.

I spent most of my time working with her sorting through a lifetime of material for her memoirs. In the evenings, Tatiana, Emmett, and I played cards or watched movies. I hung out a couple of nights with Sadie, and my family had our first appointment with the Ohrist therapist that Jude had recommended. My life was calm, my House of Bricks steady.

Finally, I woke up one morning and that stupid tattoo was gone. I sent word to Zev that we were on but didn't tell anyone else. After all the posturing and game-playing of last time, this could be a quick one and done session.

He came that night. Nav's people had done a good job running off demons, though Eli's apple tree was trashed and there was a huge crack in my kitchen window.

Unlike the last time, we completed the ward with no trouble or drama. There was a click inside me when it kicked in and a new awareness of our property. It was blissfully anti-climactic.

That night, I slept in my own bed, having the best rest in weeks. The vibrator helped.

Sadie and Eli came home the next day and my daughter immediately came over to stay with me, bringing all her laundry with her. To celebrate our return, I went for takeout at her favorite Italian restaurant.

They were running a bit behind, so I wandered up and down the block to kill time, a flash of color catching my eye. I swiveled, backtracking to the window of a high-end furniture boutique to stare at the beauty in the window.

She was the deep burgundy of a fine wine, the line of her back curving sensuously, and her cushions full and plump. She wasn't the orange sofa I'd drooled over, she was even better, and I had to have her. But she was a twelve-hundred-dollar velvet impracticality.

Dejected, I walked away, and then stopped. I wanted to be the woman who bought a gorgeous showpiece of a sofa because she deserved beauty and fun.

With that, I strode back and flung open the shop door. Hello, new me.

Thank you for reading A SHADE TOO FAR!

Things heat up in A SHADE OF MYSELF (MAGIC AFTER MIDLIFE #4)

Vanquisher of evil. Wrangler of offspring. Seriously in need of a coffee.

Miriam Feldman's life is happily bobbing along. Her family and close friends support her magic and things are getting interesting with the wolf shifter. But smooth sailing turns to shark-infested waters when she plumbs the dark depths of her past to investigate her parents' last con.

Being chum was never on her bucket list.

In comparison, Miri's new assignment should be easy: track down a demon to check a necklace for dark magic. Of course, nothing about demons is simple and she finds herself forced to strike hard bargains with both demon hunters and an ancient vampire. Awesome.

The farther out she drifts seeking answers, the tighter she's caught in a net of secrets, lies, and deadly revelations. And this time, she might not break free.

Just keep swimming ...

A Shade of Myself features a later in life romance, a heart-pounding mystery, and a magical midlife adventure.

Get it now!

Every time a reader leaves a review, an author gets ... a glass of wine. (You thought I was going to say "wings," didn't you? We're authors, not angels, but *you'll* get heavenly karma for your good deed.) Please leave yours on your favorite book site. It makes a huge difference in discoverability to rate and review, especially the first book in a series.

Turn the page for an excerpt from *A Shade of Myself* ...

EXCERPT FROM A SHADE OF MYSELF

Phone calls at 3AM meant only one thing: someone was dead.

The caller was Tatiana, so clearly the dead person wasn't her, even though my boss was in her eighties. My adrenaline rush blunted my grogginess while I quickly sorted through which of my friends or loved ones had bit the dust. It made for an interesting cocktail of super wired and slow on the uptake, and by the time I'd understood that Tatiana was phoning about a quick job, I was halfway to my car, keys in hand, hospital bound.

Yawning and knocking on the wood and glass front door of the client's mansion on swanky Point Grey Road, I wished that I'd worn more than a light sweater over my pajamas. When no one answered, I double-checked the address, though with the electronica on full blast inside that sent vibrations up through my feet out here on the stoop, that was hardly surprising. I tentatively pushed the door open, following the music down a hallway past an Ansel Adams photograph on the wall. Unlike the identical one that I'd hung in my dorm room, this wasn't a mass reproduction.

"Hello?" I called out. "Tatiana sent me."

I'd been working for the elderly artist as her archivist and

313

magic fixer minion for almost two months now, and it had its ups and downs. Tonight's job promised to be a quick in and done, though the last time I'd assumed the assignment would be simple, I'd ended up with a human heart on my passenger seat, vaulting me into one of the top spots as the murder suspect.

The slap of my shoes on the intricate mosaic tile made me suspicious that—yup, I was wearing slippers. They were green and fuzzy with a fake fur trim that clashed with my orange pajamas, although given how much the place stank of weed, our client, Davide Forino, probably wouldn't notice my lapse in professional attire. Tatiana had warned me he was a snowboarding celeb and rumored to be constantly stoned.

I put my hand over my mouth and nose to minimize the chances of getting a contact high. I had no problem with pot, especially not now that marijuana was legal, but I had to drive home. Unfortunately, that left only one hand free to plug my ears against the pounding bass and its sassy conga line in my back molars. With my right hand over my mouth and my left in my ear, I felt like I was playing a children's game.

I stopped on the threshold to the airy living room and bellowed out, "Could you please turn that down?"

A pause, and then the music was lowered to barely tolerable levels, but my ears still rung.

"What?" a man drawled in a dazed voice.

I snorted.

He was sitting, back toward me, in a chair shaped like a scorpion spine that probably cost as much as a new car and resembled a Delia Deetz creation from *Beetlejuice*. Presumably the sitter was staring out the floor-to-ceiling windows at the gently rippling waves with crests of foamy white, which met the inky darkness of an endless night sky.

Oh, to have a view like that. Give me this guy's decorating budget and I'd have installed long bookcases and comfortable seating in decadent fabrics, not this ridiculously shaped bull-shit that no one could lounge on. Other than a pizza box tossed on the ground, the all-white room was spotless, which meant he had a cleaning service, because he sure as hell wasn't applying that elbow grease.

I hated him a little more.

"I'm Miriam." I stepped over the pizza box and entered the room. "You texted Tatiana Cassin about sensitive material that you needed magically disposed?"

"I did?" Davide spun the chair around, looking like Shaggy after a bender. Which, come to think of it, was what Shaggy always looked like. Except Davide was also scratched up. He took a drag off a joint, ashes dropping onto a ratty plaid bathrobe that fell almost to his knees. At least it was tied tightly, sparing me the sight of dark, thick chest hair covering his torso like a pelt. Or worse.

I took a very long, very slow breath. "Yes. You did."

Davide darted a wary look behind his sofa at—I tried to follow his gaze—his laptop sitting on a bookshelf crowded with snowboarding trophies? Was there a file he wanted scrubbed? My hacker skills only went as far as emptying the trash.

"If it's something electronic—" I said.

"It's not." He exhaled hard then stood up with a grim expression. With the joint clamped in the corner of his mouth, he scratched his scrawny belly, picking the bathrobe out of his ass with his other hand. Who said men couldn't multitask? "Over here, dude."

BECOME A WILDE ONE

If you enjoyed this book and want to be first in the know about bonus content, reveals, and exclusive giveaways, become a Wilde One by joining my newsletter: http://www. deborahwilde.com/subscribe

You'll immediately receive short stories set in my different worlds and available only to my newsletter subscribers. There are mild spoilers so they're best enjoyed in the recommended reading order.

If you just want to know about my new releases, please follow me on:

Amazon: https://www.amazon.com/Deborah-Wilde/e/B01MSA01NW

or

BookBub: https://www.bookbub.com/authors/deborah-wilde

ACKNOWLEDGMENTS

The upside of being mostly stuck at home during the Pandemic was that my husband and daughter had nowhere to run to when I wanted to discuss the story with them. Heh. Heh.

Special thanks to the child for letting me shamelessly mine both our relationship and her personality in the creation of Sadie. I love that character, but not half as much as I love you, kid.

One of my favourite moments in the writing process is when I've finished my first draft and sent it off to my editor, Dr. Alex Yuschik. I've created something out of nothing, which is so satisfying, and while it's still rough, I know that I'm sending to someone with a keen eye who will help me refine it into the best version of this story. I couldn't do what I do without them in my corner and for that I give endless thanks.

And now to you, my dear reader. If you emailed to say hi, chatted with me on FB, or messaged me to tell me how funny you think my books are (my very favourite compliment), thank you. These connections get me through the rough patches and I treasure them.

ABOUT THE AUTHOR

A global wanderer, former screenwriter, and total cynic with a broken edit button, Deborah (pronounced deb-O-rah) writes funny urban fantasy and paranormal women's fiction.

Her stories feature sassy women who kick butt, strong female friendships, and swoony, sexy romance. She's all about the happily ever after, with a huge dose of hilarity along the way.

Deborah lives in Vancouver with her husband, daughter, and asshole cat, Abra.

"Magic, sparks, and snark! Go Wilde."

www.deborahwilde.com

Made in the USA
Coppell, TX
30 December 2023

27050069R10194